1979

Boris Pasternak

COLLECTED SHORT PROSE

Boris Pasternak

COLLECTED SHORT PROSE

Edited with an Introduction by
Christopher Barnes

Praeger Publishers
NEW YORK

The translation of "Without Love" by Max Hayward was earlier published in *Dissonant Voices in Soviet Literature,* by Max Hayward and Patricia Blake. Copyright © 1961 by Partisan Review. Reprinted by permission of Pantheon Books, a Division of Random House, Inc., New York. British copyright © by George Allen & Unwin, Ltd., Hemel Hempstead, England.

The quoted extract from Pasternak's letter to Stephen Spender was first published in *Encounter,* August 1960. Stephen Spender and the editors of *Encounter* are thanked for their permission to reprint it in the present volume.

Parts of "A District in the Rear" and "Before Parting" appeared in Russian in Boris Pasternak, *Fragmenty romana.* Copyright © 1973 by Collins & Harvill Press, London.

Published in the United States of America in 1977
by Praeger Publishers
200 Park Avenue, New York, N.Y. 10017

© 1977 by Praeger Publishers

789   074   987654321

Library of Congress Cataloging in Publication Data
Pasternak, Boris Leonidovich, 1890–1960.
    Collected short prose.

    CONTENTS: Autobiography: A safe-conduct.—Fiction:
The mark of Apelles. Letters from Tula. Without love.
The childhood of Zhenya Luvers. Aerial ways. Three
chapters from a story. The story. Fragments of a
novel. [etc.]
    I. Barnes, Christopher J.
PG3476.P27A22 1977   891.7'8'4208   73-189901
ISBN 0-275-50390-9

Printed in the United States of America

Contents

Preface

Boris Pasternak's reputation in the Soviet Union has always rested mainly on his poetry, and latterly also on his verse translations of foreign poets and dramatists. But there has been no separate edition of his prose in the Soviet Union since before World War II. In Western countries, on the other hand, it is Pasternak's prose fiction—notably, the novel *Doctor Zhivago*—that has enjoyed the greatest prominence. Although some of the splendors of Pasternak's poetry are apparent in the English versions by Lydia Pasternak Slater (the poet's sister), Robert Lowell, and others, the problems of translating much of his earlier verse are enormous, and there seems little prospect at present of a translated anthology that would do justice to the brilliance and range of the originals. With Pasternak's prose, however, we are more fortunate. It has sometimes been described as "the prose of a poet." But it would be quite mistaken to suppose that Pasternak was principally a poet who simply happened, incidentally, to write some prose. Pasternak usually worked concurrently in both verse and prose genres, which in effect complemented one another. But while his prose often displayed themes and devices to be found also in his dense and more complex poetry, it was often only in prose that some of his most important artistic statements were possible.

This book is intended to present in one volume the best of Boris Pasternak's short prose. The first item—by way of autobiographical introduction —is the earlier of his two autobiographies, *A Safe-Conduct,* which appeared in 1931. This is followed by works of fiction, most of which were written between 1915 and the late 1920s. Finally, there are a few short items that display Pasternak as an essayist and show his position in relation to the literary and political scene at the time when most of his fiction was written. Almost all the works in this book thus come from the first major phase of Pasternak's creativity, which ended in the early 1930s. For several years thereafter, until World War II, he published very little apart from translations, the only significant original works of the period being some short snatches of fiction published between 1937 and 1939. These new pieces—two of which, "A District in the Rear" and "Before Parting," are printed here—are in a simpler, more transparent style. Although they preserve some links with Pasternak's earlier prose, it is more correct to regard them as first drafts of *Doctor Zhivago,* a book that, though absent from the present anthology, can be regarded as its vicarious climax and completion.

Some of the pieces in this book have been included in earlier English anthologies of Pasternak, often in somewhat unsatisfactory translations. But the present volume is the fullest collection of Pasternak's short prose to date, and it contains a number of novelties: the "Three Chapters from a Story," which form a little-known attendant piece to *The Story*; "A District in the Rear," newly translated from the unabridged manuscript text, and "Before Parting," which has not appeared before either in Russian or translated; and, finally, a short essay, "Some Propositions," together with Pasternak's responses to circular questionnaires from various journals in the 1920s, none of which is familiar to the majority of readers.

Alas, with space limited, there have been numerous regrettable but necessary omissions. I should have liked to include Pasternak's various dramatic works and fragments, his early "Story of a Contraoctave" (1913), and the other four draft fragments of *Doctor Zhivago;* the *Essay in Autobiography* had to be left out; Pasternak's fascinating letters and speeches are also totally unrepresented here; and the laconic "Propositions" and other short items are hardly an adequate demonstration of his abilities as essayist or polemicist. But readers will find here some of Pasternak's most inspired prose creations. Works such as "The Childhood of Zhenya Luvers" and *A Safe-Conduct* are some of Russian literature's finest masterpieces and require no apology.

This book is intended mainly for the nonspecialist reader with little or no knowledge of the Russian language and literary background. Some guidance on these is, therefore, provided in the Introduction and the notes at the end of the book. The Introduction is a brief essay on Pasternak's prose writings, placing them in the context of his complete works and offering some clues to their interpretation. Although *Doctor Zhivago* really lies outside the scope of this volume, some attempt has been made to show how it relates to the works that are included here. Also, because *A Safe-Conduct* offers no coverage of any event after 1931, this has been compensated for in the Introduction by the provision of slightly more detailed biographical information for the last thirty years of Pasternak's life. There is no attempt in the Introduction to give exhaustive and detailed commentary. Where further comment or explanation seemed necessary, this has been provided in the notes at the end of the book. Those notes presume a certain familiarity with Western European cultural references and, therefore, concentrate mainly on Russian figures and phenomena.

The transliteration of Russian proper names always presents problems, and the system used here is a compromise among traditional, though non-English, spelling (as in "Scriabin" and "Tchaikovsky"), the demands of strict transliteration, and the need for a phonetic rendering to help the nonspecialist reader. I hope that the versions used in these pages will be found acceptable to the majority of readers.

This anthology arose originally from the initiative of Max Hayward and Praeger Publishers. Many have helped in its preparation. Particular thanks are due to Angela Livingstone and Nicholas Anning for preparing new translations specially for this edition, and for their help with the explanatory notes. The translators gratefully acknowledge the generous and welcome advice of Tatyana Chambers, Valentina Coe, and members of Boris Pasternak's family on translation of some of the complex Russian texts.

St. Andrews, Scotland　　　　　　　　**CHRISTOPHER BARNES**
January 1977

Boris Pasternak

COLLECTED SHORT PROSE

Introduction

The two climactic stages in Boris Pasternak's creative life were his early
fame as the lyric poet of the books *My Sister Life* (1922) and *Themes and
Variations* (1923) and his later, international celebrity as author of the novel
Doctor Zhivago (1957). This sequence in itself suggests a gravitation from
lyric miniatures to more ambitious large-scale works as Pasternak reached
maturity, and a closer examination of his writings confirms this shift of
emphasis. But, during most of his career, Pasternak worked on both prose
and poetry with equal attention, regarding them as related aspects of the
same basic creative process. As he said in an early article, "Poetry and prose
are two poles, indivisible one from another."

Writing about Pasternak's short prose in the 1930s, Roman Jakobson
described it as "the characteristic prose of the poet in a great poetic epoch."
In stating this, he was not pointing out shortcomings so much as indicating
a certain quality or accent in Pasternak's prose style that is not normally
considered germane to the genre. It is perhaps symptomatic that the central
character of Pasternak's first published short stories, "The Mark of
Apelles" (1918) and "Letters from Tula" (1922), is a poet. Moreover the
close and permanent symbiosis of verse and prose was also later confirmed
in *Doctor Zhivago,* where the two genres were shown to combine: Zhivago's
life, a sustained piece of objectified autobiography, was written in prose,
whereas the creative essence of his personality was distilled in the verses
that form the concluding chapter of the novel. In fact, some form of poetic,
or poetically inclined, alter ego figure appears in most of Pasternak's prose
and is used largely to illuminate and explore an aspect of the author's
artistic personality. Thus, in these works, the author's vision is rarely that

3

of a detached, "realist" observer but, rather, that of a poet who in the landscapes, situations, and characters depicted invariably discovers a function of himself.

Described in this way, Pasternak's prose must appear, like his poetry, to be the work of an incorrigible romantic, and though he would have disliked the label, it is nevertheless applicable to him. Certainly the emphasis on subjectivity and the subconscious in *A Safe-Conduct* (1931) and the description of poetic inspiration as a form of madness in "Some Propositions" (1922) are ideas found in the romantic tradition. But Pasternak was a romantic in the manner of Keats rather than Byron. (He actually translated both poets into Russian, but his Keats was rendered with particularly fine understanding.) He could share the Keatsian claim to empathy with all of creation, which results in a quite "unpoetical" loss of personal identity, and a number of Pasternak's early writings were concerned with countering romanticism in the "grand manner," which was endemic in the works of his contemporaries. When the twenty-three year old Pasternak made his literary debut in 1913, the main poetic groups of Moscow represented either the Symbolist or the Futurist trend. Yet, despite their experimentation and hostility to traditions and norms, even the Cubo-Futurist extremists perpetuated a modified version of the Symbolist generation's romantic myth-making. As Pasternak explains in Part III of *A Safe-Conduct,* this involved a quasi-theatrical, unnatural self-dramatization by the poet, and it presupposed a contrast between the poet's sensitive, passionate, and coruscating personality and the dull, philistine outlook of the general public. Such an approach was epitomized by the life and art of Vladimir Mayakovsky, and "Some Propositions," written by Pasternak in 1918, without naming Mayakovsky, inveighed against his influence, which during World War I and the Revolution infected much of contemporary poetry with theatrical pretensions. But Pasternak's first few stories, composed before and during World War I, were part of a personal experience of the Mayakovskian romantic manner and of a later attempt to shed it.

The earliest of Pasternak's short prose pieces, "The Story of a Contraoctave" (which is yet to appear in English), was written in 1913 and left in the form of a rough and ready manuscript that was not to be printed until after the author's death. It tells the story of a nineteenth-century German organist who, while surrendering to inspiration as he plays an extemporized fantasia, unwittingly causes his son to be crushed to death in the organ's mechanism. The distraught musician soon afterward leaves town. Several years later, however, he returns and applies for reappointment to the post of organist, but his request is refused and he is ignominiously obliged to leave once more. The story thus rehandles the traditional romantic myth of superhuman forces wielded by the artist, of art's disregard for the lives of ordinary folk, and of the artist's supposed criminal guilt before society.

It also reflects Pasternak's deep interest in the literature and culture of Germany and contains strong echoes of E. T. A. Hoffmann and of Kleist's "Saint Cecilia, or The Power of Music," as well as a native link with Tolstoy's *The Kreutzer Sonata*.

If Pasternak's first story is a plain restatement of neoromantic themes, his next (his first published fiction) is a polemical and satirical work. Although, again, its opening clearly recalls Kleist ("The Marchioness of O."), this work is no fanciful pastiche. Written in 1915 while Pasternak was under Mayakovsky's strongest influence, "The Mark of Apelles" is an expression of the author's own dilemma and conflict with romanticism. Relinquimini, whose very name implies that he is destined for abandonment, had previously appeared as the hero of several of Pasternak's unpublished early sketches in prose. In "The Mark of Apelles," his exaggerated romantic posturing is made to look stupid when his rival, the poet Heinrich Heine, answers his challenge to a literary contest by transferring it from the realm of literature to that of real life and seduces Relinquimini's mistress. Heine's sortie to Ferrara and his merry exploits there are thus a serious probing of the frontiers between literary invention and reality. Heine quickly identifies his rival's literary heroine Rondolfina as his mistress Camilla Ardenze (another symbolic name), and thus discovers the reality behind the romantic illusion, establishing the banal truth that "all the world's a stage"—all people are actors, not just Relinquimini and his beloved. Heine's name is his own, but it is no coincidence that he is a namesake of that nineteenth-century German poet who used irony to expose the naïveté of romantic statement. Paradoxically, Heine's apparent frivolity is thus the sign of seriousness and down-to-earth realism that contrast totally with Relinquimini's ponderous make-believe. Moreover, Heine is successfully recognized by Camilla as a true poet. Although he has cunningly planned in advance how his visit to Camilla will end, all trace of artifice is erased in the genuine passion they finally awaken in each other. In this way, Heine simply and unpretentiously traces his "mark of Apelles."

"Letters from Tula" was written three years later, in 1918,but it deals with a similar problem and presents it in more or less the same dialectical manner. This time, however, the setting is in contemporary Russia. Tormented by powerful romantic passion, the young letter-writing poet sees the shamelessness and vulgarity of his attempts to express it mirrored in the behavior of a rowdy troupe of film actors. But their shooting of various film sequences is also witnessed by an old retired actor. He too is perturbed by what he sees (the story, incidentally, reflects the then current controversy about the legitimacy of film as an art form), but, unlike the young poet, the actor is able to consummate his feelings back at home: With masterly stage technique he plays a little scene for himself in his rooms, and in this way he brings to life part of his own past. The successful artist is thus shown as the one who does not strive to articulate his passion before a public. The old actor's art is equally effective at home, away from the stage, and as Pasternak wrote in an article in 1916, art is only "a peculiar homework assignment, whose sole requirement is that it be executed brilliantly." The artist, therefore, requires no platform posturing before an audience. He needs only to achieve "complete physical silence within his soul," sublimating passion and allowing accumulated impression and living experience to speak through him.

This idea of the poet as a medium, rather than an agent, is of central importance in Pasternak's art. In fact, it transcends mere aesthetics and, as "Letters from Tula" suggests, it has become a matter for the artist's conscience. The same idea is expressed also in "Some Propositions," which were written at nearly the same time as the story. In the third of these, characteristically, Pasternak made hardly any mention of the first person singular. A book, he says, has a life of its own, its own memories and experiences, and the artist is only there as a means for these to find verbal expression. As Pasternak states in his first autobiography, "In art the man is silent, and the image speaks," and his early lyric poetry indeed shows the personality of the poet virtually indistinguishable amid a shower of objective impressions. Yet another powerful restatement of Pasternak's artistic principle, in which he also underlined the basic oneness of prose and verse, was presented in 1934 at the First Congress of Soviet Writers. This was the fatal gathering where the Soviet literary management imposed Socialist Realism as the sole permitted style for Soviet writers, and Pasternak's speech included the following telling remarks:

> Comrades, what is poetry, if its birth is such as we have witnessed here? Poetry is prose. Prose, not in the sense of someone's complete prose works, but prose itself, the voice of prose, prose in action, not narration. Poetry is the language of organic fact, that is, fact that has live consequences. And of course, like everything in this world, it can be good or bad according to whether we preserve it undistorted or contrive somehow to spoil it.

* * *

The artistic reticence and the refusal to romanticize the poet's role implied in his early stories largely explain the apparent evasiveness of Pasternak's first autobiography, *A Safe-Conduct*. Although nominally concerned with the first four decades of the author's life, the work is by no means a consistent, detailed, or balanced account of facts and events. It was, in fact, begun as a short literary tribute to Rainer Maria Rilke, who had died in 1926, and it only gradually evolved into an autobiography. In the opening pages, Pasternak issues a disclaimer: "I am not writing my autobiography."

The poet's life, he writes, "cannot be found under his own name and has to be sought under those of others." Thus the name of Rilke figures prominently, along with the names of Scriabin, Mayakovsky, and others who "gave" Pasternak his biography, and they are all closely involved in the vivid episodes of childhood, youth, and early manhood recounted in *A Safe-Conduct*. But the author's choice of material is highly selective: It is limited to the memorable events and impressions that contributed to his growth as an artist, the experience on which he inwardly fed and to which he constantly returned for inspiration in his later years. The other memories are discarded or mentioned only fleetingly.

Interwoven with the recollections, however, is a series of fascinating and original discourses on art, culture, history, psychology, and many other topics. But the most crucial passages of *A Safe-Conduct* are those in which Pasternak describes the creative process and demonstrates how poetry originates. Although initially triggered by the poet's emotive reaction to his surroundings, poetry is not an outpouring of emotion or a fulfillment of some preconceived scheme. It is, rather, a form of "escape" from emotion, and it seems to burgeon forth from surrounding reality and life itself, as though independently of the poet. The persona of the artist hardly figures in the resulting poetic landscape. Only the excitement or distortion of the landscape through metaphor and other devices betrays the quality and intensity of the artist's emotional involvement. The creative process described in *A Safe-Conduct* is not, of course, limited to Pasternak's poetry. It is equally evident in his early prose and accounts for the many passages of brilliant impressionism, thematic fragmentation, and dislocation of plot and structure, and the synaesthetic amalgamation of sight and sound, time and place that one finds in both *A Safe-Conduct* and Pasternak's prose fiction.

* * *

Russia has enriched world literature with some unique evocations of childhood. One thinks, in particular, of the well-known accounts by Tolstoy, Gorky, and Bunin, but the list can be extended and should certainly contain Pasternak's masterly "Childhood of Zhenya Luvers." This was written during the Russian Civil War as part of a full-length novel. But the novel was destroyed before publication, apart from this one section, which was printed separately in 1922 and now stands alone as a complete story. In one of her poems, Anna Akhmatova describes Pasternak as "endowed with a sort of eternal childhood," and the studied naïveté of his artistic approach—allowing "Sister Life" to write itself—corresponds closely to the childlike vision re-created in this story. "The childhood of some people takes place in towns that do not at all resemble everything that is said about them by those making up the population," Pasternak wrote in an early review article. He was, of course, not the first to discover the disparity between language and immediate experience. Many Russian and Western poets, philosophers, and philologists of the past had known of it, but it was experienced with especial acuteness and vigor by the Russian twentieth-century avant-garde, who displayed new techniques and even created a new "transmental" language to convey this new awareness. The Formalist critic Viktor Shklovsky described and explained how Tolstoy had used *ostranenie* ("making strange") in the nineteenth century, and some new prose writers of the 1920s, including Olesha, Nabokov, and Pasternak, began cultivating their own novel form of vision, showing the world as viewed through fresh and "innocent eyes."

As in *A Safe-Conduct,* conventional biographical elements are only nominally present in "The Childhood of Zhenya Luvers." The author hastens over the introductory formalities—"Zhenya Luvers was born and brought up in Perm. . . . Her father managed the affairs of . . . ," and so forth—and plunges as quickly as possible into his young heroine's world of vivid, immediate sensations. These surround Zhenya as she experiences her first encounter with life, and it is in terms of this fresh and inchoate perception that such adult concepts as "cards," "town," "Asia," and the factory at "Motovilikha" are first presented to the child's mind. The world of grown-ups is, in contrast, one of dull and readily articulated thoughts, conventions, and prohibitions, which serve only to obscure the true essence of "living life." There are, as Pasternak explains, very few adults who "know and sense what it is that creates, fashions, and binds their own fabric."

If the first part of Pasternak's account of Zhenya's childhood is concerned with language and cognition, the second part shows her growing moral awareness and her developing perception of other human beings. She learns the meaning of being a woman, the suffering involved in loving, the giving and receiving of compassion. But, as in the first part, all these are instilled into her in terms of freshly experienced sensation, for which at the time there is no name, and which differs altogether from an adult moral system of abstract principles and rules. It is, therefore, only at the end of the story that Zhenya realizes that what she has experienced is what the Ten Commandments had in mind; only then is the essentially Christian message of the story made explicit.

* * *

As a young Futurist in 1916, Pasternak once described lyricism and history as opposite poles, incompatible and irreconcilable, both of them "equally a priori and absolute," and he defended the right of the artist to refrain from "preparation of history for tomorrow." These words were spoken in reaction against the increasing social and political commitment of Mayakovsky and other contemporary poets during World War I, but they are by no means the statement of an irresponsible aesthete. Pasternak climbed no platforms, yet his lyric verses of those years contain unmistakable echoes of World War I and the Revolution; his "Dramatic Fragments" of 1917 are an obvious reaction to events in Russia, and they show Saint-Just's ecstatic involvement in the French Revolution, just as Doctor Yurii Zhivago in Pasternak's novel would later express his thrill at the Russian Revolution's "splendid surgery."

What Pasternak was incapable of was to suppress subjective emotion or politicize artistic inspiration in the way demanded by the new Bolshevik rulers. The artistic and human disaster when a poet dragooned his muse into revolutionary service would eventually be demonstrated in the case of Mayakovsky; and later on, in *Doctor Zhivago,* Pasternak was to sketch a detailed portrait of Pasha Antipov-Strelnikov, whose "living human face became the embodiment of a principle, the image of an idea [when] he handed himself over to something lofty but deadening and pitiless, which would not spare him in the end." But the barrenness of abstract political schemes for the betterment of mankind is also demonstrated in some of Pasternak's early works written under the immediate impact of the Revolution. Even the relationship between Antipov and Zhivago is clearly adumbrated in the contrast of Robespierre and Saint-Just in the "Dramatic Fragments" and of the characters of Kovalevsky and Goltsev in a prose piece entitled "Without Love," which was penned and published in 1918.

"Without Love" is described in its subtitle as a "chapter from a tale." Like "The Childhood of Zhenya Luvers," it was, in fact, originally intended as part of a longer prose work, and it eventually contributed some of its material to *Doctor Zhivago* (the episode of the accident and the characters of Galliula, Gimazetdin, and Mekhanoshin all reappear there). The story also has an autobiographical basis. Pasternak spent much of the World War I period in the Urals, and the sleigh ride described in the story is clearly based on his own return journey to Moscow in the spring of 1917 (he recounts this in his *Essay in Autobiography*), and the author and his traveling companion, Boris Zbarsky, evidently served as prototypes for the day-dreamer Goltsev and the revolutionary Kovalevsky. In "Without Love," the lyrically musing Goltsev is described paradoxically as being in close touch with reality—the reality of remembered experience—whereas the activist Kovalevsky is shown as living in a fantasy world. Like the grim adults in "The Childhood of Zhenya Luvers," he simply misses the point of what life is really about. But, as Pasternak's next story, "Aerial Ways," demonstrates, the unbending rules and stringencies imposed by history can be more cruel by far than any of the Luvers' mild parental prohibitions.

The war and the Revolution and their aftermath caused a total disruption of Russian life and brought an end to the settled Chekhovian world of before. The universal upheaval was both described in Russian literature and reflected in the Russian language. Pasternak's and Mayakovsky's Futurist poetry and the prose of such writers as Isaak Babel, Boris Pilnyak, and Paternak bore witness in their form and substance to the general violation of norms and the destruction of order and causality. In "Aerial Ways" (1924) the very sequence and flow of time are disrupted; objects swing back and forth between past and future, and the author deliberately withholds information or else jumps ahead of his narrative, constantly changing his point of view from rapt impressionism to detached reportage or Tolstoyan "omniscience." The mannequin-like characters in the story are deprived of human volition. They are snatched up and swept along by events and circumstances. Their helplessness is that of the half-witted shepherdess, with her cry of "Where, oh where, are you going?" in the story's prerevolutionary opening episode. Her answer comes in the course of the tale. Unlike natural objects and animals, people are "borne only from the past into the future"—to the past there is no return. Thus, at a private family level in prerevolutionary Russia, it is possible for a mother to recover her child straying in the fields. But neither she nor the Bolshevik officer Polivanov can hope to prevent his execution later on in accordance with the revolutionary order of 1920.

In "Aerial Ways" Pasternak deploys the narrative devices and metaphoric speech habits familiar from his earlier prose. But here they are used for more than to define a private artistic morality or aesthetic, or to record sensation. It is not that the opposite poles of lyricism and history have begun to converge. But, without actually entering the hemisphere of historical concerns, Pasternak is now skirting its extremities and charting those "aerial ways" of history that only men like Lenin or Liebknecht can safely tread. Clearly, the story is partly a form af Aesopian comment on the fate of modern Russia, and a number of Pasternak's other writings also show the war and Revolution as a final tragic frontier separating the cruel modern world from a bygone lyrical age. *The Story* (1929), for instance, also spans the two epochs, and it records its hero's haunting memories of the prewar period. A novel that Pasternak planned in the 1930s but never completed was to have drawn a similar sharp dividing line between the old order's nostalgic memories and the Soviet age. Even Pasternak's *Essay in Autobiography* of 1957 breaks off, like the earlier *A Safe-Conduct,* at a point where the author considers he has written "sufficient to demonstrate how in [his] particular case life was realized in art, and how this realization was born of fate and experience." This time, a concluding note from Pasternak explains the reasons for the curtailment:

> To continue would be excessively difficult. . . . If one were consistent, he would have to talk about years, circumstances, men, and human fates seized within the frame of revolution. He would have to speak of a world of aims and

aspirations, feats and problems unknown before, of a new restraint, a new severity, and of new trials that this world has set for the human personality, for the honor, pride, diligence, and endurance of man.

* * *

Despite the difficulties of readjustment, Pasternak was forced to adapt in his own way to the new postrevolutionary realities. Never an admirer of Tsarism, he accepted the Russian Revolution, but not in a manner that met all the demands of the Marxist-Leninist literary establishment. Unlike the initial elemental spontaneity of the Revolution, the dull and doctrinaire aftermath was unpalatable to him as an artist, and he resisted all pressures to emerge from his shell of subjectivity into the realist arena of social commitment. But despite his disdainful response to the Central Committee's Resolution on Literature in 1925, and his scorn for the mediocrity sponsored and encouraged by officialdom, there was no hypocrisy in his professed desire to "breathe the air of history." The mid-1920s were years of arduous but steady productivity for Pasternak. The works he wrote then show a new awareness of the role of art in history and of an idiosyncratic but deeply felt responsibility toward it.

In a long poem called *The Lofty Malady,* published first in fragments and then complete in 1928, Pasternak attempts to find a place for the poet in the Revolution. He dwells, as Blok and others did earlier, on the alleged failure of the intelligentsia to pass this final, great historical test. Yet, though the poem appears to end in a major key, with a spectacular portrait of Lenin, it also issues a reminder, if any is needed, that the leader "avenged his departure with oppression." Another, longer poem, on *The Year 1905* (1927), depicts the revolutionary sweep of the 1905 Revolution in a series of brilliant impressionistic episodes, and this time the author has sought to rehabilitate the intelligentsia and show how its successive generations prepared and carried out the Revolution. *Lieutenant Schmidt* (1926) is artistically perhaps the most successful of these longer poems. Its hero is the historical leader of the naval revolt of 1905. But, though founded on fact, his character bears a number of Pasternakian traits. There is emphasis on his awareness of being a preordained sacrificial victim and on his contemplative qualities, rather than on any blazing revolutionary convictions. A fourth poem, or "novel in verse," entitled *Spektorsky,* was written in the late 1920s in an attempt to "graduate" from 1905 to the more demanding subject of 1917. In it, a firm association between the narrator and his hero is established, and the recurrent question of the intellectual's place in the Revolution is posed. But this time, in 1917, Spektorsky turns out like Goltsev: He remains a passive dreamer and a drifter who never commits himself to any cause and never really tries to control his individual fate.

All Pasternak's major poetic works of the 1920s show evidence of his
concerned effort to reassess his position as a litterateur in an age that placed
little value on intellect, sensitivity, and lack of commitment. Also, his
changing awareness inevitably colored his assessment of other writers. A
short note "On the Classics" (1927), for instance, explains how his earlier
impressionistic view of Pushkin has recently broadened to include new,
ethical elements. Strictly speaking, of course, he had always been acutely
aware of the artist's moral obligations, but initially, in "Some Propositions"
and "Letters from Tula," the pressures of conscience were mainly of a
private kind, prompted by the urgent need to justify talent and find a literary
expression adequate to inspiration's demands. But the Christian moral
concerns hinted at in "The Childhood of Zhenya Luvers" and *Lieutenant
Schmidt* point to new, "extraliterary" commitments to mankind at large,
which will ultimately transform the whole of Pasternak's art. *The Story*
presents the first unmistakable evidence of this new moral orientation. In
it, the hero's pity for a prostitute and a Danish woman moves him to
compose the story of Y_3, a poet and pianist, who plans to auction himself
to the highest bidder. The money raised through this act of self-sacrifice is
to be used to relieve the sufferings of mankind. Thus Pasternak forges a link
between creativity and sacrifice—a motif that will receive its fullest development in the prose and poems of *Doctor Zhivago*.

The material of *The Story* is closely bound up with that of the earlier
"Three Chapters from a Story" (1922) and of *Spektorsky*. As the author
puts it in the opening of *The Story*, they share "one and the same life"
and have characters and motifs in common: Lemokh figures in both "Three
Chapters" and *The Story*; Schütz in "Three Chapters" is clearly the
prototype of Baltz in *Spektorsky* and *The Story*; and the central hero of
all three works is basically the same semi-autobiographical projection of the
author. Although interrelated, the three works are complete in themselves,
and even the isolated "Three Chapters" seem to have their own emotional
coherence. Yet all these works are an attempt by Pasternak to move in a
new direction, using material from his own life in a broader, epic framework. As we saw earlier, the aspiration toward longer forms was evident
already in "Without Love" in 1918, but it was reinforced in the 1920s.
Pasternak rightly sensed that "the age demands the epic," and he therefore
undertook the difficult transition "from the lyric way of thought to the
epic." With varying degrees of success, this is embodied in the longer poems
and the prose works of the 1920s. As before, poetry and prose continue to
complement and coexist with one another, but there is now an apparent
distinction between their functions. In 1929, while working on both *The
Story* and *Spektorsky,* Pasternak wrote a note to a literary journal, explaining that the events of the war and Revolution had been dealt with in prose

"because the characterizations and formulations that in this part [that is, in *The Story*] are most binding and obvious are not possible in verse." Pasternak's subsequent experience seemed to confirm this conviction.

* * *

When Mayakovsky shot himself in 1930, it was the close of an era and the end of a generation that, as Roman Jakobson said, had "squandered its poets." Pasternak conveys some of this sense of finality in *A Safe-Conduct*, which ends with the death of Mayakovsky. (It may also be recalled that his later hero Yurii Zhivago died at the end of the 1920s.) The next years were ones of suffering and tragedy for all of Russia, not least for its writers and poets. Scores of them were purged, gagged by censorship, or, like Pasternak, hounded by the press and the literary bureaucracy and forced to resort to translation work as a safer means of livelihood. Yet Pasternak was aware that Mayakovsky's death placed a new artistic responsibility on his own shoulders, and as more and more voices fell silent in the 1930s, his lonely and still unarticulated sense of mission grew. Although the title of *A Safe-Conduct* seems to suggest the presence of some force that could safeguard the poet and his artistic integrity in the years to come, his survival through the worst period of the Great Terror must, in retrospect, be regarded as a near miracle.

The poet's tragic involvement with his age was expressed in 1932 in a new book of verse, *Second Birth,* where in one poem he appears—as later in Yurii Zhivago's "Hamlet"—in the role of an actor: "Oh, had I known when I made my debut that lines with blood in them can flood the throat and kill! . . . When feeling dictates a line of verse, it sends a slave out onto the stage. Then art comes to an end, and there is a breath of soil and of fate." This is not a Mayakovskian performance in which the poet's fictional literary biography is extended into real life. Instead the poet's literary persona and pronouncements have become an extension of the real life outside. The opening cycle of *Second Birth* articulates Pasternak's new wish: "Instead of the life of a poet, let me rather live the life of the poems themselves!" But the tragic potential is no less than in the case of Mayakovsky. The poet and his works are ultimately just as ineluctably bound together.

In his new collection of verse, Pasternak achieved a fresh, "unprecendented simplicity" of expression and explored new and broader themes than in earlier books. But the renewal promised in the title was short-lived. The 1930s as a whole were an unfruitful decade for Pasternak. The unpropitious political climate coincided with, and probably brought on, a virtual nervous breakdown in 1935. Moreover, Pasternak's painful sense of duty as a witness to the age, which was frustrated outwardly by political tyranny and from within by his still imperfect artistry, led to a crisis in his art.

After *Second Birth*, Pasternak's output of verse in the next decade was negligible, and he was displeased with what little he did compose. At a writers' conference in Minsk in 1936, he explained publicly that for some time to come he would be writing badly—"like a cobbler"—until he could adapt himself to the novelty of the themes he wished to treat. At the First Writers' Congress in 1934, he had warned against the stifling patronage of the Communist Party, and now in Minsk he again made it clear that he had little sympathy with the official treatment of literary work as if it were produced by mechanical pump and were not an organic entity with a life of its own. Yet, though the official brand of Socialist Realism was unacceptable to Pasternak, he was gravitating in both verse and prose toward his own original form of realism. World culture provides many instances of artists who move from a florid and exuberant youthful virtuosity to a wiser, more mature serenity and profundity, and Pasternak's desire to eschew his earlier metaphoric flamboyance in favor of plain statement was partly a result of a natural evolution. As he explained to one of his correspondents, "Direct formulation and metaphor are not opposites, but different stages of thought —early thought born of the moment and still unclarified in metaphor, and seasoned thought that has defined its meaning and is merely perfecting its expression in a nonmetaphoric statement." Another letter, written to his parents in 1934, explained that he was attempting to become a "poet in the manner of Pushkin" and to transform himself into a "writer of a Dickensian sort." In fact, the major work that occupied Pasternak in the later 1930s was a new novel in prose.

In 1938, Pasternak announced in *Literaturnaya gazeta* that he proposed to "write the first part of a novel. The novel will be in three parts. I do not know what it will be called. The first part will be about children." So far as we can tell from archive materials and a few fragments published between 1937 and 1939, this novel was in its early part a reworking of semi-autobiographical material from Pasternak's younger days. Two titles that he considered for the work were "The Notes of Patrick" and "The Notes of Zhivult." No doubt, the latter name contained a hint of the later "Zhivago," but the titles must also inevitably recall Rilke's *Notebooks of Malte Laurids Brigge*, which was a favorite work of Pasternak's and one he mentioned as a seminal influence on *Doctor Zhivago*. The opening of the novel was evidently meant to contain the fragments that we know as "A District in the Rear" and "Before Parting." In them, the fictional narrator recounts some events that took place in 1916, during World War I and on the eve of the Revolution—"that major event that overshadows all others." But, instead of continuing the narrative, the writer announces at the end of "Before Parting" that he will now recount some of his earlier memories. Thereupon, he delves back into his childhood recollections from the dawn of the twentieth century, and these are presented in four further short fragments. The first of these, "A Beggar Who Is Proud," tells how Patrick, the narrator, was transferred as a boy from one guardian to his eventual foster parents; "Aunt Olya" introduces the stepsister of the narrator's adoptive father and describes her association with Terentyev, a political activist friend; and two further fragments, "A Night in December" and "The House with the Galleries," describe episodes from the 1905 Revolution, which was evidently intended to figure prominently in this uncompleted novel. However, it is not known exactly how the work was to continue after the initial flashbacks. Pasternak left no general outline of his intentions, and it is probable that had it not been abandoned, the work would have been allowed to grow organically and naturally rather than compelled to follow any pre-established scheme.

Even in their unfinished state, however, it is clear that the novel fragments of the late 1930s occupy an intermediary position between Pasternak's early prose fiction and the later *Doctor Zhivago*. For instance, the personality and circumstances of Evgeniya Istomina in "A District in the Rear" and "Before Parting" firmly link her with Zhenya Luvers in Pasternak's early story. But she also shares certain features with Zhivago's Lara, such as her husband's teaching post in the Urals and departure to the front as a volunteer, and her prolonged sojourn in Yuryatin, where Lara meets the novel's hero. The fragments also introduce other familiar characters from Zhivago's family: Tonya, his wife; Shura (or Sasha), their son; and Aleksandr Aleksandrovich Gromeko, Zhivago's father-in-law. Moreover, the events described in the fragments bear a general correspondence to the Varykino episode in *Doctor Zhivago* (except that in the later work the Zhivago family does not reach the Urals until after the Revolution). Condensed to a few short sentences dealing with the hero's boyhood, the contents of "A Beggar Who Is Proud" also entered the later novel, and the revolutionary stirrings of 1905 and the accident that precipitated the death of Zhivago's mother-in-law are also prefigured in the other short prose fragments.

At the time of its writing, in the late 1930s, Pasternak once referred to his novel as being "about the year 1905." On the other hand, "A District in the Rear" and "Before Parting" take us already up to 1916. But in none of the known sketches from this period does Pasternak meet the great challenge of recording the postrevolutionary age. The difficulty of thinking creatively beyond the year 1917 was evidently then as great as it had ever been. Perhaps Pasternak needed World War II and the aftermath of the death of Stalin to enable him to see the events of the Soviet period in proper artistic perspective. In the 1930s, he still seemed to be grappling unsuccessfully with his autobiographical material and using the somewhat unsatisfactory technique of half narrative and half reminiscence already employed in *The Story*. Although the sober narrative style of *Doctor*

Zhivago had now been discovered, Pasternak still retained the poetic
luxury of a first-person storyteller. But he had not yet established *Doctor
Zhivago*'s central and deeply autobiographical thematic thread, which
binds the work together as the chronicle of a great poet's destiny in a tragic
age.

* * *

When World War II came, the period of Pasternak's involvement with
short prose stories and fragments was over. *Doctor Zhivago* was the product
of a new phase of his development, which, strictly speaking, had little
connection with the short-prose genre. Yet an account of Pasternak as a
prose-writer would be incomplete without mention of his novel, and even
in absentia it must be regarded as the proper conclusion of a definitive prose
anthology.

World War II took Pasternak away from his work on the novel. After
his country became embroiled in the war in 1941, he was for a time evacuated to the Urals along with several other Soviet writers, but he later
returned to Moscow and paid a visit to the battle front. Much of the war
period he spent working on the Shakespeare translations that were soon to
add a new facet to his fame. Perhaps it was under this theatrical influence
that he tried out some of the Zhivago material in a version for the stage
entitled *In This World.* However, this version was never completed or
published. Between 1941 and 1945, lyric poems again flowed freely, and
they appeared in two books, *On Early Trains* (1943) and *Terrestrial Expanse* (1945). But, under the renewed cultural and political oppression of
the postwar years, publication of original works ceased again. Pasternak
devoted himself, instead, to a translation of Goethe's *Faust.* Privately and
with no prospect of immediate publication, he wrote some lyric verse and
worked on a new novel in prose. The main substance of *Doctor Zhivago* was
ready by the beginning of the post-Stalin "thaw" in 1953, and it was
completed and some of its poems were published as a preview the following
year. The novel was rejected for publication in the Soviet Union, but in 1957
it appeared in the West despite pressure from the Soviet authorities, and it
was widely acclaimed. Partly on the strength of *Doctor Zhivago,* Pasternak
was awarded the Nobel Prize in 1958. This led to a storm of criticism back
home, and the award was eventually and regretfully declined. The same
year, there appeared in the West Pasternak's *Essay in Autobiography* (published in the United States as *I Remember: Sketch for an Autobiography*),
written as the Introduction to a projected Soviet edition of his collected
verse that was later canceled. The following year, a book of verse, *When
the Sky Clears,* also found its way to a Western publisher. Pasternak's final
literary project was a dramatic trilogy entitled *The Blind Beauty.* It was

never completed, and the author died at his home near Moscow in May 1960.

Pasternak regarded *Doctor Zhivago* as his crowning achievement. It fed on, and grew naturally out of, his earlier writings, developing Christian motifs, aesthetic, ethical, and historical views, and strands of literary and personal experience, combining them in a bold new poetic revelation of man's place in the modern world. The novel is also a fulfillment of its author's prophecy in a poem of the early 1920s: "O verses, my mania, I'll bid you *adieu.* I've appointed the novel our next rendezvous." And in *Doctor Zhivago* verse and prose are organically combined, each playing a vital role in the whole composition. As Pasternak explained to a visitor, lyric poetry alone can no longer convey the immensity of modern man's experience, for he has "acquired values which are best expressed in prose." The main ideological weight of *Doctor Zhivago,* therefore, rests on the prose narrative, and readers of Pasternak's novel have been quick to make comparisons with Tolstoy, Dostoevsky, and the Russian nineteenth-century novel tradition whose influence was apparent despite the author's alleged pursuit of Pushkinesque or Chekhovian simplicity and modesty. Certainly, the texture of the language is clearer and more "realist" than before. And, despite the Soviet critics' displeasure, the outlines of the story are an object lesson in Marxist history, depicting the downfall and death of a bourgeois-intellectual poet cast into the historical "ash can" by the forces of revolution. Yet the prose remains that of a poet: Some of the descriptive passages show no lessening of Pasternak's earlier verbal magic and deft observation, while the improbable, symbolic coincidences with which the plot is riven are but a transfer of poetic metaphor to the macrostructure of the novel. Moreover, the final words of the novel and the full Christian essence of Zhivago's spiritual message are reserved for the poet.

What many had regarded as *Doctor Zhivago*'s major shortcomings—its arbitrary coincidences and pale characterization—were justified by the author in a letter he wrote in 1959. Written in colorful and idiosyncratic English and addressed to the poet Stephen Spender, this message described how Pasternak had always perceived reality and attempted to convey it in his writings. For Pasternak,

> ... the top pleasure consists in having hit the sense or taste of reality, in having been able, in having succeeded in rendering the *atmosphere of being,* the surrounding whole, the total environment, the frame where the particular and depicted thing is having been plunged and floating. . . . Always my sense of the whole, of the reality as such was that of a reached sending, of a sudden unawaited coming, of a welcomed arrival and I always sought to reproduce this trait of being sent and launched, that I thought to find in the nature of the appearance. . . . There is an attempt in the novel to represent the whole

sequence of facts and beings and happenings like some moving entireness, like a developing, passing by, rolling and rushing inspiration, as if reality itself had freedom and choice and was composing itself out of the numberless variants and versions.

Thus Pasternak underlined the essential unity of vision and *Weltgefühl* that had inspired a lifetime of writing in prose and verse and had finally borne fruit in *Doctor Zhivago*.

* * *

This anthology contains neither Pasternak's poetry nor his novel, and readers must look elsewhere for texts of, and critical commentary on, those works. When Pasternak had written all the short prose works printed here, he had still another twenty years of creativity before him. Yet it can be claimed that the short prose writings contain the best essence of his art: In comparison with *A Safe-Conduct* and "The Childhood of Zhenya Luvers," the later novel must in some respects appear as a faulted masterpiece. But the basic unity of Pasternak's vision means that his prose, even in translation, contains some of the most original virtues of his poetry, enriched with other qualities that only a supreme master of prose idiom can express.

Autobiography

A Safe-Conduct

To the memory of Rainer Maria Rilke

PART I

1

One hot summer morning in the year 1900 an express train was leaving the Kursk Station in Moscow. Just before its departure someone wearing a black Tyrolean cloak came up to the window from outside. With him was a tall woman. She seemed to be his mother or older sister. They talked to my father about something into which they were all initiated, all three speaking with the same animation; the woman, though, exchanged a word in Russian now and then with my mother, while the unknown man spoke only German. Although I knew the language perfectly, I had never heard it spoken as he spoke it. For this reason, there on the crowded platform, between two jangles of the bell, the foreign man seemed to be a silhouette among bodies, a fiction in the midst of the unfictitious.

On the journey, as we drew near Tula, this couple appeared again in our compartment. They were saying that the express was not scheduled to stop at Kozlovka-Zaseka and they were afraid the guard would not tell the driver in time to make a brief halt at the Tolstoys'. From the rest of their conversation I concluded that they were going to see Sofiya Andreevna, because she went to symphony concerts in Moscow and she had been at our house not long before. But that matter of infinite importance symbolized by the letters

Ct. L. N., which in our family played a brain-racking role hidden in endless smoking, did not yield itself to any embodiment. It had been seen too early in infancy. Its hoariness, subsequently retouched in the sketches by my father, Repin, and others, had long been assigned by my childish imagination to another old man, one seen more often, and probably later in life— Nikolai Nikolaevich Gay.

Then they said good-bye and went to their own compartment. Not much farther on, the embankments' flight was sharply braked. There was a flashing of birch trees. Coupling plates down the whole length of track snorted and clashed. Then out of a whirl of singing sand a cumulous sky tore loose with relief, and, low to the ground as if dancing the russkaya, an empty carriage and pair made a half turn out of the copse and came flitting up to the people who had left the train. Stirring as a sudden shot, came the brief silence of a railway halt that knew nothing of us. We were not to stop there. They waved good-bye with handkerchiefs; we waved back. We were still just able to see them being helped in. Now the coachman had handed the lady the rug and was half standing up, in his red sleeves, to arrange his sash and gather the long skirts of his coat beneath himself. Any second now he would be off. At this moment a curve in the line caught us up and, slowly turning like a page that has been read, the railway halt disappeared. Face and incident were forgotten, so it seemed, forever.

2

Three years went by; it was winter outside. Dusk and fur coats shortened the street by one-third. Along it flew the noiseless cubes of carriages and lanterns. An end was put to the inheritance of conventions, already broken off more than once. They were washed away by the wave of a more powerful kind of succession—that of faces.

I shall not describe in detail what preceded this: How nature was revealed to the ten-year-old in a sensation resembling Gumilyov's "Sixth Sense"; how, in response to the five-petaled stare of a plant, botany became his first passion; how the names he sought and found in the catalog brought peace to those sweet-scented eyes that rushed unquestioningly toward Linnaeus, as if from obscurity to fame. How in the spring of 1901 a detachment of Dahomean horsewomen was put on show in the Zoological Garden. How for me the first awareness of woman was linked with a sense of naked ranks, of serried anguish, a tropical parade to the sound of drums. How I became the slave of forms earlier than I should have done because, in these women, I had seen too early the form of slaves. How in the summer of 1903, in Obolenskoye, near where the Scriabins lived, a girl brought up in a family we knew, who lived beyond the Protva, was almost drowned while swimming. How the student who jumped in to save her perished, and later she herself went mad after several attempts at suicide from the same precipice. How later, when I had broken my leg, escaping two future wars in a single evening, and was lying motionless, encased in plaster, the house of these friends the other side of the river caught fire, and the shrill alarm bells of the village shook in delirium, crazed as a village idiot. How the slant-angled glow beat away at the air, stretching itself like a kite being launched, then suddenly curling the splints of its framework into a funnel, dived down head over heels into the pie-soft layers of gray and crimson smoke.

How, as he galloped that night with a doctor from Maloyaroslavets, my father's hair turned gray at the sight of the wreathing reflection that rose like a cloud two versts away above the forest road, convincing him that what was burning was the woman he loved, with three children and a hundred pounds of plaster of Paris that she could not lift without risk of permanent crippling.

I shall not describe any of this. The reader will do it for me. He enjoys horrors, and stories with plots, and regards history as an uninterrupted, ever continuing tale. It is not clear whether he wishes it to have a rational ending. He likes those places beyond which his walks have never taken him. He is immersed in forewords and introductions, but for me life has revealed itself only at the point where he tends to sum things up. Even without mentioning how the inner articulation of history was thrust upon my under- standing in an image of unavoidable death, I only came completely alive, within life itself, on those occasions when the dreary simmering of ingredi- ents was done and, having dined from the finished dish, a feeling equipped with all conceivable spaciousness tore loose from its moorings and escaped to freedom.

So, it was winter out of doors. The street was chopped a third shorter by dusk and was full of errand-running all day long. A whirl of streetlamps chased along after the street, lagging behind in the whirl of snowflakes. On my way home from school, the name Scriabin, covered with snow, skipped down from a poster onto my back. I carried it home on the flap of my satchel; water flowed from it onto the windowsill. This adoration attacked me more cruelly and undisguisedly than any fever. Whenever I saw him I turned pale, then straightaway, ashamed of the very pallor, I turned deep red. If he spoke to me, I would lose all power of thought and would hear myself answer with something quite off the point, while everyone laughed, though *what* I said I did not hear. I knew that he guessed everything; yet not once did he come to my aid. That meant he did not spare me, which was just the unshared, unrequited feeling for which I thirsted. This alone, and the fiercer it was, the more surely it protected me from the ravaging effect of his indescribable music.

Before leaving for Italy he dropped in on us to say good-bye. He played —this cannot be put into words—had supper with us, talked philosophy, chatted simply and unaffectedly, and joked. All the time it seemed to me he was suffering an agony of boredom. The moment of leave-taking came, good wishes resounded, my own dropped like a clot of blood into the common heap of farewells. All these things were said on the move, and the exclamations, crowding in the doorway, gradually crossed over into the entrance hall. Here it was all repeated once again with the abruptness of recapitulation, like the hook of a collar that for ages has refused to go into its tightly sewn loop. The door banged; the key turned twice. Passing the grand piano, which with all the radiant loops of its music stand still spoke of how he had played, my mother sat down to look through the études he had left. And no sooner had the first sixteen bars formed themselves into a sentence that was full of some sort of astounded readiness, unrewardable by anything on earth, than I raced coatless and bareheaded down the stairs and through Myasnitskaya Street in the night, to bring him back or at least set eyes on him once more.

This has been experienced by everyone. To all of us tradition has appeared; to all it has promised a face; to all, each in a different way, it has kept its promise. We have all become people only to the measure to which we have loved people and had the opportunity to love. Never, under cover of its nickname, "milieu," has it been content with the compound image people make up about it, but it has always detailed some one of its most decided exceptions to us. Then why have the majority departed in the form of a bearable, yet only just tolerated, commonness? To personality they preferred nonentity, afraid of the sacrifices tradition demands from childhood. To love selflessly and unreservedly, with a strength equal to the square of the distance—this is the task of our hearts while we are children.

3

Of course I did not catch up with him, and indeed scarcely thought I would. We met six years later, on his return from abroad. This period fell full on my adolescent years. And everyone knows the vastness of adolescence. However many decades are heaped upon us afterward, they are powerless to fill this hangar, to which they come flying back for memories, day and night, separately or flocking together, like trainer aircraft coming in for fuel. In other words, these years in our life constitute a part that exceeds the whole, and Faust, who lived through them twice, lived something utterly unimaginable, to be measured only in terms of a mathematical paradox.

He arrived, and straightaway rehearsals of *L'Extase* began. (How I should now like to exchange this name, which smacks of a tight little soap wrapping, for something more suitable!) They took place in the mornings;

the way to them lay in soupy darkness along Furkasovsky Lane and Kuznetsky Bridge Street sunk in an icy pulp. Down the sleepy road, the tongues
of belfries hung plunged in mist. From each a solitary bell gave out a single
boom. The rest stayed unanimously silent with all the self-denial of Lenten
copper. Nikitskaya Street, at the end of Gazetny, whipped egg and cognac
in the resonant pool of the crossroads. Wailing, the iron sleigh runners
drove into puddles, and the flintstone clicked beneath the canes of the
concertgoers. At these hours the Conservatoire looked like a circus at the
time of its morning clean-out. The amphitheater cages lay empty; the stalls
were slowly filling. Forced into its winter season, like a wild beast driven
back with sticks, the music slapped its paw out onto the wooden paneling
of the organ. All of a sudden the public would begin to arrive in a steady
stream, as if a city were being evacuated and left to the enemy. The music
was let loose. Colorful, countlessly breaking and multiplying with lightning
speed, it scattered in leaps and bounds across the platform. They ordered
it, and with feverish haste it sped toward harmony. Then suddenly, attain-
ing a thunder of noise unprecedentedly blended, it would break off, while
all the bass whirlwind sounded, and go dead still, lining up along the edge
of the footlights.

This was the first settlement of man in the worlds that Wagner had
opened up for chimeras and mastodons. And on this area an unchimerical,
lyrical dwelling was being erected, materially equal to the whole universe,
which had been ground down to make its bricks. Above the wattle fence
of the symphony blazed the sun of Van Gogh. Its windowsills were covered
with the dusty archive of Chopin. The inhabitants were not poking about
in this dust, but in their whole way of being they were realizing the finest
behests of their forerunner.

I could not hear it without tears. It had engraved itself on my memory
before it lay on the zinc plates of the first proofs. There was nothing
unexpected in this. The hand that wrote it had lain on me six years earlier,
with no less weight.

What else had all those years been but subsequent transformations of that
living imprint, handed over to the will of growth? It is not surprising that,
in the symphony, I met a friend of my own age and one enviably fortunate.
Its nearness could not but tell upon the people close to me, upon my work,
and upon my whole daily life. And this is how it told.

More than anything else in the world I loved music; more than anyone
else in music—Scriabin. My musical babblings had begun not long before
my first acquaintance with him. By the time of his return, I was the pupil
of a certain composer alive to this day. The only thing I had still to learn
was orchestration. All sorts of things were said, but what matters is that,
even if the opposite things had been said, I could not have imagined a life
outside music.

But I did not possess absolute pitch. This is the name of the ability to recognize the pitch of any note sounded at random. My lack of a quality that had nothing to do with musical talent in general, yet was possessed to perfection by my mother, gave me no peace. Had music been my true career, as it seemed to outsiders, I would not have cared about absolute pitch. I knew that outstanding composers of my time did not have it, and that both Wagner and Tchaikovsky were also thought perhaps to have lacked it. But music was to me a cult, that is, the destructive focal point at which everything that was most superstitious and self-abnegating in me gathered, and therefore every time my will took wing after some evening inspiration, I hastened next morning to humble it again by recalling this defect.

Nonetheless, I had written several serious pieces. Now I was to show them to my idol. A meeting was arranged, quite naturally in view of the acquaintance between our families, but I regarded it with my usual extremeness. Such a step would have seemed an importunity to me under any circumstances, and in the present case, it assumed in my eyes the proportions of something like blasphemy. And, when on the appointed day I was on my way to Glazovsky Lane, where Scriabin was temporarily living, I was bringing him not so much my compositions as a love that had long exceeded all possible expression, and my apologies for the imagined tactlessness of which I felt myself to be the involuntary cause. The overcrowded No. 4 gripped and tossed these feelings, carrying them inexorably toward their formidable goal, along the tawny Arbat Street, which was dragged toward Smolensky Lane by shaggy, sweating black horses and pedestrians up to their knees in water.

4

It was then I appreciated how well our facial muscles are schooled. My throat tightened with agitation; I mumbled something with parched tongue, slaking my answers with frequent gulps of tea so as not to choke or commit any other blunder.

Over my jawbone and the bumps of my forehead the skin was twitching. I jerked my eyebrows, nodded, smiled, and each time I touched on the bridge of my nose the wrinkles of this mimicry, ticklish and vexing as spiderweb, I found a convulsively squeezed handkerchief in my hand, repeatedly wiping large drops of sweat from my brow. Behind my head, tied up with curtains, a mist of spring was drifting the length of the road. In front of me, between my hosts, who were trying with redoubled loquacity to draw me out of my embarrassment, tea breathed in the cups, the samovar hissed, pierced with an arrow of steam, and sunshine billowed, hazy with water and manure. Smoke from a cigar end, fibrous as a tortoiseshell comb, stretched from the ashtray up to the light and, reaching it, satedly crawled along it sideways, as along a piece of woolen cloth. I do not know why, but this spinning of dazzled air, steamy waffles, smoking sugar and silver burning like paper aggravated my nervousness unbearably. It subsided when I crossed the room and found myself at the piano.

The first piece I played with agitation; the second—almost in control of it; the third—surrendering to the pressure of the new and unforeseen. My glance happened to fall on my listener.

Following the gradual progress of the performance, he had first raised his head and then his eyebrows, and finally, he himself stood up, beaming, and accompanying the changes of the melody with scarcely perceptible changes in his smile, he floated toward me along its rhythmic perspective. He liked it all. I quickly finished. At once he began assuring me that it was absurd to talk of mere musical gifts when there was something incomparably greater there, that I had the ability to say something of my own music. Referring to the episodes that had just flashed by, he sat down at the piano to repeat one that had particularly attracted him. It was a complicated phrase, and I did not expect him to reproduce it exactly, but what happened was something else unexpected: He repeated it in a different key, and the defect tormenting me all these years splashed out from beneath his hands as his own.

And again, preferring the hazards of divination to the eloquence of fact, I gave a start and made a wager with myself. If to my confession he should object, "But Borya, I haven't got it either," then—all right, it would mean I was not imposing myself upon music, but music itself was meant as my destiny. But if in his answer there should be any talk of Wagner and Tchaikovsky, of piano-tuners and all the rest of it—but already I was approaching the alarming subject, and, interrupted in mid-question, was already swallowing down the answer: "Absolute pitch? After all I have said to you? What about Wagner? What about Tchaikovsky? And the hundreds of piano-tuners who have it? . . . "

We walked up and down the salon. He kept putting his hand on my shoulder or taking me by the arm. He was talking of the harmfulness of improvisation, of when and why and how one should write. As models of the simplicity one should always aspire to, he mentioned his own new sonatas, which were notorious for their difficulty. Examples of a reprehensible complexity he found in the most platitudinous parlor songs. I was not disturbed by the paradox in this comparison. I agreed that lack of personality was a more complex thing than personality; that an unguarded prolixity seemed accessible because it was without content; that because we are corrupted by the emptiness of clichés, we think, when after long desuetude we come across something unprecedentedly rich in content, that *that* is only formal pretentiousness. Imperceptibly he moved on to more definite exhortations. He inquired about my education, and when he learned that I had chosen the Law Faculty because it was easy, he advised me to transfer without delay to the philosophy section of the Historical and Philological Faculty—which indeed I did the next day. And while he talked I was thinking about what had happened. I did not go back on my bargain with fate, but thought of the sorry issue of my wager. Was my god dethroned by this chance event? Not in the least—it raised him from his former loftiness to a new height. Why had he refused me the simple answer I had longed for so much? That was his secret. Sometime, when it would be too late, he would present me with the omitted confession. How had he overcome his own doubts in his youth? That was his secret too, and it elevated him to his new height. But it had been dark in the room for a long time now; the lamps were lit in the street outside; it was time to leave.

As I said good-bye, I did not know how to thank him. Something was mounting up in me. Something was tearing and trying to get free. Something was weeping; something was exulting.

The first stream of coolness in the street had a taste of houses and distances. Like a great Tower of Babel they rose to the sky, lifted from the cobbles by the single-heartedness of the Moscow night. I remembered my parents and the questions they were impatiently waiting to ask me. However I told it, my news could have only the most joyful meaning. And as I yielded to the logic of the tale I was to tell, only now, for the first time, did I consider the happy events of the day as facts. In such a form they did not belong to me. They became a reality only when destined for others. No matter how exciting the news I was taking home, my soul was disquieted. Yet the consciousness that this very sadness was something I would never be able to pour into anyone else's ear, and that, like my future, it would stay below, in the street, with all Moscow, my Moscow, mine at this moment as never before—this consciousness more and more resembled happiness. I went along side streets, crossing over more often than I needed to. Entirely without my knowledge, a world was melting and cracking in me that only the day before had seemed inborn forever. I went on, quickening my step at every turning, and did not know that in that night I was already breaking with music.

Greece had an excellent understanding of the different ages of life. She took care not to mix them up. She knew how to think of childhood as something closed upon itself and independent, like a central nucleus of integration. How greatly she possessed this ability can be seen in the myth of Ganymede and a great many similar myths. The same views formed part of her conception of the demigod and the hero. In her view, a certain amount of risk and tragedy had to be gathered sufficiently early and held in the hand, obvious at a glance. In the interest of its future good proportions, certain parts of the building had to be laid, simultaneously, at the very beginning, and among them the fundamental arch of fatality. And lastly, perhaps in some memorable analogy, death itself had to be lived through.

This is why, with all its art of genius, always unexpected and enthralling as a fairy tale, antiquity knew no romanticism.

Brought up on a rigorous demand, which no one was ever to repeat, on the superhumanity of deeds and tasks, it knew nothing whatever of super-humanity as a matter of personal passion. It was insured against this because it prescribed entirely for childhood the whole dose of extraordinariness contained in the world. And when, after taking it, a person entered with gigantic strides into a gigantic reality, both his stride and the world around him were accounted ordinary.

5

One evening very soon after, as I set out for a meeting of "Serdarda," a drunken fellowship founded by a dozen poets, musicians, and artists, I remembered I had promised Yulian Anisimov, who had previously read some excellent translations from Dehmel, that I would bring him another German poet, the one I preferred above all his contemporaries. And again, as many a time before, the collection of poems *Mir zur Feier* found itself in my hands at my most difficult hour. And off it went through the slush toward wood-built Razgulyai, to a damp interlacement of ancient times, heredity, and youthful promises, to be stupefied by rooks in the attic under the poplars, and come back home with a new friendship—that is, with the awareness of one more door in the town, where at that time there were few. But it is time I told how this collection of poems came my way.

What happened was that six years earlier, in the December dusk that I have set out to describe twice already, together with the noiseless street that mysterious, grimacing snowflakes lay in wait for everywhere, I too was shuffling about on my knees, helping my mother set my father's bookshelves in order. The printed entrails, well wiped with a rag and shoved into a rough pile, were being replaced in regular rows on the disemboweled shelves, when all of a sudden from one of the heaps, an especially wobbly and disobedient one, there fell a little book in a faded gray cover. It was wholly by chance that I did not push it back but picked it up from the floor and later took it to my room. A long time passed and I came to love this book—and soon another one as well, which had joined it and which had been dedicated to my father by the same hand. But still more time passed before one day I realized that their author, Rainer Maria Rilke, must be that very same German whom we had once left in mid-journey, long ago in the summer, on the slowly turning section of a forgotten railway halt in a forest. I ran to my father to check my guess and he confirmed it, wondering why it should excite me so.

I am not writing my autobiography. I turn to it when someone else's demands that I should. Together with its principal character, I consider that only the hero deserves his actual life story to be told, while the history of a poet is unpresentable in this form. It would have to be assembled from inessential matters bearing witness to compromises with pity and coercion. The poet deliberately gives the whole of his life such a steep incline that it cannot exist in the vertical line of biography, where we expect to meet it. It cannot be found under his own name and has to be sought under those of others, in the biographical columns of those who follow him. The more the productive individuality is closed within itself, the more collective—and this is no allegory—is his story. The realm of the subconscious in a genius does not submit to measurement. It consists of everything that happens to his readers and that he does not know. I am not presenting my reminiscences in memory of Rilke. On the contrary, I myself received them from him as a gift.

6

Although my story has inclined this way, I have not asked the question of what music is or what leads up to it. I have not done so, not only because I woke up one night in my third year of life and found the whole horizon flooded with it for more than fifteen years ahead, and thus had no occasion to experience its problematics, but also because it now ceases to bear on our theme. However, the same question in relation to art as such, art as a whole, in other words, in relation to poetry, cannot be passed over. I shall answer it neither theoretically nor in a sufficiently general form, but much of what I shall relate will be the answer I can give for myself and for my poet.

The sun used to rise behind the post office and, slipping down Kiselny Lane, would set over the Neglinka. When it had gilded our part of the house, it would make its way from lunchtime on into the dining room and kitchen. The apartment was government property; its rooms were made up from classrooms. I was studying at the university. I was reading Hegel and Kant. It was a time when, at every meeting with friends, gulfs would yawn and first one, then another of us would emerge with some new discovery.

Often we would get each other up in the dead of night. The reason for it always seemed of utmost urgency. Whoever was woken was ashamed of his sleep, as if it was an accidentally exposed weakness. To the fright of the unfortunate inhabitants of the house, all without exception considered nonentities, we would instantly set off—as if to an adjoining room—to Sokolniki and the Yaroslavl railway crossing. I had made friends with a girl from a wealthy family. It was obvious to everyone that I loved her. She took part in these walks only in the abstract, on the lips of those more used to going without sleep and adapted to such a life. I was giving a few meagerly paid lessons so as not to take money from my father. In the summers, when my family went away, I used to stay on in the town at my own expense. The illusion of independence was obtained by means of such moderation in food that on top of everything else there was hunger too, which conclusively transformed night into day in the uninhabited apartment. Music, which I was still just putting off saying good-bye to, was already becoming interwoven with literature. The depth and charm of Bely and Blok could not but be revealed to me. Their influence was combined in a singular way with a force that went beyond mere ignorance. My fifteen-year abstinence from words, which I had sacrificed to sounds, doomed me to originality as a certain kind of maiming forces a person into performing acrobatics. Along with some of my acquaintances I had connections with "Musaget." From others I learned of the existence of Marburg. Kant and Hegel were replaced by Cohen, Natorp, and Plato.

I am characterizing my life of those years with intentional randomness. I could multiply these tokens or exchange them for others. However, the ones I have given are enough for my purpose. Using them to mark out approximately—as on a technical sketch—what reality was for me at that time, I shall ask myself at this point by what virtue and whereabouts in reality poetry was born. I do not have to spend a long time pondering the answer. This is the only feeling my memory has preserved in all its freshness.

It was born from the interruptions of these series, from the diversity of their speed, from the way the more sluggish lagged behind and piled up far in the rear, on the deep horizon of memory.

Love raced along most impetuously of all. Sometimes it found itself at the head of nature and would overtake the sun. But as this happened only rarely, one could say that the force that gilded one side of the house and then began to bronze the other, which washed weather away with weather and turned the heavy winch of the four seasons, moved forward with constant superiority, nearly always competing with love, while the remaining orders dragged along at the back, at various distances. I often heard the hiss of a yearning that had not originated with me. Catching up with me from behind, it filled me with fright and pity. It issued from the point at which everyday life had torn away, and it either threatened to put brakes on reality or else begged for everyday life to be joined to the living air, which in the meantime had moved a long way ahead. And what is known as inspiration consisted in this turning around to look back. The most tumid, uncreative parts of existence called for a special vividness because of the distance to which they had rolled away. Inanimate objects acted still more strongly. They were models for still life, a branch of art especially beloved of artists. Piling up in the very farthest distance of the living universe, and in a state of immobility, they provided the fullest possible idea of its moving entirety, as does any limit that appears to us as a contrast. Their disposition marked a frontier beyond which wonder and pity had nothing to do. There, science was at work, seeking the atomic foundations of reality.

But because there was no second universe from which one could have lifted reality up out of the first, taking it by its tops as if by the hair, the manipulations it itself called for required that a representation of it be taken, as in algebra, which is limited quantitatively by a similar singleness of plane. But to me this representation always seemed a way out of the difficulty, not an aim in itself. I always conceived the aim as being to shift the thing represented from cold axles onto hot, to make what had already been lived set off to pursue and catch up with life. This is how I reasoned at that time, not very differently from how I think now. We represent people in order to throw a cloak of weather upon them. Weather—or what is the same thing, nature—we represent in order to throw our passion about its shoulders. We drag the everyday into prose for the sake of poetry. We draw prose into poetry for the sake of music. This is, in the broadest sense of the word, what I called art, set by the clock of the living race, which chimes by the generation.

This is why the sensation of the city never corresponded to the place in it where my life was being lived. An inward pressure always flung it back into the depth of the perspective I have described. There puffing clouds kicked their heels, and, thrusting its way through the crowd of them, the mingling smoke of innumerable stoves hung athwart the sky. There, in lines, as if along embankments, collapsing houses plunged their porches into the snow. There the frail squalor of a dragged-out existence was fingered by quiet guitar pluckings of drunkenness. And, having sat at the bottle until they were boiled as hard as eggs, large, stately ladies, red in the face, emerged with swaying husbands out into the nightly tide of cabs, as if they were coming from the feverish uproar of tubs in the bathhouse out into the birch-twig coolness of the anteroom. There people poisoned themselves and burned away, threw acid at rivals, drove in satin to weddings and pawned their furs. There the varnished grins of a way of life that was cracking apart exchanged winks on the quiet, and as they waited for me to give them a lesson, my alumni—school pupils who were repeating the year—would arrange themselves, setting out their textbooks, their faces painted saffron-bright with unintelligence. There too, with its hundred auditoriums, the gray-green, much littered university ebbed and flowed with sound.

With the glass of their spectacles glancing across that of their pocket watches, the professors raised their heads to address the galleries and vaults. The heads of students detached themselves from their jackets and hung on long cords, pairing off in even numbers with the green lampshades.

During these visits to the city, in which I arrived each day as if from another, my heartbeat invariably speeded up. Had I gone to a doctor then, he would have thought I had malaria. Yet these attacks of chronic impatience could not have been cured by quinine. This strange perspiring was caused by the obstinate crudeness of those worlds—their turgid visuality, which nothing within them spent to their advantage. They lived and moved as if striking attitudes. Among them, uniting them into a kind of colony, the antenna of universal preordainment rose up mentally. Just at the base of this imagined post came the attacks of fever. It was generated by currents sent by the mast to its opposite pole. Conversing with the distant mast of genius, it summoned from those regions some new Balzac into its own small settlement. Yet one had only to go a little way from the fatal rod for immediate tranquillity to set in.

Thus, for example, I didn't feel feverish at the lectures given by Savin, because that professor was not one to serve as a type. He lectured with real talent, which grew in proportion as his subject grew. Time did not take offense at him. It did not go tearing away from his assertions, leaping into ventilators or flinging itself headlong toward the doors. It did not blow the smoke back up the chimneys or slither down the roof to catch hold of the hook of a trolley sweeping away into the snowstorm. No, it would plunge head and ears into medieval England or the Robespierre Convention, pulling us in with it and, together with us, everything we could imagine alive beyond the high university windows fashioned at the very cornices.

I stayed healthy, too, in a room in some cheap furnished lodgings where, with several other students, I led the studies of a group of grown-up pupils. Nobody there shone with talent. Without expecting a legacy from anywhere, it was quite enough that instructors and instructed joined in a common effort to shift themselves from the standstill to which life was preparing to nail them. Like their teachers, among whom were some who had stayed on at the university, they were not typical of their professions. Clerks and employees, workers, domestic servants and postmen, they came here in order that one day they might become something else.

I was not feverish in their active midst, and in rare harmony with myself I often used to turn off from there into a nearby side street where in one of the courtyard buildings of the Zlatoustinsky monastery lived whole guilds of flower-sellers. This was where boys would come and load themselves with all the flora of the Riviera, to go and peddle it on the Petrovka. Ordered from Nice by peasant wholesalers, these treasures could be obtained from them on the spot for a mere trifle. I was especially drawn to them at the turn of the academic year, when, on discovering one fine evening that studies had long been taking place without lamps, the bright March twilight started coming more and more often into the dirty lodgings and soon was not even getting left behind on the hotel porch after the lessons were over. With its head uncovered, contrary to its custom, by the low kerchief of winter night, the street seemed to grow up suddenly at the porch from underneath the earth with a kind of dried fairy tale on its scarcely stirring lips. Spring air shuffled jerkily over the hardy cobbles. And, as if they had a live skin drawn tightly over them, the outlines of the street shivered a chilly shiver, tired of waiting for the first star, whose appearance the insatiable, fabulously leisurely sky kept putting off.

The reeking gallery was packed to the ceiling with empty wicker boxes that had foreign stamps under their sonorous Italian postmarks. In reply to the felted grunt of the door, a cloud of paunchy steam would billow outside, as if to relieve itself, and even in the steam one guessed at something unspeakably exciting. Directly opposite the vestibule, in the depth of the gradually sloping room, youthful peddlers crowded at a small fortress window, taking the roughly counted goods and stuffing them into their baskets. There too, on the other side of the broad table, the proprietor's sons were silently slicing open new parcels that had just been brought from the Customs. Bent open in two like a book, the orange lining laid bare the fresh core of the wicker box. Serried tangles of chilled violets were lifted out all in one piece like dark blue layers of dried Malaga. They filled the room— a sort of janitor's lodge—with such a stupefying fragrance that the columns of early evening dusk and the shadows lying in layers over the floor seemed cut out from a damp, dark lilac turf.

But the real miracles were still to come. Going through to the very end of the yard, the owner would unbolt one of the doors of the stone shed, raise a trapdoor by its ring, and in that moment the tale of Ali Baba and the forty thieves would come true in all its dazzling splendor. On the floor of the dry cellar, explosively, like suns, there burned four globe lightnings and, frenzied in their huge tubs, rivaling the lamps, were hot sheaves of peonies, yellow daisies, tulips, and anemones, sorted out according to color and kind. They were breathing and swaying, and seemed to be vying with one another. The dusty sweetness of mimosa was washed away by a wave of bright scent that came pouring with unexpected force, a watery scent threaded through with liquid needles of aniseed. This was the scent of daffodils, vivid as a sweet brandy diluted to pure whiteness. Yet even now all this jealous storm was conquered by the black cockades of the violets. Secretive and half insane, like pupils of eyes without whites, they hypnotized you with their indifference. Their sweet and uncoughed breath filled the broad frame of the trapdoor from the bottom of the cellar. They coated one's chest with a kind of woody pleurisy. This scent would recall something, then slip away, leaving the mind fooled. It seemed that the notion of the earth that persuades them to return every year had been made up by the months of spring on the pattern of this scent, and somewhere near at hand lay the origins of the Greek beliefs about Demeter.

7

Then, and for a long time to come, I regarded my attempts at poetry-writing as an unfortunate weakness and did not expect any good to come of them. There was one person, Sergei Durylin, who supported me with his approval even then. This was explained by his uniquely responsive nature. From my other friends, who had seen me practically start my career as a musician, I took care to hide these signs of a new immaturity.

On the other hand, I studied philosophy with undivided enthusiasm, sensing that somewhere in its neighborhood lay the rudiments of what would later apply to my work. The range of topics lectured on to our group was as far removed from the ideal as was the method of teaching. It was a curious jumble of antiquated metaphysics and unfledged enlightenmentism. For the sake of agreement, the two tendencies waived the last remnants of what meaning they might still have possessed if taken separately. The history of philosophy became a literary dabbling in dogmatics, while psychology degenerated into a mindless, inane journalese.

Young lecturers like Shpet, Samsonov, and Kubnitsky could not change this state of things. Yet the older professors were not so very much to blame. They were bound by the demand, already making itself felt, that lectures be popular and use only words of one syllable. Although the participants were not distinctly aware of it, the campaign for the eradication of illiteracy was begun just around that time. Students who had any grounding in their subject tried to work on their own, growing more and more attached to the excellent university library. Sympathies were divided among three names. A large group enthused over Bergson. Adherents of the Göttingen Husserlianism found support in Shpet. Followers of the Marburg school had no one to guide them and, left to their own resources, were united by the chance ramifications of a personal tradition that began as far back as Sergei Nikolaevich Trubetskoi.

A remarkable phenomenon in this circle was the young Samarin. A direct scion of the best Russian past, and moreover linked by various gradations of kinship with the history of the very building at the end of Nikitskaya Street, he would put in an appearance about twice a term at some seminar meeting or other, like a cut-off son turning up in the parental apartment at the hour when all were assembled for dinner. The leader of the seminar would stop reading and wait while the lanky eccentric, embarrassed by the silence he had caused and was prolonging by his choice of seat, clambered up the snapping boards to the farthest bench of the plank-built amphitheater. But the moment discussion of the paper began, all that crashing and creaking that had just trailed so laboriously up to the place under the very ceiling came back down again in a renewed and unrecognizable form. Seizing upon the speaker's first slip of the tongue, Samarin would hurl down some extemporization from Hegel or Cohen, rolling it down like a ball that went clattering over the ribbed ledges of an enormous store of boxes. He would get excited and swallow his words, and he spoke with a voice innately loud, sustained on that acquired, even note that never changed from cradle to grave, knows neither whispering nor shouting, and which with its constant rounded and throaty "r" sound, is always an immediate sign of breeding. I lost sight of him later but was involuntarily reminded of him when I reread Tolstoy and came across him in Nekhlyudov.

8

Although the summer coffeehouse on the Tverskoi Boulevard had no name of its own, everyone called it the Café Grec. It did not shut down for the winter, and its function then became a strange riddle. Once, by chance, without having arranged it, Loks, Samarin, and I met in this bare pavilion. We were the only visitors it had had, not only that evening but perhaps for the whole of the past season. It was just at the turning point toward warm weather; there was a whiff of spring. Samarin had scarcely arrived and sat down with us when he began philosophizing, arming himself with a dry biscuit and using it, like a choirmaster's tuning fork, to beat out the logical articulations of his speech. A piece of Hegelian infinity stretched itself across the pavilion, composed of alternating affirmations and negations. I had told him, probably, of the subject I had chosen for my doctoral thesis, and immediately he had leapt from Leibniz and mathematical infinity to the dialectical kind. Suddenly he started talking about Marburg. This was the first account I had heard of the town itself, rather than of the school. Later I realized there was no other way to talk of its antiquity and poetry, but at that moment this enamored description, uttered to the rattling of the ventilation fan, was a new experience for me. Abruptly recollecting that he had come in only for a moment and not in order to philosophize over coffee, he startled up the café-owner, who was nodding in a corner behind his newspaper and, learning that the telephone was out of order, tumbled out of the icy dovecote even more noisily than he had tumbled into it. Soon we got up too. The weather had changed. A wind had risen and begun lashing down a February sleet. It was falling to the earth in regular windings like a figure eight. In its frenzied looping there was something of the sea. This was how men piled up hawsers and nets in wavy layers, swinging stroke upon stroke. As we went along, Loks began several times on his favorite theme of Stendhal, but I kept silent, helped considerably by the blizzard. I could not stop thinking of what I had heard, and I grieved for the little town that I thought I was no more likely ever to see than my own ears.

That was in February, and one morning in April my mother announced that, by collecting her earnings and economizing on the housekeeping, she had saved two hundred rubles, which she was giving to me with the advice to travel abroad. Neither my joy nor the complete unexpectedness of the gift can be described, nor how undeserved it was. No small amount of strumming on the piano had had to be endured to make up such a sum. However, I had not the strength to refuse. There was no need to choose a route. In those days, European universities were constantly informed about

one another. That very day I began hurrying around to the various adminis-
trative offices, and together with a small number of documents I brought
a certain treasure away from Mokhovaya Street. This was the detailed list,
printed in Marburg two weeks before, of lecture courses proposed for the
summer term of 1912. I studied this prospectus, pencil in hand, and could
not part with it whether walking along or standing at the grids of office
counters. My absorption smelt of happiness a mile away and, without
realizing, I infected the secretaries and clerks with it, thus hastening the
already quite straightforward procedures.

My program was naturally a Spartan one. Third-class travel and abroad,
if necessary, even fourth, the slowest trains, a room in some small village
outside the town, bread and sausage and tea. My mother's self-sacrifice
bound me to a tenfold avarice. I wanted to get to Italy, too, on her money.
Besides this, I knew that a very perceptible sum would be swallowed by the
university entrance fees and the fees for particular seminars and courses.
But even if I had had ten times the money, I would never, as I was then,
have abandoned this program. I do not know how I would have disposed
of the remainder, but at that time nothing in the world would have moved
me into the second class or inclined me to leave any trace on a restaurant
table cloth. My tolerance of comforts, and of the need to be comfortable,
appeared only after the war. Those years placed such obstacles in the way
of a world that had not allowed anything decorative or indulgent into my
room that for a while my whole character could not but change as well.

9

At home the snow was still melting and the sky swimming out in pieces
onto the water from under the crust of ice, like a transfer sliding out from
under its tracing paper, but all over Poland apple trees were warmly blos-
soming and the whole land sped from morning to night and from west to
east in a summery sleeplessness like some Romanic part of the Slav design.

Berlin seemed to me a city of young boys who had just been presented,
the day before, with broadswords and helmets, canes and pipes, real bicycles
and grown-ups' frock coats. I came upon them as they were making their
first appearance, not yet used to the change and each of them pluming
himself on what had yesterday fallen to his lot. On one of the most splendid
streets, I was hailed from the window of a bookshop by Natorp's manual
of logic, and I went in to buy it with the sensation that tomorrow I would
see the author himself. In forty-eight hours of travel I had already spent one
sleepless night on German territory, now a second one lay ahead of me.

It is only here in Russia that folding bunks have been introduced in
third-class carriages; once over the frontier, you have to pay for the cheapness of the transport by nodding, all night long, four in a row, on a deep-

seated bench divided up by armrests. Although this time both benches in the compartment were at my disposal, I did not feel like sleeping. Only now and then, at long intervals, single passengers, students for the most part, came in and stayed for a station or two, then, silently bowing, sank into the warm unknown of night. Each time they changed, sleeping towns came rolling in beneath the platform roofs. The immemorial Middle Ages were discovered to me for the first time. Their authenticity was fresh and terrifying, like everything that is original. Clanking the familiar names like naked steel, the journey took them out one after the other from descriptions I had read in books, as if from dusty scabbards manufactured by historians.

Flying toward them, the train's ten riveted carriages stretched themselves out like a chain-mail wonder. The leather casing of the carriage joints swelled and sagged like blacksmiths' bellows. Beer, blotched by the lights of the station, sparkled clearly in tall, clean glasses. On their thick, stonelike rollers, empty luggage carts moved smoothly down the stone platforms. Under the vaults of colossal landing stages the torsos of short-snouted engines sweated. They seemed to have been carried up to that height by some game that the low wheels had been playing as they suddenly came to a halt when fully wound.

From all sides there came the 600-year-old forefathers of the desolate concrete. Quartered by a slanting trellis of beams, the walls stretched their drowsy decoration. Pageboys crowded on them, with knights, maidens, and ginger-bearded ogres, and the checkered lathing of the lattice-work was repeated like an ornamental design in the gridlike visors of the helmets, the slits of the ballooning sleeves, and the crisscross lacing of the bodices. Houses came almost up to the lowered window. Completely stunned, I leaned on its broad rib, spellbinding myself by murmuring over and over again a short and now outmoded exclamation of rapture. But it was still dark, and the leaping paws of wild vine were a scarcely visible black against the stucco. And when the hurricane struck anew, redolent of coal and dew and roses, and I was suddenly spattered by a fistful of sparks from the hands of the night flying past in rapture, I quickly raised the window and started to think of the unforeseeable events of the next day. But I must say something at least of where I was going, and why.

Created by the genius Cohen, and prepared for by Friedrich Albert Lange, his predecessor in the chair and well known in our country for his *History of Materialism*, the Marburg school of thought won me over with two special peculiarities. First, it was original; it dug everything over to the very foundations and built upon a clear space. It did not join in the lazy routine of all conceivable "isms," which always cling to their rewarding tenth-hand omniscience and are always ignorant and always, for one reason or another, afraid of any re-examination out in the open of man's age-old culture. Unruled by terminological inertia, the Marburg school turned to the primary sources, that is, to the authentic signatures left by thought in the history of knowledge. If fashionable philosophy speaks of what one or another writer thinks, and fashionable psychology of what the average man thinks; if formal logic teaches you how to think in the baker's shop to make sure you get the right change—the Marburg school was interested in how science itself thinks in its twenty-five centuries of continuous authorship, at the burning origins and sources of world-important discoveries. With such a disposition, and authorized, as it were, by history itself, philosophy grew young and clever again beyond all recognition, and changed from a problematic discipline into a primordial discipline about problems, which is indeed what it ought to be.

The second characteristic of the Marburg school proceeded directly from the first and consisted in a scrupulous and exacting attitude toward the heritage of history. Quite alien to this school was the abominably condescending attitude that sees the past as a kind of poorhouse where a knot of old men in chlamys and sandals, or periwigs and camisoles, fib up some impenetrable mumbo jumbo, excused by the whimsicalities of the Corinthian order, Gothic, Baroque, or some other architectural style. Homogeneity in the structure of knowledge was for this school as much a principle as the anatomical identity of historical man. In Marburg, history was known to perfection, and they never grew tired of pulling treasure after treasure out of the archives of the Italian Renaissance, French and Scottish rationalism, and other little-studied schools. In Marburg, history was looked at through both Hegelian eyes, that is with the generalizing of genius, and yet at the same time within the strict boundaries of common-sense probability. Thus, for example, the school did not speak of the stages of the world spirit but, let us say, of the postal correspondence of the Bernoulli family, but it knew all the while that every thought, however distant in time, when it is caught on the spot and in action, is bound to be wholly accessible to our logical commentary. Were this not so, it would lose its immediate interest for us and fall into the province of the archaeologist, the historian of costumes, manners, literatures, sociopolitical trends, and so forth.

These two features (its independence and its historicism) say nothing of the content of Cohen's system, but I did not intend, and would certainly not undertake to speak about its essence. They, nonetheless, explain its attractiveness. They speak of its originality, that is, of the living place it occupies in a living tradition for one part of contemporary consciousness.

As a particle of that consciousness, I was speeding to the center of attraction. The train was crossing the Harz. In the smoky morning, leaping forth from the forest, thousand-year-old Goslar went flashing by like a medieval coal-miner. Sometime later Göttingen rushed past. The names of towns were growing louder and louder. The train flung most of them out of its path in full flight without even stopping. As they rolled away, I looked on the map for the names of these spinning tops. Ancient details rose up round some of them, to be drawn into their vortex like astral rings and satellites. Sometimes the horizon spread out as in "The Terrible Vengeance" and, smoking simultaneously in several orbits, the earth, all separate town-lets and castles, began to grow as exciting as the night sky.

10

In the two years preceding this journey, the word Marburg had not left my lips. In every secondary-school textbook there was a mention of the town in the chapters on the Reformation. Mediator Publishers had even brought out a small book for children about Elizabeth of Hungary, who was buried there at the beginning of the thirteenth century. Any biography of Giordano Bruno mentioned Marburg when listing the towns where he lectured on his fatal journey from London to his native country. Yet, in Moscow, unlikely as it may seem, I did not once guess that the Marburg of these references was identical with the Marburg for whose sake I gnawed at derivative and differential tables and jumped from Maclaurin to Maxwell, who was ultimately beyond me. It was not until I walked, clutching my suitcase, past the old post station and the medieval hostelry that I came face to face for the first time with this identity.

I stood with my head thrown back, gasping. Above me towered a dizzy slope on which in three tiers stood the stone maquettes of the university, the *Rathaus*, and the 800-year-old castle. After ten steps I ceased to realize where I was. I recalled that I had left my connection with the rest of the world in the carriage of the train, and now it could no more be got back than the hooks, luggage rack, and ashtrays. Clouds stood idly above the tower clock. To them the place seemed familiar. But even they did not explain anything. It was obvious that, as watchmen of this nest, they never left it at all. A midday silence reigned. It communed with the silence of the plain that spread below. Between them they seemed to sum up my stupefac-tion. The upper one exchanged languorous winnowings of lilac with the lower. Birds chirruped, as if waiting for something. I scarcely noticed any people. The motionless contours of roofs were curious to see how all this would end.

Streets clung to the steep slopes like Gothic dwarfs. They were arranged one below the other, the cellars of one gazing over the attics of the next. Their narrow gorges were crowded with miracles of the craft of building with boxes. The stories of the houses, widening out upward, rested on protruding beams and, almost touching roofs, they reached out their hands to one another over the roadway. There were no pavements. In some roads it was impossible for two people to pass.

Suddenly I realized that Lomonosov's five years of trudging over these same cobbles must have been preceded by a day when he entered this town for the first time, carrying a letter to Leibniz's disciple Christian von Wolff, and did not yet know anyone there. It is not enough to say that the town had not altered since that day. One needs to realize, it might have been just as unexpectedly tiny and ancient in those days too. And one could turn one's head and experience the shock of repeating exactly a bodily movement from terribly long ago. Just as it had done then, in Lomonosov's time, the town, scattered at one's feet with its blue-gray swarm of slate roofs, resembled a flock of doves, bewitched in midair as they swooped toward their replenished feeding ground. I shuddered as I celebrated the two hundredth anniversary of another man's neck muscles. Coming to, I observed that the scenery had now become real, and I set off to look for the cheap hotel Samarin had recommended.

PART II

1

I rented a room on the edge of the town. The house stood in the last row on the Giessen road. At this spot the chestnut trees planted along it, standing shoulder to shoulder as if obeying a command, wheeled about to the right, still keeping their formation. The highway glanced back one last time at the sullen hill with the small ancient town, then vanished behind the forest.

The room had a miserable little balcony looking out on the next-door kitchen garden. The carriage of an old Marburg horse trolley stood there, taken off its axles and converted into a hen coop.

The room was let by an old woman, the widow of a civil servant. She lived alone with her daughter on her meager pension. Mother and daughter were as alike as two peas. As always happens with women afflicted with goiter, they kept catching my glance, which was furtively directed at their collars. At these moments I kept recalling children's balloons that are gathered into an earlike point at one end and tightly tied. Perhaps they guessed this.

Through their eyes, from which I would have liked to release a little air by placing a palm to their throats, an ancient Prussian pietism looked out at the world.

Their type, however, was uncharacteristic of this part of Germany. Here another type, the Middle German, prevailed, and even into nature herself there crept the first suspicions of a South and a West, of the existence of

Switzerland and France. So it was most fitting, in the presence of her leafy surmises, green at the window, to be leafing through French volumes of Leibniz and Descartes.

Beyond the fields that advanced on the ingenious hen house, the village of Ockershausen could be seen. This was a long encampment of long barns, long carts, and massive Percherons. From there another road trailed along the horizon. As it entered the town it became christened the Barfüsser-strasse. For "barefoots" were what Franciscan monks were called in the Middle Ages.

This must have been the very road along which winter arrived here each year, for if one looked out from the balcony in that direction one could imagine many things appropriate to winter. Hans Sachs. The Thirty Years' War. The sleepy, unexciting nature of historical calamity, when it is measured not in hours but in decades. Winters, winters, and winters and then, when the century had lapsed, a century as deserted as an ogre's yawn, the first arising of new settlements under the vagrant skies, somewhere far off from the wild Harz, with names as black as the sites of fires—Elend, Sorge and other such names.

At the back, away from the house, the River Lahn flowed, crumpling beneath itself bushes and reflections. Beyond it stretched the railway line. In the evenings, into the muffled snorting of the spirit lamp in the kitchen there would burst the accelerated jingling of a mechanical bell to whose sound the railway swing beam would come down all by itself. Then, in the dark, a man in uniform would loom up at the crossing and quickly sprinkle it from a watering can in anticipation of dust, and in the very same second the train would rush by, convulsively thrusting itself up and down and in all directions at once. Sheaves of its thrumming light dropped into my landlady's saucepans. And the milk always got burned.

Down onto the fluvial oil of the Lahn slid a star or two. In Ockershausen the cattle that had just been driven in bellowed. Marburg lit up, operatically, on the top of the hill. If the brothers Grimm could have come here once again, as they did a hundred years ago, to study law with the celebrated lawyer Savigny, they would once again have gone away collectors of fairy tales. I made sure I had the key to the front door on my person and set off for the town.

The old-established citizens were already asleep. Only students crossed my path. They all looked as if they were performing in Wagner's *Meistersinger*. The houses, which even in daytime had seemed a stage set, were pressing still more closely together. The hanging lamps, strung over the roadway from one wall to the other, had nowhere to let themselves go. With all its might their light crashed down onto sounds. It drenched with lily-shaped patches the noise of receding heels and the explosions of loud German speech. As if the electricity knew the legend about this place.

Long, long ago, some half a thousand years before Lomonosov, when the New Year upon earth, then a very ordinary year, was the year one thousand two hundred and thirty, there came down these slopes from the Marburg castle a living historical person, Elizabeth of Hungary.

This is so far away that, if imagination ever reaches it, a snowstorm will arise of its own accord, at the point of its arrival. It will come about from the increasing cold, by the law of the vanquishing of the unattainable. Night will set in there; the mountains will clothe themselves in forest; in the forests wild beasts will appear. But human ways and customs will be covered with a crust of ice.

The future saint, who was to be canonized three years after her death, had a tyrant for her confessor, that is—a man without imagination. This sober, practical man perceived that the torments imposed on her at confession brought her into a state of ecstasy. Seeking tortures that would be true suffering for her, he forbade her to help the poor and the sick. Here legend takes over from history. It seems she had not the strength for this. And to whiten the sin of her disobedience, a whirlwind of snow used to screen her with its body on her way down to the lower town and, for the length of her nocturnal journeys, transformed the bread into flowers.

Thus nature sometimes has to step aside from her laws when a convinced bigot insists too much on the fulfillment of his own. It does not matter that the voice of natural law is here robed in the shape of miracle. Such is the criterion of authenticity in a religious epoch.

Flying downhill, the street grew more and more twisty and narrow the nearer it came to the university. In one of the housefronts, baked in the cinders of the centuries like a potato, was a glass door. It opened into a corridor that led out on one of the precipitous northern slopes. There was a terrace there, covered with tables and flooded with electric light. The terrace hung above the lowland that had once given so much disquiet to the countess of that land. Since that time the town, establishing itself along the path of her nightly excursions, had set firm on the height in the form it had taken by the middle of the sixteenth century. But the lowland that had harassed her spiritual peace, the lowland that had made her break the Rule. The lowland, set astir by miracles as before, walked fully in step with the times.

Night dampness wafted from it. Iron resounded on it sleeplessly, and sidings shifted back and forth, flowing together and apart. Every moment something noisy fell and rose again. Till morning the watery thunder of the dam sustained on one level the deafening note it had taken up in the evening. At a third lower, the slashing squeal of the sawmill accompanied the oxen in the slaughterhouse. Something kept bursting and lighting up, letting out steam and toppling over. Something kept fidgeting and veiling itself with a painted smoke.

The café was chiefly frequented by philosophers. Others had their own cafés. On the terrace sat G—— and L——, Germans who subsequently received chairs in their own country and abroad. Among the Danes, the English girls, the Japanese, and all who had traveled here from all corners of the world to hear Cohen, a familiar, excitedly melodious voice could already be heard. It was the voice of an advocate from Barcelona, a pupil of Stammler's, active in the recent Spanish revolution, continuing his education here for the second year—he was declaiming Verlaine to his acquaintances.

Already I knew a number of people and was not shy with anyone. Already my tongue had run away with me into two promises and I was anxiously preparing for the days when I would be examined on Leibniz by Hartmann and on one of the parts of the *Critique of Practical Reason* by the head of the school. Already the image of the latter, long guessed at but turning out terribly inadequate at first acquaintance, had become my property; that is, it had begun to have an existence of its own within me, altering according as it plunged to the bottom of my disinterested enthusiasms or floated to the surface when, with the delirious ambition of the novice, I tried to guess if I should ever be noticed by him and invited to one of his Sunday dinners. This was something that immediately raised one in the local esteem, for it marked the beginning of a new philosophical career.

Already I had confirmed, by his example, how a great inner world is dramatized when presented by a great man. Already I knew how the shock-headed, bespectacled old man would raise his head and step backward as he told of the Greek conception of immortality, and would sweep his arm through the air in the direction of the Marburg fire station as he interpreted the image of the Elysian fields. Already I knew how on some other occasion, stealthily creeping up on pre-Kantian metaphysics, he would croon away, pretending to woo it, then suddenly utter a raucous bark and give it a terrible scolding with quotations from Hume. How, after a fit of coughing and a lengthy pause, he would then drawl forth, exhausted and peaceable, *"Und nun, meine Herren . . . ,"** which meant he had finished telling the century off, the performance was over, and it was possible to move on to the subject of the course.

Meanwhile, almost no one was left on the terrace. The electric lights there were being switched off. It was growing apparent that it was morning. We looked down over the rails and saw that the nocturnal lowland had completely vanished. The panorama that had taken its place knew nothing of its precursor in the night.

*"And now, gentlemen . . . ."

2

About that time the V—— sisters came to Marburg. They belonged to a wealthy family. In Moscow, while I was still at grammar school, I had been friends with the elder girl and had given her occasional lessons in goodness knows what. Or rather, the family had paid me to have discussions with her on the most unpredictable topics. But in the spring of 1908, the dates on which we were finishing our grammar-school careers coincided, and at the same time as I prepared myself for the examinations, I undertook to coach the elder V—— girl as well.

The majority of my exam questions were on matters I had thoughtlessly neglected at the time when they were gone through in class. I had not enough nights to get these subjects up. Yet, off and on, heedless of the hour and oftenest of all at break of day, I would hurry around to V—— for the study of subjects that invariably differed from my own because, naturally enough, the order of examinations in our different schools did not coincide. This confusion made my position still more complicated. I did not notice it. My feeling toward V—— was not new; I had known about it since I was fourteen.

She was a charming, pretty girl, excellently brought up, and spoiled since infancy by an old Frenchwoman who worshiped her. This old lady knew better than I did that the geometry I was bringing into the house for her favorite at such unearthly hours was more Abélardean than Euclidean. And, cheerfully underlining her own shrewdness, she never absented herself from our lessons. I was secretly thankful for her interference. In her presence my feelings could remain inviolate. I did not judge them and could not be judged by them. I was eighteen years old. In any case, temperament and upbringing prevented me giving rein to my feelings, nor would I have had the boldness to do so.

It was the time of year when people dissolve paint in pots of boiling water, and gardens, left to their own devices, warm themselves idly in the sunshine, all cluttered with snow shoveled down from everywhere. To their very brink they are filled with a bright, quiet water. And overboard, on the other sides of the fences, along the horizon, gardeners, rooks and bell towers stand in columns, exchanging two or three words a day in loud remarks heard all the way across the town. Against the top of the window frame rubs a damp, woolly gray sky. It is full of undeparted night. It keeps its silence for hours on end, silence, silence, then all of a sudden there rolls into the room a round piece of cartwheel thunder. It stops as abruptly as if this were all a game of "magic stick" and the cart had no other purpose but up from the roadway and in through the window. And now it was no longer the cart's turn. And still more mysterious was the empty silence, pouring like springwaters into the hole that had been hewn out by the sound.

I do not know why all this impressed itself on me in the image of a school blackboard with the chalk not quite rubbed off. Oh, if we had been made to stop then, and the blackboard wiped to a gleaming wetness, and if instead of theorems about isometric pyramids, they had expounded to us in fine copperplate, with carefully thickened strokes of the pen, just what lay ahead of us both. Oh, how dumbfounded we should have been!

But where does this notion come from, and why does it occur to me at this point?

Because it was Spring, which had completed in rough its eviction of the cold half-year, and all around on the earth, like mirrors not yet hung up, lakes and puddles lay face upward telling how the insanely spacious world had been cleaned and the premises were ready to be let again. Because, whoever first wished to, then, was given the chance to embrace and experience afresh all the life that there is upon earth. Because I loved V——.

Because the very *perceptibility* of the present is itself already the future, and the future of man is love.

3

There is in the world, however, a so-called elevated attitude toward woman. I shall say a little about this. There is that immense sphere of phenomena that provoke suicides in adolescence. There is the sphere of mistakes made by the infantile imagination, of childish perversions and adolescent starvations, the sphere of Kreutzer sonatas and sonatas written against Kreutzer sonatas. I was once in this sphere and stayed in it a shamefully long time. But what exactly is it?

It tears you to pieces and nothing ever comes of it but harm. And yet there will never be a liberation from it. Everyone who enters history as a human being will always have to go through this. For these sonatas, which are the threshold to the only complete moral freedom, are written not by Tolstoys and Wedekinds but—through their hands—by nature itself. And only in their mutual contradictoriness lies the fullness of her purpose.

Having founded matter upon resistance and divided fact from fantasy by a dam called love, she takes care to keep this firm, that is, to keep the world entire. Here is the point where her craziness and her morbid exaggerations center. It can be truly said that here, at every step, she turns a mouse into an elephant.

But excuse me—she does make real elephants too! This is said to be her main business. Or is that just a phrase? Well, what about the history of species? And the history of human names? Moreover, the place where she makes them is here, in these sluiced-off sections of living evolution, at the dams where her agitated imagination has such free play.

So might it not be said that the reason we exaggerate in childhood and have disordered imaginations is that at that time we are mice and nature is making elephants of us?

Holding to the philosophy that only the *almost impossible* is real, she has made feeling extraordinarily difficult for all things living. She has made it difficult for the animal in one way, for the plant in another. The way she has made it difficult for us shows her astoundingly high opinion of man. She has made it difficult for us not through any sort of mechanical tricks but through what she considers has absolute power for us. She made it difficult for us through the sense of our mouselike vulgarity which seizes each of us the more strongly, the farther we move away from being mice. This is stated with genius by Hans Christian Anderson in his "Ugly Duckling."

All literature about sex, like the word "sex" itself, smacks of an exasperating vulgarity, and in this lies its purpose. It is solely and precisely through this repulsiveness that it is useful to nature, for her contact with us is founded on this very fear of vulgarity, and anything not vulgar would fail to strengthen her means of control.

Whatever material our thoughts might supply in this connection, the *fate* of that material is in her hands. And by means of the share of instinct that she has allocated to us from her entirety, nature always manages that material in such a way that all the efforts of pedagogues, directed as they are toward making it easier to be natural, invariably make it harder, and *this is just how it ought to be*.

This is necessary in order that feeling itself should have something to overcome. If not dumbfounded one way, then another way. And it does not matter of *what* nastiness or nonsense the barrier is built up. The movement that leads to conception is the purest movement of all those known to the universe. And this purity alone, which has triumphed so many times in the course of the centuries, is enough to make everthing that is not it seem by contrast infinitely dirty.

And there is art. Art is concerned not with man but with the image of man. But the image of man, it turns out, is bigger than man. It can have its conception only in motion, and even then not in just any. It can have its conception only in the transition from mouse to elephant.

What is it the honest man does when he speaks *only* the truth? While he is telling the truth time goes by; in that time life moves ahead. His truth lags behind, it deceives. Is this the way man must speak, everywhere and always?

And so in art his mouth is shut for him. In art the man falls silent and the image begins to speak. And it turns out that *only* the image can keep pace with the progress of nature.

In Russian "to fib" means "to say more than is necessary," rather than "to deceive." It is in this sense that art "fibs." Its image encompasses life and does not seek a spectator. Its truths are not depictive but are capable of eternal development.

Only art, speaking for centuries about love, is *not* at the disposal of the instinct for strengthening the means of impeding feeling. A generation, when it has taken the hurdle of a new spiritual development, *preserves* the lyric truth and does not reject it, so that from a very great distance one might imagine mankind to be gradually composing itself from generations in the form of lyric truth.

All this is extraordinary. All this is breathtakingly difficult. Taste teaches morality, but power teaches taste.

4

The sisters were spending the summer in Belgium. They had heard from someone that I was in Marburg. At this time they were called to a family gathering in Berlin. They decided to look me up on their way there.

They put up at the best hotel in the little town, in its most ancient quarter. The three days I spent constantly in their company were as unlike my usual life as festivals are unlike workdays. I was endlessly telling them something or other, and was intoxicated by their laughter and by the signs of understanding from people who happened to be with us. I took them places. They were both seen with me at lectures in the university. And so the day of their departure came.

On the evening before, as he laid the table for supper, the waiter said to me, "Das ist wohl Ihr Henkersmahl, nicht wahr?" i.e., "Eat for the last time, tomorrow it's the gallows for you, isn't it?"

In the morning I entered their hotel and ran into the younger sister in the corridor. She looked at me and realized something, stepped back without a greeting, and shut herself in her room. I went on to the elder sister and in dreadful agitation I said that things could not go on like this any longer, and that I was begging her to decide my fate. There was nothing new in this at all except for my insistence upon it. She got up from her chair and backed away from the eloquence of my agitation, which seemed to be advancing upon her. As she reached the wall, she suddenly remembered that there existed a means of putting a stop to all of this at one blow—and she refused me. Soon a noise started up in the corridor. A trunk was being dragged from the next room. Then they knocked at our door. Quickly I set myself to rights. It was time to leave for the station. The walk there would take five minutes.

At the station the ability to say good-bye abandoned me completely. Just when I realized that I had only said good-bye to the younger sister and had not yet even begun to with the elder, the smoothly gliding express from Frankfurt loomed up beside the platform. Almost in a single movement it swiftly gathered up its passengers and took off. I ran alongside the train and at the end of the platform, with an extra run, jumped up onto the step of the carriage. The heavy door had not been slammed. A furious conductor barred my way, at the same time grasping me by the shoulder so that I should not, God forbid, take it into my head to sacrifice my life, shamed by his remonstrations. My travelers ran out onto the landing from their compartment. They started pushing banknotes at the conductor to rescue me and purchase a ticket. He gave way to mercy and I followed the sisters into the compartment. We sped to Berlin. The fairy-tale holiday, almost interrupted, went on, enhanced tenfold by the frenzy of movement and by a blissful headache from all that I had just experienced.

I had leapt onto the moving train solely in order to say good-bye, but again forgot to, and again remembered only when it was too late. I had still not come to my senses when day was done and evening had come and, pressing us to the ground, the resonant breathing of the Berlin station roof was moving upon us. The sisters were to be met. It was not desirable that they should be seen with me in my disordered state of emotion. They persuaded me our farewells had really been made already; I had just not noticed it. I sank in the crowd, which was gripped by the gaslike roaring of the station.

It was night, a nasty drizzle was falling. Berlin had no interest for me whatever. The next train in the direction I wanted left in the morning. I could easily have waited at the station for it. But I felt I could not possibly stay among people. My face was jerking and twitching; tears were continually coming to my eyes. My thirst for a final farewell, one that would be utterly and wholly devastating, had remained unquenched. It was like the need for a great cadenza, which shakes an aching music to its roots in order to remove it, the whole of it at once, with the single pull of the final chord. But this relief was denied me.

It was night, a nasty drizzle was falling. On the asphalt outside the station it was just as smoky as it was on the platform, where the glass of the roofing swelled in its iron like a ball in a string net. The tapping here and there about the street was like the popping sounds of carbon dioxide; everything was wrapped in a quiet ferment of rain. As the occasion was unforeseen, I had on me what I had had when I left home—that is, no coat, no luggage, no documents. I was shown out of hotels at the first glance, with polite excuses about all the rooms being taken. At last I found a place where my traveling as light as this was no obstacle. It was the lowest kind of hotel. Alone in the room I sat down sideways on a chair that was standing by the window. Beside it was a table. I dropped my head onto it. Why do I specify my posture so exactly? Because I spent the whole night in it. Now and then, as if at someone's touch, I raised my head and did something to the wall, which slanted obliquely away from me under the dark ceiling. As if with a yardstick, I measured it from below with a fixed, unseeing stare. Then the sobbing started again. Again I sank my face into my hands.

I have specified the posture of my body so exactly because this had been its posture that morning, on the footboard of the flying train, and it had remembered the position. It was the pose of a person who has fallen down from something high that had held and carried him for a long time, then had let him go, passed noisily over his head, and vanished around a turn for ever.

At last I got to my feet. I looked around the room and flung a window open. Night had gone; rain hung in a misty spray. It was impossible to say whether it was still falling or had stopped. The room was paid for in advance. There was not a soul in the hall. I went away, without a word to anyone.

5

Only now did something leap to my eyes that had probably started before but had been eclipsed all the time by the nearness of what was happening and by the ugliness of a grown-up person crying.

I was surrounded by changed things. Something never before experienced had crept into the essence of reality. The morning recognized my face and made its appearance for the very purpose of being with me and *never* leaving me.

The mist dispersed, promising a hot day. Little by little the town began to move. Small carts, bicycles, vans, and trains began slipping in all directions. Above them human plans and desires wound like invisible plumes. They rose like smoke and moved with the conciseness of familiar parables that are clear without explanation. Birds, houses and dogs, trees and horses, tulips and people had all become shorter and abrupter than childhood had known them. The fresh laconism of life revealed itself to me, crossed the road, took me by the hand, led me along the pavement. Less than ever did I deserve brotherhood with this vast summer sky. But there was no talk of that as yet. For the time being, all was forgiven me. Sometime in the future I would have to repay the morning for its trust. And everything around was dizzily reliable, like a law that says that one never remains indebted for *that* sort of loan.

I got a ticket without any trouble and took my place in the train. I did not have to wait long for its departure. Then I was rolling along again from Berlin to Marburg, but this time, in contrast to the first time, I was traveling by day, with expenses paid, and—a completely different person. I traveled in comfort on the money borrowed from V——, and a picture of my Marburg room kept appearing before my mind's eye.

Opposite me, with their backs to the engine, there sat swaying in a row and smoking: a man in a pince-nez that was awaiting its chance to slide off his nose into the newspaper held close beneath it, a clerk from the Forestry Department with a game bag over his shoulder and a gun at the bottom of the luggage rack, and someone else, and again someone else. They did not hamper me any more than the Marburg room I could see in my mind. The nature of my silence hypnotized them. Occasionally I broke it on purpose, to test its power over them. They understood it. It was traveling with me; I was officially attached to its person for the journey and wore its uniform, one that is familiar to everyone from his own experience. If it had not been, my neighbors would certainly not have rewarded me with silent sympathy for the way I was courteously slighting them rather than associating with them, and not so much sitting in the compartment as striking a pose toward it, though without actually posing. In that compartment there was more kindness and doglike sensitivity than cigar and engine smoke; ancient towns flew up to meet us, and the setting of my Marburg room kept becoming mentally visible to me. What was the reason for this?

Some weeks before the sisters' brief visit, a trivial thing had happened that was far from unimportant to me at the time. I had given papers in both the seminars. My papers were successful. They received approval.

I was pressed to develop my arguments in more detail and present them before the end of the summer term. I seized on this idea and began working with redoubled zeal.

Yet from this very ardor an experienced observer would have diagnosed that I would never make a scholar. I *lived* my scientific studies more powerfully than their subject required. A vegetable kind of thinking dwelt in me. Its peculiarity was that any secondary idea would boundlessly unfold in my interpretation of it and start demanding sustenance and attention, so that when, under its influence, I turned to books, I was drawn to them not from pure interest in knowledge but by the wish to find literary references in support of my idea. And despite the fact that my work was being accomplished by means of logic, imagination, paper and ink, I loved it most for the way in which in the course of the writing it became overgrown with a thicker and thicker ornamentation of comparisons and quotations from books. And because, with the limited time available, I had at a certain stage had to give up copying pieces out and had begun, instead, simply leaving the authors open at the pages I needed, a moment arrived when the theme of my work had materialized and the whole of it lay visible to the naked eye from the doorway of my room. It spread across the room in the likeness of a tree fern, heavily unfurling its leafy coils on my desk, divan, and windowsill. To disarray them meant upsetting the course of my argument, while to tidy them up completely was tantamount to burning a manuscript of which no fair copy has been made. With utmost strictness the landlady was forbidden to touch them. For some time the room had not been cleaned.

And when on my journey I saw this room in my imagination, I was really seeing in the flesh my philosophy and its probable fate.

6

I did not recognize Marburg on my arrival. The hill had grown taller and drawn in, the town had turned gaunt and black.

The landlady opened the door to me. Looking me up and down, she requested me on any future occasions of this kind to give advance notice either to her daughter or to herself. I said that I had not been able to warn her because I had suddenly had to go to Berlin very urgently, without coming home first. She looked at me still more mockingly. My sudden appearance from the other end of Germany, as lightly equipped as if from an evening walk, did not fit in with her way of thinking at all. It seemed to her a clumsy fabrication. Shaking her head all the time, she handed me two letters. One was sealed; the other was a local postcard. The sealed one was from my Petersburg cousin, unexpectedly in Frankfurt. She wrote to say that she was on her way to Switzerland and would be in Frankfurt for three days. The postcard, of which one-third was covered with a neat, characterless handwriting, was signed by another hand, all too familiar from the signature at the foot of university notices—Cohen's. It contained an invitation to dinner the following Sunday.

Between the landlady and myself the following conversation, more or less, took place in German: "What day is it today?"—"Saturday."—"I won't be having any tea. And while I remember: I've got to go to Frankfurt tomorrow; please wake me in time for the first train."—"But, if I am not mistaken, Herr Geheimrat . . ."—"It's all right; I'll manage."—"Impossible. At the Herr Geheimrat's they sit down to table at twelve, and you'll . . ." But there was something improper in this solicitude about me. With an expressive glance at the old lady, I went into my room.

I sat down on my bed, unable to collect my thoughts. But this scarcely lasted more than a minute, after which, mastering a surge of useless regret, I went down to the kitchen to get a dust pan and brush. I threw off my jacket, pushed up my sleeves, and set to work dismantling the many-jointed fern. Half an hour later the room was just as it had been on the day I arrived, and even the books I had borrowed from the library did not disturb its tidiness. I tied them up neatly in four bundles so that they would be handy when there was a chance to go to the library, and kicked them under the bed. At this moment the landlady knocked at my door. She had come to tell me the exact time of departure of tomorrow's train by the timetable. At the sight of the change that had taken place she froze to the spot; then, suddenly, shaking her skirts, blouse, and cap as if puffing out a ball of feathers, she floated through the air toward me, quivering and stiffened. She held out her hand and with wooden solemnity congratulated me on the completion of my difficult work. I did not feel like disappointing her a second time. I left her in her noble delusion.

Then I got washed and, wiping my face, went out onto the balcony. Evening was coming. I rubbed my neck with the towel and looked into the distance, at the road that joined Ockershausen and Marburg. It was no longer possible now to recall how I had gazed in that direction on the evening of my arrival. The end, the end! The end of philosophy, that is, of any thought of it at all.

Just like my fellow passengers on the train, it too would have to come to terms with the fact that every love is a crossing over into a new faith.

7

It is strange that I did not then leave for home immediately. The town's value had lain in its school of philosophy. I did not need this any longer. But it turned out to have another.

There exists a psychology of creation, the problems of poetics. Meanwhile what is experienced most immediately of all in the whole of art is precisely its coming into being, and about this there is no need to make guesses.

We cease to recognize reality. It presents itself in some new category. This category seems to us to be its own, not our, condition. Except for this condition everything in the world has been named. It alone is unnamed and new. We try to name it. The result is art.

The clearest, most memorable, and most important thing in art is its origination, and the world's best works of art, while telling about the most varied things, are really telling about their own birth. I first understood this in its whole magnitude in the period I am describing.

Although all the while I was talking with V— nothing happened that could have altered my situation, it was all accompanied by unexpected things that resembled happiness. I despaired; she comforted me. But her mere touch was such bliss that it swept away with a wave of rejoicing the distinct bitterness of what I heard, which was not subject to alteration.

The circumstances of the day seemed all a rapid, noisy dashing to and fro. We seemed to be incessantly flying at full speed into darkness and flying out again fast as an arrow without a pause for breath. So that, without once being able to stop and look about us, we found ourselves, some twenty times in the course of the day, in the crowded hold from where time's rowing galley is set in motion. This was none other than that grown-up world for which I had been so violently jealous of V—— ever since childhood, when I had loved her, a schoolgirl, in my schoolboy fashion.

When I got back to Marburg, I found I had parted not from the girl I had known for six years but from the woman I had seen a few moments after her refusal of me. My shoulders and my hands were no longer mine. Like someone else's, they begged to leave me and enter the fetters by which man is chained to a common cause. For now I could not think even of her except as of someone chained up, and I loved her only as someone in chains, only as a prisoner, only for the cold sweat in which beauty serves its sentence. Every thought of her instantly fused me with that cooperative singing in chorus which fills the world with a forest of movements ecstatically learned by heart, and is like a battle, like hard labor, like medieval hell and craftsmanship. I mean what children do not know and what I shall call the sense of *the real.*

At the beginning of *A Safe-Conduct* I said that sometimes love outstripped the sun. I had in mind the patency of feeling that every morning outdistanced the whole of the surrounding world with the reliability of a piece of news that has just been confirmed anew for the hundredth time. In comparison with this, even the sunrise acquired the character of a local rumor still needing verification. In other words, I had in mind the patency of a power that outweighed the evidential nature of light.

If, given the knowledge, ability and leisure, I were to decide now to write a creative aesthetics, I would construct it upon two concepts—upon the concepts of power, or energy, and symbol. I would show that as distinct from science, which takes nature in the section of a shaft of light, art is interested in life at the moment when the beam of energy *is passing through it.* I would take the concept of power, or energy, in that broadest sense in which it is taken by theoretical physics, only with the difference that it would be a question not of the principle of power but of its voice, its presence. I would explain that, in the context of self-awareness, this power is called "feeling."

When we suppose that in *Tristan, Romeo and Juliet,* and other memorable great works a powerful passion is portrayed, we underestimate their content. Their theme is wider than this powerful theme. Their theme is the theme of power.

And it is from this theme that art is born. Art is more one-sided than people think. It cannot be directed at will, wherever one wishes, like a telescope. Focused upon a reality that has been displaced by feeling, art is a record of this displacement. It copies it from nature. How then does nature become displaced? Details gain in sharpness, each losing its independent meaning. Each one of them could be replaced by another. Any one of them is precious. Any one, chosen at random, will serve as evidence of the state that envelops the whole of transposed reality.

When the signs of this condition are transferred onto paper, the characteristics of life become the characteristics of creation. The latter stand out more sharply than the former. They have been better studied. There is a terminology for them. They are called devices.

Art is realistic as activity, and it is symbolic as fact. It is realistic by virtue of the fact that it did not itself invent metaphor but found it in nature and faithfully reproduced it. The transferred sense means nothing in isolation but refers to the general spirit of all art, just as the parts of the transposed reality mean nothing if taken separately.

And in the configuration of its whole pull, art is symbolic. Its only symbol is in the sharpness and nonobligatory nature of the images, which character-ize it *as a whole.* The interchangeability of images is the sign of a situation in which the parts of reality are mutually indifferent. The interchangeability of images, that is, art, is the symbol of power.

Actually, only power needs the language of material proofs. The other aspects of consciousness are durable without any signs. For them there is the direct path to the visual analogies of light: to number, precise concept, and idea. But there is nothing except the mobile language of images, that is, the language of attendant attributes, for power to express itself by, the fact of power, power durable only at the moment of its manifestation.

The direct speech of feeling is allegorical, and there is nothing by which it can be replaced.*

8

I went to visit my cousin in Frankfurt, and also my family which had by then arrived in Bavaria. I was visited by my brother and then by my father. But I noticed nothing of all this. I had begun writing poetry and was completely taken up with it. Day and night, at every opportunity, I wrote, about the sea, the dawn, the southern rain, the coal of the Harz.

Once I was especially carried away. It was one of those nights that laboriously make their way to the nearest fence and, quite worn out, bemused with weariness, hang above the earth. Utter windlessness. No sign of life but this black profile of sky leaning against the wattle fence, drained of strength. And one other. The strong scent of stocks and of flowering tobacco plants, which is the earth's reply to that exhaustion. What can the sky not be compared to on such a night? Big stars like a party, the Milky Way like a big social gathering. But even more, the chalky streakings across those diagonal expanses of space recall a bed of flowers at night. In it there

---

* For fear of misunderstandings, let me remind you that I am speaking not of the material content of art but about the ways in which art can be filled and expanded, about the meaning of its appearance and its place in life. The individual images in themselves are visual and are based on the analogy of light. The individual words of art, like all concepts, derive their vitality from the act of cognition. But the complete pronouncements of art as a whole, which cannot be quoted, consist in the mobility of the metaphor itself, and this is a symbolic indication of power, or energy.

are heliotropes and matthiolas. They have been watered in the evening and pushed aslant. Flowers and stars are so close together, it seems the sky itself was under the watering can and now the stars and the white-speckled grass cannot be disentangled.

I wrote with passionate absorption, and a dust different from before covered my desk. The previous, philosophical kind had accumulated from the splinters of nonconformity. I had trembled for the wholeness of my work. But is was out of solidarity that I did not wipe away the present dust, out of sympathy with the gravel of the Giessen highway. And at the far end of the desk's oilcloth the tea glass, long unwashed, shone like a star in the sky.

Suddenly I got up, assailed by the sweat of this stupid dissolving away of everything, and started to pace about the room. "What a dirty trick!" I thought. "Isn't he still a genius for me? Am I breaking with *him?* It's more than two weeks now since his postcard came and I began this mean game of hide-and-seek with him. I must give him an explanation. But how can it be done?"

I remembered how pedantic and severe he was. "Was ist Apperzeption?"* he would ask a nonspecialist at the examination, and when the latter said, translating from Latin, that it meant *durchfassen* (to grasp through), his answer would ring out: "Nein, das heisst durchfallen, mein Herr" ("No, sir, it means to fail an exam").

The classics were read in his seminars. He would interrupt the reading to ask what the author was driving at. One was expected to snap out the main idea, with a single noun, like a soldier. Not only vagueness was unendurable to him, but so was any approximation to the truth, instead of the truth itself.

He was somewhat deaf in the right ear. And it was on his right side that I sat when I had to analyze the passage from Kant set before me. He let me get well under way and lose myself in the argument, then when I was least expecting it, disconcerted me with his usual "Was meint der Alte?" ("What does the old man mean?").

I do not recall what it was, but suppose that on the multiplication table of ideas the right answer was the answer to the question "What is five times five?" "Twenty-five," I replied. He frowned and waved his hand to one side. A slight modification of my answer followed, which had failed to satisfy him because of its timidity. Obviously, so long as he prodded into space and appealed to those who knew, my answer kept reappearing in increasingly complex variants. At least, though, we were talking about two and a half tens or, roughly, half a hundred divided by two. But it was precisely the

*Apperception is an act of perception involving cognition on the basis of earlier-established concepts.

increasing clumsiness of the answers that made him more and more irritated. Yet nobody dared to repeat what I had said, after the look of disgust
on his face. Then with a movement that seemed to say, "Up to you now,
in the back row!" he heaved over toward the others. And in a merry clamor
on all sides calls of sixty-two, ninety-eight, and two hundred and fourteen
were heard. He raised his hand, barely calming the storm of jubilant nonsense, and, turning toward me, he quietly and dryly repeated to me my own
answer. There followed a new storm, in my defense. When he had grasped
the whole situation, he took a good look at me, patted me on the shoulder,
and asked where I came from and how many terms I had spent in Marburg.
Then, snorting and frowning, he asked me to go on, repeating all the time,
"Sehr recht, sehr richtig. Sie merken wohl? Ja, ja. Ach, ach, der Alte!"
("Correct, correct. You see? Aha, the good old fellow!"). And I remember
a great deal more.

Well, how does one approach such a person? What should I say to him?
"Verse?" he would drawl. *"Verse!"* Had he not sufficiently studied the
whole of human mediocrity and its subterfuges? *"Verse!"*

9

All this must have happened in July, for the lime trees were still in flower.
The sun fought its way through the diamonds of their waxy blooms as if
through pieces of kindling glass, and scorched the dusty leaves with small
black circles.

I had often walked past the parade ground before. At noon, the dust
moved above it like a steamroller, and there was a muffled noise of something shuddering and clanking. Soldiers were trained there, and during the
drill hours, sausage-shop boys with trays on their shoulders and schoolboys
from the town used to linger in front of the parade ground a long time and
stare. There was certainly something to look at. In every direction, all over
the field, spherical dummies, looking like cockerels in sacks, were galloping
up to each other by twos and pecking at each other. The soldiers were
wearing quilted jackets and helmets of steel net. They were being taught to
fence.

This spectacle was nothing new to me. In the course of the summer I had
seen my fill of it.

Yet on the morning after the night I have described, when I was walking
into town and just drawing level with the field, I suddenly remembered that
less than an hour ago I had seen this field in a dream.

In the night I had not decided what to do about Cohen. I had gone to
bed at dawn, slept all morning, and, just before waking, had had the dream
about the field. It was a dream of a future war, adequate as the mathemati-
cians say—and necessary.

It has long been observed that, however insistently the regulations
drummed into regiments and squadrons go on repeating things about wartime, the mind in peacetime is unable to make the transition from premises
to conclusion. Every day, because no military unit could pass through the
narrow streets of Marburg, pale riflemen, dusty up to their foreheads and
dressed in sun-faded uniforms, marched around the town by the road below.
Yet the most one could call to mind at the sight of them was the stationers'
shops where those very same riflemen were sold by the sheet, with a pot of
gum as a free gift with every dozen bought.

It was a different matter in the dream. Here impressions were not limited
to the requirements of habit. Here it was the colors that moved and drew
conclusions.

I dreamed of a deserted field, and something told me it was Marburg
under siege. Pale, lanky Nettelbecks were going by in single file, pushing
wheelbarrows. It was some dark hour of the daytime, such as does not exist
in the real world. The dream was in a Frederick the Great style, with
fieldworks and entrenchments. Just visible on the battery mounds were the
outlines of men with field glasses. They were enveloped, with physical
tangibility, by a silence such as does not exist in the real world. Like a
blizzard of loose earth, it pulsed in the air, not merely being, but happening.
It seemed to be constantly being tossed up with spades. This was the saddest
dream of all the dreams I have ever had. I probably wept in my sleep.

What had happened with V—— had lodged deep in me. My heart was
healthy. It worked well. Working at night, it would pick up the most
accidental and worthless of the day's impressions. And now it had latched
onto the parade ground, and one push was enough to set the mechanism
of the training ground in motion, and the dream itself, on its circular path,
quietly chimed, "I am a dream about war."

I don't know why I was going into town, but there was such a weight
in my soul that my very head seemed packed with earth for some sort of
fortification purposes.

It was lunchtime. At this hour no one I knew was in the university. The
seminar reading room was empty. Private houses of the town advanced
right up to it from beneath. The heat was merciless. Here and there at
windowsills, drowned people appeared with their chewed-looking collars
awry. The half-dark of drawing rooms smokily drifted beyond them. From
within came haggard female martyrs, the fronts of their housecoats looking
boiled through as if in laundry coppers. I turned toward home, deciding to
go by the higher ground, where there were many shady villas under the
castle wall.

Their gardens lay prostrate in the furnace of heat, and only the stalks of
roses, as if they had just come from the anvil, haughtily stooped in the slow,
blue fire. I was dreaming of a small street that descended steeply behind one

of those villas. There was shade there. I knew this. I had decided to turn
off into it and have a short rest. What was my astonishment when in the
very same stupefaction in which I was preparing to settle myself there, I
saw Professor Hermann Cohen. He noticed me. My retreat was cut off.

My son is in his seventh year. When he does not understand a French
phrase but simply guesses its meaning from the situation in which it is
spoken, he says, "I understood, not from the words but *because*." Full stop.
Not because of this or that but: I understood because.

I shall adopt his terminology and shall call the mind that is used in order
to *arrive* somewhere as distinct from the mind that is taken out riding for
the sake of exercise—the *"because" mind*.

This because mind was the kind that Cohen had. Talking to him was
rather frightening, and going for a walk with him was no joke at all. Beside
you, leaning on a stick and moving along with frequent stops, went the very
spirit of mathematical physics, which had assembled its basic principles,
step by step, by way of just such a gait as this. In his roomy frock coat and
his soft hat, this university professor was filled to a certain degree with the
valuable essence that in olden times had been bottled in the heads of
Galileos, Newtons, Leibnizes, and Pascals.

He did not like talking while he walked but merely listened to the chatter
of his companions, always uneven because of the stepwise structure of the
Marburg footpaths. He would stride, listen, suddenly stop, deliver a caustic
utterance about what he had just heard, and, pushing off from the pavement
with his stick, solemnly proceed as far as the next aphoristic breathing
space.

And this was just how our conversation went. Mention of my blunder
only aggravated it—this he let me know in a deadly fashion, without words,
adding nothing at all to the mocking silence of his stick propped on a stone.
He inquired about my plans. He did not approve of them. In his opinion
I ought to stay on till the doctoral examination, take it, and only then go
home and take our state examinations, to come back later perhaps and settle
in the West. I thanked him with all fervor for this hospitality. But my
gratitude told him much less than did my longing to return to Moscow. In
the way I presented it to him he rightly detected a quality of insincerity and
silliness, which offended him because, in view of the enigmatic shortness of
life, he could not endure enigmas that shortened it artificially. And restraining his irritation he slowly went down from slab to slab, waiting to see if
the fellow would at last talk some sense after such obvious and tiresome
trivialities.

But how could I tell him that I was abandoning philosophy forever, that
I was going to finish my studies in Moscow like everyone else, solely in order
to get them finished, that I was not even thinking of ever returning to
Marburg? To him, whose final words before his retirement were about

fidelity to great philosophy, and were uttered to the university in such tones that, along the benches where a number of young ladies were sitting, there was a flutter of pocket handkerchiefs.

10

At the beginning of August my family moved from Bavaria to Italy and invited me to Pisa. I was running out of funds; there was scarcely enough for my return to Moscow. One of those evenings, many of which I imagined to lie ahead of me, I was sitting with G—— on our time-honored terrace, complaining of the sorry state of my finances. He talked it over. At various times he had had occasion to live in real penury, and it was precisely at those times that he had done a great deal of roaming around the world. He had been to England and to Italy, and he knew ways of living on practically nothing while traveling. According to his plan, I ought to get to Venice and Florence on the remainder of my money and then go on to my parents for a remedial feed and a fresh subsidy for the return trip, which might even be unnecessary if I was miserly enough with what I had left. He began putting figures down on paper that really did add up to a most modest total.

The headwaiter in the café was friendly with us all. He knew the ins and outs of all our lives. When at the height of my examinations my brother had come to visit me and begun to hinder my work in the daytime, this eccentric fellow discovered in him rare potentialities for billiards and got him so interested in the game that he would go to him in the early morning to improve his play, leaving me my room for the whole day.

He took the liveliest interest in our discussion of the Italian plan. Although he absented himself every few moments, he kept coming back to us, and, tapping at G——'s sum with his pencil, he found even this insufficiently economical.

He hurried back from one of his absences with a thick reference book under his arm, placed on the table a tray bearing three glasses of strawberry punch, and, ramming the book open, chased through it all twice, from the beginning and from the end. And finding in the whirl of pages the one he was looking for, he announced that I had to leave that very night by the express that departed at three-something A.M., in token of which he proposed that we should all drink with him to my journey.

I did not waste much time in hesitation. "Yes, indeed," I thought, following the line of his reasoning. A formal discharge had been received from the university. All the marks for my written work were in order. It was now half past ten. To wake the landlady was no great sin. There was more than enough time for packing. Right, I'll go.

He was as delighted as if it were he who was to see Basel the next day. "Listen," he said, smacking his lips and collecting the empty glasses. "Let's take a good look at each other; that's a custom of ours. It might come in useful; you never can tell what the future holds." I laughed in answer, assuring him that this was superfluous, for I had done it long ago, and that I would never forget him.

We said good-bye. I went after G——, and the vague clinking of nickel-plated cutlery fell silent behind us—as it seemed to me then—forever.

Several hours later, having talked ourselves dry and stupefied ourselves in a walk about the small town that had quickly exhausted its small supply of streets, G—— and I went down into the suburb that adjoined the station. We were enveloped in mist. We stood in it motionless, like cattle at a watering place, doggedly smoking with that wordless obtuseness that time and again puts cigarettes out. Gradually day began to glimmer. Dew, like gooseflesh, tightened the kitchen gardens. Out of the haze burst forth little rows of satiny seedlings. And suddenly, just at this stage in the coming daylight, the town—the whole of it at once—stood outlined on its characteristic height. There were people asleep in it. There were churches, a castle, and a university. But they were still merged with the gray sky like a shred of spiderweb on a damp mop. It even seemed to me that scarcely had the town taken shape before it started to dissolve like a trace of breath cut short half a pace from a windowpane. "Well, it's time!" said G—.

It was growing light. We walked quickly up and down the stone platform. Pieces of the approaching roar flew into our faces out of the mist, like stones. The train came in with a rush; I embraced my friend and, flinging my suitcase up, leaped into the carriage. The flints of the concrete rolled away with a shriek; the train door clicked; I pressed against the window. The train cut off in the shape of an arc everything I had experienced, and, sooner than I expected, the Lahn, the crossing, the highway, and my recent home flashed past, tumbling upon each other. I tore at the window to let it down. It would not yield. Suddenly it went down by itself with a bang. I leaned out with all my might. The carriage was swaying on a headlong bend; there was nothing to be seen. Good-bye philosophy; good-bye youth; good-bye Germany!

11

Six years passed. When all was forgotten, when the war had dragged by and come to an end and the Revolution had broken out, one low dusk that did not even reach to the second story, there crept over the snow and out of the darkness a ring of the telephone, out of another time, and resounded in our apartment. "Who's there?" I asked. "G—" came the answer. It was so surprising—I was not even surprised. "Where are you?"—I forced myself to say, out of another time. He replied. A further absurdity. The place was right next to us, just across the courtyard. He was phoning from what had previously been a hotel and was now a Narkompros hostel. A minute later, I was sitting in his room. His wife had not changed in the least. His children I had not known before.

But the unexpected thing was this. It turned out that he had lived upon earth all these years like everyone else and—though abroad—had lived beneath the overcast sky of that very same war for the liberation of small nations. I learned that he had recently come from London. And he was either in the party or fiercely in sympathy with it. He had a job. With the government's move to Moscow, he had automatically been transferred along with the corresponding Narkompros department. This explained his being our neighbor. And this was all there was to it.

And I had rushed to him as to a Marburger. Not, of course, in order to take up my life again, with his help, from that far-off misty dawn when we had stood in the darkness like cattle at a ford—a little more carefully this time, and if possible without a war. Oh, of course not in order to do that. But knowing in advance that such a reprise was unthinkable, I had rushed to check just what made it unthinkable in my own life.

Later, I had the good fortune to visit Marburg once more. I spent two days there in February 1923. I went there with my wife but did not manage to bring the two of them together. Thus I was guilty toward them both. But it was hard for me as well. I had seen Germany before the war, and now I was seeing it after. What had happened in the world was presented to me in the most terrible foreshortening. It was the period of the occupation of the Ruhr. Germany was cold and starving, deceived about nothing and deceiving no one, her hand stretched out to the age like a beggar (a gesture not her own at all), and the entire country on crutches.

To my surprise I found my landlady alive. She and her daughter threw up their hands at the sight of me. Both were sitting, when I appeared, in exactly the same places as eleven years ago, sewing. The room was to let. They unlocked it for me. I would not have recognized it but for the road from Ockershausen to Marburg, visible as before from the window. And it was winter. The empty, cold, untidy room, the bare willows on the horizon —it was all unfamiliar. The landscape that had once spent too much thought on the Thirty Years' War had ended by bringing war upon itself through its prophecies. Before my departure I went into a bakery and sent the two women a large nutcake.

And now about Cohen: I could not see Cohen. Cohen was dead.

12

And so—stations, stations, stations. Stations flying by to the rear of the train, like moths of stone.

In Basel there was a Sunday quiet, and you could hear the swallows scraping the eaves with their wings as they scurried about. Glowing walls rolled upward like eyeballs under the sloping tiled roofs, black as cherries. The whole town was blinking with them as with eyelashes, now half closed and now wide open. And the same kiln heat that burned in the wild vines of the private houses burned in the ceramic gold of the Primitives in the clean and cool museum.

"Zwei francs vierzig centimes"—the peasant woman in the shop, in her Canton costume, pronounced with amazing purity, but the merging place of the two pools of language was not here but farther over to the right, past a low, hanging roof, away to the south of it across the wide-spreading, hot federal azure, and uphill all the way. Somewhere below Saint Gotthard and —they say—in the depths of the night.

And I slept through such a place, tired out by the nightly vigils of a two-day journey! The one night of my life when I ought not to have slept —almost a sort of "Simon, sleepest thou?"—may it be forgiven me. Yet there were moments when I did wake up, standing at the window for a disgracefully short time, "for their eyes were heavy." And then . . .

All around, the hubbub of a rural assembly of peaks that had crowded together motionlessly. Aha! So while I was dozing, we had drilled our way, screwlike, from tunnel to tunnel, whistling incessantly in cold smoke, and now we were surrounded with a breath three thousand meters superior to the breath to which we were born.

There was an opaque darkness, but echo filled it with a bulging sculpture of sounds. Chasms conversed unashamedly loudly, like old gossips pulling the earth to pieces. Everywhere, everywhere, everywhere, the prattle and scandalmongering and filtering of streams. It was easy to picture them, hung out all over the steeps and let down into the valleys like twisted threads. While down onto the train from above leaped vertical overhangs that settled themselves on the carriage roofs and, with shouts to one another and dangling their feet, enjoyed a free ride.

But sleep overcame me, and I kept falling into an impermissible slumber on the threshold of the snows, under the blind, white Oedipal eyes of the Alps, on the peak of the planet's demonic perfection. At the level of the kiss that, in love with itself, the earth places upon its own shoulder like Michelangelo's Night.

When I woke up, a pure Alpine morning was looking in at the window. Something, a landslide or other such obstacle, had brought the train to a halt. We were asked to cross over to another train. We walked along the track of the mountain railway. The ribbon of the line went twisting through disconnected panoramas, as if the path were continually being pushed around a corner, like something stolen. My luggage was carried by a barefoot Italian boy, who looked exactly like those depicted on chocolate wrappings. Somewhere near at hand, his flock was making its music. The jingling of the little bells fell in lazy shakings, toward and away. Gadflies sucked the music in; its skin probably moved with sudden twitches. There was a fragrance of chamomile flowers, and everywhere invisibly slapping waters were idly pouring from hollow to hollow, never ceasing for an instant.

The effect of not sleeping enough was soon felt. Although I spent half a day in Milan, I retained nothing of it. Only the cathedral, which constantly changed its face while I was going toward it through the town, and looked different according to which of the successive crossroads it was revealed from, dimly stamped itself upon my mind. Like a melting glacier, it loomed forth repeatedly against the deep blue, vertical slant of August heat and seemed to be feeding the numerous cafés of Milan with ice and water. When at last a rather small square set me at its foot and I craned my neck to look at it, it slid down into me with all its choir and its rustling of pilasters and turrets, like a plug of snow sliding down the jointed column of a drainpipe.

But I could scarcely stand on my feet, and the first thing I promised myself when I should get to Venice was to have a thoroughly good sleep.

13

When I came out of the station building with its provincial awning in a kind of Customs and Excise style, something smooth slid quietly up to my feet. Something malignantly dark, like sink dregs, touched by two or three sequins of stars. Almost imperceptibly it rose and fell and was like a painting, darkened with age, set in a swaying frame. I did not grasp at first that this depiction of Venice *was* Venice. That I was *in* it, and not dreaming about it.

The canal by the station went, like a blind gut, away around a corner toward other wonders of this floating gallery upon a sewer. I hurried to the place where the cheap steamboats stopped, which here did the work of trams.

The *vaporetto* sweated and panted, wiped its nose and spluttered. And over the same unruffled surface where it dragged its drowned mustaches, the palaces of the Grand Canal floated in a semicircular path, gradually dropping behind us. They are called palaces, and they could be called temples, and still no words could give any idea of those carpets of colored marble, hung plumb down into the nocturnal lagoon as if onto the arena of a medieval tournament.

There exists a special Christmas-tree East, the East of the Pre-Raphaelites. There exists the image of a starry night, as in the legend of the adoration of the Magi. There exists an age-old Christmas carving: a gilded walnut, its surface splashed with blue candle wax. There exist such words

as khalva and Chaldea, magicians and magnesium, India and indigo. With
these belong the nocturnal coloring of Venice and her watery reflections.

As if to establish its walnut scale the more firmly in the Russian ear, cries
ring out on the *vaporetto* for the information of the passengers: "Fondaco
dei turchi! Fondaco dei tedeschi!" as the boat draws in now to one bank,
now to the other. But of course, the names of the different quarters have
nothing to do with *funduki*, the Russian for hazelnuts; they enshrine recollections of caravansaries founded here once by Turkish and German merchants.

I do not remember in front of which one of these innumerable Ven-
draminos, Grimanis, Corneros, Foscaris, and Loredanos I saw my first
gondola, that is, the first to strike me. But it was certainly on the other side
of the Rialto. It came out noiselessly from a side-turning onto the canal and,
leaning as it moved across it, proceeded to moor at the nearest palace portal.
It seemed to have been sent up from backyard to front porch on the round
belly of a wave, which came slowly rolling out. Behind it remained a dark
crevice, full of dead rats and capering melon peel. Before it ran the streaming lunar desert of the wide road of water. The gondola had a female
hugeness, the way everything is huge that is perfect in form and incommen-
surate with the place its body occupies in space. Its bright crested halberd
flew lightly along the sky, carried high by the rounded nape of the wave.
And just as lightly, the black silhouette of the gondolier sped among the
stars. While the small cowl of the cabin seemed to vanish, pressed down into
the water at the saddle between stern and prow.

Even before coming here, from what G——had told me about Venice,
I had decided that the best place to stay would be the quarter near the
academy. And this was where I left the boat. I do not remember whether
I crossed the bridge onto the left bank or stayed on the right. I remember
a tiny square. It was surrounded by palaces just like the ones on the canal,
only they were grayer and sterner looking. And they had their feet on solid
ground.

The square was flooded with moonlight, and in it people were standing,
walking about, or half reclining. There were not very many of them, and
they seemed to make it a drapery of moving, slightly moving, and unmoving
figures. It was an unusually calm evening. One couple in particular caught
my attention. Without turning to face each other, enjoying a shared silence,
they were gazing intently into the distance on the opposite bank. Most likely
they were servants from the palace taking a rest. What first attracted me
was the calm demeanor of the manservant, his grizzled, close-cut hair, the
gray of his jacket. There was something un-Italian about these things. There
was something northern in them. Then I saw his face. It seemed to me a
face I had seen before, though I could not recall where.

I went up to him with my suitcase and poured out to him my concern for a lodging, using a nonexistent dialect concocted from past attempts to read Dante in the original. He courteously heard me out, thought for a little, and asked the housemaid beside him something. She shook her head negatively. He took out a watch with a lid, looked at the time, clicked it shut, replaced it in his waistcoat, and, still thoughtful, with a nod of the head invited me to follow him. From the moonlight-flooded façade we turned a corner into utter darkness.

We walked down narrow stone streets no wider than apartment corridors. Now and again they lifted us up onto short bridges of humpback stone. There the dirty sleeves of the lagoon stretched out on both sides, the water in them so densely packed it was like a Persian carpet rolled into a tube and forced with effort into the bottom of a crooked case.

People came toward us over the humpy bridges, and every time a Venetian woman appeared her approach was heralded long in advance by the rapid clicking of her shoes on the stone with which this quarter was paved.

High above us, laid sheer across the pitch-black cracks that we were wandering through, shone a bright night sky, forever receding. The down of a dandelion shedding its seeds seemed to be scattered all over the Milky Way, and it was solely in order to let through a shaft or two of this moving light that the alleyways now and then stepped apart to form squares and crossroads. And, surprised by my odd sense of knowing him, I talked away to my companion in the nonexistent dialect, lurching across from pitch to down and from down to pitch, while with his help I sought out the cheapest possible lodging.

But on the embankments, where there was a way out to the open water, other colors reigned and the quietness gave way to commotion. Arriving and departing *vaporetti* were crowded with people, and the oil-black waters burst in snowy spray like shattered marble, breaking to bits in the mortars of those engines now feverishly working, now stopping dead. And right next to its gurgling came the vivid hiss of the burners in the fruit merchants' stalls, where tongues were at work and where fruits were bouncing and pounding about in the nonsensical columns of a kind of half-cooked fruit stew.

In the scullery of one of the restaurants by the shore we received some useful information: The address we were given sent us all the way back to the beginning of our pilgrimage. We retraced our whole path in reverse as we went toward it. So when my guide installed me in one of the hotels near the Campo Morosini, I had the feeling that I had just traversed a distance equal to the starry sky of Venice, going in the direction contrary to its own movement. If I had then been asked what Venice was . . . "Bright nights," I would have said, "and tiny squares and peaceful people who seem oddly familiar."

14

"Well, my friend!" the landlord growled at me, loudly as if I were deaf.
He was a sturdy old man of some sixty years in a dirty unbuttoned shirt.
"I'll fix you up like one of the family." Blood rose to his face, he eyed me
with lowered head, and, his hands stuck behind the buckles of his braces,
he drummed on his hairy chest with his fingers. "Want some cold veal?"
he bellowed, not softening his glance and deducing nothing whatever from
my reply.

He was, no doubt, a good-hearted fellow who, with his mustaches à la
Radetzki, was pretending to be a fearsome monster. He could remember
Austrian rule, and, as soon became apparent, he spoke a little German. But
to him it was chiefly the language of Dalmatian sergeant majors, and my
fluent pronunciation led him to sad reflections on the decline of the German
language since his soldiering days. Besides which he probably suffered from
heartburn.

Raising himself up behind the counter as if he were standing on stirrups,
he bawled out something to somebody in a murderous voice and came
bouncing down into the little yard where we made each other's acquaintance. Several tables stood there, covered with dirty cloths. "Took a liking
to you the moment you came in," he snarled at me with evil glee and, with
a gesture inviting me to take a seat, sank onto a chair himself two or three
tables away from me. Someone brought me beer and meat. The courtyard
served as a dining room. The hotel's guests, if it had any, must have had
supper long ago and gone off to their rooms, except for one seedy little
old man sitting it out in the farthest corner of that guzzling-rink and
making obsequious sounds of agreement each time the landlord turned
to him.

I had noticed once or twice already, while tucking into the veal, how the
moist, pink slices kept vanishing and reappearing on the plate. Evidently
I was falling asleep. My eyelids were sticking together.

All of a sudden, just as in a fairy tale, there appeared at the table a dear
little wizened old woman whom the landlord briefly put in the picture about
his ferocious liking for me. Straight after which I went with her somewhere
up a narrow staircase and, remaining alone, groped for the bed and lay
down on it without another thought, having undressed in the dark.

I woke to a vivid, sunny morning from ten hours of uninterrupted,
headlong sleep. All the unbelievable happenings were confirmed. I was in
Venice. The tiny patches of reflected brightness swarming on the ceiling, as
they do in the cabin of a riverboat, told me this, and they told me that I
would now get up and rush out to look at it all.

I examined the place in which I was lying. On nails hammered into a
painted partition hung skirts and blouses, a feather duster on a ring, and

a carpet-beater hanging from its nail by a loop. The windowsill was heaped with jars of ointment. There was a candy box full of unrefined chalk.

Behind a curtain drawn across the whole width of the attic I could hear a shoe brush knocking and rustling. It had been audible for a long time now. They must have been cleaning the shoes for the whole hotel. In addition to this noise I could hear the soft murmur of a woman and a child's whisper. In the murmuring woman I recognized my little old lady of the day before.

She was a distant relative of the landlord's and worked for him as his housekeeper. He had given up her kennel of a room to me, but when I tried to set this right somehow, it was she who anxiously begged me not to interfere in their family affairs.

Stretching myself before getting dressed, I once again surveyed everything around me, and suddenly the events of the previous day were illumined by a moment's clarity. My guide of yesterday had reminded me of the headwaiter in Marburg, the very one who had hoped he might still come in useful to me.

The probable touch of imputation in his request may have increased this resemblance even more. So that was the reason why I had instinctively picked out one person from the others in the square.

This discovery did not surprise me. There is nothing miraculous in this sort of thing. Our most innocent hello's and good-byes would have no meaning at all, were not time threaded through with the unity of life's events, that is, with the intercrossing effects of a common, everyday hypnosis.

15

And so I too knew the touch of this happiness. I too had the fortune to discover that one could go day after day to meet a piece of built-up space as if it were a living personality.

From whichever side the Piazza is approached, on every path to it there lies in wait the moment when your breathing quickens and, with hurrying step, your feet begin carrying you to meet it of their own accord. Whether from the Merceria or from the Telegraph, at a certain moment the road acquires the likeness of a threshold and the square, opening out a boldly sketched horizon of its own, leads forth as if to a reception: the Campanile, the Duomo, the Doges' Palace, and the three-sided gallery.

As you gradually grow attached to it, you come to have the sensation that Venice is a city inhabited by buildings. The four just mentioned, and several others of their kind. In this assertion there is nothing figurative. The word spoken in stone by the architects is so lofty no rhetoric can reach up to it. Besides, it is all overgrown, as though with seashells, with centuries of tourists' rapture. Their ever growing delight has forced out of Venice the last trace of declamation. No empty places remain in the empty palaces. Every spot is occupied by beauty.

When Englishmen, before getting into the gondola hired to take them to the station, linger a last moment on the Piazza in poses that would be natural at a farewell scene with a living person, you envy them the square the more keenly because, as is well known, no European culture has approached the Italian so closely as the English.

16

Once, beneath these standard-bearing masts, their generations interlacing like golden threads, three centuries thronged, magnificently woven together. And not far from the square slumbered the fleet of those centuries, a motionless thicket of vessels. It seemed a continuation of the plan of the city. Rigging thrust forth from behind garrets; galleys peeped through; movements were identical on land and on board the ships. On a moonlit night some three-decked vessel, glaring straight into the street, would weld the whole street with the dead thunder of its unwound and immobile thrust. And in that same funereal grandeur, frigates stood at anchor, picking out from beyond the port the quietest and deepest halls.

For those times it was a very powerful fleet. Its strength was amazing. In the fifteenth century it already numbered three and a half thousand trading vessels, not counting the military ones, with seventy thousand seamen and shipworkers.

This fleet was the unfictitious reality of Venice, the prosaic underpinning of her fairy-tale quality. One might say, paradoxically, that its swaying tonnage was the city's terra firma, her landed stock, the subterrain of her commerce and her prisons. Captive air pined in the snares of the ropes. The fleet was oppressive and wearisome. But just as between a pair of communicating vessels, something redeeming rose in response from the shore, equal in level to its pressure. To understand this is to understand how art deceives its client.

The derivation of the word "pantaloons" is curious. Once, before its later sense of "trousers," it designated a character in Italian comedy. But still earlier, in its original meaning, *pianta leone* expressed the idea of the victoriousness of Venice and meant: the hoister of the lion (on the flag), that is—in other words—Venice-Victrix. There is even something about this in Byron, in *Childe Harold:*

> Her very byword sprung from victory,
> The "Planter of the Lion," which through fire
> And blood she bore o'er subject earth and sea.

Concepts are reborn in remarkable ways. When people grow accustomed to horrors, these become the foundations of good taste. Shall we ever understand how, for a while, the guillotine could be the model for a lady's brooch?

The emblem of the lion has figured in many different ways in Venice. Thus the movable slot for secret denunciations on the stairway of the Censors, next to paintings by Veronese and Tintoretto, was carved in the form of a lion's maw. It is well known what terror this *bocca di leoni* inspired in the people of the time, how it gradually became a sign of ill-breeding to mention the persons who had mysteriously fallen into the exquisitely carved slot in those cases where the state itself expressed no regret on their account.

When art raised palaces for conquerors, people trusted it. They thought it shared the general views and would in the future share the common fate. But this is just what did not happen. The language of the palaces turned out to be the language of oblivion, and not at all that pantaloon language mistakenly ascribed to them. The pantaloon purposes disintegrated; the palaces remained.

And Venetian painting remained. From my childhood I was acquainted with the taste of its hot springs, through reproductions and in the export overflow of museums. But one needed to be at their birthplace to see, instead of particular pictures, the painting itself, like a marsh of gold, like one of the primal pools of creativity.

17

I looked at this spectacle more deeply and more diffusely than my formulations of it now can express. I did not try to make conscious sense of what I saw in the direction in which I am now interpreting it. But over the years the impressions have settled in me by themselves in this form, and my compressed conclusion will not be a departure from the truth.

I saw what is the first observation to strike the painter's instinct. How one suddenly understands what it is like for the visible object, when it begins to be seen. Once noticed, nature moves aside with the obedient spaciousness of a story, and in this condition, like one asleep, is quietly transferred onto the canvas. One has to see Carpaccio and Bellini to understand what is depiction.

I learned, further, what syncretism accompanies the flowering of artistic talent, when the artist achieves identity with the elemental essence of the art of painting, and it becomes impossible to say which of the three is most active upon the canvas and for whose benefit: the painter, the painting, or the thing painted. One has to see Veronese and Titian to understand what is art.

Finally, though at the time I did not value these impressions sufficiently, I learned how little a genius needs in order to explode.

Who will believe it? The identity of the depiction with the depicter and the object depicted, or—more broadly—indifference to the immediate truth: This is what brings him into a frenzy. As if it were a slap in the face, given to mankind in his person. And then his canvases are invaded by a storm that purifies the chaos of craftsmanship with the definitive blows of passion. One has to see the Michelangelo of Venice—Tintoretto—to understand what is a genius, that is, an artist.

18

However, I did not go into these subtleties then. In Venice at that time, and still more strongly in Florence, or, to be quite precise, in the following winters in Moscow, after my journey, other and more particular thoughts entered my head.

The chief thing that everyone carries away from an encounter with Italian art is a sensation of the tangible unity of our culture, whatever he may have seen this in, and whatever name he may give it.

How much people have said, for instance, about the paganism of the Humanists, and what various things they have said about it, calling it both a legitimate trend and otherwise. And indeed, the collision of faith in the Resurrection with the age of the Renaissance is an extraordinary phenomenon, central to the whole of European culture. And who has not noticed the anachronism, often immoral, in the way canonical themes are treated in all these *Presentation*s, *Ascension*s, *Wedding*s *in Cana,* and *Last Supper*s, with their *grand-monde* licentiousness and their luxury?

It was in this very incongruity that the thousand-year-long peculiarity of our culture made itself known to me.

Italy crystallized for me what we breathe in unconsciously from the cradle. Her painting itself finally accomplished for me what I still had to think out because of her, and while I was spending whole days going from collection to collection, it flung at my feet the ready-made observation, finally rendered in paint.

I understood that the Bible, for instance, is not so much a book with a definitive text as the notebook of mankind, and that everything everlasting is like this. That it is vital not when it is enforced but when it is receptive to all the analogies by means of which subsequent ages, issuing from it, look back at it. I understood that the history of culture is a chain of equations in images, which link in pairs the next unknown thing with something already known, whereby the known, constant for the whole series, is legend, set at the base of tradition, and the unknown, new each time, is the actual moment in the flow of culture.

This is what interested me at that time, this what I then understood and loved.

I loved the living essence of the symbolic pattern of history—in other words, the instinct with whose help, like salangane swallows, we have constructed the world: a vast nest, glued together from earth and sky, life and death, and two kinds of time, present and absent. I understood that what prevents it from falling apart is the force of cohesion consisting in the utter figurativeness of all its parts.

But I was young, and I did not know that this does not encompass the fate of a genius and his nature. I did not know that his essence rests in the experiencing of an actual biography and not in a symbolic pattern refracted in images. I did not know that he is distinguished from the Primitives by the fact that his roots lie in the coarse immediacy of moral sentience. One of his peculiarities is remarkable. Although all the flarings of moral passion are enacted inside the culture, it always seems to the rebel that his rebellion is rolling along on the street, beyond culture's fence. I did not know that the longest-lived images are left intact by the iconoclast in those rare cases when he is not born with empty hands.

When Pope Julius II expressed displeasure at the chromatic poverty of the Sistine ceiling, Michelangelo remarked, by way of justification, referring to the ceiling, which represents the Creation of the world with the appropriate figures, "*In those times* they didn't dress up in gold. The persons depicted here were *people of modest means.*" Such is the thunderous child-like language of this kind of man.

The boundary of culture is reached by the man who conceals within himself a tamed Savonarola. The untamed Savonarola destroys it.

19

The evening before my departure there was a concert with illuminations on the Piazza, such as were often held there. The buildings enclosing the Piazza had decked themselves from head to foot with the sharp points of electric-light bulbs, and it was lit on three sides by a black-and-white banner. The faces of the listeners under the open sky were steamed in bathlike brightness as if they were in a closed, magnificently illumined hall. Suddenly from the ceiling of the imaginary ballroom a gentle rain began to fall. And scarcely had it started when it suddenly stopped again. The reflected glow of the illuminations seethed in a colorful haze above the square. The belltower of San Marco cut like a rocket of red marble into the pink mist, which half obscured its summit. A little way off swirled dark olive steam clouds, and in them the five-headed hull of the cathedral was hidden like something in a legend. That end of the square was like an underwater kingdom. On the cathedral porch the four horses, galloping headlong from ancient Greece and halting here as if on the edge of a precipice, were glittering with gold.

When the concert was over, a millstone of steady shuffling became audible; it had been turning all the time in a circle around the galleries, but till now it had been muffled by the music. It was the ring of strollers, whose footsteps resounded and merged together like the rustle of skates in the frozen bowl of an ice rink.

Among these strollers, women passed with rapid, angry gait, more menacing than seductive. They glanced over their shoulders as they walked, as if to repulse and annihilate. Curving their bodies challengingly, they quickly vanished beneath the porticoes. Every time they looked around, you were stared at by the deathly mascara face of a black Venetian head-scarf. Their quick gait in *allegro irato* time corresponded strangely to the black shivering of the illuminations among the white scratches of the diamond lights.

Twice I have tried to express in verse the sensation that for me is forever connected with Venice. In the night before my departure I was wakened in my hotel by an arpeggio on a guitar that broke off the instant that I woke. I hurried to the window, under which water was splashing, and peered intently into the distance of the night sky, as if there might still be a trace in it of the instantly silenced sound. From the way I gazed, an observer might have said that I was still half asleep and investigating whether there had risen over Venice some new constellation of which I had a dim but ready-made idea as the Constellation of the Guitar.

PART III

1

The chain of boulevards went cutting through Moscow, in the wintertimes, behind a double curtain of blackened trees. Lights gleamed yellow in the houses, like small star-shaped circles of lemon cut through the center. Blizzardy sky hung down low on the trees, and all around everything white was blue.

Poorly dressed young people went hurrying along the boulevards, bending their heads as if they were going to butt. I was acquainted with some of them; most of them I did not know. But all of them were my coevals, the countless faces of my childhood.

They had just begun to be addressed by their patronymics, endowed with rights, and initiated into the secret of the words "possess," "profit," and "acquire." The haste they displayed deserves closer analysis.

In the world there is death and foresight. The unknown is dear to us. What we know in advance is terrifying, and every passion is a blind leap aside from the inevitable, which comes bearing down upon us. Living species would have nowhere to exist and to repeat themselves if passion had nowhere to jump to, off the common path along which common time rolls, the time in which the universe is gradually demolished.

But life does have somewhere to live and passion somewhere to leap, because alongside common time there exists an infinity of other pathways, never ceasing, immortal in their reproduction of themselves, and every new generation is one of these.

Young people, bending as they ran, hurried through the blizzard. And, though each of them had his own reasons for haste, far more than by all their personal promptings they were spurred along by something they had in common, and that was their historical wholeness—their surrender to the passion with which mankind had just dashed into them as it escaped from the common path, and for yet one more innumerable time avoided its own end.

And to screen from them the duality of their career through the inevitable, and so that they should not go mad, abandon what was begun, and hang themselves, the whole earth's globe of them, a power kept watch from behind the trees on all the boulevards, a much tested, terribly experienced power, which accompanied them as they went with its intelligent eyes. Art stood behind the trees—art, which so splendidly understands our workings that one always wonders from what nonhistorical worlds it derived its ability to see history in outline. It stood behind the trees, terribly similar to life, and was endured in life because of this likeness, just as portraits of wives and mothers are endured in the laboratories of scholars dedicated to natural science, that is, to the gradual solution of death's enigma.

What kind of art, then, was it? It was the youthful art of Scriabin, Blok, Kommissarzhevskaya, Bely—advanced, gripping, original. And so astounding that not only did it not make one think of replacing it with anything else, but, just the opposite, one wished—for the sake of its greater stability—to repeat the whole of it from its very foundation, only more strongly, more hotly, more wholly. One wanted to resay it all in a single breath, but this was unthinkable without passion, and passion kept leaping aside all the time; and so in this way the new came into being. But the new did not come to take the place of the old, as is usually thought; exactly the contrary, it arose in an enraptured reproduction of the model. This is the kind of art it was. And what kind of generation was it?

The boys close to me in age were thirteen years old in 1905, and twenty-one just before the war. Their two critical periods coincided with two red-letter days in our country's history. Both their boyish maturing and their coming of call-up age immediately served as clamps to strengthen a transitional epoch. Our age was stitched through and through with their nerves and obligingly left by them at the disposal of old men and children.

When I came back from abroad it was the centennial of the war against Napoleon. The Brest line had been renamed the "Aleksandrovsky." Stations were whitewashed; the watchmen at crossings were dressed in clean shirts. Flags were stuck all over the Kubinka station building; extra guards stood at the doors. Nearby, an imperial inspection was taking place and on account of this the platform shone with a vivid profusion of loose sand as yet trodden down only here and there.

In the minds of travelers this aroused no recollection of the events being celebrated. One sensed in the jubilee decorations the reign's chief characteristic: indifference to our own history. And if anything was affected by the festivities, it was not the movement of people's thoughts but the movement of the train, which was being stopped at stations for longer than the timetable required and held up by signals in the countryside more often than usual.

I could not help calling to mind Serov, who had died the previous winter, and his stories of the time when he was painting the Tsar's family; caricatures made by artists at the Yusupovs' sketching evenings; odd incidents that had accompanied the Kutepov edition of *The Tsar's Hunt;* and a number of other trifles relevant to this moment and connected with the school of painting that was under the control of a Ministry of the Imperial Court and in which we had lived for something like twenty years. I might have recalled the year 1905 as well, the drama in the Kasatkin family, and my own half-baked revolutionism, which went no farther than braving a Cossack whip and feeling its lash on the back of my quilted greatcoat. And finally, as for the guards, stations, and flags, even they, of course, heralded a very serious drama and were not at all the innocent vaudeville act my shallow apoliticism saw in them.

The generation was apolitical, I might have said, were I not aware that the tiny part of it I came in contact with was not even enough by which to judge the whole intelligentsia. I can say that this was the side of itself that it presented toward me, but it was also the side that it turned toward the age, when it came forth with its first declarations of a science, a philosophy, and an art of its own.

2

However, culture does not just fall into the arms of the first comer. All the things listed had to be won by battle. The notion of love as a duel applies here too. Art could be passed on to the adolescent only as a result of a militant attraction experienced in all possible excitement, like an event in his personal life. The literature of the beginners abounded in symptoms of such a condition. The novices formed groups. The groups divided into epigonic and innovatory ones. These were parts—inconceivable in isolation —of the impetus that had been so urgently foretold that it already permeated everything around with the atmosphere of a love affair no longer merely expected but actually happening. The "epigones" represented enthusiasm without fire or gift; the "innovators" were militants moved solely by an emasculated hatred. These were the words and gestures of a serious discussion, overheard by a monkey and spread about in bits, disjointedly verbatim, wherever he happened to go, with no idea of what meaning had inspired this tempest.

Meanwhile the fate of whoever was to be the chosen one already hung in the air. It was almost possible to say what kind of person it would be, but not yet possible to say who it would be. To judge by appearance, there were dozens of young people identically restless, thinking identically, making identical claims to originality. As a movement the "innovators" were distinguished by an apparent unanimity. But, as in the movements of every age, it was the unanimity of lottery tickets swarming and tossing in the mixing drum. The movement's fate was to remain forever a movement, that is, just a curious case of the mechanical shifting of changes—which it would become the very moment that one of the tickets coming away from the lottery wheel blazed up as it left it, with the fire of winning, of conquest, of having a face and a precise designation. The movement was called: Futurism. The winner and the justification of the draw was Mayakovsky.

3

We made each other's acquaintance in the constrained atmosphere of group prejudices. Long before this, Yulian Anisimov had shown me his poems in *A Trap for Judges,* the way one poet shows off the work of another. But that was in the epigonic circle, "Lirika," and the epigones were not ashamed of their sympathies; in their circle Mayakovsky had been discovered as a phenomenon of great promise and imminence, like a titan.

On the other hand, in the innovators' groups, "Tsentrifuga," of which I shortly became a member, I learned (in 1914, in the spring) that Shershenevich, Bolshakov, and Mayakovsky were our enemies and that we were due to have a far from jocular confrontation with them. I was not in the least surprised by the prospect of quarreling with someone who had already made an impression on me and was from a distance attracting me more and more. Here lay the innovators' whole originality. The birth of "Tsentrifuga" had been accompanied all winter by interminable squabbles. All winter I was aware only of playing at group discipline, and did nothing but sacrifice to it conscience and taste. Now I made ready once again to betray whatever I had to when the moment came. This time, however, I overestimated my strength.

It was a hot day at the end of May, and we were already sitting in the tearoom on the Arbat when the three I have mentioned came in noisily and youthfully from the street, handed their hats to the porter, and, without moderating the sonorousness of their talk, which had been drowned till then by trolleys and drays, made their way toward us with unforced dignity. They had beautiful voices. It was here that the later declamatory style in poetry had its beginning. Their clothes were elegant; ours were slovenly. In all respects the enemy's position was superior.

While Bobrov was wrangling with Shershenevich—the crux of the matter was that they had taunted us on one occasion, we had replied even more coarsely, and an end had to be put to all this—I was watching Mayakovsky, unable to tear my eyes from him. This, I believe, was the first time I had seen him so closely.

The way he said "è" instead of "a," setting his diction rocking like a piece of sheet iron, was the trait of an actor. One could easily imagine his deliberate abruptness as the distinguishing characteristic of other professions and statuses. He was not the only striking one. Beside him sat his comrades. One of them, like him, acted the dandy; another, like him, was a genuine poet. But all these similarities, instead of diminishing Mayakovsky's exclusivity, underlined it. As distinct from playing one single game, he played all games at once; and in contrast to the playing out of roles, he played—with his life. This could be sensed at the very first glance—without any thought of how his end would turn out. And this was what riveted one to him and was frightening.

Although all people, when they walk or stand, can be seen at their full height, whenever Mayakovsky made his appearance this fact seemed a miracle and made everyone turn to look at him. The natural seemed in his case supernatural. The cause of it was not his height but another, more general, more elusive quality. Far more than other people, he was contained in the manifestation of himself. In him there was as much expressed and final as there is little in the majority of people, who rarely and only under some special shock emerge from the murk of half-fermented intentions and unrealized suppositions. He existed as if on the day after some enormous spiritual life that had been lived and stored up ready for all eventualities, and everyone who met him now met him sheafed in its irreversible consequences. He would sit in a chair as if it were the saddle of a motorcycle, bend forward, cut and rapidly swallow a Wiener schnitzel, play cards with sidelong glances and without turning his head; he would stroll majestically along the Kuznetsky, dully and nasally intone, like parts of the liturgy, especially profound bits of his own and other men's work; he scowled, he grew, he traveled, he appeared in public, and somewhere in a depth beyond all this, as behind the upright stance of a skater going at full speed, one perpetually glimpsed, preceding all his days, the one day when the amazing initial run had been taken which had set him erect so vastly and uncon-strainedly. Behind his way of holding himself one sensed something that was like a decision that has been put into action, when the results of it can no longer be revoked. Such a decision was his own genius, for the encounter with it had once so astounded him that it became a thematic prescription for him for ever, to the embodiment of which he gave himself up wholly, without pity or hesitation.

But he was still young; the forms this theme was to take still lay ahead. The theme, however, was insatiable, it endured no putting off. And so, at the beginning, in order to please it, he was obliged to anticipate his future, and anticipation, when realized in the first person, is what acting a role is.

From these poses, which are as natural in the world of highest self-expression as the rules of propriety are in everyday life, he chose for himself the pose of an outward wholeness, the hardest one for an artist and the noblest in relation to friends and intimates. He kept up this pose with such perfection that it is practically impossible now to characterize what lay beneath it.

Yet the mainspring of his brazen confidence was a wild shyness, and under his pretended willpower lay hidden a phenomenally suspicious lack of will and an inclination to causeless gloom. And the mechanism of his yellow blouse was just as deceptive. By means of it he was not fighting the jackets of the bourgeois at all, he was fighting the black velvet of the talent within himself, whose cloying black-browed forms had begun to disturb him earlier than happens in the lives of the less gifted. For no one knew as well as he all the vulgarity of the natural fire when it has not been gradually enraged by cold water. Nor did they know as he did that the passion that suffices for the continuation of the race is not adequate for creativity, which needs a passion sufficient for the continuation of the race's image, that is, a passion that inwardly resembles Christ's Passion, and whose newness inwardly resembles the Divine Promise.

The parley abruptly ended. The enemies we were supposed to annihilate went away unvanquished. On the contrary, the peace terms arrived at were humiliating to us.

Meanwhile it had grown darker outside in the street. It had started to drizzle. In our enemies' absence the tearoom seemed drearily empty. Flies became noticeable along with half-eaten cakes and glasses blinded with hot milk. But the thunderstorm did not take place. Lushly the sun struck at the pavement netted in its pattern of little mauve dots. It was May of the year 1914. The vicissitudes of history were so near! But who thought of them? The crass city glowed with enamel and tinfoil, as in "The Golden Cock-erel." The lacquered green of poplars glittered. For the last time, colors had that poisonous grassiness they were shortly to part with forever. I was crazy about Mayakovsky and already missed him. Do I need to add that those I betrayed were not at all those I had meant to?

4

Chance brought us together the next day under the awning of the Greek café. The large yellow boulevard lay flattened out, spread between the Pushkin monument and Nikitskaya Street. Lean dogs with long tongues lay yawning, stretching, and laying their muzzles comfortably on their front paws. Gossipy pairs of nannies were chattering away, bewailing something or other. Butterflies would fold their wings for a few moments and melt away in the heat, then suddenly open out again, lured sideways by irregular waves of sultry intensity. A small girl in white, who must have been wringing wet, was suspended in midair as she whipped herself up at the heels with the whistling circles of a jump rope.

From a distance I caught sight of Mayakovsky and pointed him out to Loks. He was playing at heads or tails with Khodasevich. At that moment Khodasevich got up, paid what he had lost, and, leaving the awning, went off in the direction of Strastnoi Boulevard. Mayakovsky remained at the table alone. We went in, greeted him, and got into a conversation. After a while he offered to recite something for us.

The poplars were green; the lime trees, a dryish gray. Driven out of all patience by fleas, the drowsy dogs kept jumping up onto all four paws, calling Heaven to witness their moral impotence against brute force and then dropped onto the sand again in sleepy indignation. On the Brest railway, now renamed the Aleksandrovsky line, the engines uttered their throaty whistles. And, all around us, hair was being cut and whiskers shaved, baking and roasting were in progress, people were selling things and moving about—and all of them were wholly unaware.

It was the tragedy *Vladimir Mayakovsky,* which had then just come out. I listened with held breath, my heart overwhelmed, oblivious. Never before had I heard anything like it.

Everything was in it. Boulevard, dogs, poplars, and butterflies. Hairdressers, bakers, tailors, and steam engines. What is the use of quoting? We all remember this sultry, mysterious, summery text, now available to everyone in its tenth edition.

Far off, locomotives roared like grampuses. And the very same absolute distance as upon the earth was there in the throaty territory of his creation. This was that unfathomable inspiration without which there is no originality, the infinity that can open out in life from any point and in any direction, and without which poetry is merely a misunderstanding that has not yet been clarified.

And how simple it all was! Art was called a tragedy. Which is what it should be called. The tragedy was called *Vladimir Mayakovsky.* Concealed in this title was a discovery that had the simplicity of genius: that the poet is not the author but the subject of the poem, which addresses the world in the first person. The title was not the author's name but the surname of the contents.

5

Actually I carried the whole of him away from the boulevard with me that day into my own life. But he was huge; there was no holding on to him when apart from him. And I kept losing him. Then he would remind me of himself—with "A Cloud in Trousers," "Backbone Flute," "War and the Universe," and "Man." What was weathered away in the intervals was so vast that extraordinarily vast reminders were needed too. And such they were. Each of the stages mentioned found me unprepared. At each one, grown out of all recognition, he was wholly born anew, as he had been the first time. It was impossible to get accustomed to him. What was it in him that was so unusual?

He possessed relatively permanent qualities. My admiration too was comparatively stable. It was always ready for him. It would seem that under such conditions I could have grown used to him without having to make any leaps. Yet this was how things were.

For four years, while he existed creatively, I tried to get used to him, but could not. Then I did get used to him in the space of the two and a quarter hours taken up by a reading and analysis of his uncreative "150,000,000." Then, for more than ten years, I carried the burden of being used to him. And then I was suddenly freed from it, all at once and weeping, when he reminded me of himself "at the top of his voice," as he had used to do, but now from beyond the grave.

What one could not get accustomed to was not him but the world that he held in his hands and that he would now set in motion, now bring to a halt, just as the whim took him. I shall never understand what he gained from demagnetizing the magnet, when, without any change in appearance, the horseshoe that previously had made every imagination rear up on end and had drawn to itself all possible weights "with the oaken feet of its lines," ceased now to shift so much as a grain of sand. There can scarcely be another instance in history of someone going so far in a new experience and then—at the hour he himself predicted—so completely rejecting it, just when that experience, though at a cost of discomfort, had become so vitally needed.

What one could not get accustomed to was the Vladimir Mayakovsky of the tragedy, *the surname of its content,* the poet contained in the poetry from time immemorial, the potentiality that only the strongest can realize —not the so-called interesting person.

Charged with this unaccustomedness, I had gone home from the boulevard. I was renting a room with a window looking onto the Kremlin. From over the river, Nikolai Aseev was likely to turn up at any moment. He would come from seeing the S——sisters, a profoundly and diversely gifted family. And when he entered I would recognize a disheveled, vivid imagination, an ability to transform triviality into music, the sensitivity and the guile of a genuine artistic nature. I was fond of him. He was enthusiastic about Khlebnikov. I cannot understand what he found in me. In art, as in life, we were trying to achieve different things.

6

The poplars were green, and reflections of gold and of white stone were running like lizards over the water of the river when I drove by way of the Kremlin to the Pokrovka on my way to the station and from there with the Baltrushaitises to the Oka in the province of Tula. There, right next to us, lived Vyacheslav Ivanov. The other dachas were also occupied by people from the world of art.*

Lilac was still in bloom. It came running out a long way onto the road and had just arranged a lively welcome (with no bread and salt or band) on the broad drive leading to the estate. Beyond it an empty yard, trodden down by cattle and all overgrown with patchy grass, sloped down a long way toward the houses.

It promised to be a hot, rich summer. I was translating Kleist's comedy *The Broken Jug* for the Chamber Theater, which was then just coming into existence. There were a lot of snakes in the park. People talked about them every day. They talked about snakes while eating fish soup and while bathing. And when I was asked to say something about myself, I would start talking about Mayakovsky. It was not a mistake. I had made a god of him. I had made him the personification of my spiritual horizon. Vyacheslav Ivanov was the first, as I remember, to compare him to the hyperbolism of Hugo.

7

When war was declared the sky turned gray, rains came, the women's first tears began to fall. The war was still new and quakingly terrible in its newness. One felt at a loss how to take it, and one went into it like entering cold water.

*Among them was Evgeniya Vladimirovna Muratova.

The passenger trains by which the local men traveled to the recruitment centers were still departing according to the old timetable. The train would set off and then, in pursuit of it, banging its head against the rails, there rolled a surge of cuckoo-crying, not at all like weeping but unnaturally tender and bitter, like the rowanberry. Someone's arm would gather up an elderly woman, warmly wrapped in unsummery clothes. And uttering monosyllabic exhortations, relatives of the recruit would lead her out under the vaults of the station.

This keening, kept up only in the first few months, was broader than the grief of mothers and young wives that streamed forth to sustain it. It was introduced as an emergency measure all along the line; stationmasters touched their caps as it traveled past; telegraph poles made way for it. It transformed the whole region and was visible from every side in a pewter icon setting of gray weather, because it was a thing of smarting vividness to which people had grown unused, and had not been touched since previous wars. It had been taken out only the night before from its hiding place, was brought to the station by horse in the morning, was led out by the hand from under the station vaults, and would immediately be driven home again along the bitter mud of a country road. This was how people saw their men off when, with fellow villagers or as single volunteers, they departed for the town in those green carriages.

But the soldiers who went in ready-formed marching units straight into the very heart of the terror were met and seen off without any ritual wailing. In their close-fitting clothes they jumped down onto the sand from the high trucks in a way quite unlike that of peasants, their spurs ringing and their greatcoats, flung on crookedly, blowing behind them. Others stood by the planks fixed across the truck doors, patting the horses that were stamping with proud hoofs the filthy wood of half-rotten flooring. The platform was giving away no apples, had plenty of cheeky answers, and, blushing red, hid its grins in the corners of tightly pinned kerchiefs.

September was ending. Garbage-golden, burning in the hollows like the dirt of a quenched fire, a grove of hazels, all bent and broken by winds and by climbers after nuts, made a chaotic image of ruin, twisted from all its joints by stubborn resistance to disaster.

One noon in August the knives and plates on the terrace had turned green, dusk had fallen on the flowerbed, the birds had gone quiet. The sky had begun tearing from itself the bright net of night deceptively cast upon it like a cap of darkness. The park had died and gazed obliquely upward with a sinister look at the humiliating enigma through which the earth, whose resounding glory it had so proudly drunk with all its roots, was being turned into something superfluous. Out onto the path a hedgehog rolled. A dead viper lay there in the shape of a knot, like an Egyptian hieroglyph. The hedgehog shifted it, then suddenly left off and went dead still. And again it broke and shed its dry bunch of needles, poking out then hiding its porcine muzzle. All the while the eclipse lasted, that ball of prickly suspicion gathered itself, now into the shape of a small shoe, now into that of a pinecone, till a portent of renascent certainty drove it back into its lair.

8

That winter, one of the S——sisters, Z.M.M., came to live on the Tverskoi Boulevard. People visite her. Dobrovein, a remarkable musician (with whom I was friends), used to call on her. Mayakovsky went to her house. By then I was accustomed to seeing in him the greatest poet of our generation. Time showed I was not mistaken.

There was Khlebnikov, it is true, with his subtle genuineness. But part of his merit remains inaccessible to me even now, for the poetry that I understand takes place, after all, in history and in collaboration with real life.

There was also Severyanin, a lyric poet who poured himself forth in spontaneous stanzas and ready forms like Lermontov's, and, with all his slovenly vulgarity, he was striking precisely because of the rare structure of his open, unfettered talent.

But the peak of poetic destiny was Mayakovsky, and this was later confirmed. After this, each time that the generation expressed itself dramatically, lending its voice to a poet, whether to Esenin, to Selvinsky, or to Tsvetaeva, an echo was heard of the lifeblood note that came from Mayakovsky; it was heard in the very way they were bound to their generation, that is, in the way they addressed the world from out of their own time. I am passing over such masters as Tikhonov and Aseev because, both here and in the rest of what I shall say, I am limiting myself to this dramatic line, which is closer to me, while they chose a different one.

Mayakovsky rarely turned up alone. Usually he came with a suite of Futurists, people of the movement. It was around this time that I saw a Primus stove for the first time in my life, in M——'s household. This invention did not yet give off a stench, and who would have thought it would bring so much filth into our lives and come into such wide use?

Its clean and roaring container threw out a high-pressure flame. Chops were fried on it one after the other; the elbows of our hostess and her helpers were covered with a chocolate Caucasian suntan. The cold little kitchen was transformed into a settlement in the Tierra del Fuego whenever we dropped in on the ladies from the dining room, and technologically innocent as wild Patagonians, bent over the copper disk that embodied something bright and Archimedean—and dashed out for beer and vodka.

A tall Christmas tree in the sitting room, secretly in league with the trees on the boulevard, held out its paws toward the grand piano. As yet it was solemnly dark. The whole divan was heaped with glittering tinsel, like piles of candy, some of it still packed in cardboard boxes. Special invitations were issued for the decorating of the tree. We were to come in the morning if possible. That meant three in the afternoon.

Mayakovsky recited, made everyone laugh, and ate hurriedly, almost unable to wait for the game of cards. He was bitingly polite and hid his constant agitation with great skill. Something was happening to him, a kind of crisis was taking place. He had realized what he was meant to do. He was openly acting a role, but with so much hidden anxiety and fever that the role he played was exuding beads of cold sweat.

9

However he was not always attended by the innovators. Often he came with a poet who had emerged with honor from the test that Mayakovsky's proximity usually posed. Of all the people I had seen at his side, the only one who could be put next to him without strain was Bolshakov. No matter who spoke first, both of them could be listened to without harm to one's hearing. Like the even stronger union he later had with his lifelong friend, Lilya Brik, this friendship was a natural one and easy to understand. One's heart did not ache for Mayakovsky in Bolshakov's company, he was on his own level, not lowering himself.

But more often his sympathies aroused bewilderment. This poet with such an overwhelming awareness of his own self, who had gone farther than anyone else in laying bare the lyrical element and with medieval boldness had brought it close to a theme in whose vast inventory poetry had begun to speak almost in the language of sectarian identifications—this poet took up just as hugely and broadly another, more local, tradition.

Beneath him he saw the city that had gradually risen up to him from the depths of *The Bronze Horseman, Crime and Punishment,* and *Petersburg,* a city in a haze, which with unnecessary vagueness was called the problem of the Russian intelligentsia, though in reality a city in the haze of eternal divinations of the future, an unprotected Russian city of the nineteenth and twentieth centuries. He could embrace such views as this and yet, at the same time as these enormous contemplations, still remained faithful, almost as to a debt, to all the dwarflike doings of his accidental clique, which was hastily assembled and invariably mediocre to the point of indecency. This man with an almost animal craving for truth surrounded himself with petty, finicky people of fictitious reputation and false, unjustifiable pretensions. Or, to state the main point, to the very end of his life he went on finding something in the veterans of a movement that he himself had long since and forever outgrown.

All this was surely the consequence of a fated loneliness, which, once he had discovered it, he deliberately intensified with that pedantry with which the will sometimes does move in a direction recognized to be inevitable.

10

But all this was to show itself later. There were still only faint signs then of the strange things to come. Mayakovsky read Akhmatova's, Severyanin's, his own, and Bolshakov's works about the war and the city. And that city we emerged into at night after visiting friends was a city set deep in the rear of the war.

We had already failed in the things that are always difficult for enormous Russia: transport and supplies. Out of the new words—"duty roster," "medicaments," "license," "refrigeration"—the first larvae of profiteering were beginning to hatch. And while the profiteers were thinking in truckloads, those same trucks were exporting large consignments of fresh indigenous population, night and day, in haste, with songs, in exchange for the damaged batches coming back in the hospital trains. And the best of the girls and women went as nurses.

The place for authentic positions was the front, and the rear would have fallen into a false one in any case, even if it had not also grown skilled in deliberate falsehood. The city hid behind phrases like a cornered thief, though no one at the time was attempting to trap it. Like all hypocrites, Moscow lived a more than usually intense external life and was vivid with the unnatural vividness of a flower shop in the winter.

By night it seemed the very image of Mayakovsky's voice. What was happening in this city and what was being piled up and smashed down by this voice—were as like as two drops of water. However, it was not the similarity that naturalism dreams of but the link that combines anode and cathode, artist and life, the poet and the age.

Opposite M——'s house stood the house of Moscow's chief of police. On several days in the autumn I ran into Mayakovsky there, and Bolshakov too, I think, at one of the formalities required for the registration of volunteers. We had been concealing this procedure from one another. I did not carry it through to the end, despite my father's sympathy. But, unless I am mistaken, nothing came of it in my friends' cases either. Shestov's son, a handsome lieutenant, entreated me by all that was holy to give up the idea. Soberly and positively he told me what it was like at the front, warning me that I would find there just the opposite of what I expected. Shortly after this he perished, in the first battle following his return from that leave.

Bolshakov entered the Tver Cavalry School, Mayakovsky was later called up when his turn came, and I, after being released that summer just before the war, was subsequently released every time my case was reexamined.

A year later I went to the Urals. Before that I spent a few days in Petersburg. The war was not so perceptible there as in Moscow. Mayakovsky, who had been called up by then, had been settled there for some time.

As always, the animated movement of the capital was tempered by the generous largeness of its dreamy spaces, which the necessities of life could never exhaust. The very streets were the color of winter and dusk, and their impetuous silveriness did not need much lamplight and snow to send them dashing and sparkling into the distance.

I walked down Liteiny Avenue with Mayakovsky; with sweeping strides he trampled miles of street, and I was amazed, as always, by the way he was able to be a kind of frame or setting to any landscape. In this he suited gray-sparkling Petrograd even better than he suited Moscow.

This was the time of the "Backbone Flute" and the first drafts of "War and the Universe." "A Cloud in Trousers" had by then come out as a book with an orange cover. He told me about the new friends he was taking me to, and about his acquaintance with Gorky, and about how the social theme was taking a bigger and bigger place in his projects, enabling him to work in a new way, at definite times, in measured doses. And that was the first time I visited the Briks.

Even more naturally than in the capitals, my thoughts about Maya-kovsky found room for themselves in the semi-Asiatic wintry landscape of "The Captain's Daughter" in the Urals—in the Kama region of Pugachyov.

Soon after the February Revolution I returned to Moscow. Mayakovsky had come from Petrograd and was staying in Stoleshnikov Lane. In the morning I went to visit him at his hotel. He was getting up and, while dressing, recited to me his new "War and the Universe." I did not start enlarging on my impression of it. He could read it in my eyes. In any case, he well knew the degree of his effect upon me. I talked about Futurism and said how marvelous it would be if he could now publicly send it all to the devil. Laughing, he almost agreed with me.

11

Hitherto I have shown what Mayakovsky meant to me. But there is no love without scars and sacrifices. I have told what Mayakovsky was, coming into my life. It remains to tell how my life was changed by this. I shall fill this gap now.

When I came back from the boulevard that day, completely over-whelmed, I could not think what to do. I felt myself to be utterly untalented. This would not have mattered terribly. But I was aware of a kind of guilt before him of which I could not quite make sense. Had I been younger, I would have given up literature. But my age prevented this. After so many metamorphoses I could not bring myself to yet a fourth change.

What happened was something different. The time and the sharing of common influences made me akin to Mayakovsky. There were similarities between us. I had noticed them. I realized that if I did not do something about myself, they would occur more often in the future. I had to protect him from their vulgarity. Although I could not have given it a name, I resolved to renounce everything that led to them. I renounced the Romantic manner. This was how the unromantic poetic style of *Over the Barriers* came into being.

But a whole conception of life lay concealed beneath the Romantic manner that I was to forbid myself from henceforth. This was a conception of life as the life of the poet. It had come to us from the Symbolists and had been adopted by them from the Romantics, principally the Germans.

Blok had been possessed by this idea, but only for a certain time. In the form in which it came to him naturally, it was incapable of satisfying him. He had to either heighten it or abandon it altogether. He abandoned the idea; Mayakovsky and Esenin heightened it.

In the poet who lays himself down as the measure of life, and pays for this with his life, the Romantic conception is irresistibly vivid and irrefutable in its symbols, that is, in everything that figuratively touches upon Orphism and Christianity. In this sense something permanent was incarnate in the life of Mayakovsky and also in the fate of Esenin, a fate that defies all epithets, self-destructively begging to become myth and receding into it. But outside the legend, the Romantic scheme is false. The poet, who is its foundation, is inconceivable without the nonpoets to bring him into relief, for this poet is not a living personality absorbed in moral cognition but a visual-biographical "emblem" that demands a background to make its contours visible. As distinct from the Passion plays, which needed a Heaven in order to be heard, this drama needs the evil of mediocrity in order to be seen, as Romanticism always needs philistinism, and with the disappearance of the petty bourgeois outlook loses half its content.

The notion of biography as spectacle was inherent in my time. I shared this notion with everyone else. I abandoned it while it was still mild and optional among the Symbolists, before it began to imply heroism and before it smelled of blood. And in the first place, I freed myself from it unconsciously, abandoning the Romantic devices for which it served as basis. In the second place, I also shunned it consciously, as a brilliance unsuited to me because, confining myself to my craft, I feared any kind of poeticizing that might place me in a false and incongruous position.

But when *My Sister Life* appeared, a book in which were expressed wholly uncontemporary aspects of poetry revealed to me in the revolutionary summer, I became utterly indifferent as to the name of the power that had produced the book, because it was immensely bigger than I and the poetic conceptions surrounding me.

12

Winter twilight and the roofs and trees of the quarter round Arbat Street peered from Sivtsev Vrazhek into a dining room that had not been cleared up for months. The apartment's owner, a bearded newspaperman of extreme absentmindedness and kindly nature, gave the impression of being a bachelor, though he had a family in the province of Orenburg. Whenever he had any spare time he would rake up from the table a whole month's newspapers of every possible persuasion and carry them in armfuls into the kitchen together with the petrified remains of breakfasts that had accumulated between his morning readings in regular deposits of pork rinds and loaf ends. Till I lost all conscience, a bright and odorous flame would roar beneath the cooker on the thirtieth of each month, just as in Dickens' Christmas tales of roast geese and counting-house clerks. With the approach of darkness, sentries on point duty would open an inspired fire from their revolvers.

Sometimes their cracking noise changed into a barbarous wail. And, as often happened in those days, you could not tell at first whether the sound was in the street or in the house. But amid a continuous delirium, these were the lucid moments of the sole inhabitant of the study, a portable one with a plug, craving someone's attention. It was from here that I was invited by telephone to a private house in Trubnikovsky Lane, for a gathering of all the poetic forces that could possibly be found at that moment in Moscow. And on this same telephone, though a good deal earlier, before the Kornilov revolt, I had had a disagreement with Mayakovsky.

Mayakovsky informed me that he had put me on his poster alongside Bolshakov and Lipskerov, but also along with the most faithful of the faithful, including, apparently, the one who could break thick planks with his forehead. I was almost glad of the opportunity to talk to my favorite for the first time as if to a stranger, and I became increasingly irritated as I parried his arguments one after the other, justifying myself. I was amazed not so much at his lack of ceremony as at the poverty of imagination it displayed, for this incident, as I pointed out, consisted not in his unbidden use of my name but in his annoying certainty that a two-year absence had not altered either my life or my interests. He ought first to have inquired whether I was still alive and whether I had not given up literature for something better. To this he replied quite reasonably that we had already met since the Urals, one day in the spring. But this piece of reasoning oddly failed to get over to me. And with misplaced stubbornness I demanded that he publish a correction of the poster in the press, something that was impracticable because the evening concerned was so near, and because I was unknown at that time, it was also affectedly meaningless.

But even though I was then still hiding *My Sister Life* and concealing from everyone what was happening to me, I could not endure it when those around me assumed that everything was going on as before. Besides which, the very conversation in the spring to which Mayakovsky had so unsuccess-

fully alluded was probably still obscurely alive in me, and I was annoyed
by the inconsistency between this invitation and everything that had been
said then.

13

Some months later, in the house of the amateur poet A——, he reminded
me of this telephone skirmish. Present were Balmont, Khodasevich, Baltrushaitis, Erenburg, Vera Inber, Antokolsky, Kamensky, Burlyuk, Mayakovsky, Andrei Bely, and Tsvetaeva. I could not know, of course, into how
incomparable a poetess Tsvetaeva was to develop. But without knowing
even her remarkable *Versty,* written at that time, I instinctively set her apart
from the others in the room because of her striking simplicity. I sensed in
her something that was akin to me: a readiness to part at any moment with
all privileges and habits if something lofty were to kindle her and set her
admiration aflame. On this occasion, we exchanged a few sincere and
friendly words. At that evening gathering, she was for me a living palladium
against the people of two movements, Symbolists and Futurists, who
thronged the room.

The recitations began. People read by seniority, without much perceptible success. When it was Mayakovsky's turn, he stood up, put one arm
around the edge of the empty shelf in which the back of the divan ended,
and started reciting "Man." Like a bas-relief, such as I have always seen
him against the background of the age, he towered among those present,
some sitting, some standing, and, now with one hand supporting his fine
head, now with a knee pressed into the bolster of the divan, he recited a
work of extraordinary depth, elation, and inspiration.

Opposite him, with Margarita Sabashnikova, sat Andrei Bely. He had
spent the war in Switzerland. The Revolution had brought him back to his
own country. It is possible that this was the first time he had seen and heard
Mayakovsky. He listened as if he were under a spell, and though he did
nothing to betray his rapture, his face was all the more eloquent. Astonished
and grateful, it seemed to be rushing forward to meet the reader. Part of
the audience was out of sight to me, including Tsvetaeva and Erenburg. I
watched the others. Most of them kept within the boundaries of an enviable
self-esteem. They all felt themselves to be names; all thought of themselves
as poets. Bely was the only one listening with self-abandon, carried far, far
away by the joy that regrets nothing because up on the heights where it feels
at home there is never anything but sacrifices and an eternal readiness for
them.

Chance was bringing together before my eyes two geniuses who justified
two literary movements that had exhausted themselves one after the other.

In Bely's vicinity, which gave me pride and delight, I felt Mayakovsky's presence with double force. In all the freshness of a first encounter, his essence was revealed to me. That evening I experienced it for the last time.

Many years passed after that. One year passed and when I read to Mayakovsky, before anyone else, the poems from *My Sister,* I heard from him ten times more than I ever expected to hear from anyone. Another year passed. In a small group of friends he read his "150,000,000." And for the first time I had nothing to say to him. Many years passed, during which we met each other at home and abroad, tried to be friends, tried to work together, and all the time I was understanding him less and less. Others will tell about this period, for in those years I came up against the limits of my understanding, which were not, apparently, to be overcome. My memories of that time would turn out pale and would add nothing to what I have said already. And so I shall go straight on to what remains for me to tell.

14

I shall tell of the strangeness that is repeated from age to age and that may be called the last year of a poet.

All of a sudden an end is put to projects that have not yielded to completion. Often nothing is added to their incompleteness except for a new, hitherto inadmissible certitude that now they are complete. And this certitude is conveyed to posterity.

Habits are changed, new plans are nursed, there is much boasting of spiritual *élan.* And all of a sudden—the end, sometimes violent, more often natural, but very like suicide even then, because of the lack of any desire to defend oneself. Then we suddenly realize something and start making comparisons. Plans had been nursed. *The Contemporary* was being published, preparations were being made to found a peasant journal. An exhibition of twenty years' work was being opened; steps had been taken to obtain a foreign passport.

Yet it turns out that others had seen them at that very same time, depressed, complaining, weeping. Accustomed to whole decades of voluntary solitude, they had suddenly grown afraid of it like children frightened of a dark room, and seized the hands of chance visitors, clutching at their presence, only to avoid being left alone. The people who witnessed these states refused to believe their ears. Those who had received from life far more confirmations than it grants to others argued as if they had not yet even begun to live and could find in the past no experience or support.

But who will understand or believe that it was suddenly given to the Pushkin of 1836 to recognize himself as the Pushkin of any year, the Pushkin, say, of 1936? That a time comes when the responses long since coming from other hearts in answer to the beats of the main one, which is still alive and still pulsing, thinking, and wanting to live, are suddenly fused into one heart, expanded and transmuted? That the irregular, constantly accelerating beats at last come so thick and fast that all at once they even out and, coinciding with the main heart's tremors, start to live one life with it, from now on beating in unison with it? That this is no allegory? That this is experienced? That this is a kind of age of life, impulsive, felt in the blood and real—only as yet unnamed? That this is a kind of nonhuman youth, but one that rends the continuity of one's preceding life with such sharp joy that because there exists no name for this age and because comparisons are inevitable, its sharpness makes it, more than anything else, resemble death? That it resembles death? That it resembles death but—is *not* death, not death at all, and if only, if only people did not desire complete resemblance . . . ?

And together with the heart, a shift takes place in memories and works, in works and hopes, in the world of the created and the world that is yet to be created. "What kind of personal life did he have?" people sometimes ask. You shall now be enlightened about his personal life. A huge region of utterly varied voices tightens, concentrates, smooths itself out, and, suddenly, shuddering with simultaneity in every part of its composition, begins to exist physically. It opens its eyes; it takes a deep breath and flings off the last remnants of the pose that was given it as a provisional support.

And if one recalls that all this sleeps by night and wakes by day, walks on two feet and is called a human being—it is natural to expect corresponding phenomena in its behavior too.

A large, real, and really existing city. It is winter there. Darkness comes early there; there the working day goes by in the light of evening.

Once, long, long ago it was terrible. It had to be conquered; its nonrecognition had to be broken. Much water has flowed by since then. Recognition has been wrung from it; its submission has become a habit. A great effort of memory is needed to imagine how it could once have inspired such alarm. Lamps twinkle in it; people cough into handkerchiefs and click their abaci. It gets covered with snow.

Its uneasy immensity would have swept past unnoticed were it not for this new, wild impressionability. What is the shyness of adolescence beside the vulnerability of this new birth?! And once again, just as in childhood, one notices everything. Lamps, typists, door pulleys, galoshes, storm clouds, the crescent moon, and the snow. Terrible world!

It bristles with backs of fur coats and sleighs; like a penny rolling across the floor, it rolls on its edge along the rails, rolls away into the distance, and tenderly falls off its rim into the mist, where a sheepskin-coated signal-woman bends to pick it up. It rolls about and grows tiny and teems with fortuities. It is so easy to stumble there against a slight want of attention! These are deliberately imagined annoyances. They are consciously blown up from nothing. But even when blown up, they are still utterly trivial next to the wrongs one strode over so majestically just a short while ago. But the point is, there can be no comparison, because that was in the previous life that it was such a joy to sever. Oh, if only this joy were more even and more probable!

But it is unbelievable and without comparison, and yet nothing in all one's life ever flung one so from one extreme to another in the same way as this joy.

What lapses into despondency there are here! What repetition of all Hans Christian Andersen with his unhappy duckling! What mountains here are made out of molehills!

But perhaps the inner voice is lying? Perhaps the terrible world is right? "No smoking." "Please state your business briefly."—Are not these truths?

"Him?—What, hang himself? Don't you worry!" "Love?—What him?—Ha-ha-ha! He doesn't love anyone but himself."

A large, real, and really existing city. It is winter there; it is freezing. Squeaking and willow-woven, the zero-degree air stands across the road as if on stilts hammered into the ground. Everything in it is misting over, rolling away, and becoming lost. But can things be as sad as this when they are so joyful? Is this, then, not a second birth? Is this—death?

15

In the public registry offices there is no apparatus for measuring truthfulness, no device for the X-raying of sincerity. For a record to be valid, nothing is necessary but the firmness of someone else's hand as it makes the entry. And then there are no doubts of any sort, and nothing is disputed.

Before he dies he will write a note with his own hand, setting his own great value before the world as in a will, like something obvious; he will measure and X-ray his own sincerity by a rapid action that does not allow of any alteration, and everywhere people will start discussing and doubting and making comparisons.

They compare his note with its predecessors, whereas it can only be compared with him and the whole of his previous life. They build up conjectures about his feelings, without understanding that it is possible to love not only in days, though that be forever, but also—even if not forever—with the complete gathered strength of all past days.

But these two notions, a man of genius and a beautiful woman, have long since acquired the same banality. And how much they have in common!

From her childhood she is inhibited in her movements. She is lovely, and she learns this early. The only one with whom she can be wholly herself is

God's earth, as we call it, for with others she cannot take a step without hurting someone or being hurt herself.

As a young girl she goes out of her house. What is she planning? Already she receives clandestine letters. She has let two or three friends into her secrets. All this she already has, and let us suppose she is going out to meet someone.

She goes out of the house. She wants the evening to notice her, the air's heart to miss a beat for her, the stars to pick up something about her. She wants the renown enjoyed by trees and fences and all things upon earth when they are not in the head but in the open air. Yet she would burst out laughing if anyone ascribed such desires to her. She is not thinking of anything like that. But there is in the world her distant brother, a person of enormous ordinariness, who exists in order to know her better than she knows herself and ultimately to answer for her. She has a common-sense liking for healthy nature and is unaware that she never ceases to count on the universe's reciprocating her feeling.

Spring, an evening in spring, little old women on benches, low fences, shaggy willows. A pale sky, mild, wine-green and weak-distilled, dust, homeland, dry splintery voices. Sounds as dry as chips of wood, and a flat, hot silence full of their splinters.

Someone comes along the road toward her, the very one whom it was natural to meet. Overjoyed, she keeps on saying she has come out just to meet him. To some extent she is right. Who is not to some extent dust and homeland and the quiet of a spring evening? She forgets why she has come out, but her feet remember. They walk on, he and she together, and the farther they go the more people they come across. And because she loves her companion with all her heart, her feet distress her not a little. But they carry her onward; he and she can scarcely keep pace with each other. Then unexpectedly the road leads out to some wider place where there seem to be fewer people and they could pause for breath and look around them, but often this is the very moment when her distant brother appears, coming along his own path, and they meet, and then nothing that happens can make any difference. Whatever happens now, some utterly perfect "I am thou" binds them with all the bonds conceivable upon earth, and proudly, youthfully, wearily it prints, as on a medal, profile upon profile.

16

The first days of April found Moscow in the white stupor of returning winter. On the seventh it started to thaw for a second time, and on the fourteenth, the day Mayakovsky shot himself, not everyone was yet used to the newness of spring.

When I heard of the disaster I sent for O.S. to come to the place where it had happened. Something suggested to me that this shock would be a way out of her own grief.

Between eleven and twelve the undulating circles generated by the shot were still rippling outward. The news rocked telephones, covered faces with pallor, sent people rushing to the Lubyansky Passage, across the yard, and into the house, where the whole stairway was already paved with weeping and huddling people from the town or from other parts of the building, all of them hurled and splashed against the walls by the laminating force of the event. Chernyak and Romadin, who had been the first to tell me of the disaster, came up to me. Zhenya was with them. At the sight of her my cheeks began twitching convulsively. Weeping she told me to run upstairs, but at that moment the body was carried downstairs on a stretcher, covered from head to foot with something. Everyone rushed down and dammed up the doors so that, by the time we managed to get out, the ambulance was already driving out through the gate. We streamed along after it into Hendrikov Lane.

Outside, life went on at its own pace, unconcerned, as we mistakenly call it. We had left behind us the concern of the asphalt courtyard, eternal participant in dramas of this kind.

Over rubbery mud the spring air was wandering on uncertain legs, as if learning to walk. Cockerels and children were announcing themselves for everyone to hear. In early spring their voices are strangely far-reaching, despite the busy rattle of the town.

The trolley was clambering slowly up Shvivaya Hill. There is one spot there where first the right-hand and then the left-hand footpath steals up so close to the trolley's windows that, catching at the strap, you make an involuntary bending movement over Moscow, as if stooping over an old woman who has slipped—for all of a sudden it goes down on all fours, drearily strips itself of cobblers and clockmakers, picks up and shifts its roofs and bell towers, and suddenly stands up and, shaking out its skirt, sends the trolley speeding along a level and quite unremarkable street.

This time its movements were so manifestly an excerpt from the man who had just shot himself, that is, they so forcefully brought to mind something significant in his essential being, that I began to tremble all over, and the famous telephone call from "A Cloud" began thundering away in me, just as if someone right next to me had suddenly started to recite it loudly. I was standing in the gangway beside S——, and I leaned toward her to remind her of those eight lines, but as they formed the words "And I feel that 'I' is to small for me," my lips were as clumsy as gloved fingers, and in my agitation I could not utter a single word aloud.

Two empty cars stood by the gate at the end of Hendrikov Lane. They were surrounded by a small, inquisitive group.

In the hall and dining room, people were standing or sitting, some with hats on and some bareheaded. He was lying farther off, in his study. The door from the hall into Lilya's room was open and on the threshold, pressing his head against the door frame, Aseev was weeping. In the depth of the room, by the window, Kirsanov, his head hunched between his shoulders, was convulsively trembling and sobbing silently.

Even here the damp mist of lamentation was interrupted by anxious half-loud conversations, just as at the end of a requiem when, after a service thick as jam, the first whispered words are so dry that they seem to be spoken from beneath the floor and have the smell of mice. During one such interruption the caretaker, with a chisel stuck in the top of his boot, cautiously entered the room and, removing the storm window, slowly and noiselessly opened the window. Outside, it was still shudderingly cold for anyone without a coat, and sparrows and children were cheering themselves on with shouts about nothing in particular.

Someone tiptoed out from where the dead man lay and quietly asked whether a telegram had been sent to Lilya. L.A.G. replied that it had. Zhenya took me aside to point out with what courage L.A. was bearing the terrible weight of the catastrophe. She burst into tears. I firmly pressed her hand.

The apparent unconcern of the immeasurable world was pouring in through the window. Along it, as if between the earth and sea, gray trees stood guarding the boundary. As I looked at the branches all covered with impassioned buds, I tried to imagine far, far beyond them that improbable London where the telegram had been sent. There, soon, someone would cry out, stretch out arms in our direction, and fall down in a faint. My throat contracted. I resolved to go back into his room and this time really weep my fill.

He was lying on his side, his face to the wall, sullen, tall, with a sheet drawn up to his chin and his mouth half open like that of someone sleeping. He had proudly turned away from everyone and, even while lying down, even in this sleep, was stubbornly straining to get away somewhere and depart. His face took one back to the time when he had called himself "handsome, 22-year-old," for death had set fast a facial expression that scarcely ever falls into its clutches. This was an expression with which people start life, not one with which they end it. He was pouting and indignant.

But now a movement occurred in the hall. Separately from her mother and elder sister, who were grieving inaudibly by now among the crowd, Olga Vladimirovna, the dead man's younger sister, had arrived at the apartment. Her arrival was demanding and noisy. Her voice came sailing into the room in advance of her. She came up the stairs alone, talking loudly, obviously addressing her brother. Then she herself appeared, and, walking past everyone as if over rubbish, she reached her brother's door, threw her hands in the air, and stopped. "Volodya!" she shouted, and her voice filled the whole house. A moment passed. "He won't speak!" she started to shout even more loudly. "He won't speak! He's not answering! Volodya! Volodya! How horrible!"

She began to fall, people caught her and hastily started trying to bring her round. As soon as she was conscious, she went avidly to the body and, sitting at its feet, hurriedly started up again her unquenched dialogue. I burst into floods of tears, just as I had long been wanting to.

It had not been possible to cry like this at the scene of the event, where the gunshot freshness of the fact had been speedily ousted by the common-herd sense of drama. There, like saltpeter, the asphalt yard stank of the worship of the inevitable, that is, of the false urban fatalism that is founded on apelike imitation and sees life as a chain of sensational happenings, easily recordable. There too people sobbed, but only because the shaken gullet reproduced like an animal medium the convulsions of the dwelling blocks, the fire escapes, the revolver case, and everything that sickens one with despair and makes one vomit murder.

His sister was the first to weep for him by her own will and choice, as something great is wept for, and one could weep to her words insatiably, expansively, as to the roar of an organ. And she did not stop. "They wanted their *Bathhouse*!" raged Mayakovsky's own voice, strangely adapted to the contralto of his sister. "They wanted it really funny! Roared with laughter. Called him out.—And all the time *this* was happening to him.—Why didn't you come to us, Volodya?" she wailed, sobbing, then quickly getting control of herself she moved impetuously to sit closer beside him. "Do you remember, do you remember, Volodichka?"—she suddenly reminded him, almost as if he were alive, and she started reciting:

> And I feel that *I* is too small for me!
> Someone is stubbornly trying to break out of me.
> Hallo!
> Who is it? Mother?
> Mother! Your son is gloriously ill!
> Mother! His heart is on fire.
> Tell his sisters, Lyuda and Olya,
> He's got nowhere to put himself anymore.

17

When I went back that evening, he was lying in his coffin. The people who had filled the room during the day had been replaced by others. It was rather quiet. There was almost no weeping now.

Suddenly, down below, under the window, I imagined his life, now utterly in the past. It led away at a slant from the window in the shape of some quiet tree-planted street, like the Povarskaya. And our state was the first thing that rose upon it, right by the wall, our unprecedented, impossible state, bursting its way into the centuries and taken up into them forever. It stood there below: One could call to it, take it by the hand. In its palpable extraordinariness there was something that resembled the dead man. So striking was the link between the two that they seemed to be twins.

And then I thought, in the same unforced way, that in fact this man had been practically the only citizen of that state. He it was who had the newness of the age climatically flowing in his veins. He was strange through and through with the strange features of our epoch, half of which were yet to come. I began to call to mind the traits of his character, and his independence, which in many ways was unique. They could all be explained by his being used to conditions that, though suggested by our age, had not yet attained their forceful relevance to the present day. From childhood he had been spoiled by a future that yielded to him quite early and, it seemed, without much effort.

Translated by Angela Livingstone

Fiction

The Mark of Apelles

Legend has it that the Greek artist Apelles, finding his rival Zeuxis out one day, traced on the wall a mark, by which Zeuxis guessed the identity of the visitor who had called during his absence. Zeuxis did not remain long in his debt. Picking a time when he knew for certain that Apelles would be out, he left his own sign, which has since become a byword for artistry.

I

On one of those September evenings when the Leaning Tower directs a whole horde of leaning sunsets and leaning shadows in an assault on Pisa and across the whole of Tuscany a nagging evening breeze carries the aroma of bay leaf rubbed between the fingers—on an evening such as this, why, I remember the exact date perfectly well, it was the evening of August 23 —Emilio Relinquimini, discovering that Heine was not at his hotel, demanded paper and a light from the servile footman who bowed and scraped before him. When the footman appeared with ink, pen, a stick of sealing wax, and a seal, in addition to the items requested, Relinquimini dismissed his offer of aid with a fastidious gesture. After removing his tiepin, he sterilized it in the candle flame, pricked himself on the finger, grabbed a card bearing the hotel letterhead from a pile of identical ones and bent it over at one corner, using the finger he had pricked. He then handed the card nonchalantly to the attentive footman with the words "Please deliver this visiting card to Mr. Heine. I shall call on him again tomorrow at exactly the same hour."

The Leaning Tower had burst through its chain of medieval fortifications. On the street the number of people gazing at it from the bridge increased with every minute that passed. The sun's last rays crept across the piazzas like partisans. Some streets were crammed with toppled shadows, while elsewhere there was hand-to-hand combat in the narrow alleyways. The Leaning Tower tilted backward, flailing wildly and indiscriminately, until a giant stray shadow passed across the face of the sun. . . . Day snapped off short.

As he briskly and disjointedly informed Heine about the recent visit, the hotel footman managed to hand the impatient guest the card, with its brown, congealed blotch a few instants before the sun finally set.

"What an eccentric!" But Heine had guessed immediately the name of the visitor, the author of a long, well-known poem entitled *Il Sangue*.

It did not strike Heine, the Westphalian, as a strange coincidence that Relinquimini from Ferrara had turned up in Pisa at the very time when a peripatetic poet's even more passing whim had brought him there himself. He recalled the anonymous correspondent from whom he had recently received a carelessly written and aggressive letter. The unknown writer's claims went beyond the bounds of the permissible. Sermonizing in a rather vague and casual manner about the origins and genealogy of poetry, the stranger demanded from Heine an Apelles-style proof of his identity.

"Love," wrote his anonymous correspondent, "the cloud that on occasion completely fogs our unclouded blood. You must define it no less succinctly than the mark of Apelles. Remember, Zeuxis is merely curious about your membership in the aristocracy of blood and spirit (two inseparable concepts).

"P.S. I have taken advantage of your presence in Pisa, of which I was opportunely informed by my publisher Conti, to settle once and for all a doubt that has been gnawing at me. In three days' time I shall personally call on you to view the signature of Apelles . . ."

The servant who appeared at Heine's summons was entrusted with the following commission:

"I am leaving for Ferrara by the ten o'clock train. Tomorrow evening a certain person who is already known to you, the one who presented this card, will come asking for me. You will personally hand over to him this package. Now please fetch me my bill. Call a porter."

The apparently empty package owed the wraithlike weight that it nevertheless possessed to a slender strip of paper obviously cut from some manuscript. This scrap consisted of part of a sentence without a beginning or an end: "but, casting aside their previous names with a wild shout of 'Rondolfina!' and a shriek of 'Enrico!' Rondolfina and Enrico contrived to assume names that had been purely imaginary until that moment."

II

The Pisans whiled away the fragrant Tuscan night on the pavements and asphalted piazzas, on balconies, and on the embankments beside the Arno. The black vapors of the burning night made breathing even more difficult in alleyways beneath dusty plane trees where it was stuffy enough already. Loose-clustered sheaves of stars and spiky wisps of mist added their effect to the night's lingeringly sultry, oily sheen. These pinpoints of light stretched the Italians' patience beyond endurance; at the very first sight of Cassiopeia, they wiped grubby sweat from their brows, cursing with fervent fanaticism as if uttering a prayer. Handkerchiefs fluttered in the gloom like thermometers being shaken. The testimony of these cambric temperature gauges spread a baleful depression down the street: The stifling atmosphere was transmitted by them like some chance-heard rumor, an epidemic, or a horror-stricken panic. And in just the same way that the inert town was disintegrating without objection into blocks, houses, and yards, so too the night air consisted of separate, motionless, encounters, exclamations, quarrels, bloody clashes, whispering, laughter, and undertones. These noises hung in a regular, dusty web over the pavements, rooted in the footpath in serried ranks like breathless, colorless trees lining the street in the light of gas lamps. In this capricious and willful way, night in Pisa set a firm limit on human endurance.

Chaos began right at this point, at this limit, an arm's length away. The same chaos reigned at the railway station. Here handkerchiefs and oaths disappeared from the scene. Here people who a moment before had considered natural movement the nearest thing to torture, clung to cases and cardboard boxes, swarmed around the ticket office, stormed the soot-covered carriages like lunatics, besieged the carriage steps and, soot-smudged as chimney sweeps, burst into compartments divided off by brown plywood that appeared to warp under the heat, the curses, and the battering of heavy bodies.

The carriages shimmered, as did the rails, oil tanks, engines in the sidings, signals, and even the squashed, steam-venting wails of nearby and distant locomotives. The heavy breathing of the wide-open firebox, flickering and flaring, spattered the driver's cheek and the stoker's leather jacket like an irritating insect: The driver and his stoker shimmered. The clock face shimmered; the cast-iron shoals of intersecting track and points, and the watchmen, also shimmered. All this was beyond the limits of human endurance. Yet it was possible to bear all of it.

A seat next to the window. A completely deserted platform made entirely of stone, of resonance—entirely of the conductor's shout of "All aboard!"; and at the last possible moment the conductor runs past in pursuit of his own shout. The pillars supporting the station roof slip smoothly past. Lights swarm by, crisscrossing like knitting needles. Rays of light from reflector plates leap in through the carriage windows, caught up by the draft, passing through the compartment and out the opposite windows, stretching along the tracks, trembling, stumbling over the rails, on their feet again and vanishing behind sheds. Dwarfish lanes; misshapen, mongrel alleyways. The maws of viaducts swallow them with a hollow rumble. Boisterous gardens step right up close to the blinds. The restful expanse of carpets of curly vineyards. Fields.

Heine is traveling on an off chance. There is no thought in his head. He tries to doze off. He closes his eyes.

"Something must surely come of this. There's no sense, and in fact no point, in trying to guess the outcome beforehand. Ahead lies beguiling but total uncertainty."

Apparently it was the wild oranges that were in blossom. The fragrant latitudes of orchards brimmed over. From that direction a breeze came scurrying to exact at least a droplet of moisture from the passengers' gummed-up eyelashes.

"Something must come of it, I'm certain. And why is it . . . aaa-ah . . . ," Heine yawns, "why is it that there isn't a single love poem of Relinquimini's that isn't invariably marked 'Ferrara'?"

Cliffs, chasms, fellow passengers struck down by sleep, the fumes of the carriage. A tongue of flame in the gaslight, licking its lips, licking shadows and rustlings from the ceiling, gasping when the cliffs and chasms are replaced by a tunnel. The mountain crawls along the carriage roof with a rumble, bearing down on the smoke from the engine, driving it through the window, grabbing at coat hooks and luggage racks. Tunnels and valleys. The single track weeps plaintively over a mountain stream that batters onto the rocks, rushing down from incredible peaks that glimmer faintly in the darkness. Out there too the waterfalls fume and smoke, their dull roar swirling around the train all night long.

"The mark of Apelles . . . Rondolfina. In twenty-four hours I doubt whether you can achieve anything. But I don't have any longer. I'll have to vanish without trace. But tomorrow . . . Of course, he'll tear straight off to the station the minute the footman tells him my destination!"

Ferrara! An indigo-black, steely dawn. An aromatic mist suffused with chill. Oh, how sonorous the Latin morning can be!

III

"It can't be done; this edition of *Il Voce* is already in the galley trays."

"Very well, but I won't hand over my find to anybody else under any other circumstances, for any amount of money. On the other hand, I can't stay in Ferrara for more than a day."

"You say you found his notebook in your compartment, under your seat?"

"Yes, Emilio Relinquimini's notebook. What's more, his notebook contains, among a mass of everyday entries, an even greater number of unpublished verses, a series of rough drafts, jotted fragments and aphorisms. They have been written throughout this current year, in Ferrara for the most part, as far as I can judge from the notes attached."

"Where is it? Do you have it with you?"

"No, I left my things at the station, and the notebook is in my valise."

"Pity. We could have delivered the book to him at his home. The editors have Relinquimini's address in Ferrara, but he's been away for about a month now."

"What? Do you mean to say Relinquimini isn't in Ferrara?"

"That's just the point. I personally fail to see what purpose you can possibly serve by publishing an announcement of your find."

"Only to establish, through the medium of your newspaper, a reliable link between the owner of this notebook and myself. Relinquimini can take advantage of the good offices of *Il Voce* at any time in this matter."

"What are we to do with you? Please sit down and be so good as to compose your notice."

"I'm sorry to put you to any trouble, my dear editor, but may I use your desk telephone?"

"Please do. Help yourself."

"Is this the Torquato Tasso Hotel? . . . Which of your rooms are available? . . . On which floor? . . . Fine. Reserve number eight in my name."

Ritrovamento: Found, one manuscript of a new book by Emilio Relinquimini, prepared for publication. Finder resident at Hotel Tasso, Room No. 8; will await owner of manuscript or his representatives throughout today until 11 P.M. As of tomorrow the *Il Voce* editorial office, as well as the hotel management, will be punctually and periodically notified of any further change in the finder's address.

Exhausted by his journey, Heine sleeps a deep and leaden sleep. The Venetian blinds in his room, warmed by the breath of the morning, have heated up just like the brass reeds of a mouth organ. By the window a bundle of sun rays falls on the floor like a strip of dilapidated rush matting. The straws pack together, jostling, pressing close. On the street there is the sound of indistinct conversation. Someone rambling on, his tongue stumbling over the words. An hour goes by. By now, the rush matting, flowing across the floor in a pool of sunlight, is packed closer together. On the street people chatter, drowse; tongues wag. Heine sleeps. The pool of sunlight contracts as if the parquet floor had soaked it up; then once again the scorched, plaited straws of the matting appear, growing more ragged all the time. Heine sleeps on. On the street, the sound of conversation. Hours go by, drawing out just like the expanding black gaps in the matting. On the street, the sound of conversation. The matting fades, dims, dusts over. By now it looks more like a jute doormat, rumpled and twisted. Now its seams and ties are indistinguishable from the web. On the street, still the sound of conversation. Heine sleeps on.

Any minute now he will wake up. Any minute now he will jump to his feet, mark my words. Any minute now. Just give him time to finish dreaming his last snatch of dream.

A wheel that had dried out in the heat suddenly splits all the way to the hub; the spokes stick out like a bunch of split pegs. The cart falls on its side with a thump and a rumble; bales of newspapers spill out. A crowd, sunshades, shop windows, and sun blinds. The news dealer is carried off on a stretcher—there is a pharmacy quite close.

There you are now! What did I tell you! Heine sits bolt upright. "Just a moment!"

Someone is knocking urgently and impatiently at the door. Heine, half asleep, hair tousled, still drunk with sleep, grabs his dressing gown.

"Sorry, just a second." There is an almost metallic clank as his right foot is lowered to the floor. This very minute. Yes, of course!

Heine goes over to the door.

"Who is it?"

The voice of a footman.

"Yes, yes. I have the notebook with me. Ask the *Signora*'s pardon on my behalf. Is she in the lounge?"

The voice of the footman.

"Will you ask the *Signorina* to wait ten minutes. In ten minutes I shall be entirely at her disposal. Do you hear?"

The voice of the footman.

"Just a minute, *cameriere.*"

The voice of the footman.

"And please don't forget to tell the young lady that the *Signor,* as he puts it, expresses his sincere regret at being unable to come out to her right away. He feels deeply at fault, but he will try—do you hear, *cameriere?* . . ."

The voice of the footman.

" . . . but he will try in ten minutes' time to make full amends for his unforgivable gaucherie. And please be as courteous as you can, *cameriere,* after all, I'm not a Ferraran, you know."

The voice of the footman.

"Very well, very well."

"*Cameriere,* is the lady in the lounge?"

"Yes, *Signor.*"

"Is she alone there?"

"She is alone, *Signor.* This way please, to your left, *Signor,* to your left!"

"Good afternoon, how can I be of service to you, *Signora*?"

"I beg your pardon, are you from room number eight?"

"Yes, that's my room."

"I've come for Relinquimini's notebook."

"Allow me to introduce myself: Heinrich Heine."

"Forgive me . . . Are you related to . . .?"

"Not in any way. Pure coincidence. One could even call it irritating. I also have the good fortune to . . ."

"You write poetry?"

"I have never written anything else."

"I know German and I spend all my leisure reading poetry, but all the same . . ."

"Have you read *Verses Unpublished During the Poet's Own Lifetime*?"

"Of course. So it was you who wrote them?"

"Forgive me, I hope still to learn your name."

"Camilla Ardenze."

"I am exceedingly pleased to meet you. So, *Signora* Ardenze, you happened to see my announcement in today's *Voce*?"

"Yes. About the notebook you found. Where is it? May I have a look at it?"

"*Signora! Signora* Camilla, you are probably devoted with all your heart, which the incomparable Relinquimini . . ."

"Stop talking like that. We aren't on the stage . . ."

"That's where you are wrong, *Signora.* All our life we are on a stage, and not everybody is capable of the naturalness that is entrusted to each of us at birth like a character part. *Signora* Camilla, you love your native town, you love Ferrara, whereas for me it is the first town that I find repulsive. You are beautiful, *Signora* Camilla, and my heart contracts at the thought that you are in league with this disgusting town against me."

"I don't understand you."

"Please don't interrupt me, *Signora.* You are in league, as I was saying, with a town that has drugged me, just as a poisoner might drug his drinking companion when the man's beloved comes to him, in order to awaken a spark of scorn for the victim in the eyes of his beloved, who has just walked into the tavern. And his beloved will be unfaithful to her lover. 'Milady,' our poisoner addresses her as she comes in, 'take a look at this lazy lout. This is the man you love: He has been whiling away the waiting hours telling stories about you. They have pricked my imagination like spurs. Did you gallop here saddled to my imagination? Then why did you lash it so mercilessly with your slender riding crop—it is in a sweat and a lather. What stories he told! But just take one look at him: He is drugged by his own stories of you, milady! You can see that absence acts like a lullaby on your beloved. Still, we could wake him.'

" 'Don't bother,' the drugged victim's beloved replies to the poisoner. 'Don't bother, don't disturb him; he's sleeping so sweetly, and perhaps he's dreaming about me. Better concern yourself with a glass of punch for me. It's so cold out on the street. I've gone all numb. Please will you rub the circulation back into my hands?' "

"You're a very strange person, *Signor* Heine. But please carry on; your eloquent speech amuses me."

"I'm sorry, I must not forget about Relinquimini's notebook. I'll go upstairs to my room and . . ."

"Don't worry, I shan't forget about it. This is a very entertaining story. Do carry on. 'Rub the circulation back into my hands,' I think the woman was saying."

"Yes, *Signora* Camilla. You have listened closely to what I've been saying and I thank you."

"Well?"

"Well, this town has treated me as the poisoner treated his comrade, and you, my lovely Camilla, are on its side. It eavesdropped on my thoughts about dawns long past as if they were robbers' castles, and, like robbers' castles, they stood lonely and in ruins. It drugged me in order to take sly advantage of my thoughts. It encouraged me to talk to my heart's content about orchards sailing off into the open sea of night with all their evening-red sails unfurled, and now it has set these sails, leaving me slumped in some tavern down at the port, and, you see, you won't let me be awakened when he cunningly suggests that I should be."

"Listen, my dear man, what has all this to do with me? I hope the footman did wake you up properly?"

" 'No,' you will say, 'night is coming on. If we're not to get caught in a storm, we must hurry. It's time to go; don't wake him.' "

"Oh, *Signor* Heine, how terribly mistaken you are. 'Yes,' I should say, 'Yes, yes, Ferrara, give him a good shake if he's still asleep. I am busy. Wake him as quickly as you can; gather all your crowds; let your squares echo until you do wake him. Time will not wait.' "

"Yes, of course, the notebook! . . ."

"Later, later."

"My dear *Signora,* Ferrara has miscalculated very seriously. Ferrara has been duped. The poisoner runs off; I am waking up; I am awake and on my knees before you, my love!"

Camilla jumps up.

THE MARK OF APELLES

"Enough! Enough! True enough, all this suits you very well. Even these clichés. Just these clichés, in fact. But all the same, you shouldn't behave like this. You know, you're a sort of wandering clown. We are hardly acquainted; we only met half an hour ago. Good God, it makes me laugh to even discuss it, but here I am discussing it. You see, I have never felt so stupid in my life before. This whole scene is like one of those Japanese flowers that bloom the instant they are dropped into water. Nothing more, nothing less! But then, you know, those flowers are made of paper. And they are cheap at that!"

"I'm hanging on your every word."

"I would far rather be hanging on yours, *Signor*. You are very intelligent, apparently even sarcastic. On the other hand, you stoop to clichés. It's strange, yet there's nothing contradictory about it . . . Your melodramatic pathos . . ."

"I beg your pardon, *Signora*. *Pathos* means "passion" in Greek, but in Italian it is a blown kiss. Sometimes force of circumstance dictates that kisses should be of this kind."

"That sort of talk again! Please stop; it's intolerable! There's something in you which you are hiding; explain yourself. And listen, please don't be angry with me, my dear *Signor* Heine. Take all this away and you are still —you won't reproach me for my familiarity?—you are a sort of child prodigy. No, that's the wrong word—you are a poet. Yes, yes, how was it I didn't pick on the word at once, since one only has to look at you to realize it? You're God's chosen idler, Fate's spoiled darling."

"*Evviva!*" Heine leaps onto the window ledge and leans his whole body out.

"Be more careful, *Signor* Heine," cries Camilla. "Be more careful. You're scaring me!"

"Don't worry, my dear *Signora*. Hey, you rascal, catch this!" Lira notes drift down into the square. "You'll get as much again and possibly ten times as much if you go and raid half a dozen gardens in Ferrara. I'll pay one soldo for every hole in your trousers. Get going! And just watch that you don't breathe on the flowers as you're carrying them along; the Contessa's as sensitive as a mimosa. On the double, you rogue. Did you hear that, enchantress? That boy will return dressed as a Cupid. But to get down to business. How perceptive you are! At one stroke, the mark of Apelles, you conveyed my whole essence, the whole crux of the situation."

"I don't understand you. Or is this another entry you're making? Are we on the stage again? What exactly is it you want?"

"Yes, it's the stage again. But why not let me stay a little in this pool of bright light? After all, it's not my fault that in real life the most dangerous places—bridges and crossings—are the most brightly lit. How harsh it is!

Everything else is sunk in gloom. On such a bridge, or let us say a stage, a man flares up in the light of the flickering rays as if he had been put on show, surrounded by a railing against the backdrop of the town, of chasms and signal lights on the river bank . . . *Signora* Camilla, you would not have listened to half my words if we hadn't bumped into each other in such a dangerous place. I'm assuming it's dangerous, although I don't know for certain; I'm assuming this because other people have used a vast amount of light to illuminate it, and I am not to blame if we are lit up so crudely and harshly."

"Fine. Have you finished? All this is true. But it's the most amazing nonsense! I want to confide in you. It isn't a whim; it's almost a need. You aren't lying. Your eyes don't lie. Well, what is it I wanted to say to you? . . . I've forgotten . . . Wait a minute . . . Listen, my dear man, after all, only an hour ago . . ."

"Stop! These are just more words. There are such things as hours and eternities. A whole wealth of eternities exist, and not one of them has any beginning. At the first opportune moment they come bursting forth, and this is coincidence itself. And then—away with words! *Signora,* do you know when words are defeated and by whom? Are you familiar with mutinies of this sort, *Signora?* Every fiber in my body is in revolt against me, *Signora,* and I shall have to give way to them as one would to a mob. And now to the last point. Do you remember what you called me just now?"

"Of course, and I'm prepared to repeat it."

"That's not necessary, but you possess such vital vision. You have already mastered a line as unique as life itself, so don't abandon it. Don't break it off at me; extend it as far as it will allow. Take the mark farther . . . and what do you get, *Signora?* How do you turn out? In profile? Half-face? Or how?"

"I understand you." Camilla offers her hand to Heine. "But just the same, after all, I'm not a schoolgirl, heaven knows. I must come to my senses. This is like some hypnosis."

"*Signora,*" exclaims Heine melodramatically, falling at Camilla's feet. "*Signora.*" he gives a stifled cry, hiding his face in his hands. "Have you made your mark already? . . . What torment!" he sighs in a half whisper, abruptly pulling his hands away from his pale face . . . and, glancing up into the eyes of an increasingly confused Camilla Ardenze, notices to his utter amazement that . . .

IV

. . . that this woman is really attractive, almost unrecognizably beautiful, and that the beating of his own heart is like a rising tide gurgling in the wake of a boat. It completely inundates her knees as she moves closer to him,

THE MARK OF APELLES

and the lazy, lapping waves wash about her figure, billowing the silk of her dress, drowning her shoulders beneath their unruffled surface, raising her chin the tiniest of fractions, higher, higher, and—miracle of miracles!—the *Signora* stands up to her neck in his heart. One more such wave and she will go under! Heine seizes the drowning Camilla at this point. They kiss —and what a kiss it is! By its own strength it bears them away, groaning under the pressure of two excited hearts, tugging and staggering upward, forward, God knows in which direction. Meanwhile, she offers not the least resistance. No, sings her body, extended, led on by the kiss, fettered by the kiss—if you wish, I'll be the ark to bear such kisses, just carry it—carry me —away . . .

"Someone's knocking!" A hoarse cry escapes Camilla's throat. "Some-one's knocking!" And she tears herself from his embrace.

And it's true.

"Damnation! Who's there?"

"*Signor,* it is not right of you to lock the lounge door. We don't permit such things."

"Silence! I may do as I please."

"You are ill, sir."

A string of Italian oaths, passionate, fanatical as a liturgy. Heine opens the door. In the corridor stands the footman, still cursing, a few paces behind him is a ragged youngster, his head half hidden by a forest of vines, oleanders, *fleurs d'orange,* lilies . . .

"This rascal . . ."

                    . . . roses, magnolias, carnations . . .

"This rascal demanded at all costs to be admitted to the room whose windows look out onto the square—that can only mean the lounge . . ."

"Yes, that's right, the lounge," growls the youngster in a gutteral voice.

"Of course he should come to the lounge. It was I myself who instructed him."

" . . . because," the footman continues impatiently, "it couldn't possibly have been the office, the bathroom, and most certainly not the reading room. In any case, his dress is completely unsuitable, so . . ."

"Ah, yes," exclaims Heine, looking as though he has only just woken up. "Rondolfina, look at his trousers. You transparent creature, did someone make you that pair of trousers out of a fishnet or something?"

"*Signor,* every year the thorns on Ferrara's prickly hedges are re-sharpened by special gardeners . . ."

"Ha, ha!"

" . . . considering his dress was thoroughly indecent . . . ," the footman goes on, impatiently, putting special emphasis on this expression in the presence of the *Signora,* on whose face a shadow of sudden bewilderment vies with rays of utterly irrepressible gaiety, " . . . considering his dress was thoroughly indecent, we told the boy that he should give what the *Signor* had asked for to us to pass on, while he waited in the street. But this swindler . . ."

"No, no, he's right." Heine cuts the orator short, "I myself ordered him to come to the *Signora* in person . . ."

" . . . this swindler . . . ," by now the footman, a hot-tempered Calabrian, can hardly contain himself and is gabbling, "this swindler started making threats."

"Oh, what threats exactly?" asks Heine curiously. "How picturesque all this is, *Signora,* don't you think?"

"The rascal referred to you. 'The *Signor,*' he threatened us, 'the *Signor* -businessman will start using the services of another *albergo* when he passes through Ferrara in the future, if you don't let me in to see him, against all his wishes.' "

"Ha, ha! What a comedian! Don't you agree, *Signora*! Take this tropical plantation . . . Just a minute . . ." Turning around, Heine awaits instructions from Camilla, " . . . to room number eight for the moment," Heine continues, not waiting for her reply.

"To your room, for the moment," Camilla repeats, blushing slightly.

"Certainly, *Signor.* But as for the boy . . ."

"Hey, you monkey, how much do you value your trousers at?"

"Giulio is all covered with scratches, blue with cold. Giulio has no other clothes, no father, no mother," the ten-year-old trickster snivels tearfully, breaking out in a sweat.

"Well, how much then? Answer me!"

"One hundred soldi, *Signor,*" the youngster pronounces with a dreamy, uncertain air, as though through some hallucination.

"Ha, ha, ha!" everybody laughs. Heine laughs, Camilla laughs too, and particularly the footman, who bursts out laughing when Heine takes out his wallet and, still laughing, draws from it a ten-lira note and gives it to the ragamuffin.

The latter's prehensile paw shoots out like lightning to grab the proffered note.

"Stop," says Heine. "I daresay this is your first commercial venture. I wish you all the best. Listen, *cameriere,* I assure you that in this instance your laughter is positively misguided. It's cutting this young man to the quick. Isn't it true, young fellow, that in your future operations in Ferrara you're never ever going to show yourself at the doors of the inhospitable Torquato Tasso Hotel again?"

"Why no, *Signor,* on the contrary . . . But how many days does the *Signor* intend to stay in Ferrara?"

"In two hours' time I'm leaving here for good."

"*Signor* Enrico . . ."

"Yes, *Signora.*"

"Let's go out for a walk. After all, we don't want to go back into that stupid lounge, do we?"

"All right . . . *Cameriere,* take these flowers to room number eight. Wait a minute; this rose must be allowed to open a little more. For this evening the gardens of Ferrara entrust it to you, *Signora.*"

"*Merci,* Enrico . . . This dark carnation has not the least vestige of discretion. The gardens of Ferrara, *Signor,* entrust to you the custody of this licentious bloom."

"Your hand, *Signora* . . . Very well, *cameriere,* these can go to room number eight. And please bring my hat—it's in my room."

The footman goes off.

"You mustn't do it, Enrico."

"Camilla, I don't understand you . . ."

"You must stay—oh, please don't give me any answer—you must stay on another day in Ferrara at least . . . Enrico, Enrico, you've got a smudge of pollen on your eyebrow from the flowers. Let me wipe it off for you."

"*Signora* Camilla, there's a furry caterpillar on your shoe. I'll knock it off . . . I'll send a telegram to my home in Frankfurt . . . and your dress is covered with petals, *Signora* . . . and I'll send express letters until you tell me to stop."

"Enrico, I don't see any sign of a wedding ring on your finger. Have you ever worn such an ornament?"

"On the other hand, I noticed one on your finger ages ago, Camilla . . . Ah, there's my hat! Thank you."

V

Every alley in Ferrara is saturated by the fragrant evening, which floods its maze of streets in a huge echoing globe, like a drop of seawater that gets into your ear and fills your whole skull with buzzing.

In the café it is noisy, but the lane that leads to it is quiet and fragile. The main reason why the dazed and astonished town, holding its breath, has surrounded it on all sides is to be found in the café itself: Evening has burrowed into one of the town's back streets, into the very one on whose corner the café stands.

Camilla is momentarily lost in thought as she waits for Heine. He has gone to the telegraph office next door to the café.

"Why didn't he want under any circumstances to write his telegram in the café and send it by messenger? Couldn't he be satisfied with a simple official express letter? Is this some firm attachment that rests wholly on emotion? Mind you, on the other hand, he would have completely forgotten about her if I hadn't reminded him about the telegram. And this Rondolfina

... I'll have to ask about her. But can I? After all, it's a bit personal. God!
I'm acting just like a little girl! Can I? I must! Today I receive the right to
do anything and today I lose that same right. These artists certainly have
got you in a muddle, my girl. But what about this one? And Relinquimini?
... What a far-off figure! Was it spring when I last saw him? No, no, earlier
than that—that New Year's party? ... Well, anyhow, he was never close
to me ... But what about this one?"

"Why so pensive, Camilla?"

"And why are you so sad, Enrico? Don't upset yourself—I release you.
Some telegrams can be taken down from dictation by a footman. Send one
like that home—you've spent only three hours over your time; there are
night trains from Ferrara to Venice and to Milan too. If you're late it'll only
be by a few ..."

"What is all this about, Camilla?"

"Why are you so sad, Enrico? Tell me something about Rondolfina."
Heine gives a start and jumps up from his seat.

"How do you know that? Is he here? He's been here while I was away!?
Where is he, where is he, Camilla?"

"You've gone pale, Enrico. Who are you talking about? I was asking you
about a woman, wasn't I? Or am I pronouncing the name wrongly? Rondolfina? It's all a question of that last vowel. Sit down. People are looking
at us."

"Who told you about her? Have you had news from him? If so, how did
it reach you here? After all, we're here by chance—what I mean is, well,
nobody knows we're here."

"Enrico, nobody has been here and nothing happened while you were at
the telegraph office. I give you my word of honor. But this is getting more
interesting every minute. So there are two of them?"

"Then it's a miracle! I can't grasp it—I must be going out of my mind.
Who mentioned this name to you, Camilla? Where did you hear it?"

"Tonight, in a dream. Good Lord, it's such a common name! But you
still haven't answered me. Who is this Rondolfina? Plenty of miracles
happen in this world. Let's leave them out of it. Who is she, Enrico?"

"Oh, Camilla, Rondolfina is *you*!"

"You are an incorrigible actor! No, no! Let me go! Don't touch me!"

They both jump up. Camilla stands in one sweeping, definitive movement. Only the table separates them. Camilla grasps the back of the chair;
she falters in her decision; something has come over her and suddenly the
whole café lurches sideways in a circular wave, like a merry-go-round.

"I'm done for! I must get this off—this necklace ..."

A string of faces begins to move, drifting and floating on the same
nauseous, wavelike merry-go-round ... goatees, monocles, and lorgnettes.

With every second a growing number, directed at her. At every other table conversations stumble over this one unfortunate table. She can still see him. She is still propped against the chair. Perhaps it will pass ... No, the orchestra is out of tune and is losing the beat ...

"*Cameriere,* water!"

VI

She has a slight fever.

"What a tiny room you've got ... Yes, yes, like that, thanks. I think I'll lie down a little while longer. It's malaria"—and then, later ... "I've got an entire apartment. But you mustn't leave me. It might come over me again any minute. Enrico!"

"Yes, darling?"

"Why aren't you saying anything? ... No, no, don't bother; it's better like that. Oh, Enrico, I can't remember if there was such a thing as this morning. And are they still standing there?"

"Are who still standing where, Camilla?"

"The flowers. They should be taken outside for the night. What a heavy perfume! I wonder how many tons it weighs."

"I'll have someone remove them ... What are you doing, Camilla?"

"I'm going to get up ... No, I can manage on my own, thank you. There you are—it's completely past; I just had to get up on my feet ... Yes, you must have them removed. But where would be the best place? Wait a moment, I have a complete apartment on the Piazza Ariosto, you know. You can probably see it from here ..."

"Nighttime already. It seems to be a bit cooler."

"Why are there so few people in the street?"

"Sshh, they can hear every word."

"What are they arguing about?"

"I don't know, Camilla. They look like students. They're bragging about something. Perhaps the same thing we're doing ..."

"Let me go a minute. They've stopped on the corner. Good God! He's just thrown the little one over his shoulder! Now it's quiet again. How weirdly the light is catching in the branches! But I can't see any streetlight. Are we on the top?"

"What do you mean, Camilla?"

"Is there another floor above ours?"

"Yes, I believe so."

Camilla leans out of the window, peering upward from beneath the overhanging guard rail.

"No . . ." But Heine will not let her finish. "No, there's nobody there," she repeats, extricating herself from his embrace.

"What are you talking about?"

"I thought there was a man standing there holding a lamp up at the window and that he was tossing crushed leaves and shadows out of the window and down into the street. I wanted to put my face under them and catch them on my cheek. Well, there's nobody there."

"But that's poetry itself, Camilla."

"Really, I don't know. There it is. Right over there by the theater. Where there's a mauve glow."

"Who's there, Camilla?"

"My place, you silly, that's who. Still, these nervous spells that come over me . . . If we could arrange somehow . . ."

"I've already booked a room for you."

"Really? How thoughtful of you! At long last. What time is it? Let's go and see what kind of room I've got. Most interesting."

They leave room number eight, smiling and excited as schoolchildren staging the siege of Troy in the backyard.

VII

Long before it arrived, the bells of the Catholic church began their gossipy chatter about the new morning, jerkily, and performing their cold bows from the somersaulting belfry beams. In the hotel only one light was burning. It had flickered on when the telephone bell gave its astringent trill, and nobody bothered to put it out afterward. The lamp was a witness to the scene in which the sleepy night porter came running to the phone, left the receiver lying on the stand after some altercation with the caller, and was swallowed up in the depths of the corridor, only to surface again after a short time from the same half-lit depths.

"Yes, the *Signor* is leaving sometime this morning. He'll ring you in half an hour if it's so urgent. Could I trouble you for your number. Who shall I say to call?"

The lamp continued to burn even when the man from number eight, as he was referred to over the phone, in his stocking feet, buttoning his dressing gown as he came, emerged from one of the smaller transverse corridors into the main one.

The lamp was situated directly opposite number eight. However, the man from number eight had made a detour along this corridor in order to get to the telephone. This detour began somewhere in the region of rooms eighty to ninety. After a short consultation with the night porter, during which the expression on his face changed from anxious agitation to a sudden carefree curiosity, he boldly grabbed hold of the receiver and, after going through the usual technical formalities, found himself talking to the editor of the newspaper *Il Voce* in person.

"Listen, what an ungodly thing to do! Who told you I suffered from insomnia?"

. . .

"It looks as though you've gotten on the telephone by mistake on your way up to the rooftops. Why are you shouting it around? Well, what's the matter?"

. . .

"Yes, I've been delayed by twenty-four hours."

. . .

"The footman is right. I haven't left a home address and I don't intend to leave one."

. . .

"Give it to you? No, I can't do that either. Well, by and large, I hadn't considered publishing it at all, and certainly not today, as you apparently imagined."

. . .

"It will never be the slightest use to you."

. . .

"Don't lose your temper, my dear editor, a little more decorum all around. Relinquimini won't even think of using you as an intermediary."

. . .

"Because he doesn't need it."

. . .

"May I remind you once again how much I would appreciate your calmness. Relinquimini never lost a notebook at any time."

. . .

"Have it your way, though that's the first unequivocal expression you've used. No, absolutely not."

. . .

"Again? All right, I admit it. But it's only blackmail in the context of yesterday's edition of *Il Voce.* Beyond that context it's nothing of the sort."

. . .

"Since yesterday. About six o'clock in the evening."

. . .

"If you had the faintest inkling of what has developed out of this scheme of mine, you would seek another, harsher name for it all, and it would be even farther from the truth than the one you've just seen fit to propose."

. . .

"Willingly. With pleasure. I can't think of any objection today. Heinrich Heine."

. . .

"That's right."

. . .

"Very flattering to hear it."

. . .

"What do you mean?"

. . .

"Willingly. How can I do that? I'm sorry, but I do have to leave today. Come to the station. We can spend an hour or so together."

. . .

"Nine thirty-five. However, time brings a constant series of surprises. Better not come."

. . .

"Come to the hotel. In the afternoon—that'll be safer. Or come to the apartment. In the evening. In tails, please, and bring flowers."

. . .

"Yes, yes, my dear editor, you are a prophet."

. . .

"Perhaps tomorrow on the dueling ground outside town."

. . .

"I don't know. Perhaps I'm in deadly earnest."

. . .

"Well if you're fully booked for these two days, do you know what to do? Come to Campo Santo the day after tomorrow."

. . .

"Do you think so?"

. . .

"Do you think so?"

. . .

"What a strange conversation at such an ungodly hour! Well, please forgive me, I'm tired and I want to get back to my room."

. . .

"I can't hear you . . . To room number eight? Ah, yes. Yes, yes, to room number eight. It's a wonderful room, my dear editor, with a climate all its own. It's been like spring in there for at least four hours. Good-bye, my dear editor."

. . .

Like an automaton, Heine turned off the light.

"Don't put it out, Enrico"—the sound of a voice came from the depths and darkness of the corridor.

"Camilla?!!"

1915

Translated by Nicholas J. Anning

Letters from Tula

I

The skylarks in the open freely poured forth their song, and in the train from Moscow a suffocating sun was borne along on the many striped bench seats. The sun was setting. A bridge with the inscription "Upa" sailed across a hundred carriage windows at the very instant when the stoker, racing in the tender at the head of the train, discovered the town on the side away from the track and through the roar of his own hair and the fresh excitement of the evening saw it speeding to meet them.

Meanwhile people over there were greeting one another in the street and saying, "Good evening." To this some added, "Have you been there?" "No, just going," others replied. "You're too late," they were told. "It's all over."

"Tula, the 10th.

"So you changed compartments then, as we agreed witn the conductor. Just now the general who gave up his seat went over to the bar, and he bowed to me on the way, as he might to an old acquaintance. The next train to Moscow goes at three o'clock in the morning. He was saying good-bye as he left just now. The porter is opening the door for him. Out there the cabmen are clamoring like sparrows from a distance. My dear, that leave-taking was madness. Now the separation is ten times more painful. Now imagination has something real to work on. It will gnaw me quite away. Out there a horse trolley is drawing up, and they are changing the team. I shall go and look around the town. O, what anguish! I will choke it back, this raging anguish; I will soften it with verses."

119

"Tula.

"Alas, there is no middle road. One must leave at the second bell, or else set off together on a journey to the end, to the grave. Look now, it will be dawn already when I make this entire journey in reverse—and in every detail too, in every trivial detail. And now they will all have the subtlety of some quite exquisite torture.

"What misery to be born a poet! What torment is imagination! Sunshine in beer. Sunk to the very bottom of the bottle. Across the table sits an agriculturist, or something of the sort. He has a ruddy face. And with a green hand he stirs his coffee. Oh, my dear, they are all strangers around me. There was one witness, but he has gone (the general). There is another still, the magistrate—they do not recognize him. Nonentities! Why, they think it is *their* sun they sip with milk from the saucer. They do not realize that their flies stick in yours, or in ours, and kitchen boys' saucepans clash, seltzer spatters, and rubles clatter sonorously like clicking tongues onto the marble tabletop. I shall go and look around the town. It has remained so far remote. There is the horse trolley, but it is not worth it; on foot, they say, it is about forty minutes. I have found the receipt; you were quite right. I will hardly have time tomorrow; I must have my full sleep. The day after tomorrow. Don't you worry—it's a pawnshop; the matter is not urgent. Oh, to write is mere self-torment. But I have not the strength to break off."

Five hours passed. There was a quite extraordinary stillness. It became impossible to tell where the grass ended and where the coal began. A star twinkled. Not a living soul remained by the pumphouse. Water showed black through a moldering cavity in the moss-covered swamp. The reflection of a birch tree trembled there. It quivered feverishly. But all this was far away. Far, far away. Apart from the birch tree there was not a soul on the road.

There was quite extraordinary stillness. Lifeless boilers and coaches lay on the flat earth like piles of low storm cloud on a windless night. Were it not April, summer lightning might have played. But the sky was troubled. Stricken with transparency, as though with some illness, and sapped from within by spring, it was a troubled sky. The final horse-drawn coach of the Tula trolley line came up from the town. The reversible backrests of the seating banged. The last to alight was a man carrying letters, which jutted from the wide pockets of his broad overcoat. The others made their way into the waiting room, toward a group of very strange young people noisily dining at the end of the room. But this man remained outside at the front of the building, searching for the green letter box. But one could not tell where the grass ended and where the coal began, and when a tired pair of horses dragged the towing shaft across the turf, harrowing the path with its iron tip, still no dust could be seen, and only a lantern by the stables gave a dim impression of events. The night uttered a long-drawn-out guttural sound—then everything was silent. It was all far, far away, beyond the horizon.

"Tula, the 10th [crossed out], the 11th, one o'clock in the morning. Look it up in a textbook, my dear. You have Klyuchevsky with you; I put it in the case myself. I do not know how to begin. I still understand nothing. So strange it is, so terrible. As I write to you, everything pursues its normal course at the far end of the table. They act as if they were geniuses, declaiming and hurling phrases at each other, and theatrically flinging their napkins on the table when they have wiped their clean-shaven lips. I have not said who they are: the worst form of bohemians [carefully crossed out]. A cinema troupe from Moscow. They have been shooting *The Time of Troubles* in the Kremlin and in places where the ramparts were.

"Read Klyuchevsky's account—I have not read it myself, but I think there must be some episode with Pyotr Bolotnikov. This is what brought them to the River Upa. I find they have set the scene at the exact spot and filmed it from the far bank. Now they have the seventeenth century stowed away in their suitcases while all the remnants linger on over the dirty table. The Polish women are horrid, and the boyars' children even more dreadful. My dear one, it sickens me! This is a display of the ideals of our age. The fumes that they produce are my own—fumes common to us all. This is the burning smell of woeful insolence and ignorance. This is my own self. My dear, I have posted two letters to you. I cannot recall them. Here is the vocabulary of these [deleted and nothing substituted]. Here is the vocabulary they use: genius, poet, ennui, verses, mediocrity, philistinism, tragedy, woman, I and she. How dreadful to see oneself in others. It is a caricature of [left incomplete].

"2 o'clock. My heart's faith is greater than ever, I swear to you, the time will come—no, let me tell you about it later. Savage me, come savage me, O night; all is not over yet; scorch me to a cinder; that word that thrusts through all accumulated dross, burn, burn bright and clear, the forgotten, angry, fiery word 'conscience' [heavily underscored with a line that tears through the paper in places]. Blaze, O furious oil-bearing tongue that illuminates the floor of darkness!

"A fashion has established itself in life, such that now there is no place left in the world where a man may warm his soul at the fire of shame; for shame has everywhere gone damp and will not burn. Falsehood and disordered dissipation. Thus for thirty years already men of singularity have lived, both young and old, damping down their shame, and now this has spread to the world at large, to men obscure and undistinguished. Now for the first, for the very first, time since the distant years of childhood I am consumed with fire [crossed out]."

Another fresh attempt. The letter remains unposted.

"How can I describe it to you? I shall have to start from the end. Otherwise nothing will come of it. Very well—and allow me also to tell it in the third person. I surely wrote about the man who was strolling past the baggage office? Well now, the poet (who will henceforth be set in inverted commas—until purged in the fire—the 'poet' observes himself in the disgusting behavior of the actors and in the outrageous spectacle that exposes his fellow men and his age for what they are. Perhaps this is only his pose?—Not so. For they confirm his identity is no illusion. They rise to their feet and approach him. '*Colleague,* have you got change for a three-ruble note?' He dispels their illusion: Actors are not the only ones who shave. There are three rubles' worth of twenty-kopeck pieces. He gets rid of the actor. But it is not a question of shaving one's upper lip. '*Colleague,*' the scum had said. Yes indeed! And he was right! Here was the witness's evidence for the prosecution. At this point something new occurred—a mere trifle, but one that in its way shivered all the events and all he had experienced in the waiting room up until this moment.

"The 'poet' at last recognizes the person strolling by the baggage office. He has seen that face before. From somewhere locally. He has seen it on several occasions in the course of a single day, at different times and in different places. It was when they were assembling the special train at Astapovo, with a freight car as a hearse, and when the crowds of strangers left the station in different trains, which then wheeled and crossed the whole day around the unexpected turns of that tangled junction where four railroads converged and parted, returned and split again.

"In an instant, realization now weighs in on all that has so far happened to the 'poet' in the waiting room, and it acts as a lever to set the whole revolving stage in motion. And why?—Indeed, this is Tula! This night is a night in Tula. Night in a place bound up with the life of Tolstoy. Is it any wonder that compass needles start to dance here? Such events are in the very nature of this place. This is an occurrence on the *territory of conscience,* in its gravitational and ore-bearing sector. There will be no more of the 'poet.' He swears it to you, that when he someday sees *The Time of Troubles* on the screen (it will be shown eventually, one imagines), the sequence on the River Upa will find him utterly alone, if actors have not reformed by then, and if dreamers of every sort can spend a whole day stamping on the mine-sown territory of the spirit and still survive unharmed in their ignorance and braggadocio."

While these lines were being written, the trackmen's lamps emerged from their huts and, creeping low, moved away down the tracks. Whistles began to sound. Iron was awakening and bruised chains screamed. Coaches slipped ever so gently down the platform. They had long been sliding past and were already countless. Behind them—the swelling approach of something breathing heavily, something unknown and coming from the night. For down the jointed tracks behind the locomotive there came that sudden sweeping clear of rails, the unexpected appearance of night in the deserted platform's vision, the emergence of silence across a whole expanse of stars and signals, and the advent of a rural peace. And this moment came snoring in the rear of the freight train, bent low under the covered overhang and made its gliding approach.

While these lines were being penned, they began to couple up the passenger-freight train for Yelets.

The man who was writing went out onto the platform. Night lay spread down the whole extent of the dampened Russian conscience. It was illuminated by lanterns. Across it, bending the rails beneath them, freight cars slowly moved with winnowing machines under tarpaulin. It was trampled by shadows and deafened by flocks of steam, which screeched like cockerels from beneath the valves. The writer went around the station. He walked out to the front of the building.

While these lines were being written, nothing had changed in the entire space of conscience. From it rose the smells of putrefaction and of clay. Far, far away, from its farthest extremity, a birch tree gleamed and a cavity in the swamp showed up like a fallen earring. Strips of light broke from within the waiting room and fell outside beneath the seats on the floor of the trolley. The strips of light skirmished together. The rattle of beer, madness, and stench followed them and fell in turn beneath the seats. And still, whenever the station windows faded, crunching and snoring were heard somewhere nearby. The man who had been writing strolled up and down. He thought of many things. He thought of his art and of how he might find the right path. He forgot with whom he had been traveling, whom he had seen off, and to whom he was writing. He supposed that everything would begin again when he ceased to hear himself, and when there was complete physical silence within his soul. Not an Ibsen silence but one in the *acoustic* sense.

Those were his thoughts. A shiver ran through his body. The east was turning gray, and a perplexed and rapid dew settled on the face of all conscience, still plunged in deepest night. It was time to think about his ticket. The cocks were crowing and the ticket office was coming to life.

II

It was only then that in his apartment in town on Posolskaya Street an extremely strange old man finally settled down to sleep. While letters were being written at the station, this apartment had quivered with soft footsteps and the candle at the window had caught a whisper broken by frequent silences. It was not the voice of the old man, though apart from him there was not a soul in the room. It was all amazingly peculiar.

The old man had spent a quite unusual day. He had left the meadow, saddened, when he realized that this was not a play at all, but for the moment merely some free flight of fantasy that would turn into a play only when shown in the "Magic" movie theater. When he first saw the boyars and governors milling on the far shore, and the commoners leading in bound men and knocking off their hats into the nettles—when he saw the Poles clinging to laburnum bushes on the scarp, and their battle-axes, which gave no response to sunlight and no bright ring, the old man began to rummage through his own repertoire. He found no such chronicle there. He decided this must be from something before his period, Ozerov or Sumarokov. It was then that they pointed out the cameraman to him; they mentioned the "Magic," an institution he detested wholeheartedly, and reminded him that he was old and lonely, and times had changed. He went away, dejected.

He walked along in his old nankeens and reflected that now there was no one left in the world to call him "dear old Savva." The day was a holiday. It basked in the warmth of scattered sunflower seeds.

Through their deep chesty speech they spat their raw novelty at him. High above, the moon crumbled like a round loaf and melted. The sky appeared cold and amazed at its own remoteness. The voices were greased by food and drink. Even the echo that mellowed across the river was steeped in saffron mushroom, rye loaf, fat, and vodka. Some of the streets were thronged. Crude flounces gave the skirts and womenfolk a particular mottled patchwork look.

The steppe grasses kept pace relentlessly with strollers. Dust flew up, causing eyes to squint and obscuring the burdocks that beat in whirls against the wattle fences and clung to people's dress. The walking stick felt like a fragment of senile sclerosis. He leaned on this extension of his knotted veins, cramped, with gouty grip.

All day he felt as if he had been at some inordinately noisy rag fair. It was the consequence of that spectacle he had seen. It had left unsatisfied his need for the human speech of tragedy. And it was this silent lacuna that now rang in the old man's ears.

All day he was sick at having heard not a single line of pentameter from the far bank of the river.

And when night fell, he sat down at the table, propped his head on his hand, and immersed himself in thought. He decided that this must be his death. This mental turmoil was so unlike his recent years of steady bitterness. He decided to take his decorations from the cupboard and warn someone—the janitor, at least—no matter whom—and yet he still sat, expecting that maybe it would just pass off.

A horse trolley jingled as it trotted by outside. It was the last trolley to the station.

Half an hour passed. A star gleamed brightly. There was not another soul around. It was late already. The candle flamed, shivered, trembled. The bookcase's softened silhouette stirred its four undulating strips of blackness. The night uttered a long-drawn-out guttural sound. Far, far away. A door banged in the street below, and people began speaking in the low, excited tones befitting such a night in spring with not a soul about and only one upper flat with a light still burning and an open window.

The old man rose. He was transformed. At last! Found! Both himself and her! They had helped him to it, and he hastened to assist their promptings, to avoid missing both, to prevent their slipping away, to fasten on and sink in them. In a few steps he reached the door, half closing his eyes, flourishing a hand and covering his chin with the other. He was remembering. Suddenly he stood erect and walked back briskly with a gait not his own but that of a stranger. He appeared to be acting some part.

"Well, there's a snowstorm, there's quite a snowstorm blowing, Lyubov Petrovna," he said, and he cleared his throat and spat into his handkerchief. He began again: "Well, there's a snowstorm, there's quite a snowstorm blowing, Lyubov Petrovna," he said, this time without coughing, and now it was more real.

He began to shake his arms and flail, as if coming in from the weather, unwrapping himself and throwing off his fur coat. He paused for some reply to come from beyond the partition, then, as if unable to wait, he asked, "Aren't you at home, Lyubov Petrovna?" still in the same stranger's voice. And he gave a start when after five and twenty years he heard—just as he was *supposed* to—from behind that *other* partition the beloved, gay reply: "Yes, I am at home!" Then he continued again, this time authentically, and with a skill at illusion that a colleague might have been proud of in such a situation. As if fumbling with his tobacco, and breaking up his speech with sidelong glances at the partition, he drawled out: "M-mm-er, sorry, Lyubov Petrovna—I don't suppose Savva Ignatyevich is, er, here?"

It was altogether too much. He could see both of them. Her and himself. The old man was stifled with silent sobbing. Hours passed. He kept weeping and whispering. There was an extraordinary stillness. And while the old man shuddered and feebly dabbed his eyes and face with a handkerchief, trembled and crumpled it, shook his head and made dismissive waves of the hand like a person giggling, who chokes and is amazed how it is that, God forgive him, he is still there and has not really burst—on the railway track they began to assemble the passenger-freight train for Yelets.

For a whole hour he kept his youth preserved in tears, as though in spirits, and then, when he had no tears left, everything collapsed, everything fled and disappeared. He immediately faded and seemed to gather dust. And then, sighing, as if guilty of some wrong, and yawning, he began to get ready for bed.

Like everyone in the story, he too shaved his mustache. And like the main character, he too was in search of physical silence. He was the only one in the story to find it, having made another to speak through his own lips.

The train was heading for Moscow, and an enormous crimson sun was borne along on the bodies of many sleeping passengers. It had just appeared from behind a hill, and it was rising.

April 1918.

Translated by Christopher Barnes

Without Love

A Chapter from a Tale

He had a brother, and it was the brother who walked around the house, his feet crunching in the snow and on the frozen steps as he went up them, to knock on the door, to knock as one does on the door of a blizzard-swept house when the wind turns your fingers to ice, and, whistling and howling, roars into your ears that you should knock even louder, if you know what's good for you . . . and all the time the same wind hammers on the shutters to drown your knocking and confuse the people inside.

They heard him and opened. The house stood on a hill. The door was torn from his grasp together with one of his gloves, and, as the door flew to and fro and they tried to catch it, the gray snow-swept countryside rushed into the hall and breathed on the lamps, bringing with it the distant tinkle of a sleigh bell. The sound sank in the vast snow field and, gasping for breath, called to the rescue. It was carried to the house by the overwhelming onrush of the blizzard, which had gripped the door in its clutches, and by the dips in the sleigh track, which had been caught up in some demoniac movement and was slithering under the runners, throwing up swirling columns of choking snow for all to see for miles around.

When the door had been caught and shut, they all got up to meet the specter in the hall; in his high boots of reindeer skin he was like a wild animal standing on its hind legs.

"Is it coming?" Kovalevsky asked.

"Yes, they're on the way. You must get ready." He licked his lips and wiped his nose. There was pandemonium as bundles and baskets were brought out; the children had sulked since nightfall (till then, for want of something better to do and on learning that everything was packed, and that there would still be a long wait and nothing to talk about, they had point- lessly weighed out raisins on the bare table) and now they set up a great wail, putting the blame on each other ("It's not me; it's Petya who's howling because Papa's going away.") and, seeking fair play and a refuge from the night, the raisins, the blizzard, the chaos, their papas about to depart, the traveling baskets, the oil lamps, and the fur coats, they tried to bury their heads in their mothers' aprons.

But instead they were snatched up, as though on a signal, by their nurses and mothers and carried with a sudden gust of feeling into the passage, and in the hall, which echoed the voices of the coachmen through the folding door, they were held up to their fathers. They all stood bareheaded and, crossing themselves with emotion, exchanged hurried kisses and said it was time to go.

Meanwhile the Tatar coachmen (they were three in number, but there seemed to be ten), carrying lights that splashed the snow without spilling into it altogether, dashed up to the horses harnessed in file and, ducking down to look at the girths and fetlocks, jumped up again at once and began to race around like madmen, brandishing their flares and lighting up in turn the trunks standing around the sleigh, the snow, the underbellies and flanks of the horses, and their muzzles, which together formed a slender garland, borne aloft, as it seemed, by the wind. The moment of departure depended on the Tatars. Round about the snow sang in the forest and raved in the open country, and it seemed as though the surging sound of the night knew Tatar and was arguing with Mininbay, who had climbed onto the roof of the sleigh, and, clutching at his hands, was telling him to fasten down the trunks not in the way Gimazetdin was shouting, nor in the way suggested by Galliula, who was hardly able to keep his feet because of the storm and had gone quite hoarse.... The moment of departure depended on the Tatars. They could hardly wait to take up their whips, whistle at the horses, and abandon themselves to the final devil-may-care *aida*. After this no power on earth would hold the horses back. Like drunkards to the bottle, the Tatars were drawn irresistibly, more and more eagerly with each passing minute, to the mournful whoops and cajolery of their trade. Hence the feverish movements of their frenzied alcoholic hands as they rushed to help their masters into their heavy fur coats.

And now the flares sent a last farewell kiss to those who were being left behind. Goltsev had already stumbled into the depths of the sleigh, and Kovalevsky, floundering in the tails of his three coats, climbed after him under the heavy traveling rug. Unable to feel the floor through their broad felt boots, they nestled down in the straw, the cushions, and the sheepskins. A flare appeared on the far side of the sleigh but suddenly bobbed down out of sight.

The sleigh shuddered and heaved. It slithered forward, lurched over, and began to turn on its side. A low whistle came from the depths of an Asian soul, and after righting the sleigh with their shoulders, Mininbay and Gimazetdin leaped into their seats. The sleigh shot forward as though borne on wings and plunged into the nearby forest. The open country, disheveled and moaning, rose up behind it. It was glad to see the end of the sleigh, which disappeared without a trace among the trees with branches like carpet slippers, at the junction with the main road to Chistopol and Kazan. Mininbay got off here and, wishing his master a good journey, vanished in the storm like a flurry of powdered snow. They sped on and on over the arrow-straight highway.

"I asked her to come here with me," one of them thought, breathing in the dampness of thawing fur. "I remember how it was." A lot of streetcars had gotten stuck in front of the theater, and an anxious crowd was milling around the first one . . . "The performance has begun," the usher said in a confidential whisper and, gray in his cloth uniform, he drew back the cloth curtain separating the stalls from the lighted cloakroom with its benches, galoshes, and posters. In the intermission (it went on longer than usual), they walked around the foyer, peering sideways at the mirrors, and neither of them knew what to do with their hands, which were hot and red. "So there now; thinking it all over," she took a sip of seltzer water, "I just don't know what to do or how I should decide. So please don't be surprised if you hear that I've gone to the front as a nurse. I shall enroll in a few days' time . . ." "Why don't you come with me to the Kama River?" he said. She laughed.

The intermission had gone on so long because of the musical item at the beginning of the second act. It could not be played without an oboe, and the oboist was the unfortunate cause of the streetcar stoppage in front of the theater. "He's badly hurt," people whispered to each other, taking their places when the painted hem of the curtain began to glow.

"He was unconscious when they pulled him from under the wheels," their friends told them as they padded over the cloth-covered carpet in heavy galoshes, trailing the ends of kerchiefs and shawls.

"And now they'll be surprised," he thought, trying to synchronize the flow of his thoughts with the movement of the sleigh and lull himself to sleep.

The other man was thinking about the purpose of their sudden departure, about the reception awaiting them at their destination, and about what should be done first. He also thought that Goltsev was asleep, not suspecting that Goltsev was wide awake and that it was he himself who was asleep, plunging in his dreams from pothole to pothole together with his thoughts about revolution, which now, as once before, meant more to him than his fur coat and his other belongings, more than his wife and child, more than his own life, and more than other people's lives, and with which he would not part for anything in the world—even in his sleep—once he had laid hold of them and kindled them within himself.

Their eyes opened languidly, of their own accord. They could not help their surprise. A village lay in a deep otherworldly trance. The snow glittered. The three horses had broken file, they had left the road and stood huddled together. The night was bright and still. The lead horse, its head raised, was gazing over a snowdrift at something left far behind. The moon shone black and mysterious behind a house tightly swathed in frosty air. After the solemnity of the forest and the blizzard-swept loneliness of the open country, a human dwelling was like an apparition in a fairy tale. The house seemed conscious of its awesome magic and was in no hurry to answer the coachman's knock. It stood silent, unwilling to break its own oppressive spell. The snow glittered. But soon two voices, unseen to each other, spoke loudly through the gate. They divided the whole world between them, these two, as they talked to each other through the timbers, in the midst of infinite stillness. The man who was opening the gate took the half that looked north, unfolding beyond the roof of the house, and the other man, who was waiting for him, took the half the horse could see over the edge of the snowdrift.

At the previous station, Gimazetdin had wakened only Kovalevsky, and the coachman who had driven them to this point was a stranger to Goltsev. But now he immediately recognized Dementii Mekhanoshin, to whom he had once issued a certificate in his office—a good sixty miles from here— to the effect that, being the owner of a troika and plying the last stage between Bilyar and Syuginsk, he was working for defense.

It was odd to think that he had certified this house and its coach yard and that, knowing nothing at all of them, he had underwritten this magic village and the starry night above it. Later, while the horses were being reharnessed and the sleepy wife of the coachman gave them tea; while the clock ticked and they tried to make conversation, and bugs crawled sultrily over calendars and portraits of crowned persons; while bodies sleeping on the benches snored and wheezed fitfully like clockwork devices of different systems, Dementii kept going out and returning, and each time his appearance changed, depending on what he had taken down from a nail or dragged from under his bed. When he came in the first time to tell his wife to give the gentlemen sugar and to get out the white bread for them, he was wearing a smock and looked like a hospitable peasant; the second time, coming for the reins, he was a laborer dressed in a short Siberian jacket; and finally he appeared as a coachman in a heavy fur coat. Without coming in, he leaned through the doorway and said that the horses were ready, that it was past three in the morning and time for them to leave. Then, pushing open the door with the stock of his whip, he went into the dark world outside, which reverberated loudly at his first steps.

The rest of the journey left no trace in their memories. It was getting light when Goltsev woke and the countryside was covered in a haze. An endless, straggling convoy of sleighs was lumbering by in a cloud of steam. They were overtaking it, and it looked therefore as though the timber-loaded sleighs were creaking and swaying without moving forward and that the drivers were just marking time, stomping their feet on the ground to keep warm. The broad cart road ran to one side of the track over which they were racing, and it was on a much higher level. Legs rose and fell, trampling the still lit stars, and there was a movement of hands, horses' muzzles, cowled heads, and sleighs. It seemed as though the gray and weary suburban morning was itself drifting over the clear sky in great damp patches toward the place where it sensed the railroad, the brick walls of factory buildings, heaps of damp coal, and the drudgery of fumes and smoke. The sleigh raced on, flying over ruts and potholes, its bell jingling frantically. There was still no end to the convoy, and it was high time for the sun to rise, but the sun was still far away.

The sun was still far away. They would see it only after another five versts, after a short stop at the inn, after the message from the factory manager and the long, restless wait in his anteroom.

Then it appeared. It entered the manager's office with them, flooded rapidly over the carpet, settled behind the flowerpots, and smiled at the caged chaffinches by the window, at the fir trees outside, at the stove, and at all forty-four volumes of the leather-bound Brockhaus Encyclopedia.

After this, during Kovalevsky's conversation with the manager, the yard outside was alive and at play, tirelessly scattering turquoise and amber, wafts of pungent resin from the sweating pines and beads of molten hoarfrost.

The manager glanced toward Goltsev. "He's my friend," said Kovalevsky quickly. "Don't worry, you can talk freely. . . . So you knew Breshkovskaya?"

Suddenly Kovalevsky got up and, turning to Goltsev, shouted in panic, "And what about my papers? Just as I said! Kostya, now what shall I do?"

Goltsev didn't at first understand: "I've got our passports . . ."

"That bundle of papers!" Kovalevsky interrupted him angrily. "I asked you to remind me."

"Oh, I'm sorry, Yura. We left them behind. It really is too bad of me. I can't think how I . . ."

Their host, a short, thickset man who had difficulty with his breathing, attended in the meantime to his managerial business. He kept looking at his watch and, puffing and blowing, stirred the logs in the stove with a poker. Sometimes, as though changing his mind about something, he would suddenly stop in his tracks halfway across the room, swivel around, and dart over to the desk at which Kovalevsky was writing to his brother, ". . . in other words, all is well. I only hope it goes on like this. Now for the most important thing. Do exactly as I tell you. Kostya says that we left a bundle with all my illegal stuff lying on Masha's suitcase in the hall. Open it up, and if there are any manuscripts among the pamphlets (memoirs, notes on the scope of the organization, letters in code relating to the secret rendezvous in our house, to the period of Kulisher's escape, etc.), wrap it all up, seal it, and send it to me in Moscow at the office in Teploryadnaya with the first reliable person—depending of course on how things work out. But you know what to do as well as I do, and if there is a change of . . ."

"Do come and have some coffee," whispered the manager with a shuffle and a click of the heels. "I mean you, young man," he explained to Goltsev with even greater care, and he paused respectfully at the sight of Kovalevsky's cuff, which was poised over the paper, waiting to pounce on the needed word.

Three Austrian prisoners of war went past the window, talking and blowing their noses. They carefully walked around the puddles that had formed.

". . . if there is a change of climate," Kovalevsky found the word he needed, "don't send the papers to Moscow, but hide them in a safe place. I'm counting on you for this and all other things we agreed on. We have to catch the train soon. I'm dead tired. We hope to have a good sleep in the train. I'm writing to Masha separately. Well, all the best. . . . P.S.: Just imagine, it turns out that R., the manager, is an old Socialist Revolutionary. What do you make of that?"

At this moment Goltsev looked into the office with a slice of buttered bread in his hand. Swallowing the half-chewed piece he had just bitten off, he said, "You're writing to Misha, are you? Tell him to send," he took another bite at his bread and butter and continued chewing and swallowing, "my papers as well. I've changed my mind. Don't forget, Yura. And come and have some coffee."

November 20, 1918.   *Translated by Max Hayward*

The Childhood of
Zhenya Luvers

The Long Days

I

Zhenya Luvers was born and brought up in Perm. Just as once her little boats and dolls, so later on her memories sank deep into the shaggy bearskins, of which there were many in their house. Her father managed the affairs of the Lunyev mines and had a large clientele among the factory-owners on the Chusovaya.

The bearskins were gifts, deep brown and sumptuous. The white she-bear in her nursery was like an enormous chrysanthemum shedding petals. This was the skin acquired specially for "young Zhenya's room," admired and bargained for at the shop and delivered by special messenger.

In summer they lived on the far bank of the Kama at the *dacha*. In those days Zhenya was put to bed early. She could not see the lights of Motovilikha. But once something scared the angora cat, and it stirred suddenly in its sleep and woke Zhenya up. Then she saw grown-ups on the balcony. The alder overhanging the railings was dense and iridescent as ink. The tea in the glasses was red, the cuffs and cards were yellow, and the cloth was green. It was like a delirium—except that this one had its name, which even Zhenya knew: They were playing cards.

However, there was no way of determining what was happening far, far away on the other bank. *That* had no name, and no precise color or definite outline. And as it stirred it was familiar and dear, and was not delirious as was the thing that muttered and swirled in clouds of tobacco smoke, throwing fresh shadows that flitted around the tawny beams of the gallery.

Zhenya burst into tears. Father came in and explained things to her. The
English governess turned her face to the wall. Father's explanation was
brief: "That is Motovilikha. For shame! A big girl like you! . . . Go to sleep!"

The little girl understood nothing and contentedly swallowed a rolling
tear. In fact, this was all she needed to know: what the mysterious thing
was called—Motovilikha. That night it still explained everything, because
that night the name still had a complete and reassuring significance for the
child.

But next morning she started asking questions—what Motovilikha was
and what they did there at night—and she learned that Motovilikha was
a factory, a government factory, and that cast iron was made there, and
from cast iron . . . But now that no longer concerned her; she was more
interested in knowing whether the things called "factories" were special
countries, and who lived there. . . . But she did not ask these questions and
for some reason deliberately concealed them.

That morning she emerged from the state of infancy she had still been
in at night. For the first time in her life she suspected there was something
that phenomena kept to themselves—or if they revealed it they did so only
to people who knew how to shout and punish, smoke and bolt doors. For
the first time, just like this new Motovilikha, she did not say everything she
thought, but kept to herself what was most essential, vital, and stirring.

The years passed. Ever since their birth, the children had gotten so
accustomed to their father's absences that in their eyes it had become a
special feature of fatherhood to lunch only rarely and never dine. But more
and more often they would play and squabble, write and eat in completely
empty, solemnly deserted rooms, and the cold instructions of the English
governess could never replace the presence of their mother, who filled the
house with the sweet oppression of her ready anger and obstinacy, like some
native electricity. The quiet northern daylight streamed through the curtains. It was unsmiling. The oaken sideboard seemed gray. And the silver
lay piled there, heavy and severe. The lavender-washed hands of the English
governess moved above the tablecloth. She always served everyone his fair
portion and had an inexhaustible supply of patience, and a sense of justice
was germane to her to the same high degree as her room and her books were
always clean and neat. The maid who brought the food stood waiting in the
dining room and only went away to the kitchen to fetch the next course.
It was all pleasant and comfortable, but dreadfully sad.

But for the little girl these were years of suspicion, solitude, and a sense
of sin, and what in French might be called *christianisme* (because none of
this could be called Christianity), and it therefore sometimes seemed to her
that things could be no better—nor, indeed, ought they to be so in view of
her perversity and impenitence—and that it all served her right. Yet, in fact
—though the children never became aware of this—in fact, it was quite the
reverse: Their whole beings shuddered and fermented, utterly bewildered by

their parents' attitude to them whenever they were there—whenever they returned "to the house," rather than returning "home."

Their father's rare jokes invariably failed and sometimes were misdirected. He was aware of this and sensed that the children realized it also. A suspicion of sad embarrassment never left his face. When he was irritated he became a stranger—a stranger totally and at the very instant when he lost his self-control. And a stranger awakes no feelings. The children never answered him back.

But for some time now the criticism coming from the nursery and silently present in the children's eyes had found him quite insensitive. He failed to notice it. Totally vulnerable, and somehow unrecognizable and pathetic, *this* father was genuinely terrifying, unlike the merely irritated stranger. He produced more effect on the little girl; his son was less moved.

But their mother bewildered them both. She showered them with caresses and loaded them with gifts and spent hours with them when they least desired her to, and this merely stifled their children's consciences with its undeservedness, and they failed to recognize themselves in the affectionate pet names lavished on them by her thoughtless instinct.

And often, when a calm of rare clarity came to their souls and they ceased inwardly to feel they were criminals—when their consciences were relieved of all the mystery that evaded discovery, like fever before a rash, they saw their mother as aloof, remote from them, and irascible without cause. The postman would come. The letter would be taken to its addressee—Mama. She would take it without a word of thanks. "Off to your room!" The door banged. They quietly hung their heads and miserably surrendered themselves to a long and mournful bewilderment.

At first they would sometimes cry; later, after one especially sharp outburst, they began to take fright; then, over the years, it turned into a concealed and increasingly deep-rooted antagonism.

Everything that passed from parents to children came inopportunely and from outside, elicited not by them but by some external cause—and as is always the case, it had a touch of remoteness and mystery, like whimpering outside the city gates at night when everyone is going to bed.

This circumstance nurtured and educated the children. They were unaware of it because there are few adults even who know and sense what it is that creates, fashions, and binds their own fabric. Life initiates very few people into the secret of what it is doing with them. It loves its purpose too well, and as it works it speaks only to those who wish it success and love its workbench. No one has power to assist it, though anyone can hinder it. And how might one hinder it? For instance, if a tree was entrusted with the care of its own growth, it might sprout uncontrollably, become totally absorbed in its own roots, or squander itself on a single leaf, because it has forgotten the surrounding universe, which should serve as a model, and in producing one thing in a thousand it will start to produce thousands of that one thing.

And to guard against dead branches in the soul—to prevent its growth from being retarded and man from involving his own stupidity in the formation of his immortal essence—several things have been introduced to divert his vulgar curiosity away from life, which dislikes working in his presence and tries every means to avoid him. For this purpose all proper religions were introduced, all general concepts and all human prejudices, and the most resplendent of these, and the most entertaining—*psychology.*

The children had already emerged from primordial infancy. The concepts of punishment, retribution, reward, and justice had in a childish way already penetrated their souls, distracting their consciousnesses and allowing life to do with them whatever it thought most necessary, impressive, and lovely.

II

Miss Hawthorn would not have done so. But in one of her bouts of gratuitous tenderness toward the children *Madame* Luvers had spoken harshly to the English governess on some utterly trifling pretext, and the latter had disappeared from the house. Shortly, and somehow imperceptibly, her place was taken by a weakly French girl. Afterward, Zhenya could recall only that the French girl had looked like a fly, and that nobody liked her. Her name was lost completely, and Zhenya could not even tell which syllables and sounds one might have to search among to come across the name again. She remembered only that the French girl had first shouted at her, then taken scissors and shorn away the patch of bearskin that was bloodstained.

It seemed to her that now people would always shout at her, her head would ache continually and never clear, and she would nevermore understand that page in her favorite book, which now dully swam together before her gaze like her lesson book after lunch.

That day was terribly drawn out. Mama was away that day. Zhenya was not sorry. She even believed she was glad at her mother's absence.

Soon that long day was consigned to oblivion among the forms of the *passé* and the *futur antérieur,* watering the hyacinths, and walks along the Sibirskaya and Okhanskaya. Indeed, so forgotten was that day that she only noticed and sensed the duration of the other, the second in her life, toward the evening, as she read by lamplight and the lazily advancing narrative suggested hundreds of quite idle thoughts to her. Whenever she later recalled that house on the Osinskaya where they lived then, she always imagined it just as she had seen it in the evening of that second long day. It certainly had been long. It was spring outside. Sickly and ripening laboriously at first, spring in the Urals later bursts through broad and vigorous in the course of a single night, and it continues broad and vigorous thereafter. The lamps only highlighted the emptiness of the evening air. They gave no light but swelled up inside like sickly fruits, with a clear and lackluster dropsy that distended their dilated shades. They went missing. They turned up in their places, where they should have been, on tables and coming down from stucco ceilings in the rooms where the girl was used to seeing them. And yet the lamps had far less to do with the rooms than with the spring sky to which they seemed to have been thrust close, like drinking water to the bedside of an invalid. At heart they were out there in the street, where the servants' babbling teemed in the wet earth, and where the now sparse droplets of melting snow froze and congealed for the night. Here was where the lamps disappeared in the evenings. Their parents were away. But Mama was apparently expected that day. On that long day, or in the next few days. Yes, probably. Or maybe she had arrived suddenly, unawares . . . Maybe that was it.

Zhenya started getting into bed and saw that the day had been long for the same reason as before, and at first she was about to think of taking scissors and shearing those pieces out of her nightdress and the sheet. But then she decided to take some of the French girl's powder and rub them white, and she had already seized the powder box when in came the French girl and slapped her. Her entire sin became concentrated in the powder.

"She's powdering herself! That really is the limit!"

Now at last she realized. She had noticed it for some time already.

Zhenya burst into tears from the slapping, the shouting, and a sense of injury, and because, while she felt innocent of what the French girl suspected, she knew she had done something that—this was what she *felt*— that was far viler than her suspicions. She had to—she sensed it with stupefying urgency, sensed it in her calves and temples—without knowing why or wherefore, she had to conceal it at all costs and no matter how. Her joints ached and fused in a total hypnotic suggestion. Tormenting and enervating, this suggestion was the work of her organism, which concealed the meaning of everything from the girl, and behaving like a criminal, made her imagine this bleeding was some foul and revolting form of evil. *Menteuse!* She could only deny it and stubbornly disavow the thing that was most vile of all—somewhere between the shame of illiteracy and the disgrace of a scene in the street. She could only shudder, grit her teeth, and press herself against the wall, choking with tears. She could not throw herself into the Kama, because it was still cold and the last ice floes were still floating down the river.

Neither she nor the French girl heard the bell in time. The commotion they raised disappeared into the density of the deep brown skins, and when mother came in it was already too late. She found her daughter in tears and the French girl blushing. She demanded an explanation. The French girl announced straightway that—not Zhenya but *votre enfant,* she said—that *her daughter* was powdering herself, and that she had noticed and suspected this for some time already. Mama did not allow her to finish—her horror was genuine: The girl was still not yet thirteen.

"Zhenya—you? . . . Good Lord, what have things come to?" (Her mother imagined at that moment that these words actually meant something, as though she had known earlier that her daughter was degenerating but she had failed to take measures in time and now she found her sunk to this depth.) "Zhenya, tell me the whole truth . . . It'll be the worse! . . . What were you doing . . .?"—"With the powder box?" *Madame* Luvers probably meant to say, but in fact she said, "with this thing?"—and she seized "this thing" and waved it in the air.

"Mama, don't believe *Mademoiselle;* I never . . ."—and she burst into sobs.

But her mother detected in this weeping a certain note of malice, which was not really there; she sensed that she herself was to blame and was inwardly terrified of herself; she would have to set everything right, she believed: Even against her maternal instincts she must "show herself capable of taking prudent educative measures." She decided not to yield to sympathy. She proposed to wait till this flood of tears that so tormented her subsided.

And she sat down on the bed and directed her serene and vacant gaze at the edge of the bookshelf. She smelled of expensive perfume. When her daughter had recovered herself, she began once more to ply her with questions. Zhenya cast a tearful glance toward the window and gave a sob. The ice was moving downstream and, presumably, crackling. A star shimmered. The deserted night showed rough and black and was malleable, chill, but unchanging. Zhenya looked away from the window. A note of threatening impatience sounded in her mother's voice. The French girl stood against the wall, all solemnity and concentrated pedagogy. Her hand was in adjutant pose, resting on her watch ribbon. Zhenya once more glanced at the stars and at the Kama. She had made up her mind. Despite the cold and the ice floes. And—in she plunged. Getting tangled in her words, she gave her mother an unlikely and terror-stricken account of *it.* Mother let her finish only because she was struck by how much feeling the child put into her story. Indeed, she understood everything from Zhenya's very first word. No, not even that: from the way the little girl gulped deeply as she started her tale. Mother listened, rejoicing, loving, and consumed with tenderness for this slender little body. She felt like throwing her arms around her daughter's neck and weeping. But—educational principle! She rose from the bed and pulled back the bedspread. She called her daughter to her and began to stroke her head very slowly, very gently.

"Good girl . . ." The words came rattling out. She swept noisily over to the window and turned away from the two of them.

Zhenya could not see the French girl. Only tears, only her mother— filling the whole room.

"Who makes the bed?"

It was a senseless question. The girl gave a shudder. She was sorry for Grusha. Then in the French tongue, she knew, something was said by a tongue she failed to recognize: harsh words. Then, again to her, in quite a different voice: "Zhenya dear, go down to the dining room, darling, and I'll come myself right away, and I'll tell you what a lovely *dacha* Daddy and I have taken for you . . . for us, for the summer."

The lamps were again themselves, as in winter, at home with the Luvers —warm, zealous, faithful. Mama's sable frisked across the blue wool table-cloth. "Won—remaining Blagodat—await end Holy Week . . ." The rest could not be read—the telegram was folded over at the corner. Zhenya sat down on the end of the settee, tired and happy. She sat down modestly and correctly, just as she sat six months later on the end of a cold brown bench in the corridor of the Ekaterinburg *lycée,* when she gained top marks for her answers in the Russian orals and was told she "may go."

The next morning Mother told her what she must do on such occasions —it was nothing serious, she need not be afraid, it would keep on happen-ing. She mentioned nothing by name and gave no explanation, but added that from now on she would be giving her daughter lessons, because she would not be going away again.

The French girl was dismissed for negligence, having spent only a few months in the family. When a cab had been hired for her and she started down the stairs, she met the doctor coming up on the landing. He responded to her bow in most unfriendly fashion and spoke no word of farewell; she guessed he must know everything already. She frowned and shrugged her shoulders.

In the doorway stood the maid who had been waiting to let in the doctor, so that in the hall where Zhenya stood the ring of footsteps and echoed answer of the stone sounded on for longer than it should. And this was how the story of her maidhood's first maturity imprinted itself on her memory: the resonant echo of the chirruping morning street, which lingered on the stair and freshly penetrated into the house, the French girl, the maid, and the doctor—two criminals and one initiate, bathed and disinefected by the daylight, chill, and sonority of shuffling steps.

It was a warm and sunny April. "Your feet—wipe your feet!"—the bright, bare corridor echoed the words from end to end. The bearskins were packed away for the summer. The rooms rose clean and transformed, and sighed sweetly with relief. Throughout the day, throughout the wearisome, unsetting, clinging day in all the corners, in all the rooms, in panes left leaning by the wall, and in mirrors, glasses of water, and the blue air of the garden, the blinking, preening cherry blossom laughed and raged and the honeysuckle choked and bubbled insatiably, unquenchably. The boring chatter of the courtyards continued around the clock; they announced the overthrow of night, and all day long their fine patter kept swelling forth and acting like a sleeping potion, reiterating that there would be no more evening, and that no one would be allowed to sleep. "Feet, feet!"—but they arrived hotfoot. They came in intoxicated from the open air with ringing in their ears, so they failed to understand properly what was said and rushed in to gulp and chew as fast as possible before shifting their chairs with an agonizing crash and running back once more into that soaring daylight that forced its way through suppertime, where drying wood gave out its brittle tapping, where the blue chirruped piercingly and the earth gleamed greasily like baked milk. The boundary between house and courtyard was erased. The floorcloth failed to wash off all the footprints. Floors were streaked with dry, light-colored daubs and crunched underfoot.

Father brought them sweets and other marvels. A wonderfully good mood filled the house. Moistly rustling, the stones gave warning of their appearance through the gradually coloring tissue paper, which grew more and more transparent as these packets, white and soft as gauze, were unwrapped layer by layer. Some of them were like drops of almond milk, others—like splashes of blue watercolor, while others resembled a solidified tear of cheese. Some were blind, somnolent, or dreamy, while others had a gay sparkle like the frozen juice of blood oranges. One feared to touch them. They were lovely, displayed on the frothing paper, which exuded them like the dark juice of a plum.

Father was unusually affectionate to the children and often accompanied Mother into town. They would return together and seemed full of joy. Most of all, both were serene in spirit, even-tempered, and friendly, and when Mother on odd occasions cast a playfully reproachful glance at Father, it seemed as though she drew tranquillity from his small and ugly eyes in order then to pour it forth from her own, large and beautiful, upon the children and those around them.

Once their parents rose very late. Then for some unknown reason they decided to go and have lunch on a steamer anchored by the harbor, and they took the children with them. Seryozha was allowed to taste some cold beer. All this pleased them so, they went for lunch on the steamer again. The children could not recognize their parents. What had happened to them? The little girl lived in a state of uncomprehending bliss and imagined that now life would always be like this. They were not downcast when told that they would not be taken to the *dacha* this summer. Soon their father left.

There appeared in the house three huge, yellow trunks with stout metal bands around them.

III

The train departed late at night. Mr. Luvers had moved one month before and had written that the apartment was ready. Several cabs went jogging down to the station. One could tell when they were nearing it by the color of the road. It turned black and the streetlights struck against brown iron. At that moment a view of the Kama opened up from the viaduct, and a pit, black as soot, all heavy mass and panic, crashed open beneath them and escaped. It darted away again, and there in the distance at its farthest reach it took fright, rolled off, and trembled with the winking beads of signals far away.

It was windy. The outlines fled from cottages and fences like the frame from the grating of a sieve, and they rippled and fluttered in the churning air. There was a smell of potato. Their cabman edged out from the line of baskets and carriage backs that jogged ahead and began to overtake them. From a distance they recognized the dray with their own luggage. They drew even. Ulyasha shouted loudly to her mistress from the cart but was drowned out by the jolting wheels, and she shook and leaped up and down, and her voice leaped too.

With the novelty of all these nocturnal noises, blacknesses, and freshness the little girl was unaware of sadness. Far, far away, something loomed black and mysterious. Beyond the huts of the harbor, lights were bobbing: The town was rinsing them in the water from boats and shore. Then there were a lot of them, and they swarmed dense and greasy, blind as worms. At the Lyubimov wharf the funnels, warehouse roofs, and decks were a sober blue. Barges lay gazing at the stars. "This is a rat hole," thought Zhenya. They were surrounded by workmen in white. Seryozha was first to jump down. He looked around and was astonished to see that the drayman with their baggage was also here already. The horse threw back its muzzle, its collar rose and reared up like a rooster, the horse leaned against the rear and began to backstep. And he had been wondering the whole journey how far behind the others would be. . . .

The young boy stood in his clean, white school shirt, reveling in the imminence of their journey. Traveling was a novelty for both of them, but he already knew and loved the words "depot," "locomotive," "sidings," "through carriage," and the sound pattern of the word "class" seemed to have a bittersweet taste. His sister enjoyed all this too, but in her own way, without the boyish methodicalness that distinguished her brother's enthusiasms.

Suddenly Mother appeared at their side, as though sprung from a hole in the ground. She gave instructions to take the children along to the buffet.

She then strutted off proudly through the crowd and went straight to the man who was first referred to in the open air by the loud and menacing title of "stationmaster," and who was often later mentioned in varied tones in various places by a variety of people in the throng.

They were overcome by yawning. They were seated at one of those windows, so dusty, standoffish, and huge that they seemed like some institutions made of bottle glass where you had to remove your hat. The little girl looked through the window: She saw not a street but another room, only more serious and gloomy than the one here—in this decanter; into this other room engines slowly came and stopped, spreading darkness, but when they left and cleared the room, it turned out not to be a room, because there was the sky, behind the pillars, and on the far side—a hill and wooden houses with people going away toward them; perhaps the cocks were crowning there right now, and the water-carrier had recently been and left a trail of sludge. . . .

This was a provincial station without the commotion and the glow of those in the capital; departing passengers turned up in good time from the benighted town; there were long waits, silence, and migrants sleeping on the floor, surrounded by their hunting dogs, trunks, engines packed in bast, and uncovered bicycles.

The children settled down on the top bunks. The boy fell asleep immediately. The train was still standing. It was getting light, and gradually the little girl realized that the coach was dark blue, clean, and chilly. And gradually she realized . . . But she too was now asleep.

He was a very portly man. He read his newspaper and swayed about. One glance at him was sufficient to reveal the swaying, which flooded the whole compartment like the sunshine. Zhenya surveyed him from above with the lazy attentiveness of a newcomer, fully awakened, who thinks about or looks at something but continues to lie there only because he is waiting for the decision to get up to come of its own accord without assistance, clear and unforced like the rest of his thoughts. She surveyed him and wondered where he had come from to sit in their compartment, and when he had managed to wash and dress. She had no idea of the real time of day. She had only just woken, so it must be morning. She observed him, but he could not see her: The upper birth sloped in toward the wall. He could not see her, because occasionally he too glanced up from the news, or aslant, or sideways, and when he looked up at her bunk their eyes never met: He either saw only the matress or else . . . but she quickly tucked them up beneath her and pulled her slackened stockings up again. "Mama is in this corner: She has already tidied up and is reading a book," Zhenya decided indirectly by studying the fat man's gaze. "But Seryozha is not down there either. So where is he?"—and she yawned sweetly and stretched. "It is terribly hot" —she realized it only now and glanced down from the head of the bunk at the half-lowered window. "But where is the earth?"—the question gaped inside her soul.

What she saw was beyond description. The sighing hazel grove into which their train was sliding snakelike had become an ocean, a whole world —anything and everything. It ran downward, bright and murmuring, broad and sloping, then fragmenting, condensing, and glooming, it fell away sharply, already completely black. And the thing that rose there on the far side of the chasm resembled some enormous green-yellow thundercloud, all curling and whirling, lost in thought and stupefied. Zhenya held her breath and immediately felt the swiftness of the boundless and oblivious air— immediately she realized that the storm cloud was some country, some locality, and that it had a loud and mountainous name that had rolled all around and been cast with stones and sand down into the valley; she realized that the hazel grove was aware only of whispering and whispering that name—here and there, and awa-a-a-ay over there—only that name.

"Is this the Urals?" she asked the whole compartment, leaning over.

She spent the entire remainder of the journey by the window in the corridor and never left it. She clung to it and constantly leaned out. She was greedy. She discovered that looking backward was much more pleasant than looking forward. Majestic acquaintances misted over and receded into the distance. And after a brief separation from them, during which cold air blew down the nape of your neck as grinding chains served up some new marvel right before you with a precipitous roar, you began to search for them again. The mountain panorama expanded outward, constantly grow- ing and enlarging. Some of them blackened, others brightened. Some of them spread dark, while others darkened. They met and parted, fell and rose again. All this was accomplished in a slow-moving circle, like the rotation of the stars, with the careful restraint of titans one hair's breadth from catastrophe, with a concern for the world's entirety. And these com- plex movements were ruled by a steady, mighty roar that eluded the human ear and was all-seeing. It surveyed them with eagle eye. Mute and obscure, it held them in review. Thus the Urals were built, rebuilt, and built up yet again.

She went to the compartment for a moment, eyes screwed up with the harsh lighting. Mama was chatting with the strange gentleman and laugh- ing. Seryozha was shifting restlessly about the crimson plush and holding on by a wall strap. Mama spat the last seed out into her clenched fist, brushed off her dress the ones she had dropped, then bent forward lithely and swiftly and flung all the rubbish under the seat. Contrary to expectation, the fat man had a husky, cracked little voice. He apparently suffered from shortness of breath. Mother introduced Zhenya to him and handed her a mandarin orange. He was amusing and probably a kind man, and as he talked he constantly lifted a plump hand to his mouth. His speech would often swell up and then break off, suddenly constricted. It turned out that he himself was from Ekaterinburg, had traveled the length and breadth of the Urals and knew them well, and when he took a gold watch from his waistcoat pocket and lifted it right up to his nose before popping it back, Zhenya noticed what kindly fingers he had. As is the nature of stout people, he took things with a gesture of actually giving, and all the time his hand kept sighing as if proffered for someone to kiss, and bobbing gently as though bouncing a ball on the floor.

"It won't be long now"—he squinted, and though addressing the boy, he spoke away from him and puffed out his lips.

"You know, there's a post, they say, on the frontier of Asia and Europe, and it has 'Asia' written on it," Seryozha exclaimed, as he slid off the seat and ran out into the corridor.

Zhenya had understood nothing, and when the fat gentleman explained things to her, she too ran out to the same side to wait for the post, fearing she had already missed it. In her enchanted head, the "frontier of Asia" arose in the form of some phantasmagoric barrier, like those iron bars, perhaps, which laid down a strip of terrible, pitch-black, stinking danger between the public and the cage with pumas in it. She awaited that post as if it was the curtain rising on the first act of a geographical tragedy, which she had heard many tales about from witnesses, and she was full of solemn excitement to think that now she too had come and would shortly see it for herself.

But meanwhile the thing that had compelled her to rejoin the adults in the compartment still continued monotonously: There was no foreseeable end to the gray alder through which the railroad had started half an hour before, and nature was making no preparations for what shortly awaited her. Zhenya was annoyed by dull and dusty Europe for sluggishly withholding the appearance of the miracle. And how put out she was when, as if in answer to Seryozha's furious shriek, something resembling a small tombstone flashed past the window, turned sideways to them, then rushed away, bearing the long-awaited, fairy-tale name off into the alders and away from more alders that came chasing after! At that instant, as if by arrangement, several heads leaned out of the windows of all classes, and the train came alive as it raced down the slope in a cloud of dust. Asia had already claimed at least a score of versts, but kerchiefs on flying heads still fluttered, people exchanged glances, there were men clean-shaven or with a growth of beard, and they all flew along through clouds of swirling sand. On and on they flew past the same dusty alders, which recently had been European, and were for some time now already Asian.

IV

Life began afresh. Milk was not brought around to the kitchen by a delivery girl; it was brought each morning by Ulyasha, two cans at a time, together with special loaves, quite different from the ones in Perm. The pavements here were made of something like marble or alabaster and had an undulating white gloss. Even in the shade, the flagstones dazzled one like icy suns, avidly engulfing the shadows of the elegant trees, which flowed away, melting on them and liquefying. Here there was quite a different way out onto the street, which was broad and bright and planted with trees.

"Just like Paris," Zhenya said, echoing her father.

He said that on the very first day of their arrival. Everything was fine and spacious. Father had had a snack before leaving for the station and did not share their dinner. His place at the table stayed clean and bright, like Ekaterinburg, and he merely unfolded his napkin and sat sideways and told some story. He unbuttoned his waistcoat, and his shirt front curved outward, fresh and vigorous. He said this was a splendid European-style town, and he rang for them to clear away and serve the next course—rang, and continued talking. And down unknown passages from rooms still unknown there came a silent maid in white, all starched and pleated, with neat black hair; she was addressed in a formal manner, and though new, she smiled at the mistress and children as though they were already friends. She was given some instructions regarding Ulyasha, who was out there in the unknown and probably exceedingly dark kitchen, where no doubt there was a window from which something new could be seen—some belfry or other, or a road, or birds. And perhaps Ulyasha was there right now, asking this lady questions and putting on her old clothes to begin unpacking their things; she would be asking questions, making herself at home, and looking to see which corner the stove was in—the same place as in Perm or somewhere else. . . .

The boy heard from his father that it was not far to the *lycée*—quite near, in fact—they must have seen it as they rode past. Father drank some Narzan water, swallowed and continued, "Didn't I show you? Well, you can't see it from here. Maybe you can from the kitchen (he made a mental estimate), but even then only the roof."

He drank some more Narzan and rang.

The kitchen turned out to be fresh and bright, exactly—it seemed to the little girl a minute later—exactly as she had guessed and imagined in the dining room: a tiled range with a whitish blue luster, and two windows, in just the order she expected. Ulyasha had slipped something on over her bare arms; the room was filled with children's voices; people were walking on the roof of the *lycée,* and the tops of scaffolding poles were showing.

"Yes, it's being repaired," Father said, when they had all filed shouting and jostling down the now discovered but still unexplored passage back to the dining room. She would have to visit the passage again tomorrow, when she had laid out her notebooks, hung up her wash glove by its loop—in fact, when she had completed all the thousand and one jobs that had to be done.

"Stupendous butter!" said Mother, sitting down.

The children went through into the classroom they had first inspected immediately on arriving, while still wearing their hats.

"What is it that makes this Asia?" she wondered aloud.

For some reason Seryozha failed to grasp what he would certainly have understood at any other time: Up till now they had lived as a pair. He turned away toward the map that hung there and ran his hand down over the Ural range. He glanced at her, and she seemed crushed by this argument.

"They agreed to mark out a natural frontier, that's all."

But then she recalled the noon of that same day, already so distant. She could not believe that a day that had all this packed into it—this actual day, now in Ekaterinburg, and even then not all of it—was still not over yet. At the thought that all this had retreated to its appointed distance and still preserved its own lifeless order, she experienced an amazing sense of spiritual fatigue, such as one's body feels toward evening after a working day. It was as if she too had assisted in shifting and removing all that weight of beautiful objects and had overstrained herself. For some reason she was certain that *they*, her Urals, were *there*, and she turned and ran off to the kitchen via the dining room, where the crockery had now grown less, although the stupendous iced butter on its perspiring maple leaves and the angry mineral water still remained.

The *lycée* was being repaired, and strident martins ripped the air like seamstresses tearing madapollam with their teeth, and down below—she leaned out—the carriage gleamed by the open coach house, sparks showered from the grinding wheel, and there was the smell of all the food they had eaten, better and more interesting than when it was served up, a persistent and melancholy smell, as in a book. She forgot why she had come running in, and failed to notice that her Urals were not there in Ekaterinburg, but she did notice that gradually, house by house, darkness was descending on Ekaterinburg, and that down in the room below they were singing, probably over some light task—probably they had washed the floor and were laying down the bast mats with their hot hands—and they were teeming water from the washing-up tub; yet, though the teeming came from below, how silent it was all around! And the tap was gurgling there like . . .

"Well now, miss . . ." (but she was still avoiding the new maid and would not listen to her)—like . . . (she was finishing her thought)—down below them they knew and were probably saying, "That's the new people come to number two today."

Ulyasha came into the kitchen.

The children slept soundly that first night, and they woke—Seryozha in Ekaterinburg and Zhenya in Asia—again the strange and broad-spreading thought occurred to her. The light played freshly on the flaky alabaster of the ceiling.

It began while it was still summer. She was notified that she would be going to the *lycée*. This was entirely pleasant. But she was notified of it! She had not invited the teacher into the classroom where sunlight hues stuck so firmly to the walls with their glue-paint wash that only by drawing blood was the evening able to rip away the clinging daylight. She had not invited him when he came in accompanied by Mama to make the acquaintance of "my future pupil." She had not given him the ridiculous surname Dikikh. And was it by her wish that from now on the soldiers always drilled at midday, stern, snorting, and sweaty, like the scarlet convulsions of a tap when the water pipes are out of order? Or that their boots were trampled by a violet thundercloud that knew far more about guns and wheels than their white shirts, white tents, and white, white officers knew? Had she asked for two objects, a basin and a napkin, to be forever now combining like carbons in an arc lamp and evoking a third thing, which instantly evaporated: the idea of death—like that sign outside the barber's where it first occurred to her? And was it with her consent that the red turnpikes with "stopping prohibited" had become the site of some illicitly halting urban secrets, and the Chinese—something personally dreadful, peculiar to Zhenya and terrible? Of course, not everything settled so heavily on her soul. There was much that was pleasant, like her forthcoming start at the *lycée*. But as in this case, all these were things of which she was notified. Ceasing to be a poetical trifle, life began to ferment as a stern, black story since it had become prose and was transformed into fact. Dull, painful, and somber, as though in an eternal state of sobering up, the elements of every-day existence entered her shaping spirit. They sank deep into it, real, solidified, and cold like sleepy pewter spoons. There at the bottom, this pewter began to melt, congealing into lumps, forming into droplets of obsessive ideas.

V

Belgians often began to appear at the house for tea. That was what they were called. That was what father called them. "Today the Belgians will be here," he would say. There were four of them. The clean-shaven one came only seldom and was not talkative. Sometimes he would pay a chance visit alone on a weekday, and he always chose nasty, rainy weather. The other three were inseparable. Their faces resembled cakes of fresh soap, unstarted, straight from the wrapper, fragrant and cold. One of them had a beard, thick and fluffy, and downy chestnut hair. They always turned up in Father's company from some meeting. Everyone in the house liked them. They talked like spilling water on the tablecloth—noisily, freshly, and all at once, away to one side where no one expected, and their jokes and stories, which were always understood by the children, always thirst-quenching and clean, left trails behind, which took a long time to dry out.

Noise arose from all around, and the sugar bowl, nickel coffeepot, clean, strong teeth, and thick linen gleamed. They joked amiably and courteously with Mother. As Father's colleagues, they had the subtle ability to restrain him in time whenever he responded to their fleeting hints and mentions of matters and men known only to themselves, the professionals sitting there, and began to speak at length in his ponderous, hesitant, and very impure French of contractors, *références approuvées,* and *férocités,* that is, *bestialités, ce que veut dire en russe* embezzlements on the Blagodat.

For some time past, one of them had taken up the study of Russian, and he often tried himself out in this new pursuit, but it still eluded him. It was awkward to laugh at their father's French periods, and his *férocités* were genuinely irksome to everybody, yet the very situation seemed to sanctify the merry laughter that greeted Negaraat's attempts.

Negaraat was his name. He was a Walloon from the Flemish part of Belgium. They recommended Dikikh to him. He noted down his address in Russian, comically tracing out the complicated letters like "ю", "я ," and " ѣ." These somehow came out in two parts, unmatching and spread-eagled. The children took the liberty of kneeling on the leather cushions of the armchair and putting their elbows on the table—everything was permitted. And everything was mixed up: "ю" was not "ю," but a sort of figure ten. There was roaring and laughter all around; Evans banged on the table with his fist; Father shook and went all red as he paced about the room saying, "No, I can't bear it!" and crumpling up his handkerchief.

"Faites de nouveau," said Evans, piling on the agony. "Commencez."

And Negaraat kept opening his mouth, hesitating like someone who stammers, and pondering how best to deliver himself of this Russian letter "ы," as unchartable as colonies in the Congo.

"Dites, 'uvý,' 'nyevýgodno,' " father suggested moistly and hoarsely, losing his voice.

"Ouvoui, niévoui."

"Entends-tu?—Ouvoui, niévoui—ouvoui, niévoui. Oui, oui—chose inouïe, charmant!" the Belgians exclaimed, bursting out in a fit of laughter.

The summer went by. Examinations were passed successfully—some even excellently. The cold, transparent noise of the passages streamed as though from a spring. Here they all knew one another. In the garden leaves turned yellow and gold. The classroom windows languished in their bright, dancing reflection. The semifrosted panes were misty and agitated in their lower portions, while the casements were racked by a blue convulsion. Their chill clarity was furrowed by the bronze twigs of maple.

She did not know that all her anxieties would be turned into such a merry joke. Divide this number of yards and inches into seven! Was it worth going through those measures of weight, the zolotniks, lots, pounds, and poods? And grains, drachmas, scruples, and ounces, which always seemed to her like the four ages of a scorpion? Why was the word " полезный " written with an "e" and not a " ѣ "? She had difficulty answering only because all her powers of reasoning were concentrated on an effort to imagine on what unfortunate grounds the word " полѣзный " might ever occur—so wild and shaggy did it appear in this rendering. She never learned why she was not sent to the *lycée* there and then, though she had been accepted and registered and her coffee-colored uniform was already being sewn, later to be meanly and boringly tried on with pins for hours at a time, and in her room new horizons were introduced, such as a bag, a pencil case, a lunch basket, and a remarkably disgusting eraser.

The Stranger

I

The little girl's head and body were wrapped in a thick woolen shawl, which reached down to her knees, and she strutted up and down the yard like a small hen. Zhenya wanted to go up and talk to the little Tatar girl. At that moment the two sides of a small window flew open with a bang. "Kolka!" called Aksinya. Looking like a peasant's bundle with felt boots hastily stuck into the bottom, the child toddled quickly to the janitor's lodge.

To take any schoolwork outside always meant grinding away at the footnote to some rule till it was blunt and had lost all meaning, and then going upstairs and beginning everything again indoors. The rooms inside seized one at the doorstep with their peculiar semigloom and chill, and with that peculiar, always unexpected familiarity of furniture that has taken up its allotted position once and for all and remained there. One could not foretell the future, but it could be glimpsed on entering the house from outside. Here its scheme was already in evidence—a distribution to which it would be subject despite its recalcitrance in all else. And there was no sleepiness induced by the moving outdoor air that could not be shaken off quickly by the fatal, cheery spirit of the house, which struck one of a sudden from the threshold of the hall.

This time it was Lermontov. Zhenya creased up the book with its binding folded inward. Had Seryozha done that indoors, she herself would have been up in arms about this "disgraceful habit." Outside it was quite another matter.

Prokhor put the ice-freezer on the ground and went back into the house. As he opened the door of the Spitsyns' hallway, there rolled forth the devilish, blustering bark of the general's little hairless dogs. The door slammed to with a brief tinkle.

Meanwhile the River Terek, "springing like a lioness with shaggy mane on back," continued to roar, as it should, and the only doubt that began to trouble Zhenya was whether it was really on its back, rather than its spine, that all this was happening. She was too lazy to follow the book, and "golden clouds from southern lands afar" had hardly had time to "accompany the Terek northward" when there they were to meet him at the general's kitchen doorstep holding a bucket and bast scrubber.

The batman set down the bucket, bent over, and after taking apart the freezer, proceeded to wash it. The August sunlight burst through the tree foliage and came to rest on the soldier's hindquarters. It settled, red, in the faded cloth of his uniform and greedily impregnated it like turpentine.

The courtyard was a broad one, complex and oppressive, with intricate nooks and corners. Paved in the center, it had not been resurfaced for many a long day, and the cobbles were thickly overgrown with short, curly grass, which in the afternoon emitted the sort of bitter medicinal smell that hangs around hospitals in hot weather. At one end, between the janitor's lodge and the coach house, the courtyard bordered on someone else's garden.

It was here, beyond the woodpile, that Zhenya headed. She propped the ladder from below with a flat billet of wood to prevent it from sliding, shook it into place among the shifting logs, then took up an uncomfortable but interesting perch on the middle rung, as though this were some outdoor game. Then she got up, climbed a little higher, and laid her book on the top row of logs, which had been partly removed, and prepared to start "The Demon" once again. Then, finding it was better sitting where she was earlier, she climbed down again, forgetting her book on top of the woodpile, and she failed to remember it because she had just noticed beyond the garden something she had never imagined was there, and she sat open-mouthed and entranced.

There were no bushes in the other garden, and as the age-old trees raised their lower branches up into the foliage as though into a night sky, they laid the garden bare below, even though it stood there and never emerged from its permanent state of solemn, airy semigloom. Fork-trunked, mauve as a thunderstorm, and covered with gray lichen, they provided a good view of the little-used deserted alleyway that the other garden gave on to on the far side. There was yellow acacia growing there. Now the shrubbery was drying, curling up and shedding.

Borne through the gloomy garden from this world to the other, the faraway alley glowed with the light that illuminates events in a dream—very brightly, very minutely and noiselessly, as if the sun over there had put on spectacles and was fumbling among the buttercups.

But what was Zhenya gaping at so?—She was gazing at her discovery, which intrigued her much more than those who had helped her to make it.

There must be a bench over there, beyond the gate in the street? . . . In a street like that! "Lucky people!" She envied those unknown girls. There were three of them.

They showed up black, like the word "anchorite" in the song. The three even necks with hair combed up under three round hats leaned as if the one at the end, half hidden by a bush, was sleeping propped on her elbow, while the other two also slept, huddling against her. The hats were a dark gray-blue and kept flashing in the sun, then fading, like insects. They were tied about with black crepe. At that moment the three strangers all turned their heads the other way. Something had, no doubt, attracted their attention at the far end of the street. For a minute they looked toward the far end— just as people look in summer when an instant is dissolved in light and extended, and you have to screw up your eyes and shield them with the palm of your hand—for just a minute they looked; then they relapsed into their former state of corporate dozing.

Zhenya was on the point of returning but suddenly missed her book and could not immediately recall where she had left it. She turned back for it, and on going around the woodpile, she saw that the strangers had gotten up and were about to leave. One by one in turn they came through the gate. A short man followed after them, walking with a strange crippled gait. Under his arm he carried an enormous album or atlas. So that was what they had been doing, peering over one another's shoulders! And she had thought they were asleep! Their neighbors came through the garden and disappeared behind the outbuildings. The sun was already sinking. As she retrieved her book Zhenya disturbed the stack of logs. The whole pile awoke and stirred as though alive. A few logs rolled down and fell onto the turf with a gentle thump. This served as a signal, like the night watchman's rattle. Evening was born, and with it a multitude of noises, soft and misty. The air began to whistle some old-time melody from across the river.

The courtyard was empty. Prokhor had completed his work. He had gone out through the gate. Low down, just above the grass, there spread the melancholy twang and strumming of a soldier's balalaika. Above her a fine swarm of quiet midges weaved and danced, plunged and fell, hanging in the air, fell and hung again, then without touching the ground rose up once more. But the strumming of the balalaika was finer and quieter still. It sank earthward lower than the swarm of midges, and without getting dusty soared aloft again more easily and airily than they, shimmering and breaking off, dipping and rising unhurriedly.

Zhenya returned to the house. "Lame . . ."—she was thinking of the stranger with the album—"Lame, but one of the gentry—no crutches." She went in through the back entrance. Outside in the yard there was a persistent sickly smell of chamomile infusion. "Lately Mama has built up quite a pharmacy—a mass of dark blue bottles with yellow caps." She slowly mounted the stairs. The iron banister was cold; the steps grated in response to her shuffling. Suddenly something strange occurred to her. She strode up two steps at once and halted on the third. It occurred to her that recently there had been a certain elusive similarity between Mama and the janitor's wife. Something quite indefinable. She stopped. Something like . . . She paused to think. Maybe something like what people mean when they say "We are all human," or "We are all cast in the same mold," or "Fate makes equals of us all . . ." With the tip of her toe she knocked aside a bottle lying there; it flew down and fell among some dusty bags and did not break. . . . Something, in fact, that was very common, common to all people. But then, why not between herself and Aksinya? Or Aksinya, say, and Ulyasha? This seemed to Zhenya all the stranger because it was difficult to find two people more dissimilar: There was something earthy about Aksinya, something of the kitchen garden, something reminiscent of potatoes swelling or the bluish green of wild pumpkin, whereas Mama . . . Zhenya smiled wrily at the very thought of comparing the two.

Nevertheless, it was Aksinya who set the tone of this compelling comparison. The association was weighted in her favor. The peasant woman gained nothing from it, but the mistress lost. For a brief moment Zhenya had a crazy notion. She had a vision of Mama imbued with a certain plebeian element and pictured her mother saying "salmond" instead of "salmon" and "we works" instead of "we work," and, she fancied, what if the day came when she came billowing in, in her new silk negligee, without a sash, and blurted out, "Thee lean it up agin't door!"?

There was a smell of medicine in the corridor. Zhenya went along to her father.

II

The house was being refurnished. Luxury made its appearance. The Luvers acquired a carriage and began to keep horses. The coachman was called Davletsha.

At that time rubber tires were a complete novelty. Whenever they drove out everyone turned around to follow the carriage with his eyes—people, fences, churches, cockerels . . .

They were a long time in opening the door to *Madame* Luvers, and as the carriage moved off at a walking pace in deference to her, she shouted after them, "Don't go far! Just to the barrier and back. Careful down the hill!"

And a whitish sun starting from the doctor's porch drew away down the street, reached Davletsha's tight and freckled purple neck, heated it and shriveled it.

They drove onto the bridge. The chatter of its boards was heard, cunning, rounded and coherent, composed once to last for all time, reverently incised by the ravine and memorable to it always, at noonday and in sleep.

Vykormysh, the homebred animal, climbed the hill and was starting on the steep, unyielding flint. He strained but was incapable. His scrambling was suddenly reminiscent of a locust crawling—and like this creature, which by nature flies and leaps, he assumed a lightning beauty in the humiliation of his unnatural efforts. . . . At any moment, it seemed, he would lose patience, flash his wings in anger, and soar away. And, in fact, the horse did give a tug, threw out his forelegs, and set off across the wasteland in a short gallop. Davletsha began to draw him in by shortening the reins. A dog barked at them, a decrepit, dull, and shaggy bark. The dust was like gunpowder. The road turned steeply to the left.

The black street ended blindly in the red fencing of the railway depot. It was in alarm. The sun beat sideways from behind the bushes and swathed the crowd of strange figures in women's jackets. The sun drenched them in pelting white light, which seemed to gush like liquid lime from a pail overturned by someone's boot and surged across the earth in a rolling wave. The street was in alarm.

The horse moved at a walk.

"Turn off to the right!" Zhenya ordered.

"There's no way across," Davletsha answered, pointing to the red dead end with his whip handle. "It's a blind alley."

"Stop, then; I'll have a look."

"It's our Chinese."

"So I see."

Realizing that the young mistress did not wish to talk to him, Davletsha sang out a long drawn "Whoaa!" and the horse's whole body heaved as it came to a halt, rooted to the spot. Davletsha began whistling softly and repetitively, with pauses to make the horse do as directed.

The Chinese were running across the road, holding enormous rye loaves. They were dressed in blue and resembled peasant women in trousers. Their bare heads ended in a knot at the crown and looked as though they were twisted together from handkerchiefs. Some of them lingered there, and these could be properly surveyed. Their faces were pale, sallow, and smirking. They were swarthy and dirty, like copper oxidized by poverty.

Davletsha took out his pouch and proceeded to roll a cigarette. At that moment, from the corner where the Chinese men were heading, there came several women. No doubt, they were also going for bread. Those on the road began to laugh loudly and steal up to them, twisting about as though their hands were tied behind their backs with rope. Their squirming movements were especially emphasized by the fact that they were dressed like acrobats in a single garment that covered their whole bodies from collar down to ankles. There was nothing frightening in all this; the women did not run away but stood and laughed.

"Now then, Davletsha, what are you doing?"

"The horse went and jerked! He jerked! Just can't keep still!" Every now and then, Davletsha kept tugging and releasing the reins to give Vykormysh a flick."

"Gently; you'll have us out! Why are you whipping him?"

"I have to."

They drove out into the fields and the horse, which had been on the point of prancing, was calmed, and only then did the wily Tatar, who had brought the mistress away swift as an arrow from that shameful scene, take the reins in his right hand and put the tobacco pouch he still held in his hand back under the flap of his coat.

They returned by another way. *Madame* Luvers had probably spied them from the doctor's window. She came out onto the porch at the very moment when the bridge, which had told them its entire story, started it once more beneath the wheels of the water-carrier's cart.

III

It was during one of the examinations that Zhenya met up with Liza Defendova, the little girl who gathered rowan sprigs on the way to school and brought them into class. The sacristan's daughter was retaking an exam in French. "Luvers, Evgeniya" was placed in the first unoccupied seat. And so they became acquainted, sitting, the two of them, over one and the same sentence:

"Est-ce Pierre qui a volé la pomme?"

"Oui. C'est Pierre qui vola . . ." etc.

The fact that Zhenya was left to study at home did not put an end to the two girls' friendship. They began to meet. But because of Mama's views their meetings were one-sided: Liza was permitted to visit them, while Zhenya for the time being was forbidden to go to the Defendovs.

The sporadic nature of these meetings did not prevent Zhenya from rapidly becoming attached to her friend. She fell in love with her; that is, she played the passive role in their relationship, became its pressure gauge, watchful and excitedly anxious. Any mention by Liza of her classmates whom Zhenya did not know aroused in her a feeling of emptiness and bitterness. Her heart would sink: the fits of first jealousy. For no reason, convinced by the mere force of her own mistrust that Liza was deceiving —though outwardly so direct, she was laughing inwardly at everything about her that was Luvers, and mocking it behind her back, in class and at home—Zhenya accepted all this as her due, as something in the very nature of affection. Her feeling was as random in its choice of an object as its origins were dictated by the powerful demands of instinct, which knows no self-love and can only suffer and consume itself in honor of some fetish as it experiences feeling for the first time.

Neither Zhenya nor Liza had the slightest influence on the other, and they met and parted—Zhenya as Zhenya, Liza as Liza—the one with deep feeling, the other without any.

The Akhmedyanovs' father traded in iron. In the year between the births of Nuretdin and Smagil he became unexpectedly wealthy. Then Smagil started being called Samoyla, and it was decided to give the sons a Russian upbringing. The father did not omit a single feature of the free, nobleman's life-style, and in a ten-year rush through all the points he overshot the mark. The children were a splendid success insofar as they followed the prescribed pattern, and they still retained the speed and sweep of their father's will, noisy and destructive as a pair of flywheels set whirling and left to spin by inertia. The most true-to-type fourth-formers in the fourth form were the brothers Akhmedyanov. They were all broken chalk, crib sheets, lead shot, banging desks, swear words, and red-cheeked, snub-nosed self-assurance that peeled away in frost. Seryozha made friends with them in August. By the end of September the boy had lost all personality. This was quite in the order of things. To be a typical schoolboy and anything else besides meant being at one with the Akhmedyanovs. And Seryozha wanted nothing so much as to be a schoolboy.

Luvers did not try to hinder his son's friendship. He saw no change in him, and even if he did, he ascribed it to the effect of adolescence. Besides, his head was filled with other cares. Some time ago he had begun to suspect that he was ill and that his illness was incurable.

IV

She was sorry, though not for him, though everyone around could only say how really awkward and how incredibly annoying it was. Negàraat was too complicated even for their parents, and all that the parents felt about others also dimly conveyed itself to the children, like spoiled household pets. Zhenya was only saddened by the fact that now not everything would be as before. Now there would be three Belgians, and there would be no more of the laughter they had had before.

She happened to be at table the evening he announced to Mama that he had to go to Dijon for some sort of muster.

"How young you must be then still!" said Mama and immediately began offering all manner of condolences.

He sat there with hanging head. The conversation flagged.

"Tomorrow they are coming to seal the windows," Mama said, and asked him whether she should close them.

He said there was no need, it was a warm evening, and back home they did not even seal them up in winter.

Soon Father came in too. He also expressed effusive regrets on hearing the news. But before starting to lament he raised his eyebrows and said in surprise, "To Dijon? But surely you are Belgian?"

"I am Belgian, but I'm a French subject."

And Negaraat began telling the story of how his "old folk" emigrated— so entertainingly, as though he were not really their son, and with such warmth, as though he were reading from a book about other people.

"Forgive me, I'm going to interrupt you," said Mama. "Zhenya, dear, all the same, do close the window. Vika, they are coming to seal them tomorrow. Well, do carry on. But that uncle of yours was a real scoundrel! Did he really, *literally* under oath . . .?"

"Yes."

And he returned to his interrupted tale. But when he got to the point, that is, the paper he received yesterday from the consulate, he guessed that the little girl understood nothing at all of this and was trying hard to grasp it. Then he turned to her and without revealing his intention, so as not to injure her pride, he began to explain what sort of thing this military service was.

"Yes, yes, I understand. Yes, I understand; I follow," the girl repeated with mechanical gratitude. "Why go so far? Be a soldier here. Train where everyone else does," she corrected herself, vividly imagining the meadows unfolding from the top of the monastery hill.

"Yes, yes, I understand. Yes, yes," the little girl repeated again as the Luvers sat with nothing to do, and thinking that the Belgian was filling the child's head with useless details, they inserted their own sleepy simplifications. And suddenly the moment came when she felt sorry for all those who long ago, or recently, had been Negaraats in various distant places, then said good-bye and set off down a road that had unexpectedly dropped from the sky and led them here to be soldiers in the strange city of Ekaterinburg.

This man explained everything so clearly to the young girl. Nobody had explained things to her like that before. The veil of soullessness, an amazing veil of obviousness, was removed from that picture of white tents; companies of men faded and became a collection of individuals in soldier's dress, and she began to pity them at the very moment when they were animated and elevated, brought close and drained of color by their newly acquired significance.

They were saying good-bye.

"I am leaving some of the books with Tsvetkov. He is the friend I've told you so much about. Please continue to use them, *Madame*. Your son knows where I live. He comes to see the landlord's family. I am handing my own room over to Tsvetkov. I will warn him."

"Tell him to come and call on us. Tsvetkov, did you say?"

"Tsvetkov, that's right."

"Tell him to come. We'll get to know him. When I was quite young I used to know some Tsvetkovs"—and she looked at her husband, who had stopped in front of Negaraat, hands tucked into the breast of his thick jacket, and distractedly awaiting a suitable juncture to make final arrangements with the Belgian for tomorrow. "Tell him to come. Only not now. I'll let him know. Here, take this; it is yours. I haven't finished it. I wept as I read it. The doctor advised me to leave it—to avoid excitement"—and she looked again at her husband, who had bowed his head, and his collar crackled and he puffed as he looked to see whether he had boots on both his feet and whether they were well cleaned.

"Well, then. There we are. Don't forget your stick. We shall see each other again I hope?"

"Oh, certainly. I'm here till Friday. What is today?"—he showed a sudden fright, common on such occasions with people leaving.

"Wednesday. Vika, Wednesday? . . . Vika, is it Wednesday?"

"Yes, Wednesday. Ecoutez,"—Father's turn finally came. "Demain . . ."

And they both went out onto the stairway.

V

They strode along and talked. Occasionally she had to break into a slight run so as not to lag behind Seryozha and to keep in step with him. They were walking very briskly, and her coat jerked to and fro because she had both hands in her pockets and was pumping with her arms to help herself along. It was cold, and the thin ice crackled sonorously beneath her galoshes. They were going on an errand for Mama to buy a present for the man who was leaving, and on the way they talked.

"So they were taking him to the station?"

"Yes."

"But why was he sitting on the hay?"

"How do you mean?"

"In the cart. All of him. Even his legs. People don't sit like that."

"I've already said. Because he was a criminal."

"Are they taking him to do hard labor?"

"No, to Perm. We don't have our own prison department. Watch where you're going."

Their way lay over the road, past the coppersmith's shop. The doors of the shop had stood wide open the entire summer, and Zhenya was used to seeing this crossroads in a general state of friendly animation dispensed by the workshop's hotly gaping maw. Throughout July, August, and September carts kept stopping here, obstructing all departure; peasants, mainly Tatars, tramped around; buckets lay about, and pieces of roof guttering, broken and rusty; it was here more often than anywhere else that the crowd was turned into a gypsy camp and the Tatars were painted up as Romanies by an awful, viscous sun, which set amid the dust at times when they were slaughtering chickens beyond the nearby wattle fencing; it was here that the buffer bars, disengaged from beneath the body of the cart, plunged their shafts into the dust with the plates on their dragbolts all rubbed up.

The same buckets and bits of iron lay scattered around, now lightly powdered with frost. But the doors were tight shut, as on holidays, on account of the cold, and the crossroads was deserted, and only through a circular vent came Zhenya's familiar breath of musty firedamp, which let out a fulminating scream, rushed up her nose, and settled on her palate like cheap pear-juice soda.

"But is there a prison board in Perm?"

"Yes, a department. I think—it's quicker going that way. There is one in Perm because it's the provincial center, but Ekaterinburg is only the main town in this district. It's very small."

The path by the private houses was laid with red brick and framed by bushes. It still bore the traces of a dull and feeble sun. Seryozha endeavored to tread as noisily as possible.

"If you tickle this barberry with a pin in spring when it's flowering, it flaps all its petals very quickly as if it's alive."

"I know."

"Are you afraid of tickling?"

"Yes."

"That means you're nervy. The Akhmedyanovs say that if anyone's afraid of tickling . . ."

And on they went, Zhenya running with her coat swinging, and Seryozha taking his unnatural strides. They caught sight of Dikikh at the very moment when their way was barred by the gate swinging like a turnpike on its post embedded in the middle of the path. They saw him from a distance. He had come from the shop to which they were heading, still half a block away. Dikikh was not alone; he was followed out by a short man who tried to conceal a limp as he walked. Zhenya thought she had seen him once before somewhere. They passed each other without a greeting. The other two headed off obliquely. Dikikh did not notice the children; he strode along in his high galoshes, frequently raising his hands with fingers splayed. He would *not agree,* and he tried to prove with all ten fingers that his companion . . . (Where was it she had seen him, now? A long time ago. But where? It must have been in Perm, when she was a *child.*)

"Stop!"—something had happened to Seryozha. He had knelt down on one knee. "Wait a bit."

"Have you caught it?"

"Yes, I have. Idiots! Why can't they knock a nail in properly?"

"Well?"

"Wait, I can't find the place. I know that man with the limp. There we are. Thank goodness."

"Have you torn it?"

"No, it's all right, thank heavens. There is a hole in the lining, but that's an old one. I didn't do it. Right, let's go. Stop, I'll just clean my knee. Right now, on we go.

"I know him. He's from the Akhmedyanovs' house. Negaraat's friend. Remember, I told you—he collects some people together, they drink the whole night, and there's a light burning at the window. Do you remember? You remember when I spent the night at their house? On Samoyla's birthday. Well, he's one of them. Remember?"

She did remember. She realized she was mistaken, and in that case she could not have seen the lame man in Perm. She had imagined it. But she still seemed to have seen him. And she still had that feeling and silently went through all her memories of Perm as she followed her brother, made some movements, took hold of something, stepped over something else, and, looking around her, found herself in the half twilight of counters, small boxes, shelving, fussy greetings and attentions, and . . . Seryozha was talking.

The bookseller, who also traded in all sorts of tobacco, turned out not to have the titles they required. But he put their minds at rest and assured them that Turgenev had been promised, just been sent from Moscow and was already on the way, and that he had only just—why, a minute ago—been talking about the same thing with Mr. Tsvetkov, their tutor. His spry manner and the delusion he was under made the children laugh. They said good-bye and left empty-handed.

When they came out, Zhenya asked her brother the following question:

"Seryozha, I keep forgetting. Tell me, you know that street you can see from our woodpile?"

"No, I've never been there."

"That's not true. I've seen you there myself."

"On the woodpile? You . . ."

"No, not on the woodpile, on that street there, beyond the Cherep-
Savvichs' garden."

"Oh, that's what you mean! That's right. You can see it as you go past.
Beyond the garden, at the far end. There are sheds and some wood. Wait
. . . So that's our yard?! That yard is ours? That's clever! How many times
have I been past and thought of getting over there—up onto the woodpile,
and from the woodpile into the garret. I've seen a ladder there. So that's
our own actual yard?"

"Seryozha, will you show me the way there?"

"What, again? But the yard's ours. Why should I need to show you?
You've been there yourself . . ."

"Seryozha, you've not understood me again. I'm talking about the street,
but you are talking about the yard. I mean the street. Show me the way to
the street. Show me how to get there. Will you show me, Seryozha?"

"I still don't understand. Why, we've been past it today already. . . . And
we'll be going by again soon."

"What do you mean?"

"Just what I said. You know the coppersmith's . . . on the corner?"

"Oh, that dusty street, you mean . . .?"

"Yes, that's the one you're asking about. And the Cherep-Savvichs are
at the end to the right. Don't lag behind. We mustn't be late for dinner. It's
crayfish today."

They began to talk of other things. The Akhmedyanovs had promised to
teach him how to plate a samovar with tin. And as for her question about
"tinplate"—it was a kind of rock, an ore, in fact, dingy-colored, like pewter.
They soldered tin cans with it and fired pots, and the Akhmedyanovs knew
how to do all that.

They had to run across, or the train of carts would have held them back.
And so they forgot: she about her request concerning the unfrequented lane,
and Seryozha his promise to show her it. They passed by the very door of
the copper shop, and here Zhenya drew a breath of warm, greasy smoke
produced when brass knobs and candlesticks were cleaned, and immediately recalled where she had seen the lame man and the three unknown
girls, and what they had been doing—and the very next moment she realized that the Tsvetkov mentioned by the bookseller was this same man with
the limp.

VI

Negaraat left in the evening. Father went to see him off. He returned from
the station late at night, and in the janitor's lodge his appearance caused

a great disturbance, which took some time to subside. They came out with lights and shouted to someone. It was pouring with rain; someone had let the geese loose, and they were cackling.

Morning rose, overcast and shaky. The wet, gray street bounced as though made of rubber. A nasty drizzle hung and spattered mud, carts came galloping up, and people in galoshes splashed as they crossed the roadway.

Zhenya was returning home. Echoes of the night's disturbance could still be heard that morning in the yard. She was not allowed to use the carriage. She set off for her friend's on foot, having said she was going to the shop to buy hempseed. But she turned back halfway, realizing she could not find her own way to the Defendovs from the merchants' quarter. Then she remembered it was still early, and Liza was at school in any case. Thoroughly drenched, she shivered. The weather was brightening but had still not cleared. A cold, white gleam flew about the street and stuck to the wet flagstones like a leaf. Murky storm clouds hurried away from the town, jostling and stirring in flighty panic at the end of the square beyond the three-branched streetlight.

The person moving out was clearly an unprincipled or slovenly man. The meager office equipment was not loaded but simply placed on the dray just as it stood in the room, and at every jolt of the cart the armchair casters peeping from beneath their white covers trundled around the dray as if on a parquet floor. Despite the fact that they were sodden through and through, the covers were white as snow. So sharply did they catch the eye that when one looked at them everything else became the same color: cobblestones gnawed by the foul weather, shivering water beneath the fences, birds flying from the stable yards and trees flying after, chunks of lead, and even that ficus in its tub, which swayed and bowed awkwardly from the cart to everybody as it flew past.

It was a crazy cartload. It could not help but draw attention. A peasant walked alongside, and listing broadly the dray moved along at walking pace, striking against the curb posts. And above everything the wet and leaden word "town" hovered in a tattered rag of rook calls, and in the little girl's head it gave rise to a multitude of thoughts, all fleeting as the cold October gleam that flew about the street and collapsed in the water.

"When he unpacks his things he will catch a chill," she reflected, thinking of the unknown owner. And she imagined the man—*any man, in fact, with a shaky and uneven gait*—setting his belongings out in different corners. She vividly pictured his mannerisms and movements, and especially how he would take a rag and hobble around the tub as he started wiping down the drizzle-clouded leaves of the ficus. Then he would catch a cold, a chill and fever. Most certainly he would. Zhenya could picture that quite vividly also. Quite vividly. The cart rumbled as it started downhill toward the River Iset. Zhenya had to turn left.

It must have been because of someone's heavy footsteps outside the door. The tea rose and fell in its glass on the little table by the bed. A slice of lemon in the tea also rose and fell. Strips of sunlight on the wallpaper swayed. They swayed in columns, like the tubes of syrup in those shops that had signboards with a Turk smoking a pipe. With a Turk . . . smoking . . . a pipe. Smoking . . . a pipe.

It must have been because of someone's footsteps. The patient fell asleep again.

Zhenya had taken to her bed the day after Negaraat's departure, on the same day she learned after her walk that Aksinya had given birth to a boy during the night, on the same day she saw the cartload of furniture and decided there was rheumatism in store for the owner. She lay in a fever for two weeks, thickly dusted with distressing red pepper for the sweat, and the pepper burned and gummed up her eyelids and the corners of her lips. Perspiration plagued her, and her feeling of disgusting obesity was combined with a sensation of being stung, as though the flame that caused her swelling had been injected by a summer wasp, as though its sting had remained in her, fine as a gray hair, and she kept wanting to pull it out over and over again in different ways: from her violet cheekbone, from her shoulder inflamed and groaning under her nightdress, or from somewhere else.

Now she was recovering. She felt an all-pervading weakness. And at its own risk and peril this sense of weakness yielded to a strange geometry all its own. It made her slightly dizzy and sick.

Beginning with some episode on the bedspread, for instance, her sense of weakness proceeded to deposit rows of gradually increasing emptiness, which soon grew vast beyond belief in the twilight's craving to adopt the form and area lying at the base of this derangement of space. Or else, separating from the pattern on the wallpaper, it chased past the girl a series of latitudes that succeeded one another, stripe upon stripe, as smoothly as if oiled, and, like all these sensations, they wearied her with their regular and gradual expansion. Or else it tormented the patient with depths that descended endlessly, betraying their fathomlessness from the very outset, from their first trick in the parquet flooring, and it lowered the bed gently, gently down into the depths, and together with the bed went the little girl. Her head became like a lump of sugar thrown into a gulf of insipid and astonishingly empty chaos, and it dissolved and streamed away in it.

This was all because of the heightened sensitivity of her aural labyrinth.

This was all because of someone's footsteps. The lemon fell and rose again. The sun on the wallpaper rose and fell.

Finally she woke. In came Mama, who greeted her on her recovery and produced on the girl an impression of reading the thoughts of others. She had already heard something similar as she awoke. These were the congratulations of her own hands and feet and elbows and knees, which she received as she stretched herself. And now Mama was here too. The coincidence was strange.

The household came in and went out, sat down and got up. She asked questions and received answers. There were things that had changed during her illness, and there were those that had remained unaltered. She did not bother with the latter, but the former she never left in peace. Apparently Mama had not changed. Her father—not at all. Things that had changed were: she herself, Seryozha, the distribution of light in the room, the silence of all the rest, and something else, many things. . . . Had snow fallen? No, there had been snowfall, now and then; it had melted; it had frozen; you could not make out; the ground was bare, no snow. . . . She hardly noticed whom she was questioning about what. The answers came in quick succession.

The healthy ones came and went. Liza came. There was an argument. Then they remembered that measles does not occur twice and let her in. Dikikh called. She hardly noticed which answers came from whom.

When everyone had gone out for dinner and she was left alone with Ulyasha, she recalled how they had all laughed in the kitchen at her stupid question. Now she was careful not to ask another one like it. She asked an intelligent and serious question in a grown-up tone of voice. She asked whether Aksinya was pregnant again. The girl jingled the spoon as she removed the glass and turned away.

"Deary! . . . Give her a rest. She can't always be at it, Zhenya, love, all at one sweep . . ." She ran out without closing the door properly, and the whole kitchen roared as though the crockery shelves had collapsed. And after the laughter there was wailing; then it passed to the cleaning woman and Galim and blazed up under their touch, and then it started as a rapid and ardent clangor, as though some quarrel was turning into a fight. Then someone came up and closed the forgotten door.

She should not have asked that. That was even more stupid.

VII

What? Could it be thawing again? Did that mean they would be going out on wheels today again and they still could not harness the sleigh? With nose growing chill and shivering hands, Zhenya stood for hours at her little window. Dikikh had left a short while before. This time he had been displeased with her. But just try studying here when the cockerels were singing about in the yards and the sky was humming, and when the ringing ceased the cockerels took up their song again! The clouds were shabby and dirty like a balding sleigh rug. The day thrust its snout up against the pane like a calf in its steamy stall. It might easily have been spring. But since lunch the air had been gripped by a hoop of livid gray frost. The sky had become drained and sunken. One could hear the wheezing breath of clouds and the passing hours as they strained northward to the winter twilight, breaking a last leaf from the trees, shearing lawns, cleaving through fissures, and rending the breasts of men. The gun muzzles of far northern lands loomed black beyond the houses; loaded with a vast November, they were aimed at their courtyard. But it was still October only.

But still it was only October. They could not remember such a winter. They were saying the winter crops had perished, and they feared a famine. It was as though someone had waved his wand around all the chimneys, roofs, and nesting boxes. Here there would be smoke; here there would be snow; there—hoarfrost. But as yet there was still neither one nor the other. The desolate, sunken twilight was pining for them. It strained its eyes; the earth ached from the early lamplight and the lights in homes, as one's head aches with the yearning stare of long waiting. Everything was tense and expectant; firewood had already been taken to the kitchens; for a second week the clouds were full with snow to overflowing; the air was pregnant with darkness. But when would the magician who drew his magic circles around everything the eye could see finally pronounce his incantation and summon up that winter whose spirit was already at the door?

But how they had neglected it! Certainly they paid no attention to the calendar in the classroom. They had torn off her own children's calendar. But still . . . the twenty-ninth of August! Clever!—as Seryozha would have said. A red letter day: the Beheading of John the Baptist. It was easy to take down from its nail. Having nothing better to do, she employed herself in tearing off the sheets. She was bored as she performed this operation and soon failed to realize what she was doing, but from time to time she repeated to herself, "The thirtieth, tomorrow is the thirty-first."

"This is the third day she hasn't been out of the house!" These words coming from the corridor brought her out of her reverie, and she saw how far she had gotten with her work. Even past the Presentation of the Virgin. Mama touched her on the hand.

"Zhenya, come, tell me now . . ." The rest was lost, as though unspoken. She interrupted her mother, and as if in a dream she asked *Madame* Luvers to say the words "Beheading of John the Baptist." She repeated it, puzzled. She did not say "Babtist." That was how Aksinya said it.

But the very next minute Zhenya was filled with amazement at herself. What could it be? What had prompted her? Where did it come from? Was it she, Zhenya, who had asked? Or could she have imagined that Mama . . . ? How fantastic and unreal! Whose invention was it?

But Mama just stood there. She could not believe her ears. She looked at her with eyes wide open. This sudden caprice had nonplussed her. The question sounded like some mockery; yet her daughter had tears in her eyes.

Her vague premonitions came true. On their drive she clearly heard the air growing flaccid, clouds falling limp, and the clop of the horseshoes getting softer. They had not yet lit the lamps when the small, gray, dry flocks began twirling and meandering in the air. But they had not had time to reach beyond the bridge when separate snowflakes ceased to be and a solid, fused coagulum came heaving down. Davletsha climbed down from the coach box and erected the hood. It became dark and cramped for Zhenya and Seryozha. They wanted to rave like the foul weather that raged about them. They perceived Davletsha was taking them home only because they heard the bridge once again beneath Vykormysh's hooves. The streets became unrecognizable; there were simply no streets left. Night fell immediately, and the maddened town began to twitch its countless thousands of thick and whitened lips. Seryozha leaned out and, propping himself on his knee, gave instructions to take them to the artisans' quarter. Zhenya was speechless with ecstasy as she learned all the secrets and splendors of winter in the sound of Seryozha's words carried on the air. Davletsha shouted back that they would have to go home so as not to wear out the horse; the master and mistress were going to the theater, and he would have to harness the sleigh. Zhenya remembered that their parents would be going out and they would be left alone. She decided to settle down by the lamp till late at night with that volume of *Tales of the Purring Puss,* which was not meant for children. She would have to fetch it from Mama's bedroom. And some chocolate. And she would read and suck the chocolate and listen to the sound of snow as it covered the streets.

And even now the snow was already sweeping down in earnest. The heavens quivered, and down from them tumbled whole white kingdoms and countries. They were countless, and they were mysterious and dreadful. It was clear that these lands falling from goodness knows where had never heard of life and earth: coming blind from the northern darkness, they covered them over without ever seeing or knowing of them.

They were ravishingly dreadful, those kingdoms—quite satanically entrancing. Zhenya was breathless as she looked at them. The air staggered and seized at what it could, and far, far away, painfully, oh, so painfully, a plaint was raised by the fields, which seemed as if flayed by whiplashes. Everything was confused. The night rushed at them, infuriated by the low-swept gray hair that flogged and blinded it. Everything was scattered, shrieking, and unable to discern the road. Call and answering cry were lost —they never met and perished, borne by a whirlwind to different roofs. Swirling snow.

For a long time they tramped in the hall, knocking the snow from their swollen white sheepskin coats. And how much water ran from their galoshes onto the checkered linoleum. On the table were many eggshells, the pepperbox had been taken from the chest and not been replaced, and a lot of pepper was scattered on the tablecloth and the running yolks, and in the half-eaten can of "saladins." Their parents had already had supper but still sat in the dining room, hustling along the dawdling children. They did not blame them; they had dined earlier in readiness for the theater. Mama hesitated, not knowing whether to go or not, and sat there very sorrowful. Looking at her, Zhenya remembered that actually she too was not at all cheerful—she finally managed to undo that horrible hook—but she was rather sad and came into the dining room and asked where they had put the nutcake. And Father glanced at their mother and said no one was forcing them, so it was better to stay at home.

"No. Why? Let's go," said Mama. "I need some diversion, and the doctor has allowed it."

"We have to decide."

"Where is the cake?" Zhenya chimed in again and was told that the cake would not run away, there was something else to eat before the cake, you did not begin with cake, and it was in the cupboard—as if she had only just arrived and didn't know the rules. . . .

So her father said, and, turning to mother again, he repeated, "We have to decide."

"I have decided. We are going." And with a rueful smile at Zhenya, Mama went away to dress.

As he tapped his egg with a spoon, watching so as not to miss, Seryozha warned Father in a businesslike voice that the weather had changed. There was a blizzard—he ought to bear that in mind—and he burst out laughing. Something peculiar was happening to his nose as it thawed out: He began to fidget and took a handkerchief from a pocket in the tight-fitting trousers of his uniform. He blew his nose as father had taught him, "without damaging the eardrums," took hold of his spoon, and, all rosy and washed from the drive, he glanced straight at Father and said, "When we went out, we saw Negaraat's friend. Do you know him?"

"Evans?" Father inquired distractedly.

"We don't know that man!" blurted Zhenya hotly.

"Vika!" a voice came from the bedroom.

Father got up in answer to the call and went out. In the doorway Zhenya collided with Ulyasha, who was bringing a lighted lamp to her. Soon the next door along banged. That was Seryozha going to his room. He had been splendid today; his sister loved it when the friend of the Akhmedyanovs became a little boy, and when you were allowed to say that he was wearing his "little school suit."

Doors opened and shut. There was the stamping of overshoes. Then at last the master and mistress left.

The letter stated that up to now she had "not ever been one bit stupid, and that they must ask her what they wanted, as before." But when "dear

sissy" had set off all festooned with memorized greetings and declarations
to be distributed to all her relatives by name, Ulyasha (who this time was
called Ulyana) thanked the young mistress, turned down the lamp, and
went off with the letter and the ink bottle and greasy octavo paper that
remained.

Then she returned once more to her task. She did not enclose the recurring figures in brackets. She continued the division, writing out one recurring set after another. There seemed to be no end in sight. The fraction in
the quotient grew and grew. "But what if measles can occur again?"—the
idea flashed through her mind. "Today Dikikh said something about infinity." She ceased to realize what she was doing. She was aware that
something similar had already happened this afternoon and she had also felt
like sleeping or weeping, but she could not think when it had been and what
it was, because she had not energy enough for thought. The noise outside
the window quietened. The blizzard was gradually abating. Decimal fractions were a complete novelty to her. There was not enough margin on the
right. She decided to begin again, write smaller, and check each stage. It
became completely quiet in the street. She was afraid she would forget what
she had borrowed from the next figure and be unable to retain the product
in her head. "The window won't run away," she thought, continuing to
pour threes and sevens into that bottomless quotient—"I'll hear them in
time—it's quiet all around—they won't be up here quickly; they are wearing
fur coats and Mama is pregnant. But the point is this: 3773 keeps recurring;
can I simply write it again or round it off?" Suddenly she recalled that
Dikikh had actually told her today that "you must not work them out—
simply throw them away." She got up and went over to the window.

It was now clear outside. Rare snowflakes came from the blackness. They
drifted to the streetlight, floated around it, then flipped and disappeared
from sight. New flakes drifted down in their place. The street shone, all
spread with a snowy sleighing carpet. It was white, glittering, and sweet,
like gingerbread in fairy tales. Zhenya stood awhile at the window, lost in
admiration at the loops and figures traced about the lamp by silvery snowflakes straight from Hans Christian Andersen. She stood awhile, then went
into Mama's room for "Puss." She went in without a light. She could see
just the same. The roof of the coach house bathed the room with shifting,
glistening light. The beds turned to ice beneath the sighing of this enormous
roof and glinted. Smoky silk lay here, scattered in disorder. Tiny blouses
gave off a stuffy, oppressive odor of armpits and calico. There was a smell
of violets, and the cupboard was bluish black, like the night outside and like
the warm, dry darkness in which these freezing sparkles moved. The metallic knob of a bed glittered like a lonely bead. The other was extinguished
by the nightdress thrown over it. Zhenya screwed up her eyes: The bead
detached itself from the floor and floated toward the wardrobe. She remem-

bered why she had come. With the book in her hands, she went over to one of the bedroom windows. It was a starry night. Winter had come to Ekaterinburg. She glanced out into the yard and began to think of Pushkin. She decided to ask the tutor to assign her an essay on Onegin.

Seryozha wanted to chat. He asked her, "Have you been putting perfume on? Let me have some."

He had been very nice all day. Very rosy-cheeked. But she thought there might not be another evening like this. She wanted to remain alone.

Zhenya returned to her room and took up the *Tales*. She read one story and with bated breath started on another. She became absorbed and did not hear through the wall when her brother turned in. The features of her countenance were strangely taken over and began to play. She was unaware of it. Now her face would spread fishlike; she hung her lip and her deathly pupils were riveted to the page in terror and refused to look up, fearing to discover the same thing behind the chest of drawers. Then she would suddenly begin nodding at the print in sympathy, as though she were approving it, like people approve some action or rejoice at some turn of events. She slowed down over the descriptions of lakes and rushed headlong into the depths of the night scenes with the scorching chunk of Bengal fire on which they depended for illumination. In one passage a man who was lost kept shouting intermittently and listening for an answer but heard only his own echo in reply. Zhenya had to clear her throat from the soundless straining of her larynx. The un-Russian name of "Mirra" brought her out of her stupor. She laid the book aside and was lost in thought. "So this is what winter is like in Asia! What can the Chinese be doing on such a dark night?" Zhenya's glance fell on the clock. "How awful it must be to be with the Chinese in such darkness as this!" Zhenya looked once more at the clock and was horrified. Her parents might appear at any moment. It was already past eleven. She unlaced her bootees and remembered she had to put the book back in its place.

Zhenya jumped up. She sat down on the bed with eyes staring. It was not a burglar. There were many of them, and they were stamping and talking loudly as in daytime. Suddenly a woman screamed with all her force as though knifed, and then chairs were overturned as something was dragged along. Little by little Zhenya recognized them all—all, that is, except the woman. An unbelievable scampering began. Doors started banging. When one of them slammed in the distance, it seemed as if they were stopping the woman's mouth. But it opened again and the house was scalded by a burning, flailing scream. Zhenya's hair stood on end. The woman was her mother—she had *guessed!* Ulyasha was wailing, and though she once caught the sound of her father's voice, she heard it no more. Seryozha was thrust into some room, and he kept howling, "Don't dare lock it! . . . We all belong here!" And Zhenya rushed out into the corridor as she was, barefoot and in just her nightie. Father almost bowled her over. Still in his overcoat, he shouted something to Ulyasha as he ran past.

"Papa!"

She saw him run back with a marble jug from the bathroom.

"Papa!"

"Where's Lipa?" he shouted in a voice not his own as he ran.

Splashing water on the floor, he disappeared through the door, and when he came out a moment later in shirt-sleeves and without a jacket Zhenya found herself in Ulyasha's arms and failed to catch the words spoken in her despairingly deep and heartrending whisper.

"What's the matter with Mama?"

By way of reply, Ulyasha simply kept repeating, "There, there, you mustn't, Zhenya, dear. You mustn't, my dear. Go to sleep, cover yourself up, lie on your side. A-a-ah! Oh, Lord! . . . Dearie! There, there, you mustn't . . ." she kept saying, covering her over like a baby and turning to go.

"You mustn't, you mustn't . . ." But what she mustn't do Ulyasha never said, and her face was wet and her hair disheveled. A lock clicked in the third door behind her.

Zhenya lit a match to see whether it would soon be dawn. It was only just after midnight. She was very surprised. Had she really slept less than an hour? But the noise had not died down in her parents' quarters. The howls came bursting, hatching forth in salvos. Then for a short moment there was a broad and age-long silence. In the midst of it there were hurried footsteps and cautious, rapid speech. Then there was a ring, and then another. Then the words, discussions, and instructions were so many that it seemed as if the rooms there were burning through with voices, like tables beneath a thousand extinguished candelabra.

Zhenya fell asleep. She fell asleep in tears. She dreamed that they had guests. She was counting them and kept getting the number wrong. Each time she came out with one too many. And each time she was seized with the same dread at this mistake as that moment when she realized it was not someone else but Mama.

How could one fail to rejoice at the pure, clear morning? Seryozha had a vision of games out there, snowball fights with the children in the yard. Tea was served to them in the classroom. The floor-polishers were in the dining room, they were told. Father came in. It was immediately apparent that he knew nothing about floor-polishers. And indeed he did know nothing of them; he told them the real reason for their being moved. Mama had been taken ill. She needed quiet.

Crows flew by above the street's white shroud with a broad-resounding cawing. A sleigh ran past, urging on the horse that pulled it. It was not yet accustomed to the new harness and kept missing its step.

"You are going to the Defendovs. I have already made arrangements. And you . . ."

"Why?" Zhenya interrupted.

But Seryozha had already guessed why and forestalled his father.

"So as not to get infected," he explained to his sister.

But something in the street prevented him from finishing. He ran to the window as though beckoned there. The Tatar boy out in his new rig was handsome and elegant as a cock pheasant. He had on a sheepskin hat. His raw sheepskin coat blazed brighter than morocco leather. He walked with a roll and a swing, no doubt because the crimson decorations on his white felt boots knew nothing about the construction of the human foot—so freely did those patterns roam, they cared little whether these were feet or teacups or porch roofing. But most remarkable of all—at that moment the moaning that carried feebly from the bedroom increased, and father went out into the passage, forbidding them to follow—but most remarkable of all were the tracks he had traced in a clean, narrow thread across the smoothened field. Thanks to these, so sculptured and neat, the snow seemed even whiter, even more like satin.

"Here is a note. You will give it to Mr. Defendov. To him in person. Do you understand? Well, get dressed. They will bring your things here right away. You will go out by the back door. And the Akhmedyanovs are expecting you."

"Really, actually expecting me?" his son asked mockingly.

"Yes. You will put your coats on in the kitchen."

He spoke distractedly and unhurriedly saw them through to the kitchen, where their sheepskins, hats, and mittens lay heaped on a stool. There was a wintry blast of air from the staircase. "Eyeeokh!"—the frozen shrill of passing sleighs stayed hanging in the air. They were hurrying and could not get their hands into the sleeves. Their things gave off an odor of trunks and sleepy fur.

"What are you fussing about for?"

"Don't put it at the edge. It'll go and fall. Well?"

"She's still moaning." The maid gathered up her apron, bent over, and threw some logs into the kitchen range with its gasping flame. "It's not my business," she said indignantly and went back into the house.

Yellow prescriptions and broken glass could be seen lying in a battered black bucket. Towels were impregnated with tousled, crumpled blood. They were ablaze. One almost wanted to stamp them out, like a fire that puffed and smoldered. Plain water boiled in saucepans. All around stood white bowls and mortars of unimagined shape, as in a pharmacy.

In the passageway little Galim was cracking ice.

"Is there much of it left from the summer?" Seryozha inquired.

"Soon will be some new," he said in broken Russian.

"Give me some. There's no point in your crunching it up."

"Why no point? Need it crush. Crush for this bottles."

"Well! Are you ready, Zhenya?"

But Zhenya had run back inside again. Seryozha came out onto the steps, and while waiting for his sister he began drumming with a log against the iron railing.

VIII

They were sitting down for supper at the Defendovs. Their grandmother crossed herself and flopped into an armchair. The lamp burned dimly and kept smoking. At one moment it was turned down too far, and the next they let it out too much. Mr. Defendov's dry hand would often reach out for the screw, and when it slowly withdrew from the lamp and he slowly settled in his seat, his hand quivered minutely, not like an old man's hand, but as though he were lifting a glass filled to the brim. His fingernails and fingertips trembled.

He spoke in a distinct and even voice, as if he were not composing his speech from sounds but setting up each letter and pronouncing everything, right down to the silent "h."

The bulbous neck of the lamp flared, edged about by tendrils of geranium and heliotrope. Cockroaches ran to congregate by the glowing glass, and the hands of the clock stretched out carefully. Time moved at a hibernal crawl. Here it gathered, festering. Out in the yard it was numb and malodorous. Outside the window it scuttled and scurried, doubling and trebling in the gleaming lights.

Madame Defendova set some liver on the table. The dish was seasoned with onion, and it was steaming. Defendov was saying something, often repeating the words "I recommend . . . ," and Liza chattered without pause. But Zhenya did not hear them. The little girl had felt like weeping ever since yesterday. And now she really craved to, sitting there in a cardigan sewed according to her mother's instructions.

Defendov realized what was the matter. He tried to amuse her. But at one moment he would address her as if she were an infant, and at the next he would go to the opposite extreme. His joking questions scared and confused her. In the darkness he was groping the soul of his daughter's friend, as though he were asking her heart how old it was. When once he had caught one of Zhenya's traits *unmistakably,* it was his intention to work on this observation and help the child to forget about home—but by his probings he had reminded her that she was in a strange house.

Suddenly she could stand no more. She got up with childish embarrassment and murmured, "Thank you. I've really had enough. May I look at
some pictures?" And blushing deeply as she saw their general puzzlement,
she added with a nod toward the next room, "Walter Scott? . . . May I?"

"Off you go, off you go, my dear!" Grandmother mammered, and riveted
Liza to her place with her eyebrows.

"Poor child!" she remarked to her son when the two halves of the
claret-colored door drape had closed to behind Zhenya.

The bookcase was bowed by a forbidding set of *North* magazine, and
down below was the dingy gold of Karamzin's complete works. A rose-
colored lamp hung from the ceiling, leaving a couple of frayed armchairs
unlighted, while the rug, which was lost in total darkness, came as a surprise
to her feet.

Zhenya had imagined she would go in, sit down, and burst into sobs. But
the tears that welled in her eyes could still not break through her sorrow.
How could she throw off the anguish that since yesterday had pressed upon
her like a beam? Tears could not console it and were powerless to remove
the dam. In order to assist them, she began thinking of her mother.

For the first time in her life, as she prepared to spend the night in a
strange house, she was able to measure the depth of her attachment to this
dear person, the most precious in the world.

Suddenly she heard Liza's loud laughter behind the door drape.

"Oooh, what a fidget! What a little imp you are!" quavered Grandmother,
coughing.

Zhenya was amazed how she could have thought earlier that she loved
the girl whose laughter now rang out next to her, so remote and so un-
wanted. And something in her turned over, releasing tears at the very
moment when Mama emerged in her memories: suffering and left standing
in the chain of yesterday's events like one of a crowd who were seeing her
off, and now set spinning back there by the train of time, which was bearing
Zhenya away.

But utterly, utterly unbearable was the penetrating glance that *Madame*
Luvers had fixed on her yesterday in the classroom. It was carved deep in
her memory and would not go. Everything that Zhenya now felt was bound
up with it. As though this were something that should have been taken and
treasured, but which was forgotten and neglected.

This feeling could have made her lose her wits. Its drunken, crazy bitterness and inescapability spun her so giddily. Zhenya stood by the window
and wept silently; tears flowed and she did not wipe them away: Her hands
and arms were occupied, though she was holding nothing in them. Something caused them vehemently, impulsively, and obstinately to straighten.

A sudden thought dawned on her. She suddenly felt that she was *terribly*
like Mama. This feeling was combined with a sense of vivid certainty,
capable of turning conjecture into fact (if the latter were not yet estab-

lished), and of making her like her mother by the mere strength of the striking, sweet condition she was in. This sensation was piercing, sharp enough to make her groan. *It was the sensation of a woman perceiving from within, or inwardly, her outward appearance and her charm.* Zhenya was incapable of realizing what it was. She was experiencing it for the first time. In one thing she was not mistaken. This was just how *Madame* Luvers had once been as she had stood by the window, turning away from her daughter and the governess in agitation, biting her lips and tapping her lorgnette against a kid-gloved palm.

She went out to rejoin the Defendovs, drunk with tears and with a bright serenity. And she came in, walking not as before but in some way changed, with a bearing that was broad and new and dreamily uncoordinated. At the sight of her entering, Defendov sensed that the idea of the girl he had formed in her absence was quite inappropriate, and he would have set about forming another one had it not been for the samovar.

Madame Defendova went into the kitchen for the tray she had left on the floor, and everybody's gaze was fixed on the panting copper, as though it were some live thing whose mischievous caprices ended at the very moment of its transfer to the table. Zhenya resumed her seat. She decided to talk to everyone. She was vaguely aware that the choice of conversation was hers. Otherwise they might only confirm her in her former loneliness without realizing that her Mama was here, with her and in her. And this shortsightedness would cause pain to her and, more important, to Mama. And as though encouraged by *her,* "Vassa Vasilyevna," she began, addressing *Madame* Defendova, who had set the samovar down heavily on the end of the tray. . . .

"Can you have babies too?"

Liza did not answer Zhenya immediately.

"Shhh! Quiet, don't shout! Of course I can, like all girls." She spoke in whispered bursts.

Zhenya could not see her friend's face. Liza was groping around the table, unable to find the matches.

She knew much more than Zhenya about that. She knew *everything,* in the way children do, who hear it from other people. In such cases any nature admired of its Creator rises in revolt, is outraged, and turns wild. It cannot survive this ordeal without some pathological excess. It would be unnatural otherwise, and a childish madness at this stage is merely a sign that deep down all is well.

Someone had once whispered a lot of horrors and filth to Liza in a corner. She did not choke over what she heard but carried it along in her mind up the street and brought it home. She dropped nothing of what she had heard on the way, and she kept all this rubbish preserved. She had found out everything. Her organism did not blaze up, her heart sounded no alarm, and her soul inflicted no blows on her mind for having dared find out something without asking, away on the side, and not from her soul's own lips.

"I know." ("You know nothing," Liza thought.) "I know," repeated Zhenya. "That's not what I'm asking about. What I mean is do you ever feel that you might go and take a step, and suddenly have a baby, like . . ."

"Do come inside!" said Liza hoarsely, stifling her laughter. "A fine place you've picked to yell. They can hear you from the doorway!"

The conversation was taking place in Liza's room. Liza was speaking so quietly one could even hear the drips in the washbowl. She had found the matches now, but she still delayed lighting them, unable to make her parted lips look serious. She did not wish to offend her friend. And she spared her ignorance because she never suspected that one could tell her about it without using expressions that could not be spoken here at home in front of a friend who did not go to school. She lighted the lamp. Luckily the pail was filled to overflowing, and Liza hurried to wipe the floor, concealing a new fit of laughter in her apron and the slopping of the floorcloth. And finally she burst out laughing openly, having found an excuse: She had dropped her comb into the pail.

All those days she was aware only of thinking about her family and waiting for the time when they would send for her. Meanwhile in the afternoons when Liza went off to the *lycée* and only grandmother was left at home Zhenya also dressed up and went out for a walk alone.

The life of the suburb bore little resemblance to life where the Luvers lived. Most of the day it was bare and dull. There was nowhere for the eye to disport itself. Whatever it met was no good for anything except perhaps as a birch rod or a broom. There was coal lying about. Blackened slops were poured out into the street and immediately turned white as they froze. At certain hours the street was filled with common people. Factory workers swarmed out across the snow like cockroaches. The swing doors of tea-rooms opened and shut and soapy steam came billowing out as from a laundry. Strange—it seemed to be getting warmer in the street, as if spring were coming round again as laundered shirts ran along stooping and there were glimpses of felt boots worn over flimsy footcloths. The pigeons were not afraid of these crowds. They flew over onto the road where food was also to be had. Surely millet, oats, and droppings were scattered on the snow in plenty. . . . The pie woman's stall was shiny with fat and warmth. This gloss and glow disappeared into mouths that were rinsed with raw brandy. The fat heated up their throats, and farther along the way it escaped from their rapidly panting chests. Was it perhaps this that had warmed up the street?

The street emptied just as suddenly. Twilight descended. Empty sleds ran past, and low, wide sleighs, with bearded men engulfed in fur coats that mischievously rolled them on their backs and clasped them in a bear hug. In the road behind them there remained nostalgic wisps of hay and the slow, sweet melting of their receding sleigh bells. The merchants disappeared around the turn, behind the birches, which from here resembled a torn and battered stockade.

The crows that cawed expansively as they passed above the house would gather here. Only here they did not caw. Here they raised a shout and drew up their wings and, hopping, perched themselves along the fences. Then suddenly, as though on signal, they rushed in a cloud to investigate the trees and jostled as they distributed themselves about the empty branches. Ah, how one could sense then that late, late hour over the whole wide world! So late—ah, so very late, no clock could express it!

Thus a week passed, and toward the end of the second, on the Thursday at dawn, she saw him again. Liza's bed was empty. As she awoke, Zhenya heard the wicket gate close with a clatter behind her. She got up and, without lighting the lamp, went over to the window. It was still completely dark. But in the sky, in the branches of trees and movements of dogs one could feel the same heaviness as yesterday. It was the third day of this sullen weather, and there was no strength to drag it from the crumbling street, like a cast-iron kettle from some jagged floorboard.

In a small window across the way a lamp was burning. Two bright stripes fell beneath a horse and settled on its shaggy pasterns. Shadows moved across the snow; the sleeves of a phantom moved, wrapping a fur coat around itself; the light moved in the curtained window. But the little horse stood motionless and dreaming.

Then she saw him. She recognized him immediately by his silhouette. The lame man lifted his lamp and began to walk away with it. The two bright stripes moved after him, distending and elongating, and behind the stripes —a sleigh, which quickly flashed into view and plunged back into the gloom even faster as it slowly went around the house to the porch.

It was strange that Tsvetkov should still appear before her gaze even here in the suburbs. But it did not surprise Zhenya. She was hardly concerned with him. Soon the lamp appeared again. It passed steadily across the curtains and was on the point of retreating again when suddenly it turned up once more behind the same curtain on the windowsill from which it had been taken.

This was on Thursday. And on Friday they finally sent for her.

IX

On the tenth day after returning home, when lessons were resumed after a break of more than three weeks, Zhenya learned all the rest from her tutor.

After dinner the doctor packed up and departed, and she asked him to give greetings to the house in which he had examined her in spring, and to all the streets, and to the Kama. He expressed the hope that it would no longer be necessary to summon him from Perm. She went out as far as the gate with this man who had made her shudder so on the very first morning of her return from the Defendovs while Mama was still sleeping and no one was allowed to see her: When she asked what Mama's trouble was, he began by reminding her that her parents had been at the theater that night. But at the end of the show, as people started coming out, their stallion . . .

"Vykormysh?!"

"Yes, if that is his name. . . . Well then, Vykorkysh started struggling, reared up, and knocked down a man who happened to be passing and trampled him and . . ."

"What? To death?"

"Alas!"

"And Mama?"

"Mama had a nervous upset"—and he smiled, having barely had time to adapt his Latin *partus praematurus* for the little girl's benefit.

"And then my little brother was born dead?!"

"Who told you? . . . Yes."

"But when? Were they there? Or was he lifeless when they found him? Don't tell me. Oh, how dreadful! Now I understand. He was dead already; otherwise I would have heard him even so. You see, I was reading. Till late in the night. I would have heard. But when was he alive? Doctor, do such things really happen? I even went to the bedroom! He was dead. He must have been!"

How fortunate that what she had observed from the Defendovs at dawn was only yesterday, whereas that horror at the theater was the week before last! How fortunate that she had recognized him! She vaguely imagined that if she had not caught sight of him all that time, now, after the doctor's story, she would certainly have decided that it was the cripple who was crushed to death at the theater.

Now, after being their guest for so long and becoming quite one of the household, the doctor departed. And in the evening the tutor came. That afternoon they had been laundering. Now they were mangling linen in the kitchen. The hoarfrost had gone from the frames, and the garden pressed up against the windows, got entangled in the lace curtains, and came right up to the table. Short bursts of rumbling from the mangle kept breaking into the conversation. Like everyone else, Dikikh too found she had changed. She also noticed a change in him.

"Why are you so sad?" she asked.

"Am I really? It may well be. I have lost a friend."

"Do you have some sorrow too? So many deaths—and all so sudden!" she sighed.

But he was just about to tell her his story when something quite inexplicable occurred. The young girl suddenly changed her ideas about the number of deaths, and clearly forgetting the evidence provided by the lamp she had seen that morning, she said anxiously, "Wait. One time you were at the tobacconist's—Negaraat was leaving—I saw you with someone. Was it he?" —She was afraid to say "Tsvetkov."

Dikikh was dumbfounded when he heard these words. He recalled what had been said, and remembered that indeed they had gone for some paper then and asked for a complete Turgenev for *Madame* Luvers—and, yes, he had been with the dead man. She shuddered and tears came to her eyes. But the most important was yet to come.

With pauses in which the goffered rumbling of the mangle could be heard Dikikh told her what sort of young man he had been and what a good family he came from; then he lit a cigarette and Zhenya realized with horror that only this pause to inhale separated the tutor from a repetition of the doctor's story. And when he made the attempt and uttered a few words that included the word "theater," Zhenya screamed in a voice quite unlike her own and rushed out of the room.

Dikikh listened. Apart from the mangling of linen, there was not a sound in the house. He stood up and looked like a stork. He stretched his neck and raised one foot, ready to fly to her aid. He rushed to look for the girl, deciding there was nobody at home and that she had fainted. And all the time he bumped in the dark into puzzles made of wood, wool, and metal, Zhenya was sitting in a corner weeping. But he continued to rummage and grope, and in thought he was already lifting her from the carpet in a dead faint. He shuddered when a voice sounded loudly at his elbow, amid whimpers: "I am here. Be careful, there's the cabinet there. Wait for me in the classroom. I'll come in a moment."

The curtains reached down to the floor, and outside the window the starry night also hung down to the floor, and low down, waist-deep in snowdrifts, two thick, dark trees rambled into the clear light of the window, trailing the glittering chains of their branches through deep snow. And somewhere through the wall the firm rumble of the mangling went up and down, tightly constricted by the sheets. "How is one to explain this excessive sensitivity?" the tutor reflected. Evidently the dead man meant something special to the girl. She had changed greatly. He had been explaining recurring decimals to a child, whereas the person who had just now sent him back into the classroom . . . And this was only a matter of one month! Obviously at some time the dead man had made an especially deep and indelible impression on this little woman. There was a name for impressions of this sort. How strange! He had been giving her lessons every other day and noticed nothing. She was *awfully splendid,* and he was fearfully sorry for her. But when would she finally stop weeping and come? Everyone else must be out visiting. With all his heart he was sorry for her. What a wonderful night!

He was mistaken, for the impression he imagined did not fit the case at all. But he was right in that the impression that lay behind it all was indelible. Its depth was even greater than he imagined. . . . It lay beyond the girl's own control, because it was vitally important and significant, and its significance consisted in the fact that this was the first time *another* human being had entered her life—a third person, totally indifferent, with no name, or only a fortuitous one, neither arousing hatred nor inspiring love, but the *person the Commandments have in mind,* addressing men with names and consciousness, when they say: "Thou shalt not kill." "Thou shalt not steal." et cetera. . . . "As a living individual human," they say, "you must not do to this *featureless generalized man* what you would not wish for yourself as a living individual." Dikikh's greatest error lay in thinking there was a name for such impressions. They do not have one.

And Zhenya wept because she considered herself to blame for everything. For it was *she* who had brought him into the life of the family that day when she noticed him on the far side of someone else's garden. And, having noticed him quite needlessly, without sense or purpose, she had then started meeting him at every step, constantly, directly or indirectly, and even, as on the last occasion, quite contrary to all possibility.

When she saw which book Dikikh was taking from the shelf, she frowned and said, "No, I can't answer on that today. Put it back in its place. Excuse me, please . . ."

And without another word Lermontov was returned by the same hand and pushed back into the little slanting row of classics.

1918

Translated by Christopher Barnes

Aerial Ways

To Mikhail Alekseevich Kuzmin

I

Beneath the age-old mulberry tree slept the nurse, leaning against its trunk. When the huge lilac storm cloud rising at the roadside had silenced even the grasshoppers that torridly chirruped in the grass, and when the drums gave a sigh and their pattering ceased in the encampment, the eyes of the earth turned dim and there was no more life in this world.

"Where, oh where, are you going?" howled the hare-lipped half-witted shepherdess for all the world to hear; the young steer went before, and she, trailing her crushed foot and flailing her wild twig like a tongue of lightning, appeared amid a cloud of refuse from the far end of the garden where the wilderness began: nightshade, bricks, twisted wire, and moldering half darkness.

And she disappeared.

The storm cloud surveyed the low and hard-baked stubble that stretched to the very horizon. The cloud reared slightly on its haunches, and the stubble reached out still farther, to beyond the encampment. The cloud fell back on its forelegs, smoothly crossed the roadway, and crept silently down the fourth rail of the sidings. The whole embankment of bushes bared their heads and followed. They flowed along, bowing to it. The cloud made no response.

Berries and caterpillars came falling from the tree. Infected by the heat, they rolled off, pelted down into the nurse's apron, and were lost to the world.

179

The child had crept as far as the water cock. He had been crawling along for some time. He crept on farther still.

When at length it starts to pour and both sets of rails fly away past the leaning wattle fences, fleeing from the black and watery night that has been let down over them—when the raging night hurriedly calls out to you as it runs and tells you not to fear; its name is only "shower," "love," and something else—then I can tell you that the parents of the kidnapped boy had cleaned their cotton piqué the night before, and it was still early morning when, dressed in snowy white as though for tennis, they went through the still dark garden and emerged by the post with the station's name at the very moment when the bellied front plate of the engine rolled from behind the kitchen gardens and enveloped the Turkish bakery in clouds of gasping, yellowish smoke.

They were going to the port to meet the navel cadet who had once been her lover, was a friend of the husband, and this morning was expected back in the town from an around-the-world training cruise.

The husband was burning with impatience to initiate his friend into the deep meaning of fatherhood, which had still not altogether cloyed for him. Such things do happen. A simple event has confronted you for almost the first time with the splendor of its originality and significance. And this is so new to you that now, when about to meet a man who has traveled the world, seen everything, and, apparently has something to tell, you still suppose that when you meet *he* will be the listener and you the chatterbox who astonishes his mind.

Unlike her husband, she was drawn, as an anchor into water, by the iron clangor of the bustling harbor, the tawny rust of three-funneled giants, the pouring streams of grain, and the radiant splash of sky, sails, and sailors' jackets. Their motives were quite dissimilar.

The rain is pouring, pouring down in torrents. I can carry out my promise. The nut tree's branches crackle above the ditch. Two figures run across the field. The man has a black beard. The woman's shaggy mane shakes in the wind. The man wears a green kaftan and silver earrings. In his arms he holds the captivated child. It is pouring, pouring down in torrents.

II

It turned out that he was long ago promoted to midshipman.

Eleven o'clock at night. The last train from town rolls up to the station. Having first wept to its heart's content, it has cheered up on the bend and begun somehow to bustle. And now, drawing air in from the whole neighborhood, together with leaves, sand, and dew that teem into its bursting reservoirs, it comes to a halt, claps its hands, and falls silent to await an answering boom. The echo should come flowing in from all the lanes, and when the engine hears it, the woman, the sailor, and the man in civilian clothes will turn off the road and onto the footpath, and directly in front of them from behind the poplars the blinding disk of the dew-covered roof will be revealed. They will make their way to the fence and slam the wicket gate, and, spilling nothing from the gutters, roof ridges, and eaves that swing from its lobes like tingling earrings, the iron planet will begin to sink as they approach. The rumble of the departing train will spread, unexpectedly distant, and deceive itself and others as it tries for a while to pass as silence; then it will disperse as a rain of fine yet fading soapsuds. But it will then transpire that this was not the train at all, but rockets of water thrown by the sea to amuse itself. From behind the grove by the station the moon will emerge onto the road. And then as you survey this whole scene, it will seem as though composed by some totally familiar poet, whose name yet constantly eludes you, and the sort of thing they still send to children at Christmastime. You will recall that this very same fence once appeared to you in a dream, but on that occasion it was called the edge of the world . . .

By the moon-washed porch a bucket of paint gleamed white, and a painter's brush stood leaning, bristles up, against the wall. Then they opened the window onto the garden.

"They've been whitewashing today," a female voice said quietly. "Can you smell it? Let's go and have supper."

And silence returned once more. It lasted only briefly. Uproar arose in the house.

"What? How do you mean: not there? Lo-o-ost?!" a hysterical, glistering female contralto and a small, hoarse bass like a slack violin string both exclaimed together.

"Under the tree? Under the tree? Get up this minute and tell us properly. And stop howling. And let go my hands, for Christ's sake. O Lord, what on earth is all this! My Tosha, my little Tosha! Don't you dare! Don't you dare say it to my face! You shameless, brazen good-for-nothing!" The sounds ceased to be words: They ran together mournfully, faltered, and faded. They were no more to be heard.

Night was drawing to an end. But dawn was still far off. On earth dark forms like hayricks stood scattered and astounded by the silence. They were at rest. The distance between them had increased by comparison with daytime; things had separated and moved apart as though to rest more easily. In the spaces between them, chilled meadows puffed silently and exchanged snorts beneath sweat-sodden horse cloths. Rarely did any of the shapes turn out to be a tree, a cloud, or anything else familiar. More often they were obscure agglomerations without name. They were all slightly dizzy and in their semiconscious state could hardly tell whether there had just been rain, or whether it was in store and just about to drizzle. Constantly they would give a heave and swing from past into future, and from the future back into the past, like sand in a repeatedly inverted sandglass.

But far removed from them, like linen snatched at dawn from the fence by a gust of wind and carried off Heaven knows where, three human figures dimly flickered at the far edge of the field, and on the side away from them, there rolled and turned again the eternally evaporating echoed rumble of a distant sea. These four were borne only from the past into the future— to the past there was no return. The people in white ran about from place to place, bent down, and straightened; they jumped down into gullies, disappeared, and emerged at the edge of the field in a different place. From a great distance they would call to one another and wave their hands, and because these signs were misunderstood every time, they would straightway start waving differently, more urgently and impatiently, often to signal that the first signs had not been understood and should be canceled, and that they were not to return but continue searching where they were. The ordered turbulence of these figures might suggest that they had decided to play a game with bat and ball at night, had lost the ball, and were now rummaging for it in the ditches, and when they found it they would start their game again.

Among the shapes at rest reigned perfect calm, and one could believe already that dawn was near; but at the sight of these people springing up above the ground in sudden shock-headed tufts, one might imagine the clearing had been whipped up and disheveled by the wind, by twilight and anxiety, as though by some black comb with three broken teeth.

There is a law according to which things that are forever bound to occur to others can never happen to us. This rule has quite often been quoted by writers. Its irrefutability lies in the fact that while our friends still recognize us, we suppose misfortune can be remedied. But once we fully realize it is irremediable, our friends cease to recognize us, and as if to confirm the rule, we ourselves become different—we become people whose role it is to be consumed, suffer ruin, and be brought to trial or the madhouse.

While still sane people vented their wrath upon the nurse, they perhaps imagined that the fervor of their judgment ensured they could afterward go to the nursery and sigh with relief to find the little boy there, installed in his proper place by the very degree of their fear and distress. The sight of the empty cot stripped the skin from their voices. But even with their souls flayed bare, as they rushed to forage first in the garden before going still farther and farther afield in their searches, for a long time they remained people of our sort; that is, they still searched in order to find. But hour succeeded hour, the night changed countenance, and they too changed, and now with dawn approaching they were quite unrecognizable. They had ceased to understand for what sins, and why, cruel space allowed them no chance to recover breath but continued to drag and fling them from one end to another of land where they could never possibly see their son again. And they had long ago forgotten the midshipman, who now continued searching on the far side of the ravine.

But is it for the sake of this dubious observation that the author hides from the reader what he knows so well himself? For he realizes better than anyone that as soon as the bakers' shops open in the village and the first trains pass on the line, news of the sad occurrence will flash around all the *dachas* and finally inform the schoolboy twins from Olgina Street where to take their nameless young friend and trophy of yesterday's victory.

From beneath the trees, as though from under a cowl pulled low, there already showed the first beginnings of a not yet conscious dawn. Daybreak came in fits and interrupted starts. The roar of the sea was suddenly no more to be heard, and the calm was even greater than before. More and more often a sweet shiver coming from who knows where ran through the trees. One by one their ranks would splash the fence with sweating silver and lapse again into their long sleep, but recently disturbed. In the deep nests of that shadowed luxuriance two rare diamonds glistened separate and independent: a small bird and its chirruping song. Scared by its solitude and ashamed of its own insignificance, the bird tried its utmost to dissolve without trace in a boundless ocean of dew that was too distracted and too drowsy to collect its thoughts. The bird succeeded. Cocking its little head and tightly screwing up its eyes, it silently drank in the stupidity and sorrow of the newborn earth, rejoicing in its own disappearance. But its strength was not sufficient. And suddenly, breaking its resistance and betraying it utterly, its coarse-grained chatter would blaze like some cold star of constant altitude and pattern; the resilient patter scattered in piercing needles; the sprays of sound grew cold and were amazed, as if they had spilled some saucer with an eye enormous and astonished.

But now the dawn came more concertedly. All the garden was filled with moist white light. Closest of all it clung to the stuccoed wall, the gravel-strewn paths, and the trunks of those fruit trees coated with a whitish, limelike copperas compound. The same deathly patina lay also on the face of the child's mother as she now returned from the field and made her way across the garden. Without pause and stepping shakily, she cut through the garden to the back of the house, oblivious of what she trampled and where her feet were sinking. The rise and fall of garden beds tossed her up and down as she went, as though her agitation required still further shaking. Crossing the kitchen garden she approached the section of the fence beyond which one could see the road to the encampment. The midshipman was also making for this point, intending to climb the fence and avoid going around the garden. A yawning eastern sky bore him up onto the fence like a white sail of a sharply heeling boat. She was waiting for him, holding on to the cross-rails of the fencing. She was obviously about to say something and had her short speech all prepared.

The same proximity of a recent or anticipated downpour could also be sensed down on the seashore. Where could that roaring come from that they heard throughout the night beyond the railroad track? The sea lay cooling like the quicksilvered backing of a mirror, and only around its rim did it faintly stir itself and whimper. The horizon was already yellowing, sickly and malevolent. One could pardon such a dawn, pressed up against the back wall of its gigantic sty, befouled for many hundred versts, where at any moment waves might rage and rear on every side. Just now, however, they were crawling on their bellies and barely noticeably rubbing up against each other like a herd of countless black and slippery pigs.

Down onto the shore from behind a rock came the midshipman. He walked with quick and lively step, sometimes jumping from stone to stone. Up there just now he had heard something that stunned him. He picked up a flat piece of ocean-gnawed tile and skimmed it at the water. The stone ricocheted sideways as if skidding on saliva and emitted the same elusive, babyish sound as the shallows all around. Completely despairing in his search, he had just turned toward the *dacha* and started approaching it from the glade when Lelya ran out to the fence and waited till he came up close, then quickly said, "We can't take any more. Save us! Find him. He's your son."

When he seized her by the hand, she tore herself free and ran away, and by the time he had climbed over into the garden she was no more to be found. He picked up another stone and then continued skimming them as he moved away and disappeared behind a projection of rock.

But the footprints he left behind him lived on, still stirring. They too were sleepy. It was the disturbed gravel that crept, crumbled, sighed, and turned from side to side, and kept crunching as it settled down comfortably to sleep in perfect peace.

III

More than fifteen years had passed. Outside dusk was falling; indoors it was dark. For yet a third time the unknown woman asked to see the presidium member of the Provincial Executive Committee, ex–naval officer Polivanov. In front of the woman stood a bored-looking soldier. Through a window in the hallway could be seen the yard heaped with snow-covered mounds of brick. At its far end, where there once had been a cesspit, there now reared a mountain of long-accumulated rubbish, and the sky looked like a wild grove of dense forest springing on the slopes of this assemblage of dead cats and food cans, which were now resurrecting in the thaw, regaining their breath, and starting to fume with former springs and a

dripping, chirruping, jolting, and clattering space and freedom. But it was
sufficient to turn one's glance from this secluded corner and gaze upward
to be astounded at the newness of the sky.

Its present ability to broadcast the day-and-night roar of rifle and field-
gun fire from sea and station had thrust far away all memory of 1905. As
though steamrollered from end to end by a drunken cannonade that had
finally rammed it down and killed it, the sky frowned silently and, without
moving, led away somewhere—quite natural in winter for any ribbon of
railway track, monotonously unwinding. . . .

What sort of sky was this? Even in daylight it recalled the image of the
night we see in our youth or on some long journey. Even in daylight it
caught one's eye, and boundlessly conspicuous, it feasted even in daylight
on the desolate earth, bowling over the somnolent and setting dreamers on
their feet.

These were the aerial ways down which there passed each day, like trains,
the unswerving thoughts of Liebknecht, Lenin, and a few other such high-
flying minds. These were the ways set up on a level high enough to cross
all frontiers, whatever their names. One of these lines, laid down back in
the war, still preserved its former strategic height, imposed on its builders
by the nature of the fronts over which it was laid. This old military branch
line, which had its own place and hours for crossing the frontier of Poland,
and then Germany, was here at its outset quite plainly overstepping all the
limits understood or tolerated by mediocrity. It passed above the yard,
which took fright at the very distance of its destination and its oppressive
vastness, just as a railway track always scares some suburb and sends it fleeing helter-skelter. It was the sky of the Third International.

The soldier replied and told the lady that Polivanov "ain't back yet." A
threefold boredom sounded in his voice. There was the boredom of one used
to liquid mud who now finds himself in dry dust. There was the boredom
of a man accustomed in antiprofiteer and requisitioning teams to asking the
questions himself and having ladies like the one here give confused and
timid answers, and he was therefore irked at this reversal and disturbance
of the standard interview. And finally there was the feigned boredom men
use to give an appearance of complete familiarity with something utterly
unprecedented. And knowing well how unimaginable the recent order must
seem to this lady, he feigned stupidity, as though he were unaware of her
feelings and had breathed nothing since birth but the good air of dictatorship.

Suddenly in came Lyovushka. Something akin to a giant-stride loop
seemed to whisk him up to the first floor from the open air, which blew a
gust of snow and unlighted silence after him. Seizing at what turned out to
be his briefcase, the soldier stopped him as he entered—as if halting a
merry-go-round as it twirled full tilt.

"Now then," he said, "they've been from the Prisoners and Refugee
Center."

"Is it about the Hungarians again?"

"It is."

"But look, they've been told that the party can't leave just with documents!"

"Well, what was I to say? It's quite clear to me—depending on the ships.
I explained it all to them."

"So what happened then?"

"They said, 'We know all that without your help. Your business is just
to see the papers are all in order, like, ready for boarding. And once they're
there it's a matter of course, like.' And we've got to give them quarters."

"Right. What else?"

"Nothing else. That's all they talked about—just their papers and the
quarters, they said."

"No, no!" Polivanov interrupted. "Why repeat it? That's not what I
meant."

"There's a packet from Kanatnaya," said the soldier, naming the street
where the Cheka was, and, coming closer, he dropped his voice to a whisper,
as though on guard duty.

"You don't say! I see. Really?" said Polivanov absentmindedly and with
an air of unconcern. The soldier stepped away again. For a moment both
stood silent.

"Have you brought the bread?" the soldier asked, suddenly souring
because the shape of the briefcase made a reply unnecessary. And he added,
"Oh yes, there's also this woman here . . . wants to see you."

"Yes, yes, yes," drawled Polivanov with the same distracted air.

The giant-stride cable quivered and grew taut. The briefcase began to
move.

"Do come in, comrade," he said to the woman, inviting her into the
study. He did not recognize her.

Compared with the gloom of the hallway, total darkness reigned in here.
She followed behind him but stopped once she was through the door. There
was probably a carpet here, which ran the full length of the room, for he
had hardly gone two or three paces when he disappeared, and the same steps
then sounded again from the far end of the darkness. Then there were
sounds that gradually cleared a tabletop, moving glasses, scraps of dried
bread and sugar lumps, the parts of a dismantled revolver, and hexagonal
pencils. He slowly felt the table with his hand, turning things over and
brushing them in search of matches. Imagination was about to translate the
whole room hung with pictures and furnished with cupboards, palms, and
bronzes to some avenue of old Saint Petersburg, and stood there with a
handful of lights outstretched to shoot them down the whole perspective,

when suddenly the telephone sounded. Its gurgling jingle that echoed of field and wilderness instantly recalled how the wire made its way here through a town engulfed in total gloom, and how all this was happening in the provinces and under the Bolsheviks.

"Yes?" answered the annoyed, impatient, and utterly exhausted man— perhaps he also covered his eyes with a hand. "Yes. I know. I know. Nonsense. Check right down the line. Rubbish. I've been in touch with headquarters. Zhmerinka has been answering for about the last hour. Is that everything? Yes, I will, and I'll let you know. No, no, in about twenty minutes. That all?"

"Well now, comrade," he turned to the visitor, holding a matchbox in one hand and a little blue spot of sputtering sulfur flame in the other.

And then, almost simultaneous with the rattle of falling and scattering matches, came the sound of her whisper, clear and agitated.

"Lelya!" cried Polivanov, beside himself. "It can't be—forgive me! Can it really be—Lelya?"

"Yes ... yes ... How are ... ? Let me collect myself. ... God alone brought me here," she whispered, monotonously choking and weeping.

Suddenly everything vanished. In the gleam of a lighted oil wick, a man in a short unbuttoned jacket, consumed by acute lack of sleep, now stood facing a woman who came unwashed from the station. No trace now of youth and ocean. By the light of the oil flame, her arrival, the deaths of Dmitrii and a daughter, of whose existence he knew nothing, and, in fact, everything she had related in the dark were depressing in their inescapable truth—a truth that invited the listener himself to his grave, if his sympathy were more than mere empty words. Glancing at her in the oil light, he straightway recalled the story that prevented their kissing immediately on meeting. He could not help smiling and he marveled at the endurance of such prejudices. By the light of the oil flame, all her hopes for a well-appointed furnished office collapsed. And this man now seemed so alien to her that no change of circumstance could account for the feeling. So she proceeded to her business all the more determinedly and again, as once before, rushed to dispatch it blindly and by rote, as though it had been assigned by someone else.

"If your child is at all dear to you ..." was how she began.

"Again!" Polivanov boiled up instantly and began to talk and talk and talk, rapidly and without a pause.

He spoke as though writing an article—with subordinate clauses and commas. He walked about the room, then stopped and shook and spread his hands. In intervals of silence, he frowned and pinched the skin on the bridge of his nose with three fingers; he worried and rubbed this spot as though it were the seat of his fading and flaring indignation. He implored her to cease thinking that people were even more inferior than she imagined, and that she could order them about as she pleased. He conjured her by all that was holy never to talk such nonsense again, especially after she had admitted herself at the time that she had deceived him. He told her that even if one were to accept this drivel, she was still producing quite the opposite effect to the one she intended. She could not possibly drive home to a man that something he did not have a moment ago and had now suddenly acquired was not a gain but an actual loss. He recalled what relief and freedom he had felt as soon as he believed her fairy tale, and he had immediately lost all desire to carry on rummaging around dikes and ditches, and wanted only to go and bathe. So even if time could be reversed—he tried taunting her—and they had to start looking once again for one of her family, even then he would only take the trouble for her sake, or for X or Y, and certainly not for himself or her laughable . . .

"Have you quite finished?" she said finally, having allowed him to unwind. "You are quite right. I take my words back. Surely you realize? What if it was mean and cowardly? I was crazy with joy when the boy was found. How marvelous it was! Do you remember? Would I have had the heart to break up my own and Dmitrii's life after that? So I denied myself. But we are not concerned with me. He is yours. And, oh, Lyova, Lyova, if only you knew what danger he is in just now! I don't know how to begin even. Let me start from the beginning. Since that day you and I have not met. You don't know him. And he is so trusting. One day it will be his ruination. There's a certain scoundrel, and adventurer—though it's not for men to judge—called Neploshaev, Tosha's friend from school . . ."

At these words Polivanov, who was pacing up and down the room, stood rooted on the spot. He ceased to hear her. She had spoken the name uttered shortly beforehand among so many other things by the whispering soldier. He knew the case quite well—it was a hopeless one for the accused, and it was only a question of time.

"So he wasn't using his own name?"

She paled at the question. It meant he knew more than she, and that matters were worse even than she had supposed. She quite forgot whose camp she was in, and imagining the whole crime lay in a fictitious name, she hastened to try and protect her son from quite the wrong quarter.

"But, Lyova, he couldn't possibly have openly defended . . ."

And again he ceased to hear her, realizing her child may be concealed under any of these names he knew from the document, and he stood by the table and rang up somewhere or other and asked something or other and went from one conversation to another, ever deeper and farther into the city and the night, until at last the abyss of the final, correct information yawned before him.

He looked around him. Lelya was not in the room. He felt a dreadful aching in his eye sockets, and when he surveyed the room it swam before him like a mass of stalactites and rivulets. He made to pinch the skin on the bridge of his nose again, but instead rubbed his eyes with his hand, and at this movement the stalactites danced and began running together. It would have been easier had their spasms not been so frequent and so noiseless. Then he found her. Like a huge, broken doll she lay between the foot of his desk and the chair, on the same layer of rubbish and sawdust that, while conscious, in the dark, she had taken for a carpet.

1924

Translated by Christopher Barnes

Three Chapters
from a Story

I

A Few Dates

These events took place a long time ago.

"Cossacks!"

Galloping in the direction of this shout, they suddenly found themselves riding the very crest of a vast, saddleless sea of heads surging along behind and in front of them. Swiftly heading it off, the Cossacks herded the crowd down the pavements, mounted on their shaggy horses—Kurdish horses, you would probably have called them at that time. Manes shook, earrings shook. Then the riders suddenly formed ranks once more and dashed off.

"Aa-ah!" A figure picked itself up from the ground, unable to recognize Nikitskaya Street. Where had everything disappeared to? Sky, stone posts along the pavements—and not a trace remained of the black, curly Cossack hats and the roar that had been audible only a moment ago.

Schütz was the son of rich parents and a relative of very famous revolutionaries. This was sufficient for him to be regarded as a revolutionary and a rich man. Schütz's other attributes had this same distinctive feature. He possessed the puzzling kind of nature that people find striking but that can rarely be fathomed, for a score of hypotheses can be considered before diagnosing that a patient has a tapeworm. In Schütz this enigmatic tapeworm was: lying. It played about inside him, and when it needed to be fed its head tickled his throat. It sprouted and shed its coils. In Schütz's eyes all this was as it should be, and he felt that he had picked it up in larval form from reading Nietzsche.

Lemokh's past was more clearly linked with the Revolution than Schütz's. Are you familiar with night in the Ukraine? In its exact image a sensitive stream was generated in his imagination, which ate more deeply into the brain of the politically conscious than the Ukraine's dark waters into the alluvial silt of Podolsk. The words "smugglers," "stage horses," "border guards," "wagons," and "stars" fell from his lips as a recitative more romantic than the music accompanying Carmen.

Sooner or later Spektorsky was bound to encounter Schütz, for just as Spektorsky was spurred everywhere by a compulsion to be enthralled and amazed, so too Schütz, for his part, turned up everywhere to tell lies, to charm and enthrall.

In 1916, the year to which the beginning of this narrative actually relates, Spektorsky recalled Schütz not just any old way but exactly as he had begun to seem during a certain period about five months after they had first become acquainted, in July 1909.

Without actually deserting his new wife or being deserted by her, he had arrived back from abroad practically addicted to morphine. He lived in furnished rooms under an assumed name. At the same time the business of his exemption from military service was being handled under his real name.

In the afternoons he would usually be busy. He used to go to the eye clinic for belladonna. A doctor acquaintance of his assured him that when he came to them for his medical examination the oculists would issue him an absolute discharge. People began to call it the "white ticket" somewhat later.

It is generally understood that a pansy is like a yellow-and-purple cotillion ribbon; yet one does come across completely purple pansies like dilated pupils, and these always appear nearer to hand and larger than life. During this period of their acquaintance Schütz's eyes had no whites.

The imbecile gaze of flickering summer lightning darted over the town. Its flashes fell behind cupboards, into inkwells, into drinking glasses with pencils propped in them. Dust lay across the whole summer like the imprint of melancholy on a person whose mind is unhinged. Schütz's rooms were called "Vorobyov's Lodgings." A surprising impression was produced by this noiseless assembly of curtains jostling at the windows and suddenly careering across the room accompanied by the distinctive smell of disturbed foliage. Chance drops of rain dried up instantly. The flying muslin was illuminated . . .

Spektorsky was dogged by the impression that their conversations always took place in the conspicuous absence of a third party. They kept stopping to listen. The impression still lingered. The thunderless summer lightning produced these illusions. These were discourses in the absence of a storm.

II

Deva Obida – the Maid of Woe

The years were going by and passing into oblivion. Many summers elapsed, many springs and winters. Much was forgotten, including faces.

Forgotten were the snakes at whose trickling transit the hazel flexed its drooping, transparent pincer-shaped leaves. Forgotten were the snakes, the only streams of moisture the already ravaged, expiring earth could still recognize in that terrible drought. They flowed drop by drop across the whole of Rukhlovo, hissing incessantly, and all along their route the sparrows kept chirping, boiling up and instantly evaporating.

Consigned to the past was that summer, throughout the course of which a dredger worked on the shoals, directly beneath the nasturtiums growing in profusion over the parapet of the turret.

Consigned to the past was that evening when the lights on the dredger were lighted early, and with one final wheeze it turned about, emitting a parting string of increasingly frequent hoots, which soon began to grow fewer and fainter.

At its departure the river banks sighed with relief. A silence as succulent as willow shoots, as heavy as damp plaits being wrung out, as alert as a horse at water, settled over the glassy Oka to the water's very edge.

Consigned to the past too was the instant when the moon, with hardly a glance into a backwater, turned to face the specter of distant regimental music, which suddenly came drifting in her wake, as if from nowhere.

For a while the imponderability of this phenomenon retained a flavor of the miraculous. But soon its very imponderability reached such proportions that by now it was no longer frightening or intriguing. It was irksome.

The women were infected by an unaccountable agitation. They crowded onto the stone patio in blouses flushed as if from the chill. They sent the menfolk to fetch them their shawls, and as they listened to this amazing sound, gazed out over the quiet reaches of the river, on which the images of stars bobbed here and there like floats.

But the march of the Preobrazhensky Regiment—for that is what it was, and they now all recognized it—came drifting from nowhere, drifting and fading, drifting, mournful as never before.

An eternity elapsed while the funnel of a tug, apparently blissfully unaware of the march, began to appear above the promontory behind which the dredger had disappeared. The coal-black outline of a barge rose up

between the reeds and stars, between moon, forest, and silence. At the end
of its long, long stretch of cable, it headed straight for the park, for the
snakes, for Müller, for Vinogradskaya and her sister Olga Dezhnyova.

The barge was like any other. On it stood trunks, camp beds, and trestles.
There were no people on it, and it held no further clues.

But one could already sense that the music was coming from the far bank,
that the soldiers were marching through the forest, and that at any moment
now they would file out onto the water meadow and meet up with their
regimental baggage, which was traveling by river.

An hour passed, as confused as a camp being pitched, as intermittent as
sands in a mist, as timid as the limpid waters into whose current a boat was
launched three times to fetch the officers. On each occasion, as they made
the return journey, a hurricane lantern flitted before them all across the
water to the river bank, waggling its whiskers, groping around in the bushes,
and from beneath them flinging onto the banks handfuls of clumsy crayfish.
A huge, ancient alder that stood above the bathing place grinned toothlessly
and seized them in midair.

Then a conversation of varying volume and duration rang out.

"Jump, Kibiryov!"

"What did you take the lantern away for? Put it in the stern."

"Hey! What? Can't hear anyth . . .!"

"That . . . the . . . la . . . ast?"

"Hold it—no, bring her in a bit. . . . Right, lower away."

The night had gone by in which the park had reverberated to the sound
of more and more unfamiliar voices. The officers had settled for the night
in the house of the owner, Fresteln, a member of the Council of Nobility.
Not a single person remained here who might have asked them the very
same question that had been put to them by positively every hamlet, estate,
wayside shrine—every patch of wasteland and every traveler whom they
had met en route during the course of the day. But the official order to
mobilize had not yet been announced. This duty of unconditional silence
was the first in a whole sea of new feelings that burst upon them during the
next twenty-four hours. Among other people it placed them in the same
position as men among women, or adults among children. A state of affairs
was being proclaimed in which they were obliged to follow the word of the
Lord faithfully, in strict hierarchical order, and the field of battle was
accorded honors more fitting for Heaven on the Feast of Saint Elias.

Night was coming to a close. As it petered out, a heap of ash on a saucer
was merely awaiting an opportune moment to fuse with all the cigarette
butts into the yellow, tobacco-saturated, eye-watering decoction. In the
east, heaps of emaciated cloud were awaiting the same opportunity. The
sound of heavy breathing came from a muzzy head, a blanket drawn to its
chin, lying in a heap of tousled hair.

Suddenly one of them yawned. The other started to talk. "I had a dream about Kiev. Seriously. I dreamed that we were at Borki, at the *dacha,* and one night we wandered into the regimental band's headquarters with our girl friends. The soldiers were asleep. It was in a wood. But the most remarkable thing was the trumpets. You could smell them. Honestly. D'you hear, Valya?"

"Yes. Not so loud."

"They were lying on the grass, all brassy and shiny, covered with dew, and you could really smell them. You know, like almonds, or snapped-off convolvulus—like a cherry stone or cyanide. And all around it was night. Pitch black night. What's the matter, Valya?"

"I think they'll announce the declaration of war today. Eh, Spektorsky? I can't hold out much longer. It's the main thing on our minds, and yet we've got to keep quiet about it. What do you think?"

"I think you're right, Valya."

"And even then they'll still pester you. For instance, that girl from these parts—just came up without so much as a by-your-leave, and wanted you to tell her straight. Is it war? For heaven's sake. Will we find out at Aleksin? What's your guess?"

"Probably—it's possible that they've already announced the mobilization. Just that we don't know about it yet. We're on the road. That's what I think."

"That's only because you blabbed so much to her."

The gray dawn was approaching. The cigarette butts slithered into the tea. The clouds melted. A fly etched the windowpane with a buzzing as prickly as unthreshed grain.

"Valya, is it in *The Lay of Igor's Host* that *Deva Obida* comes?"

"Yes, I believe so."

"Why exactly is it *Obida?* Any idea?"

"It's translated as the modern word *beda*—trouble or misfortune."

"What do you mean 'translated'? God knows, it's all the same language. There's something about trumpets in *The Lay of Igor's Host* as well. I've forgotten it now."

The fly buzzed. The regulars were still asleep.

III

The Staircase

Spektorsky's father was an amazing man. He was a member of some board of directors, but he had given up business a long time ago. He moved in the company of literary men and professors and was a bit of an eccentric.

Whenever there was a ring at the door he would rush out himself, often straight from the bathroom or the dinner table. He would clap his hands, step back, and then embrace the visitor, roaring "How's life? How's life?" Then, turning to the door curtain, he would shake his fists and his mane of hair like the miller in *Rusalka* and shout into the suite of rooms with their diminishing series of folding wicker hampers frilled with winter semi-gloom, "It's N.N. Well? Glasha! Katya! N.N.! Come in. Don't let's stand here in the doorway like idiots! Our guests come in, take off their coats, come into the dining room in their galoshes, into the study, in to tea. Please come in. Take off your coat. Get out of your things. Come into the dining room. Tea? Glasha, Katya, what about it?"

Glasha was the maid, and Katya—his sister. Every fresh visitor unconsciously guessed. Now if after all that performance he were in addition to jump onto the window ledge or something similar, it would mean he was really out of his mind. But for the moment, blast him, it only appeared that way.

Aunt Katya's dresses rose up to her plump neck, to her throat, raising her chin slightly and flooding her face with a kindly, plaintive smile. She had the deepset eyes of a reticent, easily disconcerted depressive. She was short in stature, and the exertion of the person speaking to her, no matter how flippant his conversation might be, communicated itself to her, and this exertion possessed the property of growing, growing, growing, and breaking off with a scintillating nod when the other person's words ceased.

Four families knew each other only through the person of the porter on the bright, spacious staircase, which ran to two stories and emerged onto one of the Kislovsky lanes.

"That young priest from the seminary was right, I tell you. Right in every way. Once—that's coincidence. The second time it's coincidence. The third time, crash from the roof of the temple without being smashed to pieces— it's habit. We've grown accustomed to everything. Whatever else comes along—we'll get used to that too. Habit is the devil's own gift . . . There's the doorbell! Don't you bother, Galochka. I'll answer it."

The porter used to fetch fancy rolls and deliver the newspaper. He had small, piglike, and yet at the same time angelic eyes, as blue as forget-me-nots. On winter evenings, when he had stoked up his stove beneath the stairs, he would sit in his room sweltering with the heat, and his eyes brimmed over with tiny tears of tow-haired, meadowy amiability.

Make a casual inquiry of him and he would recount how, according to a letter from Minsk, Sergei Gennadyevich Spektorsky had a shattered foot, thank God—thank God in the sense that now there was hope. It meant his war service was over. Incidentally, he wasn't deformed or anything. Just a slight difference in their length. The old man would see to it. He knew the right people. If it had been left up to him he would have gotten the lad out of it a long time ago. All those doctors have to do is hear an uneven heartbeat, and that's enough to do the trick. "And look at the way he walks —just look!" they'd have said. Then he wouldn't have to have gone in the first place. But the old man wouldn't agree to it himself. He was ashamed. In his eyes it was a disgrace. Now it's a different matter. He's bound to be back soon. They're expecting him.

The blizzard raged and abated, abated and revived. The houses, floating past in shallow flight, almost diving into the snow, battered the streetlights with their wide-eaved wings. A sound rang out, a shower of broken glass, and then an elemental screech like dry, ripping worsted suddenly lit up the whole street at once as it lay wallowing in a gloom, mute for all eternity. Then through the gray tatters of the snowstorm a flickering glimpse of the faces of men on foot and on horseback, their helmets pulled low over their foreheads, enveloped in domes of snow. They approached and retreated, stumbled about and were lost to view, but then they kept reappearing and disappearing so frequently and with so little trace that it was impossible to say whether they were ghosts, or not even that.

Every time street rumors of the blizzard floated in and reached the lamp, the staircase gently waved the shadows of its banisters, the steps collapsed like cards, without a rustle, and a thin black tongue of soot writhed up toward the lantern glass. Vision was strained; vision weakened.

From time to time the following could be heard:

"Spiridon."

"At your service, sir."

"Spiridon, just tell me, how have you managed to get out of military service? How is it that you're still walking around a free man? Come on, come on, old fellow. Do me a favor. How did you manage it? On grounds of your stupidity, was that it?"

"You will have your little joke. I've got flat feet. D'you think Sergei Gennadyevich will return soon, sir?"

"I don't know, old fellow. I don't know. If he doesn't send a telegram, then it could be any time now. Unawares. To catch us by surprise, by surprise, Spiridon."

"What's that, sir?"

"Did you say there's a blizzard?"

"A real bad one."

"I can hear it, I can hear it. I don't need you to tell me, old fellow. So you won't be going? Well, let's say it's on grounds of your stupidity."

Or the following:

"You see, Spiridon, I'm miserable—don't be ignorant, old fellow, interrupting your elders. I'll tell you what I mean. Don't get married, Spiridon. You get married and they'll take away your son to the war, and then you'll be like me, wandering up and down the stairs."

"Surely it won't last for ever?"

"There'll be enough for our grandchildren. For our grandchildren. Wars will never end. And when will it finish, do you think? The seventh of March next year. The seventh, you mark my words. There'll be peace. But you'd better make the door fast for the night, in case of Germans."

One hour goes by, then another. After three hours Spiridon trims and extinguishes his alter ego. Only the blizzard remains out on the stairs. It sees the porter in his underpants as an oddity, but still it keeps silent. He is falling asleep. It scurries up every flight of stairs and rolls down them again like a wheel.

During the night, obliquely lit up from below by both Spiridons, nineteen-twentieths of a leg made their way upstairs, far more slowly than the old man's galoshes, with a clumping and stumbling fitting for such an . . . improper fraction.

Homecoming

"Just imagine, they couldn't agree on the price. It wasn't even worth letting them in. I'll tell you what I've come to see you about, Seryozha. Doesn't it strike you as strange, my dear boy, here you've been home for four whole days, after all? My own son, no matter what, and an officer into the bargain. Well it's all hellish interesting, damn it all, and incidentally . . ."

"Drop the subject, Dad. You want to talk about the war? Well I'm not keeping quiet by accident. I have my reasons. Someday I'll tell you everything. Someday yet to come. When I have to."

"Do me a favor, dear boy. I'm not twisting your arm. Only you must admit, it's a bit absurd. All right, all right, all right. Another time, another time. I'll remind you."

"That's the way. You remind me. Let's agree on that. You'll say to me *obida,* woe . . ."

"*Obi* . . . ? Now listen, my boy, that's no way to talk. What kind of rotten riddle is that? Well . . . but . . . but . . . You've got the Saint George Medal. Did you . . . how did you win that?"

"You poor old thing. You don't understand me. I didn't mean it like that. I'm not talking about *obida* in the sense of an insult. In that respect everything is fine with me, and with the others too. No. I'll tell you about it someday . . . about the way folksongs are born."

Translated by Nicholas J. Anning

The Story

I

At the beginning of 1916 Seryozha came to stay with his sister Natasha in Solikamsk. I have had the separate parts of this story in my mind for the past ten years now, and shortly after the Revolution some of them found their way into print.

But the reader would do better to forget these versions; otherwise he will flounder about, deciding what fate eventually befell each of the characters. I have given different names to a number of them; as to the fates themselves, they remain to this very day as I found them during those years in the snow beneath the trees; and there will be no discrepancy between my novel in verse *Spektorsky,* which I started subsequently, and this present piece of prose. They are one and the same life.

As a matter of fact Seryozha came not to Solikamsk, but to Usolye, which loomed white on the far bank of the Kama River. Even on arrival, at first sight, viewing it from the kitchen of the doctor's newly renovated home on the factory side of the river, it was easy to grasp why, for what purpose, and to what end Usolye stood where it did. The sheer commercial masonry of the cathedral and the official buildings glittered and browsed, scattered in all directions by explosive charges of surfeit and the gunpowder blast of contentment. Reducing to neat squares this spectacle across the river, the handiwork of Ivan the Terrible and the Stroganovs, the windows of the doctor's house shone just as if the fresh white paint had been stirred and spread in bags of skimmed cream over the woodwork in honor of the distant view. That was indeed the case, for the gaunt, tattered frontages of the financial quarter had little to offer.

The thaw helped the ravens peck away beneath the bushes. Solitary sounds waded in black puddles of slush. The whistling of a shunting engine at Veretye alternated with the voices of playing children. The thudding of axes from a nearby construction site distracted attention from the muffled organ hum of the distant factory, a hum more imagined than really audible, prompted by the sight of its five smoking chimney tops. Horses neighed and dogs barked. The raucous crowing of a cockerel dangled like a mote on a thread and snapped off. Meanwhile the energetic pounding of a dynamo generator floated leisurely across from the distant tributary, where the sleepy whiskers of a swaddled willow clump stuck out from beneath the snowdrifts. The sounds were scant, seemingly drunk as they drifted in the ruts. In the intervals the wintry plain's silences gaped, solemn and exultant. Somewhere close by, almost in the neighboring village, according to the locals, the plain concealed the first foothills of the Urals, hiding them away like deserters.

Seryozha bumped into his sister Natasha as she came out the door, intending to go off somewhere on some household errand. Behind her stood a little girl with a snub nose, wearing a short fur jacket fastened all askew. Natasha flung her shopping bag on the windowsill, and while they embraced and talked noisily, the girl snatched Seryozha's suitcase and, with her loose felt boots flapping, she steered around the dining-room table, sidelong, like a rolling hoop, and careered like a whirlwind into the interior of the apartment.

Before long, under a barrage of questions from his sister, Seryozha began clumsily and awkwardly to wash away with Kazan soap the grubby traces of two solid days and nights without sleep. At this point, as he stood with a towel across his shoulder, his sister could see how much thinner and taller he had grown. After that he shaved. His brother-in-law, Pasha Kalyazin, was away at work at this hour, but when Natasha brought his shaving equipment from the bedroom, Seryozha was a bit nonplussed by the number of accessories.

There was a delicious smell of sausage in the bright dining room. A thirteen-branched palm brandished ferocious fist-fronds at the black varnish of the piano, and the brass glare of the candlesticks fastened to it pressed and threatened to smash the panel. Catching Seryozha's glance as it strayed over the milk-white cosmetic shades of the oilcloth, Natasha said, "We got all this from Pasha's predecessor. The furniture is rented." Then after a pause she added, "I'm terribly curious to see what you'll think of the children. After all, you only know them from photographs."

The children were expected back from their walk at any minute.

He sat down to tea and, deferring to Natasha, explained to her that their mother's death had shaken him by its utter unexpectedness. He had feared it more during the summer when, as he put it, she really had been at death's door and he had traveled there to visit her.

"I know! Right before the exams! They wrote and told me," Natasha put in. "Well, yes," he took up her words, almost choking. "And do you know I actually took them! What an effort it cost to pass them! But now my time at the university is so much water under the bridge."

Continuing to knead a sticky mouthful of pulped roll and sip tea from the glass, he recounted how he had meant to start his revision that spring, soon after Natasha had visited him in Moscow, but had had to abandon the idea: their mother's illness, his trip to Saint Petersburg, and much more besides (here he went over it all once again). But then, a month before the winter term, he had thought better of it, though the constant distractions, which had become an ingrained habit since childhood, were the hardest thing of all to combat. When he remarked that "one talent in the hand is worth two in the bush," he felt injured because his sister did not recognize the proverb that their dead father had coined in the family, with special reference to him.

"Well, how did you manage, then?" Natasha asked, hastily disguising her embarrassment.

"What do you mean, how did I manage? I forced the pace day and night, that's how." And he began trying to convince her that there was no pleasure to equal such a race, which he defined as *the exaltation of nonleisure.* According to him, this mental sport alone had helped him to deal with his inborn temptations, the main one being his music, which he had since abandoned. And to prevent his sister's putting in another word he rapidly informed her, without any apparent transition, that when the war broke out Moscow had been at the height of a building boom and that work had gone on at first but had now come to a complete standstill in some places, so that many houses would remain unfinished for good.

"Why for good?" she objected. "Don't you have any hope that the war will come to an end?"

But he remained silent, assuming that here, as elsewhere, the topic of the war, that is, of the utter inconceivability of peace, would come up more than once, and that Kalyazin was probably the chief talker on this subject.

Suddenly Natasha was struck by the unhealthy anticipation Seryozha began to use with increasing frequency and success to ward off her curiosity. At this point she realized that he was exhausted and, eluding this mind-reading of his, she suggested that he get undressed and take a nap. At that moment there was an unexpected interruption. A bell tinkled faintly. Assuming that it was the children, Seryozha started to follow his sister, but Natasha waved him away and, muttering something, vanished into the bedroom. Seryozha walked over to the window, his hands clasped behind his back, and stared into space.

In his state of elated abstraction his ear failed to register the fury that was unleashed next door. Straining every nerve and clutching the receiver tightly, Natasha dinned some sort of pleasantries into those same spaces that spread before her brother's gaze. A man was walking off with measured, heavy tread in the direction of the endless fence at the far end of the village, a man notable only for the fact that there was not a soul near him and that no one came toward him from the opposite direction. Idly watching this departing figure, Seryozha recalled a wooded stretch of countryside through which his journey had just taken him. He could picture the station, the deserted buffet with boards propped on trestles serving as a counter, the hills beyond the signals, and the passengers who strolled, raced madly, and jostled on the heaped-up mound of snow that separated the cold railway carriages from the hot pies.

At that point the striding man skirted the fence and, turning behind it, disappeared from view.

While this was going on, changes had occurred in the bedroom. The yelling over the telephone had come to an end. Clearing her throat with relief, Natasha was inquiring how soon her jacket would be ready and explaining how to sew it.

"Did you guess who that was?" she said as she came in, catching her brother's attentive glance. "It was Lemokh. He's here on business to do with his factory, and he's coming to spend the evening with us."

"Which Lemokh? Why were you shouting like that?" Seryozha interrupted her in a low voice. "You might have warned me. When you chat away out loud, thinking you're alone in the apartment, and someone is working next door, it can put them out. You should have said that the dressmaker was in the house."

At first the misunderstanding grew serious, but eventually it was completely resolved. It turned out that no one else had been in the bedroom, and when Natasha had been cut off from her more distant caller she had carried on chatting to the operator who had disconnected her and who was sitting in an office at the far end of the village.

"A charming girl," Natasha added. "She's also a dressmaker; she can't manage on her wages. She's coming tonight, as well. Though it's not definite, because she has guests from the front."

"Do you know," Seryozha declared abruptly, "I really think I'll go and lie down."

"That's a good idea," his sister quickly agreed, and she led him to the room that had been made ready for him the moment his letter had arrived. "I'm surprised you weren't drafted," she remarked on the way, half turning to glance at her brother. "After all, you haven't got a limp at all."

"Yes, just imagine, not a single objection, by a unanimous decision of the board. What are you doing?" he exclaimed, noticing that his sister was about to make up the bed and was pulling off the bedspread. "Leave it like that. I'll sleep with my clothes on. Don't bother."

"Just as you like," she consented, and with a proprietary glance around the room, she said from the doorway, "Have a good sleep and don't worry. I'll see to it that there isn't any noise. If the worst comes to the worst we'll have dinner without you and your meal can be warmed up later. But for you to go and forget Lemokh, that's unforgivable on your part. He's a very, very interesting and admirable man, and he speaks very warmly and sincerely about you."

"But what am I supposed to do about it?" Seryozha pleaded. "I've never seen him, and this is the first time I've ever heard of him."

It struck him that even the door closing behind his sister did so in a mildly reproachful way.

He unfastened his suspenders and, sitting down on the bed, began loosening his bootlaces.

A sailor named Fardybasov, who was on a short spell of shore leave from the destroyer *Novik*, had also come to Veretye by the same train as Seryozha. He carried his small trunk from the station direct to the railway office, gave a resounding kiss to a woman relative of his who worked there, and set off right away with firm footsteps toward the Mechanical Workshop, crunching the ice and spraying water. His arrival created an uproar. However, when he failed to find Otryganyev, the man he had come to see, in the crowd that gathered around him, and learned that he now worked in one of of the recently established plants, he headed at the same pace toward Auxiliary Workshop No. 2, which he soon discovered behind the storehouse fences, at the junction of the narrow-gauge railway. The track crawled like a grubby little fringe along the brink of an abrupt rise. Its defenselessness was frighteningly obvious, for at the forest edge a sentry paced up and down, armed with a rifle. Leaving the road, Fardybasov rushed down through the field, flitting from one hummock to the next and disappearing in stagnant pits that had formed over the summer. Then he began to make his way up to the mound where the wooden shed stood. It differed from an ordinary outhouse only because it bombarded the reigning silence there with its regular, snowball-like plumes of steam.

Trotting up to the doorway, Fardybasov slapped the doorpost with the palm of his hand and grunted "Otryganyev!" into the depths of the building, where a number of peasants were dragging sacks from one place to another and a huge engine, its flywheel apparently frozen in its lightning motion, was hammering away, protected from the outside world by nothing but a clapboard siding. The wild connecting-rod lever beneath it danced, slapped its pistons, squatted and dipped through the floor, flailing its sprained leg, its tremors enough to terrorize the entire establishment.

"What's this old crap you're pumping here?" asked the new arrival, by way of greeting to a sluggish cripple who came hobbling over from the machine, rocking from one good leg onto his other, withered one, and loomed up in the doorway.

"Eryomka!" the cripple had just time to blurt out, when he was immediately seized by a spasm of bitter, course, catarrhal smoker's coughing. "Chloroform," he gurgled in a voice drink-sodden to the point of tuberculosis, and could only wave his hand in the throes of a fresh paroxysm of asthmatic wheezing.

"Tar-mixers, is that what it's come to!" the sailor said with an affectionate grin, waiting for the spasm to subside.

But it never came to that because, at that moment, two of the Tatar peasants, detaching themselves from the rest, quickly scrambled up a wall ladder to the front above and started to pour lime into the mixer, which produced an incredible din and enveloped the whole building in a billowing white screen of dust. And right in the middle of this cloud, Fardybasov began to yell how he reckoned the clerk had eaten into his time and his days were all accounted for. At which point he began urging his friend to do the very thing he had struggled up here from the station cross-country to do —to spend the whole of his leave hunting.

After a little time had passed, spent in gentle mocking at the apprentices, at those awating call-up, and at factories engaged in war work, Fardybasov, who was about to leave, recounted how not so long ago, just before Christmas, they had strayed into a German minefield one night as they were sailing out of the Gulf of Finland and been blown up. There was exaggeration and bravado only in terms of the personalities involved, for Fardybasov had been on board the *Novik,* though it was another destroyer in the flotilla that had lifted its bows, plowed the deep, and sunk, drawing over itself a watery noose of savage depth and tightness.

It was getting dark. A slight frost had set in; water was being put on to boil in the kitchen. The children came in and were shushed. From time to time Natasha stole over to listen at the door. But Seryozha could not sleep: He was only pretending to be asleep. Beyond the wall the whole household was shifting from twilight into evening. To the lament of slaving utensils, floors, and buckets, Seryozha was thinking how unrecognizable everything would be in the lamplight when this shift was accomplished. It would be as though he had arrived for a second time and, most important of all, he would have had a good sleep as well. But the first hint of novelty, already conjured up by the lamps to some extent, scurried and rattled through one incarnation to another. It inquired in childish voices where Uncle was and when he would be leaving again, and, taught a forbidding glare, it uttered a piercing shoo at the perfectly innocent Mashka. It fluttered about in a flock of maternal admonitions amid the steam from the soup, flapping its wings at aprons and plates. No amount of objections could prevent it from being wrapped up again by fussy and irritable hands and dispatched for another walk, hurried through the hallway to avoid letting cold air into the house. And eventually, much later that evening, it was embodied in the incursion of Kalyazin's bass voice, his cane, and his tall galoshes, which, in ten years of married life, had still not yielded to any argument.

To induce sleep, Seryozha doggedly tried to picture some summer noon, the first that came to mind. He knew that if such an image were to appear and he could hang on to it, the vision would seal his eyes and rush snoring to his feet and brain. But he lay there for a long time, holding the spectacle of July heat right in front of his nose like a book, and still sleep declined to visit him. It so happened that it was the summer of 1914 that cropped up, and in the circumstances this upset all his calculations. To gaze at that summer, and drink in its soporific clarity through clouded eyes, was impossible. He was forced to think instead, passing from one reminiscence to another. This same reason will also keep us away from the Usolye apartment for some time.

It was here that Natasha's commissions had originated, and with her list rendered illegible by minute jottings and frequent crossouts, she had scoured Moscow on her arrival there in the spring of 1913. She had stopped at Seryozha's on that occasion, and now from the smell of construction timber, the buzz of surrounding calm, and the state of the roads in the village, he imagined that he could already recognize the people his sister was assisting when she left the room on Kislovka Street for days at a time. The factory staff lived in real amity, like one big family. Her journey in 1913 had even been registered as a business trip with the husband's mission entrusted to the wife. Such nonsense was only conceivable because every link in that abstract chain, which ended in overnight and traveling expenses, was a human being linked to another in a kinship forged by the crowded conditions in which they had to huddle, as though on a tiny island, with their diverse degrees of literacy, amid three thousand miles of utterly illiterate snows. Taking advantage of the occasion, management had even delegated to Natasha power to negotiate for it in clearing up certain trifling misunderstandings, which could easily have been settled by mail, and this was why Natasha kept going to and fro to the Ilyinka on visits that she presented in a very ambiguous light. She set these "calls" in emphatically comic quotation marks, thereby implying that the inverted commas enclosed matters of ministerial importance. But in her free time, and particularly in the evening, she would visit her own and her husband's friends from former days in Moscow.

With them she went to theaters and concerts. As with her spells at the Ilyinka managerial office, she gave these amusements the appearance of business, but of the sort that did not require the use of inverted commas. That was because an important past bound her to the people with whom she was now sharing visits to the Moscow Art Theater and the Korsh Theater. Spontaneously open to intriguing interpretations on each occasion when they went over old times afresh, this past now remained the sole proof of their contact with one another. They met, welded firmly together by its remoteness; some were now doctors, others engineers, and still others had entered the legal profession. Those who had not managed to take up their temporarily interrupted studies again worked on the staff of *The Russian Word*. All of them had set up house, and with the exception of those who had opted for a literary career, all of them had children. They were not all alike, of course, and they lived separately, rather than on top of one another, each on a different street. When she went off to visit some of them, Natasha turned off Kislovka to the trolley stop on Vozdvizhenka, whereas when calling on another group, she walked along Gazetnaya, Kamergersky, and so on, cutting across streets each more crooked, sinuous, and crowded than the one before.

It must also be said that during this short visit of Natasha's, except for one occasion in Georgievsky Lane, where she had to look in on friends on her way to attend a benefit concert with singers and readings from Chekhov, there was no talk of the past. And even on this occasion, hardly had Natasha begun to indulge her memories following her discovery in her friend's toilet case of a red tie from the time she attended the Women's Senior Courses, when her friend, whom she herself had been urging to hurry, finished getting ready, and, moving away from the mirror, where resurrected images had already begun to flicker, they rolled out in a threesome with her friend's husband, headlong into the green, mirror-chill, spring-evening air. What is more, they did not discuss the past, because they knew deep in their hearts that the revolution would come again. By virtue of a deception forgivable even in our day, they imagined that the revolution would be staged again, like a drama that has been temporarily taken off the boards and suddenly revived again with the original cast, that is, with all of them playing their old parts. This misapprehension was all the more natural in that, given their profound belief in the widespread popular appeal of their ideas, they were all of the opinion that it was necessary to test their own convictions on living people. And at this stage, becoming convinced of the absolute and, to a certain extent, banal oddity of the revolution from the broad point of view of the average Russian, they were justified in wondering where fresh advocates and devotees of such an isolated and delicate undertaking might ever appear.

Like all of them, Natasha believed that the most worthy cause of her younger days had merely been put off, and when the hour struck she would not be passed by. This belief accounted for all the flaws in Natasha's character. It explained her self-assurance, which was mitigated only by her total ignorance of her defect. It also explained those elements of inexplicit integrity and all-forgiving understanding that illuminated Natasha from within with an unquenchable light, yet did not correspond to anything in particular.

She had learned from relations that Seryozha was involved in some sort of affair. It should be noted that she was familiar with every detail, starting with the name of Seryozha's lady friend, Olga, right down to the fact that the latter was happily married to an engineer. She did not get around to cross-examining her brother about anything. Though she acted this way from conventional decorum, she immediately ascribed it, bright spirit that she was, to some special generic virtue. She did not get around to cross-examining Seryozha, but breathing an awareness of his story's direct deference to the thoughtful and sensitive principle that she herself personified, she waited until, unable to bear his isolation, he would open his heart to her of his own accord. She laid claim to his sudden confession, awaiting it with professional impatience; and who could jeer at her, considering that her brother's story had in it an element of free love, a colorful clash with everyday matrimonial ties, the right to strong, healthy emotion, and, heavens above, almost the whole of Leonid Andreev? Meanwhile, pent-up pettiness had a worse effect on Seryozha than irrepressible and effervescent stupidity, and once, when he could not contain himself, his sister interpreted his evasiveness in her own way and deduced from his clumsily disjointed sentences that everything had gone wrong between the lovers. After that, her feeling of competence only increased because what was for her the indispensable element of drama had now been added to the inventory. For, no matter how remote her brother might have been to her as a result of being born five years and a few months later than her generation, even she had eyes in her head, and she could see beyond a shadow of doubt that trickery and mischief were not in Seryozha's character. And the word "drama," which Natasha spread among her acquaintances, was the only one not to be found in her brother's vocabulary.

II

Seryozha put a great deal of this behind him when, after successfully passing his last examination, he came out into the street as if capless and, overwhelmed by everything that had happened, gazed excitedly around him. A young cabby, his raised boot parting his kaftan, was sitting sideways on the driver's box, glancing beneath his horse every once in a while, with total confidence in the heedless purity of the March air, as he waited indifferently to be hailed from any corner of the broad square. The dapple-gray mare stood, an unwilling replica of his voluntary abeyance, blinking in the shafts as if the very rumble of the streets had transported it there bodily and harnessed it under the shaft bow. Everything roundabout imitated horse and driver. With its crest of clean cobbles the cambered street, studded with curb posts and lights, looked like a document on headed paper. The houses stood poised in a vacant prespring alert as though on a resilient base of four rubber tires. Seryozha looked around. Beyond a fence, the door that had only recently closed quietly upon his twelve years at school swung in ponderous, high-summer indolence on one of the grayest and most dilapidated façades. Those years had been immured at precisely that moment, now and forever. Seryozha set off for home on foot. A blank sunset of pinching chill unexpectedly broke upon Nikitskaya Street. A frosty purple caught the stonework. Seryozha felt too ashamed to glance at the passersby. Everything that had happened to him was written all over his face, and a dancing smile, as expansive as all of Moscow life at this hour, dominated his features.

Next day he called on one of his friends who, because he taught in a girl's *lycée,* knew what was going on in the others. On one occasion that winter he had mentioned to Seryozha a post for a teacher of literature and psychology at a private high school on Basmannaya Street that would fall vacant in the spring.

Seryozha could not bear school literature or psychology. He knew, in any case, that a girls' high school was not the place for him to teach, because he would have to sweat far too hard among the girls without any profit and unbeknownst to anyone. But now, worn out at last by all the excitement of the examinations, he was relaxing; that is, he was allowing the hours and days to shift him according to their will. It was then as if someone had cracked a jar of pussy willow marmalade near the university and he had gotten stuck together with the whole town in the bitter mass of downy berries and submitted to its viscous, pewter-colored rippling and folding. In this way he wandered into one of the side lanes of the Plyushchikha, where the aforementioned friend had his lodgings.

The rooms had shielded themselves from the rest of the world with a huge yard used by the cabmen A row of empty carriages rose up to the evening sky like the bony spine of some legendary vertebrate that had just been skinned. Here, more than in the street, one sensed the presence of recent distances, naked and compassionate, and there was plenty of manure and hay. Here there was a particular abundance of that sweet grayness on the waves of which Seryozha himself had arrived. And now, just as he was drawn along to these lodgings and their smoky conversations, supported from outside by a three-branched kerosene lantern, so at the next twilight he rushed to Basmannaya Street to the principal and her conversations of pewter, below which there bristled the branching and cawing of a large neglected garden, full of the ladies' private, silvery-mousy earth, which in places had already been churned up by rakes.

Then suddenly, for some unknown reason, on one of the pewtery sinuosities of the last week, he found himself in the Frestelns' house as tutor to the owner's son, and here he remained and shook the pewter from his feet.

Nor was this surprising. They took him in with board and lodging provided, and in addition they offered a fee double that of his school post, a huge room with three windows adjoining that of his pupil, and full use of all the leisure time he saw fit to take without prejudicing his pupil's studies.

In the event they gave him just about everything short of the Fresteln family's cloth business, for never before in his life had he found it so easy to go straight out from his books and tea, out of the marble hallway, wearing a floppy hat (he had been given a large advance), and into the bakery aroma of the sunny street, which, with its twin sloping pavements, careered busily down an incline toward the square lying concealed below, around a corner. It was in the Samotyoki district, and despite the few passersby in the neighborhood, Seryozha had two encounters during his very first walk. The first was with a young man who was walking on the other side of the street; he had been one of those present at that memorable evening at Baltz's. There had been two brothers there, the elder an engineer, while the younger had told him that as soon as he finished the Commercial School he had to do his army service, but he did not know whether to volunteer or wait to be drafted. Now he was wearing a volunteer's uniform, and the fact that he was in uniform inhibited Seryozha so much that he merely nodded to him without stopping him or crossing over. The volunteer did not stop either, because he had sensed Seryozha's restraint from across the street. Moreover, Seryozha did not know the brothers' surname, for they had not been introduced to each other, and he only remembered the elder as a very self-assured and probably successful man and the younger as more reserved and far more pleasant.

The other encounter occurred on his side of the street. Kovalenko, the editor of one of the Saint Petersburg journals, a stout, kindly man, came bustling toward him. He knew Seryozha's work and approved of it, besides which he intended, with the help of Seryozha and several other once admired eccentrics, to revive his enterprise. He always spoke with a fixed grin about the injection of vital energy and other such nonsense. This grin was characteristic of him generally because he seemed to detect comic situations everywhere, and he used this irony as a defense against them. Brushing aside Seryozha's polite remarks, he asked him what he was doing now, and Seryozha, with the Fresteln mansion on the tip of his tongue, just bit it back in time and for safety's sake quickly lied that he was busy with a new story. And as Kovalenko was bound to ask about its theme, he at once set about composing it in his mind.

But Kovalenko did not put the question and, instead, agreed to meet Seryozha in a month's time on his next trip to Moscow and, without pausing, mumbled something about some friends in whose half-empty apartment he was staying and quickly wrote their address on a loose scrap of paper. Seryozha took it without glancing at it and, folding it in four, thrust it into his waistcoat pocket. The ironic smile with which Kovalenko had done all this did not give anything away, because it was inseparable from Kovalenko himself.

Taking leave of his well-wisher, Seryozha returned to the house by a roundabout way to avoid accompanying the man with whom his conversation had ended on such a final and natural note. Moreover, he was startled by a wind that suddenly began to blow through his head at that moment. He failed to notice that it was not a wind but the continuation of his imaginary story, which concluded with the gradual fading away of the encounter, the address, and everything that had happened. Nor did he realize that its plot was his own thought-provoking susceptibility and that he was susceptible precisely because everything around him was so wonderful and he had done so well in his examinations, his job, and everything else in the world.

His arrival at the Frestelns' coincided with a period of changes in the household. Some of these had taken place before Seryozha arrived; others were still in the offing. Shortly before he came, the husband and wife had finally brought their quarreling to a lifelong conclusion and had moved onto separate floors. Mr. Fresteln occupied half of the ground floor, across the hallway to the right of the nursery and Seryozha's quarters. Mrs. Fresteln spread herself over the entire top floor, where, besides her three rooms, there was also, apart from the drawing room, a large ballroom with twin windows and a Pompeian atrium, as well as a dining room with an adjoining servery.

Spring arrived early that year, and the heady noondays were warm and appetizing. At full steam spring was rapidly outstripping the calendar and prompting the household to make arrangements for the summer. The Frestelns owned an estate in Tula province. Although until then the town house had only been ventilated when the trunks and suitcases were put out to air on warm mornings, the front door was already admitting ladies, the mothers of families applying to rent out-of-town accommodation for the summer. Previous tenants were greeted like dearly loved departed dead miraculously restored to the bosom of the family, but with new applicants they discussed both the stone wings and the timber cottages and, as they were taking leave of them in the vestibule, insisted on the famous properties of the Aleksin air, which had a certain unusually nourishing quality, and the beauties of the Oka landscape, to which no words of praise could ever do sufficient justice. All this, incidentally, was perfectly true.

In the courtyard, carpets were being beaten, clouds hung over the garden in suet lumps, and the puffs of gritty dust, stagnant in the greasy sky, seemed of their own accord to charge the air with thunder. But from the way in which the caretaker, all covered by a hair net of carpet dirt, kept looking up at the sky, it was evident that there would be no rain. Lavrentii, the footman, in a glossy silk jacket instead of tails and with a carpet-beater under his arm, passed through the vestibule into the yard. Seeing all this, breathing in the odor of mothballs and catching snatches of the ladies' conversation, Seryozha could not help feeling that the house was already dressed for the journey and would at any moment dive beneath a canopy of bitter, tremblingly moist, laurel-sultry birch trees. In addition to all this, Mrs. Fresteln's companion, without as yet mentioning her dismissal, was preparing to leave and, seeking a new post, absented herself indiscriminately, irrespective of whether it was a workday or not. Her name was Anna Arild Tornskjöld, but in the house she was called Mrs. Arild for brevity's sake. She was Danish, dressed always in black, and it was depressing and strange to observe her in the situations in which her duties often placed her.

She kept herself precisely thus, in a spirit of oppressive alienation, crossing the hall diagonally with large strides in her wide skirt, her hair piled high in a bun and with a sympathetic smile at Seryozha as if he was an accomplice.

Thus, imperceptibly, the day arrived when Seryozha, adored by his pupil and on the friendliest terms with the Frestelns (it was quite impossible to decide who of the latter was nicer because, as a substitute for the broken bond between them, they indulged in private backbiting to Seryozha), took a book in his hand and, leaving his charge chasing a cat in the yard, crossed from there into the garden. The paths were littered with fallen lilac blossoms and only two or three bushes on the shady side were still in bloom. Beneath these Mrs. Arild, her elbows on a table and her head inclined to one side, was sitting and busily writing. A branch of the ashen tetrahedrals, swaying slightly under its mauve burden, tried to peep from behind at what she was writing, but to no avail. The writer shielded both letter and addressee from the whole world with the broad thrice-wound braid of her fine, light chestnut hair. On the table lay opened letters, mixed up with her knitting. Light clouds the color of the lilac and the notepaper floated across the sky. A steely gray color itself, the sky cooled them. Catching the sound of a stranger's footsteps, Mrs. Arild first of all carefully blotted what she had been writing and then calmly raised her head. An iron garden seat stood next to her bench. Seryozha settled into it, and the following conversation in German took place between them:

"I'm familiar with Chekhov and Dostoevsky," Mrs. Arild began, looping her arms over the back of the bench and looking directly at Seryozha, "and I've been in Russia for five months now. You're worse than the French. To believe in a woman's existence you have to attribute some vile secret to her, as though in the real light she were something colorless, like boiled water. But when she casts a shadow of scandal from somewhere within onto a screen, then it's another matter: There's no disputing that silhouette, and you think it's beyond price. I haven't seen the Russian countryside yet, but in the towns your preference for alleyways proves that you aren't living your own lives and that each of you, in his own different way, is anxious to share someone else's. It's not like that where I come from, in Denmark. Wait, I haven't finished . . ."

At this point she turned away from Seryozha and, noticing a layer of fallen lilac on her letter, scrupulously blew it off. After a second, mastering some incomprehensible impediment, she continued, "Last spring, in March, I lost my husband. He died a young man. He was only thirty-two. He was a clergyman."

"Look here," Seryozha interrupted her as he had planned, though he now wished to say something quite different, "I've read Ibsen and I don't understand you. You are mistaken. It's unjust to judge a whole country by one single household."

"Ah, what do you mean by that? Are you referring to the Frestelns? You must have a nice opinion of me. I am farther from such mistakes than you, and I'll prove it to you this minute. Did you guess that they were Jews and that they were just concealing it from us?"

"What nonsense! Where did you hear that?"

"See how unobservant you are! But I'm certain of it. And perhaps that's why I hate her so implacably. But don't get me off the subject," she began with fresh intensity, without giving Seryozha time to remark that this blood, which she found so distasteful, also flowed in his veins on his father's side, while there was not even a trace of it in this house. Instead of which, and according to his original plan, he managed to interject all the same that all her ideas about debauchery were pure Tolstoy, that is, the most Russian of anything deserving of the name.

"That's not the point," she cut in impatiently, hastening to break off the argument and quickly moving to the edge of the bench nearer to Seryozha. "Listen!" she exclaimed in great agitation, taking him by the hand. "Your job is to look after Harry, but I'm sure you're not obliged to wash him in the morning. What's more, I bet it hasn't been suggested that you should massage the old man every day."

This was so unexpected that Seryozha let her hands fall.

"In Berlin this winter not a word was said about anything like that. I went to the Hotel Adlon to arrange matters. I was to be employed as Mrs. Fresteln's companion, not as her chambermaid, wasn't I? Here I sit before you—a sane, reasonable person, you'll agree? Don't answer for a minute. The post was in a distant place, in a strange country. And I accepted. Do you see how I was tricked? I don't know how it was I liked the look of her. I didn't size her up at first sight. And then all this began, on the other side of the frontier, beyond Verzhbolovoye . . . No, wait, I haven't finished. I had brought my husband to Berlin for an operation. He died in my arms and I buried him there. I have no relatives. That's not true; I have, but I'll tell you about that some other time. I was in a dreadful state and without any means of support. Then suddenly her offer came up. I read about it in a paper. And just by sheer accident, if only you knew!"

She moved away to the middle of the bench, making a vague gesture with her hand at Seryozha.

Mrs. Fresteln passed through the glass gallery that linked the kitchen to the house. The housekeeper followed her. Seryozha at once regretted that he had interpreted Mrs. Arild's movement in an unfavorable light. She had no intention of hiding from anyone. On the contrary, taking up the conversation with unnatural haste, she raised her voice and introduced into it a note of ironic disdain. But Mrs. Fresteln did not hear her.

"You dine upstairs with her and Harry, and with the guests when there are any. When you were puzzled as to why I wasn't present at table, I heard them tell you with my own ears that I was ill. It is true that I often suffer from migraine. But, another time, do you remember one day when you were larking about with Harry after dessert? Please don't nod so gaily; the point is not that you haven't forgotten about it but that when you ran into the servery I almost died of shame. They actually explained to you that I myself had wanted to dine in a corner behind the door with the housekeeper (who really prefers that). But that's nothing at all. Every morning I'm obliged to help that trembling jewel out of the bath like a child, to wrap sheets around her and then rub her with cloths, brushes, pumice stone, and goodness knows what else until I'm exhausted. And I can't tell you the whole story," she concluded in an unexpectedly low voice, coloring, and catching her breath as if she had been in a race. She wiped her flushed face with her handkerchief and turned it toward him.

Seryozha stayed silent, and from his agonized look she guessed how deeply all this had touched him.

"Don't try to comfort me," she requested, getting up from the bench. "However, that's not what I intended to say. I'm reluctant to talk German. The minute you really deserve my confidence I'll address you differently. No, not in Danish. *We shall be friends, I'm sure,*" she said, and her last remark was in English.

And again Seryozha did not give the reply he had intended, answering "*Gut*" instead of "*Good,*" forgetting to warn her that he understood English but had forgotten how to speak what little he knew. But Mrs. Arild, continuing in English, reminded him simply and warmly (later translating this much more coldly into German) that he should not forget what she had told him about the screens and shady alleyways, that she was Nordic and

religious and could not bear people taking liberties, that this was both a
request and a warning, and that he should keep it all in mind.

III

The days were stifling. Seryozha was refreshing his scant and neglected
knowledge of English, using Nurok's grammar. When it was time for dinner
he and Harry used to go upstairs to the ballroom, where they kicked their
heels as they waited for Mrs. Fresteln to appear. Letting her go ahead, they
would follow her through into the dining room. Mrs. Arild would often
precede her by five or ten minutes, and Seryozha would talk loudly with his
Danish friend until the lady of the house emerged, and then part from her
with unconcealed regret. The procession of three with Mrs. Fresteln at its
head would make its way to the dining room, and the nearer they came to
the door the more the lady's companion, who was moving in the same
direction, got headed off to the left. Thus their ways parted.

For some time now, Mrs. Fresteln had been obliged to come to terms with
the obstinacy that prompted Seryozha to refer to the main dining room as
the "small servery," and to the adjoining room, where they carved the
chickens and served out ice cream, as the "main servery." But she had
grown to expect certain peculiarities from him, for she regarded him as a
born eccentric even though she did not understand half his jokes. She
trusted the tutor, and he did not let her down. He had no grudge against
her even now, just as he bore no grudge against anyone. In a human being
he could only hate his own major enemy, that is, an extraordinarily offensive
and trite victory over life, one that avoided everything that was most
awkward and precious about it. But people fit to personify such a combination were few and far between.

After dinner, whole trayloads of shattered and broken harmonies slid
downstairs. They rolled down and scattered in unexpected bursts, more
abrupt and startling than any instances of a waiter's clumsiness. Miles of
carpeted silence stretched between these turbulent topplings. It was Mrs.
Arild upstairs, behind several pairs of burlap-lined and tightly closed doors,
playing Schumann and Chopin on the grand piano. At such moments one
had a more involuntary desire than usual to gaze out of the window. But
no changes were noticeable there, the sky was not moved by these musical
torrents. It continued to stand like a sultry pillar upon its established
principle of rainlessness, while beneath it for forty miles around danced a
dead sea of dust like a funeral pyre ignited simultaneously at different points
by wagoners at the five freight stations and in the center of the brick
wilderness beyond the wall of Moscow's Kitaigorod region.

Chaos resulted. The Frestelns stayed on for a spell in town, and Mrs.
Arild hung around at the house longer than intended. All at once, fate
provided a justification for everything just when the incomprehensibility of

their delayed departure had begun to surprise everyone. Harry came down with measles, and the move to the country estate was put off until his recovery. The sandy whirlwinds did not let up, there was no prospect of rain, and gradually everyone became accustomed to the fact. It even began to seem as if this was still the same day that had been loitering for long weeks now and had not been hauled off to the police station in time. So this day had taken heart and was driving everyone to distraction. And now every dog in the street knew it. In the end, but for the nights, which still breathed some spectral variety, one would have run for witnesses and fixed wax seals to the arid calendar.

The streets resembled random beds of poppies with wandering tree borders. Dazed, ashen shadows with drooping, half-withered heads moved along flabby footpaths. Only once, on a Sunday, did Seryozha and Mrs. Arild pluck up enough courage, after plunging their heads in a washbowl, to fight their way out of town. They traveled out to Sokolniki Park. However, here as well the same fumes hung over the ponds, the only difference being that while in town the sultriness was not visible to the eye, here it could be seen. A mingled layer of dust, mist, and locomotive smoke dangled like an office ruler across the black pinewood, and of course, this efficient specter was far more frightening than the simple suffocation of the streets.

As it happened, this miasma hovered at such a height above the water that the boats could freely slip beneath it, and when the squealing young ladies changed over from the stern to the oars, their young men, rising to let them by, actually caught their caps in this gravy-like scum. Near the bank the sunset hissed like fuming acid on the pond's surface. Its ruddy glow resembled a red-hot ingot of pig iron doused in a swamp. From the same shore the slippery, plaintively resonant clamor of frogs drifted in bursting bubbles.

Meanwhile, twilight was falling. Mrs. Arild chattered away in English and Seryozha gave timely answers. They wound their way at ever increasing speed through the maze, which always brought them back to the same starting point, and yet at the same time they were taking the shortest route to the gate and the trolley terminal. They were markedly different from the other people who were out for a stroll. In spite of all the couples crowding the wood, they reacted more and more anxiously as night fell, and they hurried to escape from it as if it were hot on their heels. Whenever they glanced back, they appeared to be measuring the speed of its pursuit. In front of them, however, on every path they took, the whole wood seemed to loom into something resembling the presence of an adult. This transformed them into children. One minute they grabbed each other's hands; the next they dropped them in confusion. At times they lost confidence in their own voices. It seemed as if they were being forced first into a loud whisper, then into a remote, distance-distorted shout. In fact, nothing of the sort was noticeable: They were enunciating their words normally. At times Anna grew lighter and more transparent than a tulip petal, while Seryozha for his part experienced a chest heat like the glass of a burning lantern. At such moments she saw how he was struggling against the hot, sooty draft to prevent it from drawing her in. In silence they stared full in each other's faces and then painfully tore apart this twin-featured smile, distorted by a prayer for mercy, as if it were a whole living creature. Here, too, Seryozha again heard the words to which he had long ago submitted.

They whirled more and more swiftly through the maze of ingenious paths and at the same time made their way out to the gate, from which point a muffled ringing already carried from the trolleys escaping the empty carts that galloped in full pursuit after them the whole length of Stromynka Street. The jingling trolley bells seemed to splash behind their illuminated glass. A cool breath of air wafted from them, as if from a well. Very soon, the endmost, dustiest section of the wood stepped from the ground onto the metaled roadway in its wooden clogs. They had entered the town.

"How great and indelible man's humiliation must be," Seryozha was thinking, "that, having made all chance circumstances tally beforehand with the past, he has grown to demand an earth that is fundamentally new and in no way resembles the one on which he has been so hurt or defeated!"

In those days the idea of wealth began to preoccupy him for the first time in his life. He was tormented by the immediate urgency of procuring it. He would have given his fortune to Mrs. Arild and asked her to distribute it more widely, all of it—to women. He himself would have named several of the first recipients for her. It would have amounted to millions, and those nominated would pass on the wealth to new recipients, and so on, and so on.

Harry was getting better, but Mrs. Fresteln remained constantly at his side. A bed was still being made up for her in the classroom. In the evenings Seryozha left the house, and he returned only at dawn. In the next room Mrs. Fresteln tossed and turned in bed and kept coughing, letting it be known in every way that she was aware of his disreputable routine. If she has asked him where he had been, he would have told her without a second thought of all the places he had frequented. She sensed this, and, guarding against the seriousness with which he would have replied and which she would have been duty-bound to swallow, she left him in peace. He returned from his outings with the same remote light in his eyes that he had had after the excursion to Sokolniki.

One after another, several women swam to the surface of the street on different nights, plucked from nonexistence by chance and their attractiveness. Three new tales of women took their place beside the story of Anna Arild. There is no knowing why these confessions had poured out upon Seryozha. He did not go to act as their confessor, because he thought that would be despicable. As if to explain the unaccountable trust that drew them to him, one of them told him that it was as if he was like them in some way.

The one who said this was the most hardened, thickly powdered, and promiscuous of them all. On familiar terms with everyone to the end of her days, she urged the coachman to hurry with unprintable complaints about feeling cold and, with every thrust of her hoarse beauty, brought everything with which she came into contact down to her level. Her little room on the second floor of a lopsided, evil-smelling five-windowed house in no way differed in appearance from any poorer merchant dwelling. Her walls were hung with cheap linens to which she pinned photographs and paper flowers. A folding table hunched between the windows, brushing both sills with its leaves. Opposite, up against a partition that did not stretch as far as the ceiling, stood an iron bed. And yet, for all its resemblance to a human dwelling, this place was its complete antithesis.

The floor mats, spreading under a guest's feet with rare servility, invited him not to stand on ceremony with the woman of the house and appeared ready themselves to set the example of how to deal with her. A stranger's benefit was their only master. Everything in the room seemed to exist in a state of openness and flux, as in time of flood. Even the windows there appeared to be turned not outward from within but inward from the outside. Lapped by public notoriety as if by floodwaters, the household things, insubordinate and disarrayed, floated under the broad title of Sashka.

On the other hand, Sashka was not beholden to them. Everything she undertook she did in motion, steadily, without rise or fall, like an enormous wave. In roughly the same way that she flung wide her supple arms as she was undressing, talking all the while, so eventually at dawn, chatting away and leaning her belly against a leaf of the table and knocking over the empty bottles, she gulped down her own and Seryozha's dregs. And in roughly the same manner and to the same degree, standing in a long chemise with her back to Seryozha and answering him over her shoulder, without shame or brashness, she urinated in the tin basin, which had been carried into the room by the same old woman who had let them in. Not one of her movements could be predicted, and her vibrant speech was raised and lowered by the same warm, ribald snore that brushed aside her locks and smoldered in her deft hands. Her answer to fate lay in the very smoothness of her nimble movements. All human naturalness, screaming and blaspheming, was hoisted there, as though on a rack, to a height of misery visible from every side. It became the duty of her surroundings, as viewed from this level, to be inspired on the spot, and from the stir of one's own excitement one could detect how rescue stations were being set up amicably and in great haste all over the wildernesses of the outside world. Of all the pungent odors here, the strongest was the characteristic pungency of Christianity.

As night was coming to an end, an invisible nudge from outside in the yard made the partition quiver. It was her man stumbling into the hall. His nose for a stranger's presence, which was his most assured income, did not betray him even at his drunkest. Treading softly in his heavy boots, he quietly collapsed somewhere close behind the partition as soon as he came in and without making a sound soon ceased to exist. His quiet couch probably stood back to back with the professional bed. Very likely it was an old chest. He had hardly begun to snore when a rat struck at him from below with its quick, greedy chisel. But silence settled again. The snoring suddenly ceased, the rat hid, and a familiar draft ran through the room. Things glued to the wall or hanging on nails recognized their master. The thief behind the partition was capable of everything they did not dare. Seryozha jumped out of bed.

"Where are you going? He'll kill you!" Sashka croaked from the depths of her being and, scrambling across the bed, hung on to his sleeve. "You can work off your temper, that's easy, but if you leave, I'll get beaten up."

But Seryozha did not even know himself where he was rushing off to. In any case, his was not the kind of jealousy that Sashka had imagined, though it flooded his heart no less passionately. And if ever a bait was dangled before a man, ensuring his eternal motion, like a carrot to make a horse run, then surely it must be this instinct. It was the kind of jealousy that we sometimes feel about a woman, or life because of death, which is like a nameless rival, and we strive to be free to have the liberty to release the object of our jealousy. And here, of course, was the same pungent odor.

It was still very early. On the opposite side of the roadway, the folding sections of the triple iron leaves on the wide granary doors could already be made out. The dusty windows glowed gray, a quarter filled with the reflection of round cobblestones. Dawn lay on Tverskaya-Yamskaya Street as if on a set of scales, and the air looked like chaff that was constantly being winnowed by it. Sashka sat at the table. Blessed drowsiness spun her and bore her along like water. She chattered without a break, and her talk resembled a healthy, drowsy animal.

"Ah, Guilty Ivanovna!" Seryozha repeated quietly, without hearing his own words.

He was sitting on the windowsill. People were already walking the streets.

"No, you're no medic," Sashka was saying, her side pressed against the partition. One minute she lay with her cheek on her elbow; the next, straightening her arm, she examined it slowly from the side, from shoulder to wrist, as though it were not an arm but, rather, a long road or her own life, which she alone could see. "No, you're no medic," she continued. "Medics are different. To be honest, I can't make you out. When one of them walks behind me, I can tell him with my tail. I bet you're a teacher? There you are. I'm frightened to death of catching 'the cold.' But if you aren't a medic there's no point in asking you. Listen, you aren't a Tatar or something, are you? Well, you must come around and see me. Come around in the afternoon. You won't lose the address, will you?"

They were chatting in low tones. One minute Sashka was convulsed in impish, beadlike laughter or overcome by yawns and fits of scratching. Insatiable as a child and as though recovering her lost dignity, she enjoyed this serenity, which likewise made Seryozha feel more human.

In the midst of their chatter, Sashka, referring to Poland as "the Kingdom of Poland" and boastfully nodding toward the wall, where in a shining nest of other photographs hung the glossy effigy of an amiable noncommissioned officer, revealed her earliest and most precious memory, in all probability the prime cause of all that came after. It was probably to him that her plump arm, outstretched from shoulder to wrist and now lost in the far distance, seemed to lead. Then again, perhaps it did not lead to him at all. Suddenly, the sunrise flared all at once, like dry hay, and like dry hay burnt itself out immediately. Flies started to crawl over the bulging, bubbly windowpanes. The streetlights and the mist exchanged feral yawns. Day was kindled and caught fire in a flurry of sparks. At this point Seryozha felt that he had never loved anyone as much as Sashka, and then in his mind's eye he saw how in the farther distance toward the cemeteries the highway was left no alternative but to have fleshy red patches, and the cobbles on it were more solid and widely spaced, just as they were at the city gates. Freight wagons, empty or filled with cattle, were sliding smoothly across this same roadway, breaking free and moving off, breaking free and moving off. Then something like a collision took place. The traffic was held up for some reason, and a severed section of the street rose out of the background. Those were empty freight wagons, linked one to another, one to another, moving at the same pace but now hidden from view by the dense wall of people and carts at the level crossing. There were nettles and buttercups here, and but for the smoke there would be a smell of field mice. And here too was Sashka, sniffing and fidgeting like a wild and boisterous six-year-old. Finally, bringing up the rear and in a terrible puffing frenzy, as though asking the bystanders whether they had seen the wagons pass by, a black, perspiring locomotive hurried past, tender first. Then the barrier was raised, the street flashed forward like an arrow, and now the carts and human detachments started advancing, intermingling from both directions. And then the smoke from the locomotive flopped down in the middle of the road like a fibrous, twice-bound sack or the warm stomach of a monster, perhaps that very same offal on which the poor people in the slums feed. And Sashka lost the thread of what she was saying and kept looking to see how frightening this smoke could be amid the tea and grocery goods, the cigar- and tobacco-sellers, the sheet iron, and the policeman. Meanwhile, somewhere a book was being written about her eyes and heels, entitled *The Childhood of a*

Woman. There was a smell of oats on the road, which had itself been signed and sealed by the sun in horse's urine until it simply caused a splitting headache. So then, in the end, unable to avoid "the cold" she dreaded so much, losing her eyes and heels, her nose and her reason, Sashka would drop in for a moment to see him before retiring to the hospital, possibly even the grave, to get the book in which, so she had been told, all this had already been described in every aspect, and now it was only too obvious that it was true: She had lived as a fool and she would die one.

She is being led by a police detachment in the roadway; she is not allowed on the pavement. Look what she's taken it into her head to do now! Someone concocted this story, and she, like a fool, took it up. It's just absurd. The book is about somebody else: It isn't a Russian surname and the town is different. Her own name is in the policeman's clothbound, braided notebook—there she is and you can read about her in it. What the hell (a momentary pressure on the vile trigger)—bang-bang-bang!—it's all the same in the end. And the policemen look a little more kindly. They escort trigger-happy girls while the noble public holds its tongue on a safety catch.

"Why are you so full of thoughts?" Sashka asked. "You should look at some of the other women. Don't stare at me. To put it bluntly, I'm a lady compared to them. Don't worry about what time it is or anything. Perhaps you'll say people are asleep now. A lot you understand about the likes of us! Oh, you make me laugh; you'll be the death of me, ha-ha-ha! Come and call here in the afternoon. Never mind *him.* Don't be scared of him; he's meek, just as long as you don't upset him. He'll go out the door the minute you come in. Or he'll just be asleep, as you can see, and you couldn't wake him if you tried. If it's dark by the time you arrive, you won't bump into him. Why he's upset you I don't understand. It would be a wonder if he turned nasty. Others have come here and didn't take offense. Wellborn gents just like yourself. Well, I'm ready, just got to powder myself, and I mustn't forget my bag. Here, hold it for me. Well, let's go; I'll walk as far as Sadovaya with you. I shan't be lonely on my way back, that I do know; it's the same old story. Day or night, you've only to wink an eye; they just come swimming right into your arms. Oh, you're not going up toward Strashnoi? Well, all right, good-bye then, but mind you don't forget. I'll go along—more likely to attract the wolves that way. You won't lose my address, will you?"

On an empty stomach the streets were impetuously straight and sullen. A lewd dove-gray shriek of emptiness still echoed down their unpeopled length. Occasionally one encountered some lean, lonely cannibal. In the distance along the boulevard, a galloping cab pounded the spot, puffed out like a pouter pigeon. Seryozha headed for the Samotyoki and, within half a mile of the Triumphal Arch, imagined he could hear people whistling after

Sashka and her slowing down in playful curiosity to see who would take the initiative—whether the man would cross the street or she would do so. Although the day had barely begun, tangled threads of sultry heat, nightmarish as crumbs in the beards of corpses, already hung in the crowded foliage of the lime trees. And Seryozha felt feverish.

IV

He felt he must make a fortune immediately. But not by work, of course. Wages are no victory, but without victory there can be no freedom. And, if possible, without public notoriety, without the flavor of legend. After all, even in Galilee the event had been local. It had begun at home, spread to the street, and finally ended out in the world. The money would be counted in millions, and if such a whirlwind should sweep through women's hands, embracing even one of the Tverskaya-Yamskaya women, it would regenerate the universe. And that was precisely what was needed—an earth restored from its very foundations.

"The main thing," Seryozha said to himself, "is not that they should undress but, rather, dress themselves. The chief thing is not that they should get money but that they should distribute it. But until my plan is realized," he told himself (no plan existed really), "I must get hold of a different sort of sum, about two hundred or at least a hundred and fifty rubles." (Here Nyura Ryumina came to his mind, and Sashka, while Anna Arild Tornskjöld was far from last on the list.) These sums were intended for something quite different. As a temporary measure he might accept such sums even from an honest source without qualms. "Ah, Raskolnikov, Raskolnikov!" Seryozha repeated to himself. "But what did the old pawnbroker have to do with it? The old pawnbroker was just another Sashka in her old age, that's all. But even if I do it legally, where am I going to get the money, that's the question? I've had two months' advance from the Frestelns and I've nothing left I can sell."

It was a day in early June. They had already begun to take Harry out for walks. In the house everybody once again began making preparations to go to the *dacha*. Mrs. Arild again began to be away more often on her own affairs, which had been interrupted by Harry's illness. Soon she was offered a post with an army family in Poltava province.

"Not Suvorov, the other," Anna lisped in throaty English, standing on the stairs, too lazy to go up and fetch the letter. "I forget always."

And Seryozha ran through all the possibilities from Kutuzov to Kuropatkin, before it turned out to be Skobelev.

"Awful, I cannot repeat it. How would you pronounce it?" she asked, again in English.

The terms of her new situation were profitable, but once again, for the hundredth time now, she was obliged to put off making a decision. The reason was this. She had hardly received the offer when she fell ill, and the severity of her illness led everyone to assume she had caught it from Harry. In the meantime, a temperature as high as in measles, which had put her to bed that very evening and which went over 104 degrees, fell steeply next morning to below 97. All this proved to be a mystery that the doctor failed to solve, but it left the poor girl extremely weak. Now the effects of the attack were wearing off, and already the house had echoed once or twice again to the thunderous sound of "Aufschwung," as in the days before Seryozha had even dreamed of Raskolnikov's dilemmas.

That same day, Mrs. Fresteln took Harry off early in the day to visit some friends by the River Klyazma, intending to spend the night there if the weather permitted and the opportunity presented itself. Mr. Fresteln had also left the house. Half the day passed as though the Frestelns were still at home. To be sure, Lavrentii, to oblige, had offered to serve Seryozha's meal downstairs, but he preferred not to upset people's established routine and, without noticing how it came about, dined upstairs at the exact hour and even in his appointed place, second from the right.

So, it was past four in the afternoon and the Frestelns were away. Seryozha thought of the millions and the two hundred rubles in turn and paced the room, engrossed in his thoughts. Then suddenly there occurred a moment of such extraordinary awareness that he froze in mid-step, forgetting everything else, and became anxious and alert. But there was absolutely nothing to be heard. Only that the room, flooded with sunshine, seemed barer and more spacious than before. He could resume his interrupted preoccupation. Yet what had distracted him had not been in the room. His ideas ceased to flow, and he had forgotten the subject of his reflections. Then he began hastily to grope for at least one verbal term for what he had been thinking, for the brain responds to the meaning of things as a whole, just as it does to one's own name, and, awakening from its paralysis, resumes its function from the lesson that it had temporarily balked at giving. However, this quest led to nothing too. It merely increased his distraction. Only extraneous matters forged into his mind.

He suddenly remembered his springtime encounter with Kovalenko. And again the falsely promised nonexistent story swam into his ken in the form of something complete and already composed, and he almost cried out when it dawned on him that here, indeed, was a possible source of the money he sought, not the miracle-working kind but the honest hundred or two. Realizing all this and drawing the curtain on the middle window to shade the table, he sat down without much reflection to write a letter to the editor. He negotiated the introduction successfully and the first vivid politenesses. It is not clear what he would have done when he came to the substance of the letter, for, at that moment, his hearing was alerted by that same strange feeling. Now he had time to analyze it. The feeling was one of nagging, nostalgic, and prolonged emptiness. The sensation was connected with the house. It declared that the house was uninhabited at that moment, that is, empty of any living being except Seryozha with his preoccupations.

"And Tornskjöld?" he thought and then remembered that she had not shown her face in the house since the previous evening. He noisily pushed his chair back. Leaving the doors of the classroom and the nursery and some other doors open behind him, he ran out into the vestibule. In the space beyond the little slanting door that led into the yard, the white heat of four o'clock in the afternoon was like baking sand. It appeared even more mysterious and ravenous to him, viewing it from above.

"How careless of them!" he thought, passing from room to room (he did not know them all). "Windows open everywhere and not a soul in the house or in the yard. The house could be ransacked and no one would make a sound. But why on earth am I drifting about like this? Anything might happen while I'm fumbling around to see if anyone's here." He ran back downstairs and out the side door into the yard as if the house were on fire. And, as if in answer to a fire alarm, the doors of the servants' quarters opened at the far end of the yard.

"Egor!" yelled Seryozha in a strange voice at the man who came running quickly to meet him, chewing a last mouthful of food as he ran and wiping his mustache and lips on the hem of his apron. "Tell me, if you'd be so good, how can I find the French woman?" (He did not have the nerve to call her "Frenchie," as the servants very precisely dubbed the Danish woman and all her predecessors.) "As quick as you can, please: Margarita Ottonovna told me to give her a message this morning, and I've only just this minute remembered."

"That window over there," gulped the caretaker gruffly, swallowing hurriedly, then, raising his arm, his cleared throat bobbing, he began chattering in a different tone about how he could find the place, staring all the time not straight at Seryozha but sideways at the neighbors' property.

It turned out that part of the humble three-storied building of unrendered brick that joined the main house at an angle and that was rented from the Frestelns as a guest house was accessible at this point at the direction of the owners and could be reached from the main part of the house through a corridor running past the nursery. In this narrow section, separated from the hostelry by a windowless wall, there was one single room to each floor. Mrs. Fresteln's companion's window was, in fact, located on the third floor.

"Where did all this happen before?" Seryozha wondered, as the sloping boards of the extra stretch of flooring that had been laid between both sections rumbled beneath his feet. He was on the point of remembering but refrained from probing further because at that very moment he came upon a spiral staircase suspended in front of him like an iron snail. Embracing him in its whorls, it checked his rush and in so doing forced him to take a breath. But his heart was still beating fast and hollow when, with its final spiral, it led him straight to Anna Arild's door. Seryozha knocked without getting an answer. He pushed the door rather harder than he needed to, and it crashed against the inner wall without producing any protest. This sound told Seryozha more eloquently than any other that there was nobody in the room. He sighed, turned, and, stooping, had already gripped the spiral banister, but remembering he had left the door open, he returned to shut it. The door had swung open to the right, and reaching for the handle would have meant looking that way, but instead, Seryozha glanced furtively to the left and stood rooted to the spot.

Mrs. Arild, in an unrumpled black skirt that had settled all about her, lay prostrate on the knitted bedspread, solemn and stiff as a corpse, her high heels pointing straight at Seryozha. Her hair looked black; her face was drained of blood.

"Anna, what's wrong?" Seryozha blurted out and choked on the gust of air that had vented this exclamation.

He rushed toward the bed and knelt down beside it. Raising Anna's head with one hand, he began feverishly and awkwardly to grope for her pulse with the other. He squeezed the icy tendons of her wrist this way and that without finding the pulse. "Lord, O Lord!" pounded in his ears and chest louder than horses' hooves, while he seemed as he stared at the dazzling pallor of her vacant, heavy eyelids to be falling rapidly in some direction, dragged down by the dead weight of her head, without ever reaching the bottom. He was choking and on the point of fainting himself. Suddenly she came to.

"You, friend?" she muttered in barely audible English, opening her eyes.

The gift of speech was restored, not just to human beings. Everything in the room began to talk, and it filled with noise as though children had been let in. Seryozha's first move was to jump up from the floor and shut the door.

"Ah, ah!" he said, repeating the syllables in a sort of ecstasy as he tramped aimlessly up and down the room, rushing first to the window, then to the dressing table. Although the room, which looked north, was swimming in lilac shadows, the labels of the medicines could be clearly made out in any corner, and in sorting out the vials and bottles there was not the slightest need to carry each one separately over to the daylight. He did this only to proclaim his joy, which required noisy expression. Anna had fully regained consciousness by now, and she obeyed his injunctions only to please him. For his sake she consented to sniff the smelling salts, and the acrid ammonia penetrated her as immediately as it would any healthy person. Her tear-stained face wrinkled in surprise, her eyebrows turned up at the corners, and she pushed Seryozha's hand away with a movement full of restored vigor. He also made her take some valerian drops. As she drained the water, her teeth knocked against the brim of the glass and she grunted the way children do when they express a need fully satisfied.

"Well, what about our mutual acquaintances? Have they returned or are they still away?" she asked, putting the glass aside on the table and licking her lips, then, propping the pillow so that she could sit up more comfortably, she enquired what time it was.

"I don't know," Seryozha replied. "It's probably around five."

"The clock's on the dressing table. Would you look, please," she asked, and she added in a tone of surprise, "I don't know what you're gaping at. It's right there in front of you. Ah, that's a photograph of Arild. The year before he died."

"A wonderful forehead."

"Yes, that's true, isn't it?"

"And what a fine looking man! What an astonishing face . . . It's ten to five."

"And now please give me the rug—there it is, on the trunk. . . . There, thank you, thank you, that's fine. I think I'll lie here for a little while longer."

With a tense push Seryozha loosened the resisting window and flung it open. The room vibrated with amplitude as if it were a bell that had been struck. There was a heavy scent of yellow dandelions and the grassy, rubbery smell of road-dividers on the boulevards. The screech of swifts darted in disorder to the ceiling.

"Here, put this on your forehead," Seryozha suggested, handing Anna a towel soaked in cologne. . . . "Well, how do you feel?"

"Oh, wonderful. Can't you tell?"

He suddenly felt that he would not have the strength to leave her, and for this reason he said, "I'll go in a moment. But you can't stay like this. You might have another attack. You should unbutton your collar and loosen your dress. Can you manage that yourself? There is no one else in the house."

"You'll not dare . . ." she began in English.

"You misunderstand me. There is no one I can send to you, After all, I said I would go, didn't I?" he interrupted quietly, and, his head sunk, he walked slowly and clumsily toward the door.

As he reached the threshold, she called to him. He looked back. Propping herself on one elbow, she was holding out her other hand to him. He went over to the foot of the bed.

"Come near; I did not wish to offend you."

He went around the bed and sat down on the floor, with his feet folded under him. His posture promised a long and unconstrained chat, but in his agitation he could not utter a word. And there was nothing to talk about.

He was happy he was not at the bottom of the spiral staircase but with her in her room and that he did not have to take leave of her at once. She was about to break the oppressive and slightly comic silence. Suddenly he knelt, pressed his crossed arms against the edge of the feather bed, and let his head drop on them. His shoulders hunched and contracted, and his shoulder blades began to move evenly and rhythmically, as though grinding something. He was either crying or laughing, but it was as yet impossible to tell which.

"Pull yourself together; pull yourself together. I didn't expect this. Stop! Aren't you ashamed!" she kept repeating rapidly when his noiseless gasps turned into unabashed sobbing.

However (and she knew this), her words of comfort only encouraged his tears, and as she stroked his head she brought on new floods of them. He did not hold back. Resistance would only have led to a blockage, but there was a large accumulated charge that he wanted to release as quickly as possible. Oh, how glad he was that all those Sokolnikis and Tverskaya-Yamskayas and all those days and nights of the last two weeks had not taken root but had finally shifted ground and started moving. He wept as though it was they that were being breached and not himself. And they really were being whirled and borne away like logs in a flood. He wept as if he were expecting some purgative effect for his concern about the millions to come from this storm, which had struck suddenly, as though out of a cloud. It was as though these tears were bound to exert an influence on the further course of day-to-day matters.

Suddenly he raised his head. She could see his face, washed by a mist and somehow transported by it into the distance. In a state of some command over himself, as if he was his own immediate guardian, he uttered several words. These words were veiled in the same grim and divisive haze.

"Anna," he said quietly, "do not be too hasty in your refusal, I implore you. I ask your hand. I know that's not the way to say it, but how can I get it out? Be my wife," he went on even more quietly and firmly, quivering inwardly at the unbearable novelty that buoyed up this word, which he had just used for the first time in his life and which was equivalent to life itself.

And pausing for a moment to control the smile that ruffled the surface of some particularly profound part of his nature, he frowned and added even more quietly and firmly than before, "Only, don't laugh, I beg you. That would be demeaning for you."

He stood up and stepped to one side. Anna quickly moved her legs off the bed. Inwardly she was in such a state that, though it was all perfectly tidy, her dress appeared crumpled and her hair unkempt.

"My dear, my dear, how can you?" she kept saying from the first, trying at each word to rise but immediately forgetting to do so and at each word spreading her arms in surprise, as though guilty of some offense. "You're out of your mind. You have no pity. I was unconscious. I can barely move my eyelids—do you hear what I'm saying? I'm trying to move them; I'm not just blinking; do you understand that or not? And suddenly to ask me such a question so bluntly! And don't you laugh, either. Ah, how you've upset me!" she exclaimed in a different sort of tone, as though in parentheses or to herself alone, and jumping to her feet she ran quickly to the dressing table, bearing this exclamation as though it were a burden. On the far side of the dressing table, Seryozha stood gloomily listening to her, his elbow against the wood, his chin on the palm of his hand.

Gripping the beading along its rim with both hands, the rocking of her whole body expressive of particularly portentous conclusions, bathing him with the light of a gradually mastered agitation, she went on: "I expected this; it was in the air. I cannot answer you. The answer lies in you. Perhaps all this will really come true some day. And how I would like it to be so! Because . . . because I am not indifferent to you. You guessed that, of course? No? Is that true? Tell me, didn't you really? How strange. Never mind. Well, anyhow, I want you to know it." She faltered and paused for a moment. "But I've been observing you all the time. There is something about you that's not right. And do you know, now, at this very moment, there is more of it in you than the situation warrants. Ah, my dear, this is not the way to propose. It's not just a matter of convention. But that's immaterial. Listen, answer me one question sincerely, as you would your own sister. Tell me, is there any shame on your conscience? Oh, don't be frightened for heaven's sake! Doesn't an unfulfilled promise or a neglected duty leave its mark? But of course, of course, I presumed so myself. All this is so untypical of you. You needn't answer. I know: Nothing that is unbecoming in a human being can be a regular part of you for long. . . . But," she spelled out the words thoughtfully, sketching something indefinably empty in the air with her hand, and there was a weary, hoarse edge to her voice, "but there are things greater than us. Tell me, don't you have something like that in you? That is equally frightening in life. It would scare me like some alien presence."

Although she did not fall silent at once, she added nothing more substantial. The yard was empty as before and the outbuildings looked devoid of life. As before, the swifts swept over them. The end of the day flared like a legendary battle. The swifts came floating like a huge cloud of slowly quivering arrows and then, suddenly turning their sharp heads about, swooped back and away, screeching. Everything was as before, only the room had grown a trifle darker.

Seryozha was silent because he was not certain he could control his voice if he broke the silence. At every attempt to speak, his chin drooped and began to tremble feverishly. For his own private reasons it struck him as shameful to howl alone without being able to blame it on the Moscow suburbs. His silence depressed Anna in the extreme. She was even more dissatisfied with herself. The most important thing was that she agreed to everything, and yet she had failed to make it obvious from her words. It seemed to her that everything was utterly dreadful and that it was her fault. As always on such occasions, she thought of herself as a soulless doll and, full of self-reproach, was ashamed of the cold rhetoric that her answers apparently contained. And so, in order to correct that imaginary sin, and certain that now everything would take a different turn, she said in a voice that echoed the whole of that evening, that is, in a voice that had acquired an affinity with Seryozha's, "I don't know whether you understood me. I replied by giving my consent. I'm prepared to wait as long as necessary. But first of all, put yourself in order—your own order, of which I know nothing, and which you yourself probably know only too well. I don't know myself to what I'm referring. These hints spring from me against my will. To guess them or surmise them is your business. Then there is also this: Waiting will not come easy for me. But enough of this now or we'll wear each other out. And now listen. If you care for me even half as much . . . Now please don't, I beg of you, don't; that way you'll destroy everything . . . There you are; thank you."

"You were going to say something," he reminded her quietly.

"Yes, of course, and I haven't forgotten. I wanted to ask you to go downstairs. Yes, really, listen to me. Go to your room, wash your face, and take a walk. You must calm yourself. You don't think so? Well, all right then. Then let me ask you another favor, my poor dear. Go to your room anyway, and make sure you wash yourself. You can't appear in public with your face in such a state. Then wait for me. I'll call for you and we'll go for a walk together. And stop shaking your head. It upsets me to look at you. It's pure self-hypnosis. Say something, try, and trust me."

Again the wilderness of sloping corridor floorboards rumbled beneath him, and once again he was reminded of the Institute courtyard. Once more the thoughts prompted by remembrance rushed on in a feverish mechanical series that bore no relation to him. He found himself once again in the sun-flooded room, which was too spacious and therefore produced the impression of being uninhabited. In his absence the light had shifted. The curtain on the middle window no longer overshadowed the table. It was the same yellow, slanting light whose rays continued their action around the angle of the building upstairs, which was casting ever thickening violet shadows on her bed and the dressing table piled with vials. In Seryozha's presence the deepening lilac tones in Anna's room still recognized some restraint and proceeded nobly enough. But how this would probably speed up in his absence, and how assertively and triumphantly the swifts, taking advantage of his absence, would assail her! There was still time for him to ward off this violation and catch up with the vanishing past. It was still not too late to begin everything all over again and bring it to a different conclusion. It was all still feasible, but very soon it would no longer be so. Why had he obeyed her then and left her alone?

"Well, all right. Let's leave it at that," he kept replying at the same time from that heated Anna series to the other feverish, mechanical thoughts that rushed by and had no relevance for him. He pulled open the middle curtain and drew the end one, which made the light shift and plunged the table into gloom, so that now instead of the table the neighboring room, through which Anna would have to pass to reach him, was bathed in light across to the far wall. The door leading to it was wide open. In performing all these actions, he had forgotten that he was supposed to wash his face.

"And then there's Maria. Well, let's leave it at that. Maria has no need of anyone. Maria is immortal. Maria is not a woman." He was standing with his back to the table, leaning against the edge with his arms folded. Through his mind's eye flashed, with revolting mechanicalness, pictures of the empty Institute, echoing steps, the unforgotten situations of the previous summer, and Maria's uncollected bags. The loaded baskets shimmered before him like abstract concepts, and the suitcases with their straps and ropes could have served as premises for a syllogism. He suffered from these cold images as he would from a welter of idle spirituality or a flood of empty enlightened rhetoric. Head bent and arms folded, he waited for Anna in irritation and longing, ready to rush to her and take refuge from this nasty surge of obsessions.

"Well, to hell with having failed! Humble thanks, and the same to you. While you spend your time messing around, somebody else got away with her, leaving no trace. Well, the best of luck to him. I don't know him and I don't want to. What if there's no news and no trace of them? Well, let's leave it at that. It's probably best that way."

While he was bandying prickly comments with his past, the tails of his jacket slid to and fro over a sheet of writing paper the upper part of which had been written over, but two-thirds of which were blank. He was perfectly aware of this, but the letter to Kovalenko also belonged to that alien series against which he was pitting himself.

Suddenly, for the first time in the year just past, it dawned on him that he himself had helped Maria Ilyina to clear up the apartment and get ready to go abroad. Baltz was a scoundrel (that was how he referred to him in his mind). Then all at once he felt confident that he had guessed right. His heart contracted. He was cut to the quick not so much by the rivalry of the past year as by the fact that in Anna's hour, he could still be interested in something unconnected with Anna that had acquired an inadmissible vigor, offensive to her. But he realized just as abruptly that outside interference might also threaten him this summer unless he became more forceful and positive.

He came to a decision and, turning on his heel, surveyed the room and the table as if they were some novel circumstance in his life. The strips of sunset burgeoned with sap and swelled to their final crimson. In a couple of places the air had been sawed down the middle from top to bottom and glowing shavings showered from the ceiling to the floor. The far end of the room seemed plunged in gloom. Seryozha placed a packet of writing paper close at hand and switched on the electric light. In doing all this he had forgotten that he had agreed to take a stroll with Anna.

"I intend to marry," he wrote to Kovalenko, "and am in desperate need of money. I am now adapting into a play the story that I was telling you about. . . . The play will be in verse."

And he set about expounding the plot:

"One day, in the real conditions of contemporary Russian life, but so depicted as to give them a wider significance, a rumor is born among the leading business circles of either Moscow or Saint Petersburg, eventually takes root, and gets embellished by all sorts of detail. It is transmitted orally; nobody tries to confirm it through the newspapers, because it is an illegal matter and, according to the recently revised legal code, it is now listed as a criminal offense. It would seem that a man has come forward who is eager to sell himself as a slave at an auction, to the highest bidder, and that the significance and benefit of the transaction would become clear at the auction. It appears that there might even be a faint ring of Wilde in this, or something else, to do with women, and though nobody bothers to identify its source the rumor echoes around the young merchant set of the kind who decorate their homes to sketches made by theatrical designers and who load their conversation with terms borrowed from the Hindu mystics. On the appointed day—for even details of the place and day of the sale have incredibly reached everybody's ears—everyone leaves town, with the misgiving that he may have been fooled by his friends and become a laughing stock for going. But curiosity wins, and besides, it is June and the weather is marvelous. It all takes place in a country residence; the house is new and no one has ever been there before. There are a lot of people, all from the same crowd: heirs to big fortunes, philosophers, music-lovers, collectors, discriminating amateurs. There are chairs set out in rows, a platform raised like a small stage on which stands a grand piano, its lid propped open, and to one side a small table with a mallet on it. Several triple windows. At this point the man appears. He is still very young. Here, of course, there is some difficulty over his name, and indeed, what can one call a man who is aspiring from the outset to become a symbol? However, there are various different symbols and because he has to be called something, let us for the time being label him algebraically— Y_3, let us say.

"It immediately becomes apparent that there will be no fireworks, no circus act, no Cagliostro, nothing from "The Egyptian Nights," and that the man was born in earnest and, what is more, with some purpose. It is evidently a serious business; everything will be carried out in the broad light of day with all of them present, without digressions into fantasy, and there will be no getting away from it. And consequently Y_3 is greeted, with all the simplicity of prose, by applause, as if he had been standing on the corner of Okhotnyi Ryad and Dmitrovka. He announces that whoever makes the largest offer will acquire the power of life or death over him, that he will take just twenty-four hours to dispose of his profit as he has planned, leaving nothing for himself, after which he will begin his total and incontestable bondage, the duration of which he now entrusts into the hands of his future master, for the latter will have not only the power to put him to whatever purpose he wishes but also to kill him, whenever and however it may suit him. He has prepared a false suicide note that will exonerate the murderer in advance. He is also ready, if necessary, to draw up when required any further kind of document that would suffice to cover with his goodwill anything that might happen to him.

" 'And now,' Y_3 declares, 'I shall play and read to you. I shall play only something unpremeditated, that is, impromptu, but the reading will be from a prepared text, though the writing is my own.'

"Then a new person walks across the platform and sits down at the table. It is a friend of Y_3's. Unlike his other friends, who have bidden him farewell that morning, this particular friend has remained at his side at Y_3's request. This one loves him no less than his other friends, but in contrast to them he does not lose his composure, because he does not believe Y_3's scheme can be realized. He is an officer of the Treasury and a very thorough, reliable man. So Y_3 has let him call the bids during this transaction, to which he, the last remaining friend, attaches no value. He has remained to help him accomplish this plan, in whose realization he has no faith, and then to wind up by toasting his friend before his long journey, according to all the rules of the auctioneer's art. At this point it begins to rain.

"At this point it begins to rain," Seryozha scribbled in the margin of an octavo sheet and then transferred from letter paper to quarto. It was a first draft of a kind a man writes only once or twice in a lifetime, all night long, in one session. Such drafts inevitably abound in water as an element that is preordained by its very nature to embody uniform and persistently powerful movements. Nothing except the most general idea, as yet unformulated and devoid of vital details, settles in written form during the first such evening, and the only remarkable feature of this sort of writing is the natural way in which the idea is born out of the circumstances of experience.

The rain was the first detail of the draft that brought Seryozha to a halt. He transferred this detail from octavo to a quarto sheet and began to cross out and correct it in an attempt to achieve the desired visual authenticity.

In places he coined words that did not exist in the language. He left them on the paper temporarily in the hope that they might eventually guide him through to more immediate torrents of rainwater in the sort of colloquial language that results from the interplay of enthusiasm and usage. He believed that these channels, recognized and accepted by all, would come to him from memory, and the anticipation of them clouded his vision with tears as if he were wearing incorrectly fitting spectacles.

If he had not been sitting, like every writer, at an angle to the table, with his back to both entrances into the room, or if he had turned his head to the right for a moment, he would have died of fright. Anna was standing in the doorway. She did not vanish at once. Retiring a step or two from the threshold, she remained standing in view in close proximity just as long as she judged it necessary to preserve a balance between faith and superstition. She did not wish to tempt fate by either deliberate dawdling or blind haste. She was dressed in her outdoor clothes. In her hand she held a tightly furled umbrella because, in the interval that had elapsed, she had not severed her connection with the outside world and there was a window in her room. What is more, as she had been about to go down to see Seryozha, she had very sensibly glanced at the barometer, which indicated stormy weather. Billowing up like a cloud behind Seryozha's back, she glittered whitely and smokily, although dressed all in black, against a sunset ribbon of dazzling intensity that poured out from beneath a gray-and-lilac storm cloud that had settled over all the gardens along the lane. The torrents of light dissolved Anna and the parquet floor, which fumed corrosively beneath her, as if they were so much vapor. From two or three movements Seryozha made, Anna guessed, as in the card game called kings, both his trouble and the fact that it could not be put right in his lifetime. Catching sight of him moving his clenched first across his eye, she turned away, gathered her skirt, and, stooping as she walked, tiptoed out of the classroom with a few long and powerful strides. Once in the corridor, she increased her pace a little and, as noiselessly as before, let the hem of her skirt fall, still biting her lips all the while.

It did not cost her much effort to refuse him. Everything happened of itself. The window of her room was already taken over to its full extent by the shifting sky. It was clear from its piled layers of purple that she would never arrive undrenched at even the nearest corner. Anna now felt even more urgently the need to take measures so as not to remain alone with this fresh misery of hers, which was rapidly turning bad. At the mere thought of being stuck alone all night in her room she turned icy with horror. What would become of her if this happened on top of everything else? Running through the yard into the lane, she hired a cab with its hood already raised, a short distance from the house. She drove to Chernyshevsky Lane, where an English lady friend of hers lived, hoping that the storm would continue to rage for a long time so that there could be no question of her being able to return home, and that her friend would be obliged, willingly or unwillingly, to put her up for the night.

"So it is beginning to rain outside the house," wrote Seryozha, "and this is what takes place outside the windows. The ancient birch trees shed their leaves in whole swarms and wave them a ceremonial farewell from the top of the rise. In the meantime, fresh flurries of leaves that get entangled in their hair writhe up in whitish spirals and disperse anew. Waving them off and losing them from sight the birches swing around toward the house. Darkness falls, and just before the first clap of thunder rings out, the grand piano begins to play.

"For his theme Y_3 picks the nocturnal sky as it looks when it emerges from the bathhouse, clad in the cashmere down of clouds, in the vitriol-and-incense vapor of the mophead forest, with a mighty bevy of stars, scoured to their last crevice and apparently a whole magnitude brighter. The glitter of these drops, which can never be isolated from space, however much they try to break away, is already strung above the instrumental thicket. Now, running his fingers over the keyboard, Y_3 abandons and then returns to the theme, committing it to oblivion and imprinting it on the memory. The windowpanes are rolled flat by torrents of mercurial chill, the birch trees move before the windows with armfuls of vast air and scatter it everywhere, showering it onto the shaggy waterfalls, while the music, for its part, bows to right and left and keeps promising something from the road.

"And what is so extraordinary, every time anyone attempts to cast doubt on the honesty of the statement, the player envelops the doubter in some unexpected, constantly recurring miracle of sound. It is the miracle of his own voice, that is, the miracle of their way of feeling and remembering tomorrow. The force of this miracle is such that, in jest, it could split the case of the piano, crushing the bones of these merchants and the Viennese chairs in passing, and yet it scatters fast silvery speech and sounds the more quietly, the more frequently and rapidly it is repeated.

"He reads in exactly the same way. He puts it thus: 'I shall read you so many passages of blank verse and so many columns of rhymed verse.' And again, each time anyone thinks it does not matter which way these blanket fantasies fall, head or heels toward the Pole, descriptions and similes of unprecedented magnetic sensitivity manifest themselves. They are images, that is, miracles of the word, examples of complete and arrow-like submission to the earth. Thus, these are the directions that their morality, their quest for truth, will follow tomorrow.

"But how strangely this man appears to experience all this. It is as if someone kept showing him the earth and then hiding it up his sleeve and he conceived of living beauty as the ultimate distinction between existence and nonexistence. His novelty resides in his grasping and elevating into a constant hallmark of poetry this difference, which is conceivable only for an instant. But where can he have seen these appearances and disappear-ances? Is it not the voice of mankind that has told him of an earth forever flickering in a succession of generations?

"All this is art, total, unimpeachable, and without omissions. Across whispering frontiers it talks constantly of infinities and is always born out of the richest, bottomlessly sincere terrestrial poverty. He intersperses his readings with playing, he hears the rustle of French phrases, and he is enveloped in scent. He is requested in low tones to forget about everything else, to continue only the piece he is performing and not to interrupt it—but this is not what he wants.

"Then he rises and addresses them, saying that their love touched him, but they did not love him sufficiently; otherwise they would have remem-bered that they were at an auction and the reason he had brought them together. He says that he cannot reveal his plans to them, for they would interfere again as they had done so many times previously, suggesting another solution and another form of help, possibly an even more generous one, but necessarily incomplete and not the kind his heart had prompted; that he has no value in that huge currency denomination in which man has been printed; that he must break himself down into small change and they must help him in this. They may think his project a whim doomed to failure. That makes no difference. They can hear him either entirely or not at all. If they hear him, then let them blindly submit to him. He resumes his playing and reading. In the intervals, numbers rattle out and work is found for his friend's idle hands and throat, and then, after about twenty minutes of senseless fever and in the very heat of glycerine hoarseness, on the ultimate crest of unparalleled perspiration, he falls to the lot of one of the most sincere prospective purchasers, a person of the strictest principles and a renowned philanthropist. But it is not at once, not the same evening, that this man allows him his freedom. . . ."

V

This is not, of course, an original of Seryozha's draft. After all, he himself did not complete it. There was much on his mind that was never recorded on paper. He was just considering a scene of city riots when Mrs. Fresteln, drenched to the skin and furious, burst into the room, dragging after her the reluctant Harry, who was evidently embarrassed about the imminent scandal.

In his plot Seryozha had planned that on the third day, let us say, after the transaction, a conversation of major significance and sincerity would take place between the philanthropist and his chattel. Seryozha had reck-oned that once the rich patron had lodged Y_3 in private quarters and exhausted him with the luxury of the way he was treated, and himself with

worries, he would no longer be able to bear the misery and would call on
Y_3 in the room set aside for him with the request that, because he did not
know how to employ him more worthily, he depart to the four corners of
the earth. This Y_3 would refuse to do. On the very same night this conversation took place, news would be brought to the countryside of riots that had
taken place in the city, which had begun with brawls in the very neighborhood where Y_3 had dispensed his millions. This news would discourage both
of them, Y_3 in particular, because in the acts of violence that had gained such
wide notoriety he would detect a return to the past, whereas he had hoped
for a mysterious renaissance, that is, something complete and irreversible.
And then he would depart. . . .

"No, it's just awful. I almost broke my umbrella!" Mrs. Fresteln exclaimed. "*Je l'admets à l'égard des domestiques, mais qu'en ai-je à penser
si* . . . But, good heavens, what's the matter with you? Are you ill? I'm a
fine one! Wait just a moment. Harry, you must go to bed this very minute,
this very minute! Varya, you will rub him down with vodka and we'll talk
tomorrow. There's no point in sniffling now; you should have thought of
it before. Off you go now, Harry dear. The heels, that's important, the heels.
And also rub his chest with turpentine. Tomorrow there'll be kind words
for all of you—for you and Lavrentii Nikitich. But Mrs. Arild will be the
first to give an account of herself."

"Why, what's she done?" Seryozha asked.

"Well, they've gone at last! I didn't want to mention it in their presence.
I didn't notice anything at first. Don't be angry. Are you having trouble?
Anything to do with the family?"

"Excuse me all the same, but how has the Mrs. displeased you?"

"Which Mrs.? I don't understand what you're talking about. You're
blushing! Aha, so that's it! Well, well. All right then. Yes, that's it—
regarding my maid. She hasn't been seen since this morning. She left the
premises with the rest of the servants, but at least the others thought better
of it in the evening . . ."

"And Mrs. Arild?"

"That's an improper question. How do I know where Mrs. Arild is
spending the night? *Suis-je sa confidente?* Now, here's why I've stopped in
to see you, my dear Sergei Osipovich. I'd ask you, my dear, to see to it that
Harry packs his games and school books first thing tomorrow morning. Let
him pack them himself as best he can. Of course you will afterward re-
arrange everything without giving the impression that it was part of your
plan. I feel you want to ask me about the linen and other things? Varya is
responsible for all that and it does not concern you. I believe that, wherever
possible, children should be given the illusion of a certain independence. In
a case like this, even appearances can stimulate beneficial habits. Having
said that, I should like you to devote more attention to him in the future.

If I were you, I'd lower the lamp shade a little. Allow me. There, a little like this, don't you think? Isn't that really better than the way you had it? But I'm afraid I shall catch a cold. We leave the day after tomorrow. Good night!"

On one occasion, in the early days of his acquaintance with Anna, Seryozha began discussing Moscow with her and checking her knowledge of the city. Besides the Kremlin, which she had seen more than enough of, she named a few other areas where friends of hers lived. It turned out now that of those names she had reeled off only two had stuck in his mind: Sadovaya-Kudrinskaya and Chernyshevsky Lane. Discarding the forgotten directions, as though Anna's choice were as limited as his memory, he was now ready to bet that Anna was spending the night at Sadovaya. He was convinced of this, because then he would be completely stuck. To find her at this hour in such a large street, without the faintest notion where or in whose house to seek her, was impossible. Chernyshevsky Lane was another matter, but it was unlikely that she could be there, judging by the way his yearning ran ahead of him along the pavement like a dog and in struggling to break free of its leash, dragged him after it. He would definitely have found her in Chernyshevsky Lane if only it was conceivable that the living Anna, of her own free will, was indeed in the place where it was merely his desire (and what a strong desire!) to situate her. Convinced of failure, he hurried to test with his own eyes this unaugured chance, because he was in the kind of state in which the heart prefers to gnaw at stale hopelessness —anything rather than remain inactive.

Morning had already completely arrived, overcast and chilly. The overnight rain had just cleared. At each step the glitter of silvery poplar trees sparkled above the almost black gray of the drenched granite. The dark sky was spattered with their whitish foliage as with milk. Leaves that had been blown down speckled the pavement like soiled scraps of torn receipts. It seemed as if, before departing, the storm had imposed upon these trees the duty of examining its aftereffects and left in their fresh, gray hands the whole of that tangled morning so full of surprises.

On Sundays Anna used to attend Communion in the Anglican church. Seryozha recalled her telling him that one of her acquaintances lodged somewhere in the vicinity. Accordingly, full of his preoccupations, he took up his station opposite the church.

He stared vacantly at the open windows of the sleeping vicarage, and his heart swallowed down morsels of the scene it picked on, greedily devouring the damp bricks of the outbuildings and the moist greenery of the trees. His anxious glances likewise hacked at the air that passed dryly into some other unknown region of his body, avoiding his lungs.

In order not to attract anyone's suspicion accidentally, Seryozha occasionally strolled unhurriedly down the full length of the street. Only two sounds disturbed its drowsy quiet: Seryozha's footsteps and the throb of some machine working nearby. That was the rotary press in the *Russian News* printing office. Seryozha felt all bruised inside; he was choking on the wealth that he had to absorb but was hardly able to.

The force that had infinitely expanded his perception was the absolutely literal nature of his passion, namely, that quality it possessed, thanks to which the tongue seethes with images, metaphors, and, even more, enigmatic forms that elude analysis. Needless to say, the whole street with its unbroken gloom had become wholly and roundly identified with Anna. In this Seryozha was not alone and he knew it. And who, in truth, had not experienced this before him? However, the feeling was more spacious and precise, and here any assistance from friends or predecessors came to an end. He saw how painful and difficult it was for Anna to be the city morning, how much the superhuman dignity of nature cost her. She gloried silently in his presence and did not appeal for his aid. Dying with longing for the real Anna, for all this splendor in its briefest and most precious abstraction, he watched how, swathed in poplars like ice-packed towels, she was sucked into the clouds and slowly threw back her Gothic brick towers. This brick, of purplish, non-Russian firing, looked imported from Scotland, for some reason.

A man in an overcoat and soft felt hat emerged from the night editorial office of the newspaper. Without turning his head, he walked off in the direction of Nikitskaya Street. So as not to arouse the man's suspicion if he should glance back, Seryozha crossed from the pavement in front of the newspaper office to the Scottish one and strode in the direction of Tverskaya. Some twenty paces from the church, he saw Anna inside a tiny room of a house across the street. At that very moment she had come from the back of the room over to the window. When they had recovered from the shock, they began to talk in hushed tones, as if in the presence of people sleeping. They did this for the sake of Anna's friend. Seryozha was standing in the middle of the street. It seemed they were talking in whispers so as not to rouse the city.

"I heard someone keep walking up and down the street for a long time, someone who couldn't sleep," Anna told him. "And then I suddenly thought, 'It's him.' Why didn't you come to the house straightaway?"

The railway-carriage corridor tossed from side to side. It looked endless. The passengers were asleep behind the rows of varnished, tightly shut doors. Supple springs muffled the rumbling of the carriage. It resembled a gloriously flounced cast-iron feather bed.

The edges of this feather bed fluttered most pleasantly of all, and a stout chief conductor, reminiscent somehow of egg-rolling at Easter, bowled down the corridor in his boots and wide breeches, a round cap on his head and a whistle dangling from a strap. He was too hot in his winter uniform, and to give himself some relief he kept adjusting his severe pince-nez as he walked along. It was surprisingly tiny against the huge beads of sweat that dotted his whole face and made it resemble a fresh slice of Meshchersk cheese. If he had noticed Seryozha's pose in a carriage of a different class, he would definitely have put an arm around him or roused him from his reverie in some other manner. Seryozha was drowsing, his elbows against the edge of the lowered window. He drowsed and then woke, yawned, admired the landscape, and rubbed his eyes. He stuck his head out of the window and bawled melodies that Anna had played at one time or another, but no one heard his bellowing. Whenever the train come out of curves into a straight stretch, a graceful, motionless current of air took over the corridor. Once they had sped about and babbled to their heart's content, the wild doors of the carriage-dividers and the toilets spread their wings, and, to the accompanying roar of increasing speed, it was amazing to feel that one was not oneself being drawn, but was simply one of the wildly straining birds, with Schumann's bravura in one's soul.

It was not the heat alone that had driven him out of his compartment. He felt awkward in the company of the Frestelns. It required a week or two more for their impaired relations to return to their former state. He blamed Margarita Ottonovna Fresteln least of all for their deterioration. He recognized that, assuming he was her adopted son and her main obligation to him was to exercise leniency and indulgence, in that case there was some cause for her despair during the recent fuss before their departure.

After her recent nocturnal reprimand, it had pleased him to disappear for the whole day on the eve of their departure, when he knew full well what a commotion would reign in the household from the first thing the next morning.

"The blinds!" someone would squeal unexpectedly and Egor would miraculously materialize out of pieces of matting, for all the world like a living person. "The blinds, Egor! . . . This is intolerable!"

"What about the blinds?"

"What d'you mean, 'What about the blinds,' you oaf? Are they to stay hanging here like this, d'you suppose?"

"But what's likely to happen to them?"

"Did you beat the dust out of them?"

"I hope you rot, Lavrentii. Leave me alone, you fiend!"

"Varya, my dear, this isn't an outing you know."

"But when all's said and done, to hell with the Arild woman," Margarita Ottonovna was thinking. "He is to be pitied, of course, poor thing: a worthless, intriguing woman, but what can you do once the scythe has struck stone. However, if that was the way things went, it is a different question altogether, and there is a human way of doing everything. He saw her off on the quarter-to-six train from the Bryansk Station—well, and that was that! And he could have managed it so that not a soul at home need mention where he had been or what he had lost. On the contrary, everyone would think, 'There's a real man, a decent, self-respecting man.' But that was obviously old-fashioned; everything is different now. He had to go and shut himself off after taking leave of her, and he's not embarrassed at their constant scrutiny to see whether he's . . . adapting and getting used to things. Well, what's one to do in such a case? Dismiss him? . . ."

"Don't bother, madam, you aren't doing it correctly. I'll tuck it under myself . . . Oh, damnation! This stuff's so rotten. That's the second one that's broken. I told you to use a rope, didn't I?"

". . . But how could I dismiss him when there was so much confusion all around and when it was absolutely clear from what had happened that his salary wasn't just for fun? But then, if you please, a job was no joke either and one must value it. You might plead as an excuse for him that a new decadent expression has been coined—'to experience.' However, to experience, that's to say to expose one's secrets to external scrutiny, could probably be done in a human way, whereas in his case he is absolutely unrecognizable and useless the morning after, a Christ, passivity incarnate. If you proposed it seriously, he would nail up a box, using his head as a hammer. But, alas, a household requires anything but that, and one does not employ a tutor in a decent family for that purpose. . . . And here they were traveling and he was with them. Why on earth was he with them? But how on earth can he be dismissed?

"Meanwhile in Tula they had all missed the passenger train with which the Moscow express was due to connect, and had watched in horror through the carriage window as it pulled out from alongside them, heading off back at an angle, toward Kaluga. That was a dreadful night. . . . But they were rewarded for their ten-hour torment. About an hour ago a long distance express came through here on the Syzran-Vyazma line, and they were now installed in it in the kind of comfort that was inconceivable on their local night train. Anton Karlovich and Harry were sleeping, but they would have to be woken up in twenty minutes, poor things."

The chief conductor found the carriage to his liking, and he kept on dropping by. The views that unfolded outside were really astonishing. Take for example this very moment, when, frozen at full speed, the noisy, dirty train floated and seemed to repose upon a widespread arc of sheer, blazing sand, while on the bank opposite this outcrop, far beyond the flood meadows, a large, shaggy estate seemed to float at rest upon a slightly tremulous hillside. When only about ten miles remained, the thought might have occurred that this was Rukhlovo; everything seemed to be so like what he had been told: the gleaming white glimpses of the manor house and the park railings, crumpled by the uneven hill, on which they seemed to have been laid out like an unclasped necklace. The park contained many silvery poplar trees. "Dear ones!" Seryozha whispered, and screwing up his eyes, he let his hair blow free in the gallop of the oncoming wind.

So it was for just such an eventuality as this that the word "happiness" existed among men. Although they had merely talked and he had merely shared her worries and helped her to prepare for the journey . . . although they would experience another, more complete intimacy . . . yet they would never be closer than they had been during those ten unforgettable hours. Everything in the world had been understood; there was nothing more to comprehend. All that remained was to live, that is, to slice up understanding with one's hands and to lose oneself in it. All that remained was to please it, just as it had pleased them, as it spread all around them with railways laid across its face and its cycles. What happiness!

But how lucky that she had spoken of her family! How easily this might not have happened. The wretches! A lot they understood about what debases or ennobles a family tree. But they would talk some other time about her unfortunate father (a remarkable case!). Seryozha now understood where she had acquired such wisdom, which made her seem twice as old as she was and ten times as austere. She had inherited it all. This explained her calm mastery of everything. What need did she have to be amazed at herself or to seek a noisy name for her gifts? She had possessed it anyway, before her marriage, and it was a very well-publicized one.

Her ancestors were of Scottish descent. The name of Mary Stuart had even cropped up. And now it was impossible not to feel that this particular name had been the one missing element all that morning on overcast Chernyshevsky Lane.

But now the chief conductor nudged the deafened passenger and warned him that he and his companions had to get off at the next stop.

This, then, was the way people had moved from place to place during that last in a series of summers when life still appeared to heed individuals, and when it was easier and more natural to love anything under the sun than to hate.

Seryozha stretched, rolled over, and gave vent to a string of yawns each less controllable than the last. Suddenly they stopped. He raised himself adroitly on his elbow and glanced soberly and rapidly about him. The reflection of a streetlight lay spilled in a pool on the floor.

"Winter," he thought immediately, "and this is my first dream at Natasha's in Usolye."

Fortunately, no one had observed his half-animal awakening. And—ah! —there was something else he must not forget. He had dreamed of something formless, and, whatever it was, it made his head ache even now. Most remarkable of all, this nonsense had a name while he could still visualize it. "Lemokh," it was called, but try as he might, he could not guess what that meant. One thing was certain: he must get up; he was feeling ravenous, and he hoped that he had not slept through the arrival of the visitors.

In a minute he was already drowning in his brother-in-law's velvety embraces, which smelled strongly of iodoform. His brother-in-law was still holding a can-opener in his fist when he rushed to greet Seryozha with his arm fully extended. This, together with the hearing aid sticking out of his pocket, like sincerity tangibly materialized, spoiled the sweetness of their embraces. And the opening of cans could not be resumed with the previous expertise and began to flag. Abrupt and artificially direct questions were bandied back and forth over the cans. Seryozha stood there feeling glad but puzzled as to why it should be necessary to play the fool when one could be a natural fool without trying. They did not like each other.

On the table stood a neat rank of lively, fresh-wakened vodka glasses and a complex assortment of wind and percussion snacks gladdened the eye. Above them, towered black bottles of wine, conductor-like and ready at any moment to burst into life and summon a deafening overture to all manner of laughter and punning. The spectacle was all the more impressive because the sale of wine had been prohibited throughout Russia, but the factory evidently worked as an autonomous republic.

It was late by now, and they agreed that Seryozha could peep at the children in their beds.

The whole room seemed to be swimming in brandy. Whether it was the effect of the light or the selection of furniture, the floor appeared to have been polished not with wax but with rosin, and his slithering foot felt beneath it not waxed-over joints, but horsehair, stained and glued together. Anything with facets or any play of light was drenched by the hot yellow of the furnishings, as if with lemon cordial ("Karelian birch, what do you think?" Kalyazin lied for some reason). Seryozha possessed these qualities too. By his reckoning the piercingly lit house should appear to the bearish blue-white night like a tiny brazier full of coals, glowing among the snowdrifts.

"Aha, there's a real frost! I'm glad!" he exclaimed, moving behind the edge of the curtain and staring into the darkness.

"Hm . . . yes, it's freezing hard," his brother-in-law grunted absentmindedly, wiping his sauce-ambered fingers on his handkerchief.

"The trouble is, I haven't any boots with me. I didn't have the sense to buy some, so I didn't bring any."

"That can be put right. You can get some here. But what are we talking about, pray? A man, so to speak, arrives here from, so to speak . . . Have some nelma—Siberian fish. And maksun. Have you heard of them, brother? No? Well, I knew myself you would never have heard of them."

Seryozha grew more and more cheerful, and it is uncertain what he might have ended up doing, but at the moment a muffled, confused trampling of feet came from the corridor. People were taking off their coats there. Soon, into the dining room, all flushed from the frost, came Natasha and a girl Seryozha did not know, and also a slim, deliberate, and very alert man, whom Seryozha rushed to meet ahead of Kalyazin and whom he greeted effusively, joyfully, and almost apprehensively. Then all his cheerfulness evaporated. In the first place, he knew this man, and besides, he was confronting something tall and alien that devalued Seryozha from head to foot. It was the masculine spirit of fact personified, that most modest and most terrible of spirits.

"And how's your brother?" Seryozha began in confusion and then stopped.

"He's still alive," Lemokh replied. "He was wounded in the foot. He's convalescing with me. I'll probably be able to fix him up at home. Glad to see you. And how are you, Pavel Pavlovich?"

"Just imagine," Seryozha mumbled even more distractedly, "he may have been concealing it as his military duty, but not one of us realized it was the mobilization. Everyone thought they were on maneuvers. I'm sorry, but I don't know what they call those training exercises. Anyhow, we all thought it was something of the sort. But they were already being taken to the front. What I mean is, I saw him in July two summers ago. Just think, their unit was traveling by in barges, and they stopped for the night just near the estate where I was working as a tutor at the time. That was two days before war was declared. We only put two and two together afterward. Do you see?"

"Yes, I know about your conversation with my brother. He told me all about it."

But the only thing Seryozha would not admit was that he had at the time been too shy to ask Lemokh the volunteer his name the night they had met.

1929   *Translated by Nicholas J. Anning*

Fragments of a Novel

A District in the Rear

I remember that evening. I see it before me now. It was at my father-in-law's mill. In the afternoon I had ridden into town on some business of his.

I left early. Tonya and Shura were still asleep as I came out on tiptoe into the light of a night that was now ending. All around, knee-deep in grass and the wail of mosquitoes stood birch trees, gazing somewhere toward the point from which autumn was approaching. I walked in the same direction.

There beyond the ravine were the farmstead and the house where we had lived previously and from which we had moved a short time before into a woodland lodge to make room for the woman who was to take the *dacha*. We were expecting her any day. Among my prospective tasks in town, I had been detailed to see her.

I had on some new boots that I had not broken in yet. As I bent to shift my heel in the heel piece of the right boot, there was a noise of something heavy passing high above me. I raised my head. Two squirrels were tearing after one another through the foliage like bullets. Here and there the branches came alive to sling and toss them from one treetop to another.

This chase, although interrupted by frequent flights through the air, took place so smoothly that it left the impression that they were scampering across the even predawn sky. Now a bucket clattered on the far side of the ravine. Demid, the workman, was opening the gates of the stable and saddling Magpie.

I had last been in town in the middle of July. Three weeks had passed, and in this time there had been new changes for the worse.

To tell the truth, it was difficult for me to judge them. Aleksandr Aleksandrovich had made his crazy purchase at the very beginning of the war. On our first visit from Moscow to "The Mill," as his woodland acquisition was called by force of habit, the Uralic countenance of Yuryatin was obscured by refugees, Austrian prisoners of war, and a multitude of soldiers and civilians from both capitals, cast here by the increasingly complex exigencies of wartime. Yuryatin itself had already lost its image and only seemed to mirror the changes taking place in the country and at the front.

The waves of evacuation had rolled this far even earlier. But when I sighted mountains of equipment from the Baltic Coast dumped in the open along the tracks of the freight station at the level crossing beyond Skobyaniki, it occurred to me that years would pass before anyone remembered these "Etnas" and "Peruns" and tube-rolling machinery from Tallinn, and that it would not be we but these heaps of rust that would one day bear witness to the way everything ended.

Despite the early hour, work at the military commandant's office was in full swing. In the courtyard the senior member of a group of Tatars and Voyaks was explaining that their village wove baskets for sulfuric acid carboys for the Maloyashvinsk and Nizhnevarynsk Union on a defense contract. In such cases peasants in whole areas were left where they were simply on request from the factories. This group's mistake consisted in having shown some sign of life and turning up in person to see someone. Their file had been lost somewhere and, weary of tedious searches, the authorities were shipping them off to the front. Although their arguments were accepted in the warm office building, nobody would listen to them outside. My papers turned out to be in order, and no one had yet questioned the article on ruptures and hernias that allowed Demid to escape the draft.

Around the corner from the military headquarters, opposite the cathedral on Sennaya Street, was an inn yard where I left Magpie, who was an embarrassment in town in view of the short distances. It was the Assumption Fast. Wine had not been sold in the state shops for more than a year. But even amid the general sobriety, the inn was remarkable for its silence and gloom. Beneath its broad roof they did a secret trade in *kumyshka*. Not counting the owner, it was a woman's domain here now. One of his daughters-in-law took the horse.

"You haven't made up your minds to sell out?" the owner asked from somewhere up above, leaning from a window, his head cupped in his hand. I did not immediately grasp what his question was about. "No, we're not thinking of it," I answered. Evidently rumors of our properties in the forest had reached here and become the talk of the town.

The street blinded me after the darkness of the inn yard. Finding myself on my feet after being in the saddle, I felt the approach of morning as though for the second time. Carts of cabbage and carrots were crawling to the market later than usual. They were getting no farther than Dvoryanskaya Street. They were being halted at every step as if they were some amazing miracle, and bought out on the way. Standing on their drays, as though elevated to national importance, the peasant women from the market gardens swore they could satisfy everyone, but this failed to appease the obstreperous, irritable crowd—unusual for the provinces—that gathered around them.

On the imitation-marble staircase leading to the city office of the Ust-Krymzhensk works I overtook a gray-bearded Yuryatin citizen in a Siberian greatcoat with gathers that gave his waist a womanish appearance from the back. He was slowly making his way up ahead of me, and on entering the office, he blew his nose into a red handkerchief, put on silver spectacles, and began examining the notices dotted all over the left-hand wall by the entrance. Apart from the monochrome and colored printed advertisements and prospectuses that had long adorned that wall, there were several white columns of typed and handwritten paper that attracted his attention.

Here were the announcements of sales of timber, both felled and standing; notices inviting offers for all types of transport; a notice to workers and employees of a lump-sum bonus equivalent to three months' salary, to cover rising costs; a summons to home guardsmen, second class, to come to the personnel offices. Here there also hung a decree about the issuance of foodstuffs to employees at the factory shops on a strict monthly quota at near-prewar prices.

"Forty-five pounds of rye flour, price three kopecks a pound; two pounds of vegetable oil . . . ," the Yuryatin gentleman read syllable by syllable. I later found him at one of the desks inquiring whether management would agree to settle for the announced contracts not in bank notes but in ration coupons, as he put it, of the type displayed. For a long time they could not grasp what he wanted, and when they did understand they pointed out to him that this was not a corn exchange. I did not hear how the misunderstanding ended. I was diverted by Vyakhrishchev.

He was standing in the main concourse of the Accounts Department, which was divided in two by a grille and series of uprights. Forcing aside the young men in their flapping jackets who rushed through the doors of the Managerial Department carrying piles of papers, he regaled the whole room with anecdotes, choking on the hot tea that the cook brought around the office on a tray at various stages, and of which he took glass after glass without finishing a single one.

Vyakhrishchev was a military man from Saint Petersburg, holding a captain's rank, clean-shaven and sarcastic, and he was attached to the works as an inspector for Central Artillery Command.

The works was sixteen miles south of Yuryatin, that is, in the opposite direction from us. It was a long journey and it had to be made on horseback. We sometimes went there to visit when they sent for us. However, this has nothing to do with Vyakhrishchev. I ought to tell you how he maintained his constant wit.

He did not have an easy part to play. He was at the works in an official capacity and lived there as a guest in the visitors' block, which they called the "Roadhouse." There were specialists all around, pushed into the foreground by the latest military requirements. The significance of factory management and owners waned in face of their authority.

They were university people for the most part, a varied bunch, but each and every one of them had passed through the school of 1905. To give just one example, Lev Nikolaevich Golomennikov, the Chief Director, who has since died but whose name is well known from the several educational institutes named after him.

In his student years Golomennikov had belonged to that particular group of Russian Social-Democrats who were destined to say so much that was new to the world. However it would be an anachronism to apply this remark, in its current sense, to those winter-evening get-togethers at which this lanky, prematurely graying, and slightly sarcastic man played host or came as a guest.

The Roadhouse stood at the factory gates near the oil-storage tanks, set apart from the factory site on wasteland toward the river. Moreover, Vyakhrishchev always claimed it was there that they kept the laboratory alcohol, a solution of which so enlivened these evening gatherings. Of course, Golomennikov also took part in all the merriment, and when conversations were toned down a little in his presence, not so much out of fear of him as from concern lest anything offend him, he was naturally upset, and in this way unwittingly furthered their revolutionary attitudes.

He recognized this anomaly only too well and on occasion would express it with some malice. He would introduce himself as "the Russian military attaché on the Krymzha," giving the impression that he thought of the works as an independent state. Or he would launch forth on a list of Russia's allies, and coming to Rumania (this was later on), he would go on: "Hydrochloric and chromic—Lev Nikolaevich Golomennikov," and everybody would roar with laughter.

On seeing me, Vyakhrishchev pretended the surprise had made him swallow too big a mouthful of hot tea. His eyes started out in fright; he crossed himself, put his glass and saucer down on the edge of the partition, and tried to ward me off, as though I were a ghost.

"So you're still alive," he gabbled, as his performance ended. "Where on earth have you been? What's happening over in those woods of yours? Haven't you concluded a separate treaty yet?"

"There's a package here for Mr. Gromeko. Do you want to take it?" asked a clerk, coming out from behind the grille.

"Why certainly. I came to pick it up. But won't it be a bit heavy? Will I manage it myself?"

"A bit heavy for your shoulder straps, I expect. It's a fair-sized bundle."

"Then I'll call back in a couple of hours' time. I haven't my horse with me at the moment.—Sorry," I addressed Vyakhrishchev. "I got sidetracked. I'm at your service."

He began dragging me from one room to another, pouring out all sorts of incredible nonsense and trying to persuade me to ride off with him there and then to the Krymzha to attend some family celebration there. Fortunately, we happened to bump into the doctor, a member of the Yuryatin medical board, who was just coming out of the Director's office.

"My dear doctor, fancy seeing you!" Vyakhrishchev exclaimed. A farcical exchange began. Taking advantage of my freedom, I hurried to our department of the Zemstvo and Town Guild, tucked away in one of the rooms of that same building facing Ermakovsky Park.

This department was actually Aleksandr Aleksandrovich's place of work, although the Guild was mainly concerned with problems of supply, about which he understood not one iota. He was attached to Reserve Section as a free-lance consultant on dairy cattle and their selection, a specialty in which he had once graduated—moreover, with some distinction—from the Geneva Polytechnical Institute. He did not often come to Yuryatin himself, relying on chance circumstances to give his consultations or sending Demid to the department with notes. There was positively nothing for him to do in the department, and he only reminded them of his existence occasionally, to avoid an unpleasant row, seeing first one colleague, then another and changing his excuses each time to make them look more plausible and lively.

Now, on the most fatuous pretext, I was to see one of the founders of the department, the editor of the progressive regional newspaper, who for some reason preferred to receive calls at the Zemstvo and Town Guild rather than at his editorial office. However it turned out that he had left for Moscow the day before. I went off to see Istomina. There was a story told about this woman. She was born locally, in Perm, apparently, and her fate was a complicated and unhappy one. Her father, a lawyer with the un-Russian surname of Luvers, had been ruined by the collapse of a certain stock and had shot himself while she was still a child. Others ascribed his death to some incurable disease. The children had moved with their mother to Moscow. Later, after her marriage, the daughter somehow found herself in home country once more. The tales told about her referred to the very recent past and will not concern us immediately.

Although teachers at educational institutions were not liable for call-up, her husband, Vladimir Vasilyevich Istomin, a physicist and mathematician at the Yuryatin *lycée*, had gone off to the war as a volunteer. For about two years now there had not been a breath of news about him. It was believed that he had been killed, and one minute his wife was suddenly convinced of her unconfirmed widowhood, the next full of doubts about it.

To see her I ran up the back stairs of the new *lycée* building, whose narrow stairwell with its slightly elongated steps had a crooked appearance. That staircase reminded me of something.

The same sense of familiarity came over me again on the threshold of the teacher's apartment. The entrance door was wide open. In the hall stood several pieces of luggage waiting to be bound up. From here the end of a dark drawing room could be seen, with an empty bookcase shifted from where it had stood and a mirror removed from its dressing table. In the windows, which probably faced north, there blazed the greenery of the *lycée* garden, illuminated from the rear. There was an unseasonable smell of mothballs.

On the floor in the drawing room a pretty little girl of about six was packing her doll family and tying them up in a roll of dirty gauze. I gave a cough. She looked up. Istomina looked out from the far room into the drawing room; she was holding an armful of colored kerchiefs, trailing the bottom ones on the floor and holding down the top ones with her chin. She was rousingly, almost offensively, attractive. Her constrained movements suited her well and were perhaps calculated.

"Well, I've decided at last," she said, without letting go of her bundle. "I really have kept you on tenterhooks for a long time." In the middle of the drawing room stood an open traveling hamper. She threw the kerchiefs into it, dusted herself down, smoothed her hair, and came over to me. We greeted one another.

"The *dacha* is furnished," I reminded her. "Why do you need to take furniture there?" I was perplexed by the thoroughness of her preparations.

"Oh, is it really?" she said in alarm. "What am I to do now? The carts are arranged for three. Dunya, what time do you make it there by the kitchen clock? Oh, of course, I sent her to the janitor's myself. Katya, don't get in the way here, for heaven's sake."

"It's twelve," I said. "You'll have to cancel the extra carters and just leave one. You still have plenty of time."

"Oh, but that's not really the point!"

This was said almost in despair. I did not understand to what she was referring. Suddenly I began to guess. She had probably been refused an official apartment and was hoping to find permanent shelter with us. This would explain her late departure. I had to warn her that we spent the winters in Moscow and boarded up the house.

At that moment the rumble of voices reached us from the staircase. Soon it filled the entrance hall too. In the doorway of the drawing room appeared a girl with several bundles of fresh bast matting and the janitor with two boxes, which he lowered to the floor with a bang. Fearing another delay, I began to take my leave. "Well then, all the best, Evgeniya Vikentyevna," I said. "We'll see you soon. The roads are dry; traveling is sheer pleasure now."

As I emerged into the street, I remembered I could not go straight home from the inn but still had to call at the office for the package put aside for Aleksandr Aleksandrovich. However, before reaching Sennaya Street, I decided to call in at the station for some lunch. The buffet there had a reputation for the cheapness and high quality of its cuisine. On the way my thoughts returned to Istomina.

Prior to this conversation I had seen her two or three times, and at every meeting I was haunted by a sense of having seen her before somewhere. For a long time I thought this feeling was illusory and never sought an explanation. Istomina herself encouraged this. She must have reminded everyone she met of something, because she often resembled a figment of memory on account of a certain vagueness in her manner.

At the station there was a scene of complete bedlam. I immediately realized I would come away empty-handed. The crowds spread in separate columns from the ticket kiosks and left no gap as they flooded the entire station. The public in the buffet was composed mainly of military. There was no space at the tables for half of them, and they milled around the diners, strolling in the gangways, smoking despite the notices hung about prohibiting it, and sat on the window ledges. At the head of the main table some soldier was attempting to jump up. His comrades were restraining him. Nothing could be heard above the general din, but to judge from the gestures of the waiter justifying himself, they were shouting at him. The manager of the buffet crossed the hall—a fat man blown up to unnatural proportions, so it seemed, by the rattle of crockery ringing through the building and the proximity of the platform.

I was about to slip onto the platform to avoid the crush and make my way into town via the railway track, but the guard would not let me pass. Through the glass windows of the exit the unusual emptiness of the platform was striking. A gang of workmen stood there looking in the direction of the open platform, which receded down the track in a continuation of the covered section. The stationmaster had gone down there with two policemen. They said that when a draft detachment was pulling out a short time before, there had been a noise of some kind at that point, which nobody could properly identify.

I recalled all this at the end of my journey back along the forest road past the official Rynva *dacha* settlement, where Magpie, as though infected by my own tiredness, began shaking his head and twitching his sides, and slowed down to a walk.

At this point the same thing happened to the forest as to myself and the horse. The little-used road passed through a clearing. It had become over-grown with grass. And it seemed as though it had not been laid by man, but, rather, that the forest itself, overwhelmed by its own immensity, had parted here of its own accord to reflect at leisure. The clearing seemed like the soul of the forest.

A white rectangle was wedged into the end of the clearing like a promon-tory enclosed by lath fencing. These were the spring crops of Yasyri. A little farther on, a poor hamlet came into view. The forest that framed it to the very horizon closed about like a wall once more. Yasyri and its oats were left behind like some insignificant island. Probably the peasants rented part of the land from the local estates, just as in neighboring Pyatibratskoye.

I rode at a walking pace, slapping at mosquitoes on my hands, forehead, and neck. I thought of my family, the wife and son to whom I was returning.

In doing so I found myself reflecting that there I would be, arriving home, and once again they would never discover that I had been thinking of them on the way, and it would seem to them that I did not love them sufficiently, that I only felt the love they desired of me for something else, something remote, like loneliness and the pacing of the horse, something like a book. But I would have no strength to explain to them that all this *was* them, and their discontent would torment me.

It was amazing to what extent the right was on their side. These things were all signs of the times. Those close to me registered them with their artless sensitivity. Something more unfathomed and remote than all these predilections of mine already hovered beyond the forest and was due to sweep like a whirlwind over the fates of men. And they could detect the breath of impending separations and changes.

There was something strange about that autumn. It was as though it had occurred to nature to pause for breath before drinking ocean and taking a bite of Heaven, and now it had suddenly caught its breath. There was something not quite right about the cuckoo's call, about the white flatness of the ripe afternoon air and the pink abundance of the fireweed. There was something not quite right about this man returning home to the family that was dearer to him than all else.

After a while the forest thinned out. Beyond a shallow ravine, which formed its boundary and into which the roadway dipped before rising again, a knoll with several buildings came into sight. The grove in which the country house stood took the place of any surrounding fence. It was so deserted that it might have envied the foresters' winter lodges, which one came across at various points in the neighboring forest. Of all the stupidities committed by Aleksandr Aleksandrovich this was perhaps the most unforgivable. Some school friend employed in local industry had hunted this little witch's lair out for him. And Aleksandr Aleksandrovich had blindly given his written agreement to the transaction instead of acquiring meadowlands somewhere in central Russia, where his knowledge of cattle-breeding would have been of greater advantage to him. But this educated, and at that time still young, man thought least of all about advantage. His thoughts, too, were directed toward remote and abstract matters. Not for nothing had I been brought up in his house along with Tonya, his daughter. However that may be, things were now getting beyond a joke. This treasure trove had to be sold as quickly as possible for firewood, seeing that there was a demand for this. The factories were being converted from mineral fuel to wood, and in town this was the main topic of conversation.

At the sight of the outbuilding with its crimson roof, Magpie broke into a gallop. From the hill I saw Tonya and Shura, laughing as they ran toward me from the direction of the cliff. The stable must have stood wide open since the morning. I had scarcely stepped to the ground when the horse wrenched the reins free and rushed into the stable for fodder and repose too tantalizing for eye and nostril. Little Shura began jumping and clapping his hands as though this had all been done on purpose to amuse him.

"Let's go and have supper," said Tonya. "What are you limping for?"

"I just can't put this foot down; it's gone numb from sitting. Nothing serious. It'll go as soon as I stretch my legs."

Demid came around the corner of the barn, gave a most doleful bow, and went to unsaddle Magpie and put him away.

"There's a present for Papa in the straps behind the saddle. It needs to be unfastened and brought inside. Where is he by the way?"

"Papa is away until Tuesday. Some people from the works came this afternoon. Today is the ninth, and some Maria or other has a birthday today. What is it?"

"His provision ration. If he's at Krymzha; all the better. He'll get a second one."

"You seem to be angry."

"Judge for yourself. It's beginning to become part of the routine. We aren't layabouts or half-wits, and your father is a simply splendid man. Nevertheless, I've spent all my childhood boarding with you, Papa with his relatives, and they with someone else, and so on ad infinitum. We could live without sponging. How often have I suggested pooling our knowledge and abilities . . . ?"

"Well, what of it?"

"It's just the fact that now it's too late. This has spread and become a general evil. In town they are all asleep and looking for ways to get themselves allotted to some well-stocked food bowl. It's a return to the age of serf labor. Do you realize what that means? It means that everyone, no matter who, is attached to some place or other, and when he is bequeathed or transferred he doesn't even know whose hands he is leaving or whose hands he will end up in. You must agree, there's little to rejoice about in that."

"Oh, how out-of-date and boring all this is! Look what you've done. That's the result of your tirades."

The boy was crying.

After our supper and reconciliation, I went off up the steep slope, which fell away abruptly at the far end of the grove above the river. It is strange that so far I have said nothing of the demon of this place, mentioned in songs and entered on maps of any scale.

This was the Rynva in its upper reaches. It emerged from the north all at once, as though aware of its fluvial name, and once it emerged, a half mile or so upstream from our cliff, it paused uncertain, as though surveying the areas due for occupation. Its every hesitation flowed out in a meander. Its contemplation created creeks. The widest of these lay below us. Here it was easy to take the river for a forest lake. On the far shore another district began.

I lay down in the grass. I had lain there for some time stretched out in it, but instead of looking at the river I idly twitched the toes of my tight boots, viewing them from the vantage point of a supporting elbow. I had only to raise my eyes just slightly to get a glimpse of the river. I was about to do so the whole time but still kept putting it off.

Nothing had been going my way, though not everything was going against me, so consequently things went no way at all. My motives lacked persistence. Being easygoing was not for the best. It was terrible to think what I would not have been prepared to renounce just then! My family would be better off without me; I was spoiling their lives.

Gradually I was possessed by a series of thoughts common to everyone in those years, varying only in quantity and personal quality, and of course in the distinctive features of the time when they occurred: uneasy in 1914, even more disturbed in 1915, and utterly cheerless in the year 1916, during the autumn of which this all took place.

I thought once again that in spite of repeated rejections, it might still perhaps be better if I could catch a whiff of gunpowder. I knew that all these regrets were not worth a penny; there might be some excuse if I did something about them.

But previously my regrets had arisen from a love of life. I regretted that a gap would be left in it if I failed to share in the military exploits of my contemporaries in this, the country's memorable hour. Now my regrets stemmed from disgust. I was sorry that my failure to participate in the war was preserving my life, a life already so unlike its former self that there was a temptation to part with it before it abandoned me itself. And one could part with it most worthily and to best advantage at the front.

Meanwhile, our shore had sunk in shadow. By the opposite bank, the water lay like a piece of cracked mirror. And the bank was repeated in it with a sheen and sinister brilliance in keeping with this ill omen. The bank was low. Contracting and dwindling reflections were sucked beneath the water meadow's grassy brow.

Soon the sun went down. It set behind my back. The river dusted over, grew bristly, and turned greasy. Suddenly its warty surface began to smoke in several places at once, as though set alight from above and below.

In Pyatibratskoye dogs started barking, barely audibly, though with apparent reason. Their barking was taken up at a nearby forester's lodge, loudly but without cause. The grass beneath me had turned noticeably damp. In it the first stars had lighted like woodland berries of delirious clarity.

Soon the distant barking was resumed, but the spacial relationships had changed. Now those nearby barked with an obvious pretext, while the distant ones merely howled in accompaniment. A rattle of wheels could be heard coming from the forest ride. The irregular sounds of the travelers' steady conversation reached my ears. The speakers were being jolted up and down in the *tarantass*. Getting up from the wet grass, I set off to meet the woman who was to be tenant of our *dacha*.

Translated by Nicholas J. Anning and Christopher Barnes

Before Parting

Istomina had not had time to move her belongings before the first signs of autumn appeared and we began to get ready for our return to Moscow. But as the city-dweller in each of us awoke, nature itself besieged us on all sides like a town.

One dark morning at the end of September, Tonya asked me to take Shura for a walk. She herself was not feeling well. The weather did not appear suitable to me. Even Katya, who used to play in the yard with Shura every morning, had not been outside. However, Tonya insisted and was already dressing him and wrapping him up. I took him by the hand, and off we went into the wood.

The gloom and dampness immediately resounded to his babbling. It was the patter peculiar to his age group, the chatter of the species. All nature's creatures whose company he enjoyed, standing as he did less than three feet above the ground, reasoned in the same way as he.

Suddenly he ran off and began calling me to come. A baby jackdaw with a trailing wing was hopping through the grass and tumbling as it tried to fly. We could not catch it at once. Finally I stood up, holding it, smoothing its wings back, and letting its hooded head protrude between my cupped hands. I stood bent for a long while, now showing it to my son, now holding it against my breast. My gaze was fixed on my hands, and they in turn were occupied by a heart that pounded away there through down and feathers. When I straightened up and looked around, my eye could not adjust to the sudden change of posture. The autumn's prime miracle, the friendly isolation of a deciduous wood amid coniferous forest, struck me almost for the first time.

The one stood amidst the other: an ornate, gilded town whose streets, roofs, and belfries were swathed in black, as if against a rainy sky, by the pines that spiraled heavenward like smoke. Everything took place in this town.

Twenty years have passed since that time. Into that period falls the Revolution, the major event that overshadows all others. A new state has been born, undescribed and unprecedented. It was Russia that gave birth to it, the same Russia discovered, then abandoned by my reminiscences.

My son, a physicist with a bright future in store, has become a person in a more direct sense than if he had perhaps grown up with me. His mother, who for so long took my place, has dealt with her ordeals more bravely than I could have done. Aleksandr Aleksandrovich is still alive, a tireless sixty-year-old specialist in genetics. It might appear that at long last I can rest easy on their account. However, each time I turn over in my mind the scenes of that autumn I suffer long periods of insomnia once more, as during the year before last, when, with the chief culprit still alive, I began for the first time to note these events down.

For them to take their course it is immaterial whether they are set out in order. Istomina's appearance gave me no peace. There was nothing particularly miraculous about that—she would have appealed to anybody. However, the madness that we call attraction only overcame me later on. At first I was aware of other forces at work.

At the outset of the third winter of the war, which brought the national calamity of utter defeat inexorably nearer, Istomina was the only one of our number whose life had obviously been ruined. She, more fully than the others, reflected my sense of the approaching end. Without being let into the details of her life history, I discerned in her the testimony of our time, a human captive placed with all her permanent qualities in the filthy cage of enslaving circumstance. Before ever I felt anything for her personally, I felt drawn into this same cage in which she found herself.

The day of our departure was approaching; the tickets were booked. In contrast to past winters, Demid asked permission to spend this one with his family in Pyatibratskoye. A new person had taken over the teacher's apartment in Yuryatin. But these preparations did not seem to perturb Istomina in any way.

"You have a word with her," Aleksandr Aleksandrovich said to me. "Shouldn't we really take her to Moscow with us?"

I do not recall what her answer was. I only remember well that under the circumstances it amounted to my not getting an answer at all. Perhaps she said that she intended to stay and guard the *dacha* if we did not turn her out. But her readiness to spend the whole winter alone with her child, surrounded by a forest echoing with the howls of wolves and scoured by blizzards—what sort of reply was that? It is a pity she did not add that she would not be left alone and that there would be people there to protect her.

I reported the conversation to Aleksandrovich, telling him that they should travel as arranged but I would stay on at the mill for a short while to try to finish an article on the historical sources of the Pugachyov legend, which I had begun at his instigation that summer. Once I had helped Evgeniya Vikentyevna to find a place in Yuryatin I would come home with the article completed—by my estimate this would be sometime in November, or in any case not later than the end of the month.

There was no ulterior motive in this. Those were my genuine intentions. Nobody had any doubt about that, but the family turned out to be more farsighted. They received my decision with great alarm, as if they knew in advance what would happen, and they began to try to talk me out of it. These conversations dragged on beyond midnight, upsetting the daily routine, and ended in tears all around. But I would not give in. Their departure had to be deferred for several days, after which it could not be postponed any further.

After one such conversation with Aleksandr Aleksandrovich, for a long time I could not get to sleep as I lay on the floor of the lodge; I had moved there from the bed so as not to disturb Tonya's deep sleep by my own tense wakefulness.

All day a motionless rain had hung in the air, verging on drizzle but never forming droplets. There were clear periods from time to time. The sky swam past, rushing low over the yard and absorbing as much freshness and light as the clouds' gills would contain. The gloom was rent from ear to ear. It lasted only an instant. The edges of darkness drew together again. It became black as night.

We talked in his room upstairs, above Istomina's basement. For some time every mention of her in her absence had pained me with a tangible sense of deprivation. I wanted to avoid this weakness. We never so much as mentioned her.

Today was the first day she had lighted the stove. It was hot and smoky up in Aleksandr Aleksandrovich's room. The whole time he kept lighting the lamp then putting it out, depending on the weather outside, and on each occasion, before he fitted the glass over the round mantle-grid he toyed with it, rolling it in his hand and warming it with his breath. This did not ease our understanding. It was fixed in his mind that I had cooled toward Tonya and did not love Shura enough; it would have been easier to move a mountain than persuade him otherwise.

"I can't go on like this," I told him. "I'm up to the eyeballs with Teutons and the Straits. I can sense how dull and coarse I'm becoming. Tonya and Shura are seeing nothing of life. Life is losing its substance because of my sitting and waiting for peace. Remember Protasov in *The Living Corpse?* I've got to get away.

"When Shura was born I felt easy on his account. How well everything was going! What an active future I saw ahead of me! I even began to hope that he would have someone to look to, as I did to you, even though you aren't my father.

"What a childhood you gave me! What pictures I was surrounded by! Admittedly, it's a pity I haven't been taught any trade, but you'll often hear such regrets voiced in Russia. For a long time we shall have to bear the curse of an education focused on deceit. But that isn't your fault. And I'm eternally grateful to you for my education.

"I wanted to bequeath something similar to my own child. But who would have thought that such an impossible string of events could befall us? Have you ever taken a really close look at Shura? In facial features he takes after Tonya, but their vitality and movement come from me. His eyes don't take after us though; they are his own, and it would have been better were it not so. There is an entreaty in them and an unchildlike fear. It's as if his pupils weren't pupils at all but arms outstretched to ward off some approaching misfortune." I could restrain myself no longer and burst into tears. "That's the way people who have been deceived look at you. It was I who deceived him, enticing him to live with quite unrealizable hopes." And finally bursting into a fit of sobbing, I covered my face with my hands.

Aleksandr Aleksandrovich blew out the lamp. The pale daylight, transformed beyond recognition by the evil weather, crept into the room. Aleksandr Aleksandrovich strode up and down and berated me for all he was worth. Downstairs they were baking potatoes in the ashes, and the oven damper kept clanking. Suddenly a tap against the windowpane made us both look around. Streams of water flattened by the wind ran across the pane like silver and mercury. Two maple leaves clung as if glued to it. I had a terrible desire to see them fly off, as though they were not leaves but my own decision to spend the winter at the mill, a decision that weighed on me no less than on my family. But the water ran streaming down the glass; yet still the leaves did not move, and this depressed me.

"Why have you stopped?" I asked Aleksandr Aleksandrovich. "You were about to say something about my parents. Ah yes, a Polish exile and the daughter of a serf-soldier . . . and I lost them at the age of three and got to know them too late, from the stories told. What next, then? Why did you bring them into this?"

"You ought to be ashamed of yourself! Whom do you take after? And anyway, if anyone is to lament about our country, God himself has decreed that I should. I am a hereditary phenomenon, Aleksandr Gromeko, member of the War Industry Committee, well, not a member, damn it, but a consultant, and it isn't a committee—I trip over my tongue talking to you, but that's not the point . . . I have faith in the future, yet you're frightened by the approach of revolution."

"Good God, how trite you make it sound! It really turns my stomach to hear it! Laugh at me by all means, but don't rub it in."

"Who's laughing? This is no time for jokes, my lad. I'd be curious to know what answer you'd have given if the remark was not meant as a joke."

"I would have reminded you of your own words when you came back from Golomennikov's—do you remember, you went there, to Maria's? And do you remember how he shot you down that time? 'The collapse of an army that realizes it has been defeated is still a far cry from a revolution.' At least, that was what you told me he said. 'The days of the working group in the War Industry Committee are numbered, and they'll be arrested any day now. If we don't gather our scattered forces before the storm breaks, then we may be in for anarchy.' And that was Golomennikov speaking, not you or I but a man who's at home with revolution, who has connections in Finland and the Petersburg underground. . . . And what are you blinking at me like that for? After all, I'm repeating what I heard from you, if you didn't simply make it up. So what's this revolution you're talking about? And is that really the point?"

The conversation slowed and returned to its former theme. I reminded Aleksandr Aleksandrovich of scenes from my childhood spent in his house. It was these scenes that haunted me during the night. Shura's mumbling could be heard from behind the stove partition. He was laughing in his sleep. Nearby came the sound of Tonya's steady breathing.

I abandoned myself to memories the more readily because they united me even more closely with those asleep than any of the ridiculous freedom I then enjoyed. I will recount some of them.

Translated by Nicholas J. Anning

Essays
and Articles

Some Propositions

I

Whenever I talk about mysticism, painting, or the theater, I can speak with all the amiable lack of constraint that a liberal-minded reader brings to any discussion. But when the subject is literature, I remember some book and lose all capacity to reason. I need to be shaken and brought around by force as though from a faint, from a state of actual dreaming about that book. And only then, and very unwillingly, can I overcome my slight revulsion and join in a conversation on some other literary topic, where the subject is anything else but that book—the stage, let us say, or poets, movements, new writing, etc. But never of my own volition and unforced, never at any price will I abandon the world of my real concern and move to this other realm of amateur solicitude.

II

Some modern movements have imagined that art is like a fountain, whereas in fact it is a sponge. They have decided that art ought to spout and gush, whereas it should absorb and saturate itself. They consider it can be resolved into means of representation, whereas it is composed of organs of perception. It should always be one of the audience and have the clearest, truest, most perceptive view of all. But in our day it has seen make-up powder and the dressing room, and it is exhibited on stage. It is as if there were two forms of art in the world, and one of them had enough in reserve to indulge in a luxury of self-perversion tantamount to suicide. It is put on show, whereas it should be hiding up in the gallery, unrecognized, hardly aware that it cannot fail to give itself away, and that when it hides in a corner it is stricken with translucency and phosphorescence as though with some disease.

III

A book is a cube-shaped chunk of blazing, smoking conscience—nothing more.

The mating call is a sign of nature's concern for the preservation of all feathered fowl. A book is like a capercaillie giving its mating call. The book hears nothing and no one, deafened and enraptured by its own music. Without it there could be no continuation of spiritual kind, and it would have been transferred elsewhere. Apes have never possessed the book.

The book was written. It grew, increased in intelligence, became worldly wise—and there it was, full-fledged and ready. It is not the book's fault that we see right through it. Such is the way of the spiritual universe. Not long ago men thought that the scenes in a book were just a series of dramatizations. This is a misconception; why should a book need them? People have forgotten that the only thing in our power is knowing how not to distort the voice of life that sounds within us.

Inability to discover and state the truth is a fault that no skill in lying can cover up. A book is a living being. It is in full possession of its memory and faculties; its scenes and pictures are the things it has preserved from the past and recorded, and that it refuses to forget.

IV

Life has not just begun. Art had no beginning. It was forever present till the very moment when it ceased.

Art is endless. And such is it, both behind me and within me here at this moment, that its fresh and urgent ubiquity and eternity come blowing over me as from a suddenly opened assembly hall—as though I was immediately summoned to take some oath.

No genuine book has a first page. Like the sighing of a forest, it is born goodness knows where, and it grows and rolls along, arousing forbidden backwoods, and suddenly, at its darkest, thunderstruck, and panic moment, it reaches its goal and speaks out all at once from every treetop.

V

Wherein lies the miracle? It rests in the fact that once there lived on earth a seventeen-year-old girl called Mary Stuart, and one October, with Puritans whooping outside her window, she wrote a poem in French that ended with the words:

> Car mon pis et mon mieux
> Sont les plus déserts lieux.

It rests secondly in the fact that once in his youth, with October reveling and raging outside his window, the English poet Algernon Charles Swinburne completed *Chastelard,* in which the quiet plaint of Mary's five stanzas was conceived as the fearful roar of five tragic acts.

It rests thirdly and finally in the fact that once, about five years ago, when the translator glanced through his window he did not know which was more surprising—the fact that the Elabuga blizzard knew Scots and was still perturbed as of yore for that seventeen-year-old girl, or that the girl and the English poet who sorrowed for her were able to tell him so well and sincerely, in Russian, what still disturbed them both as before and had never ceased to haunt them.

"What can this mean?" the translator asked himself. What is going on there? Why is it so quiet there today (yet at the same time so snow-blown)? It might seem that because we send our messages out there they should be shedding blood. Meanwhile, in fact, they smile.

This is the miracle: In the unity and identity of the lives of these three people, and of many others (eyewitnesses and spectators of three epochs, characters, biographies, readers)—in the real-life October of some year unknown that howls itself hoarse and goes blind out there, outside the window, below the hill, in . . . in art.

That is what it is.

VI

There are misunderstandings. They have to be avoided. This leaves room for boredom. They claim it is the writer, the poet . . .

Aesthetics does not exist. It seems to me that aesthetics does not exist, as a punishment for its lying, its pardoning, conniving, and condescension —for knowing nothing about man, yet bandying gossip about specialities. Portraitist, landscape artist, genre painter, still-life specialist? Symbolist, Acmeist, Futurist? What murderous jargon!

It is quite clear that this is science, classifying air balloons by the position and distribution of the holes in them that prevent their flying.

Poetry and prose are two polarities, indivisible one from another.

Through its inborn hearing, poetry seeks out the melody of nature amid the noise of the lexicon, and picking it up like some motif, it proceeds to improvise on that theme. By its feeling, through its spirituality, prose seeks and finds man in the category of speech. And when man is found lacking in an age, then it re-creates him from memory and sets him there and pretends for the good of mankind to have found him in the present. These two principles do not exist separately.

As it improvises, poetry strikes up against nature. The vital world of reality—this is imagination's sole scheme, successful once and forever more. It continues at every moment, never failing. It is still always effective, profound and endlessly absorbing. It serves much more as the poet's example than as a subject or a model.

VII

It is madness to trust in common sense. It is madness to doubt it. Madness to look ahead. Madness to live without looking. But to roll up one's eyes occasionally and with rapidly rising blood heat hear the reflected fresco of some unearthly, transient, yet forever vernal thunderstorm begin to spread and roar through the consciousness stroke by stroke, like convulsions of lightning on dusty ceilings and plaster—this is pure. . . . This, at any rate, is purest madness!

It is natural to strive for purity.

Thus we come close to the pure essence of poetry. And it disturbs us like the sinister turning of ten windmills by the edge of some bare field in a black and hungry year.

Translated by Christopher Barnes

Apropos of the Central Committee's Resolution on Literature

I ask you not to search my words for Aesopian notes, or progressive civic virtue, or conservatism, or in fact anything except what is presented to you without searching—and causes me a measure of vexation. Sometimes it seems to me that facts can be replaced by hopes, and that words spoken coherently are bound to correspond to the real state of affairs. On one such occasion in the summer I read the resolution on literature in a newspaper, and it produced the most powerful impression on me. Let me elaborate. Without your reminders about the need to respond, I might indeed have stored this profound and pathos-laden idea in my heart and overlooked its details. I began to notice them only thanks to you; you have caused me to read the resolution through several times and scrutinize it. And it was then that I was gripped by these declarations: "(1) We have thus entered the period of cultural revolution, which is a prerequisite for our further advance toward a communist society. (2) However, it would be quite wrong to lose sight of the basic fact of the working class's seizure of power and the presence in our land of a proletarian dictatorship. (3) Everything leads us to suppose that a style appropriate to our epoch will be created."

I felt a waft of the air of history, which these statements aspire to breathe: Indeed, I wish to breathe it myself, and naturally I felt drawn to breathe together with them. And then, in terms of pure approximation, I imagined forms quite unlike the present ones, and through the heated vapors of a remote but just visible distance, I imagined something akin to what Blok's barricade and street style or Mayakovsky's superhuman-collective one had been to their own age. Amid all the prophesying, I heard talk of how history might fully come to *be* history, and I—a full-fledged human being within it. The resolution has assisted me to stand apart from a multitude of things that become odious as soon as men start to admire them. I forgot my people, the messianic call of Russia, the peasant, the honor of my vocation, the multitude of writers, their hypocritical simplicity, and things too many to enumerate. Now, you may not believe this, but this is my whole point: It seemed to me that the resolution too had forgotten that *all these things* have to be hated in order to love the one thing worthy of our love—in order to love history. And now, when, thanks to your happy initiative, I have lost all my illusions, the source of my self-deception has become clear to me. I thought that the resolution would idealize the worker just as I would have wished—with the boldness, breadth, and generosity without which no one can enthusiastically throw himself into the epoch—an epoch, that is, in the full sense, understood in the way that the quoted extracts imply. But the resolution has refrained from this sort of idealization, though not through any peculiarities of its philosophy but because it has many cares and commitments and is, therefore, unable to raise any one thing to historical level. And for this same reason the quoted statements all fall down, and I would permit myself to doubt them each in turn. We are not experiencing a cultural revolution; it appears to me we are going through a cultural reaction. The presence of a dictatorship of the proletariat is insufficient to affect our culture. For this one would require a real, physical domination, which would speak through me without my knowing or wishing it, and even against my will. I am not aware of this. And that this is in fact not so is obvious from the resolution's appeal to me to work out the themes it has laid down—even if I am more willing than before. Finally, among the contradictions of our age, which are only reconcilable in terms of a statistical average, there is nothing that leads one to suppose that a style appropriate to it has been created. Or, if you wish, one could put it as follows: A style has already been found, and like any statistical average it is transparent and of no value. In general outline it is a combination of *Smenovekhovstvo* and Populism. One ought to offer his sincere congratulations. It is a revolutionary style, and most important of all—it is new. How did it arise? Quite simply. Of the nonrevolutionary forms the most mediocre one has been admitted, and of the revolutionary ones—the same again. This was inevitable; such is the logic of large numbers. Instead of leaving it to posterity to make the generalizations about our age, as we should have done, we have obliged our age itself to exist as an embodied generalization. All my thoughts take second place beside the one that is of primary importance: Am I acceptable or am I not? Am I sufficiently undistinctive to look like a black-and-white illustration and to find delight in forming the golden mean? Recently the copyright for the style of today belonged to the censor. Now he has divided it up with the modern publisher. The philosophy governing the size of an edition now works together with the philosophy of acceptability. They have occupied the whole horizon. There is nothing for me to do. A style for the epoch has already been created. There is my answer.

There is still one more thing. It is not for nothing that the resolution has stirred me so. Its prospects are close to me for another reason. I was excited even before its appearance. Recently in spite of everything I started to work, and convictions seemingly long buried have begun to come to life in me. I believe that work is wiser and more noble than man, and that the artist can expect no good but from his own imagination. If I thought otherwise, I should have said one ought to abolish censorship. The main thing, however, is that I am convinced that art should be an extreme feature of its age, and not its "resultant"; it should be linked with the age by its own growth and strength, and only then will art be in a position afterward to *recall* its age and enable the historian to assume that it reflected its epoch. This is where my optimism springs from. If I thought otherwise, there would be no sense in your approaching me.

Translated by Christopher Barnes

On the Classics

By a "classic" I understand a writer whose work provides some tangible likeness of an integrated world view. Classical literature itself is the sum total of those literary works and movements, which are later accepted as representing the philosophy of their epochs.

I have read the classics ever since my childhood.

In my own work I can feel the influence of Pushkin. The Pushkinian aesthetic is so broad and flexible that it permits different interpretations at different ages.

Pushkin's urgency and inventiveness even allow him to be understood impressionistically, as I myself understood him some fifteen years ago in accordance with my personal tastes and the literary trends prevalent at the time. But now my understanding has broadened, and new elements of an ethical sort have entered into it.

The various possibilities of artistic method are never derived from a study of the modern age, for each one of us is functionally bound up with it. This correlation might certainly be discovered by detailed analysis of the contemporary scene, but instead of going through the whole of living humanity individually by name—and coming across oneself in the process—it is easier and more sensible to begin with one's own self.

It appears to me that at the present time there is less reason than ever before to stray from the Pushkinian aesthetic. By the word "aesthetic" I mean the artist's concept of the nature of art, the role of art in history, and his own personal *responsibility* toward it.

Translated by Christopher Barnes

About Myself
and the Reader

In February 1926, I learned that the greatest poet in German and my beloved teacher, Rainer Maria Rilke, knew of my existence, and this provided a pretext for me to write and tell him what I owed him. At about the same time, there came into my hands Marina Tsvetaeva's "Poem of the End," a lyrical work of rare profundity and strength, and the most remarkable since Mayakovsky's "Man," and Esenin's *Pugachyov*. Both these facts contained such a concentration of energy that without them I could not have completed my work on "The Year 1905." I promised myself a meeting with the German poet as soon as I could finish *Lieutenant Schmidt,* and this urged me on and sustained me. However, this dream was not to be realized: He died in December of that year, when the final part of my poem still remained to be written, and it is very likely that his death is actually reflected in the mood of its final pages. My most immediate concern was then to tell about this amazing lyric poet, and about that special world contained in the works of any genuine poet. Meanwhile, as its composition progressed, the article I had planned turned into a series of autobiographical fragments on how my conception of art was formed and where its roots lay. I have not yet thought up a title for this work, which I am dedicating to his memory, and I have still not completed it. It is between sixteen and twenty-four pages in length and will appear in one of the spring numbers of *Zvezda*. Apart from this, I have yet to finish *Spektorsky,* which has been promised to *Krasnaya nov.*

Now about the reader. I require nothing of him and have only great wishes for him. The arrogance and egoism that lie at the base of a writer's

267

appeal to his "audience" are alien to me and beyond my comprehension. By his own precious native ability, the reader himself always realizes what is happening to things, people, and the actual author in a book. By drumming into him our fanciful notions about what exactly we have done and how we have achieved it, we do not enlighten him but render him barren. Moreover, the only ones among us who really understand what they are doing are those who do precious little and do it badly—a rather shaky foundation for any moralizing! The reader is undeservedly humiliated by any summons to him from the author. Our works can and should be a private affair of the heart for him. By bringing the reader out of his puzzling uncertainty into the feeble light of our own petty self-interpretations we turn the three-dimensional world of author, reader, and book into a flat illusion, which is no use to anyone. Very probably, I like the reader more than I can say. Like him, I am reticent and uncommunicative, and unlike most writers, I cannot conceive of any correspondence with him.

Translated by Christopher Barnes

Explanatory
Notes

A SAFE-CONDUCT

This work was the first of Pasternak's two autobiographies. It was begun in the late 1920s and published first in separate sections. Part I appeared in the journal *Zvezda (The Star),* issue number eight, in 1929; Part II, in *Krasnaya nov (Red Virgin Soil),* number four, in 1931; and Part III, in issues five and six of *Krasnaya nov,* in 1931. The work also appeared as a separate book in 1931 with slight textual alterations; this is the version translated here.

Page 21
Sofiya Andreevna. . . . Lev Tolstoy's wife (1844–1919).

Page 22
Ct.L.N. . . . Count Lev Nikolaevich Tolstoy (1828–1910), author.
Sketches by my father. . . . Pasternak's father was the well-known artist Leonid Osipovich Pasternak (1862–1945).
Repin. . . . Ilya Efimovich Repin (1844–1930), artist.
Nikolai Nikolaevich Gay. . . . 1831–94, artist.
Gumilyov's "Sixth Sense." . . . Nikolai Stepanovich Gumilyov (1886–1921), the Acmeist poet, wrote a poem of this title in which he suggested that man, as he evolves, is growing a new sense, of which his present inarticulate responses to beauty are a painful adumbration or promise.
Linnaeus. . . . Carolus Linnaeus (1707–78), Swedish botanist.
The Scriabins. . . . The composer Aleksandr Nikolaevich Scriabin (1872–1915) had a country house near that of the Pasternaks.

Page 24
L'Extase. . . . Scriabin's *Poème de l'Extase (Poem of Ecstasy)* for orchestra.

Page 25
A certain composer alive to this day. . . . Reinhold Moritsevich Glière (1875–1956).

Page 29
Julian Anisimov. . . . Julian Pavlovich Anisimov (1889–1940), poet and painter, founder of the "Serdarda" group; his translation of Rilke's *Stundenbuch* was published in 1913.
Dehmel. . . . Richard Dehmel (1863–1920), German poet.
Mir zur Feier. . . . A volume of poetry by Rilke.
Razgulyai. . . . An area of Moscow.
Rainer Maria Rilke. . . . Austrian poet (1875–1926). Pasternak's one personal encounter with him, recounted in the opening of *A Safe-Conduct,* took place in May 1900, during Rilke's second journey to Russia. The woman traveling with him was Lou Andreas-Salomé.

Page 31
Bely. . . . Andrei Bely, the pen name of Boris Nikolaevich Bugaev (1880–1934), Symbolist poet and writer.
Blok. . . . Aleksandr Aleksandrovich Blok (1880–1921), Symbolist poet.

"Musaget." . . . A Symbolist-oriented publishing enterprise.

Cohen. . . . Hermann Cohen (1842–1918), German Neo-Kantian philosopher, professor at Marburg University from 1876 to 1912.

Natorp. . . . Paul Natorp (1854–1924), German Neo-Kantian philosopher, professor at Marburg University from 1885 to 1924.

Page 35

Sergei Nikolaevich Trubetskoi. . . . Prince S. N. Trubetskoi (1862–1905), Russian idealist philosopher, professor at Moscow University from 1900 to 1905.

Samarin. . . . Dmitrii Samarin, school and university friend of Pasternak's, descended from the well-known Slavophile publicist and politician, Yurii Samarin (1819–76).

The very building at the end of Nikitskaya Street. . . . The Moscow University buildings stand on either side of the junction between Nikitskaya Street and Mokhovaya Street.

Nekhlyudov. . . . A name Tolstoy gave to three of his fictional characters—the young landowner in *A Landowner's Morning,* who wants to give up his land to the peasants; the serious-minded friend of the hero in the autobiographical *Childhood, Boyhood,* and *Youth;* and the hero of the novel *Resurrection.* The last of these is presumably referred to here: Having once caused a girl's downfall by seducing her, he very solemnly and single-mindedly sets out to work for her, his own, and society's salvation.

Page 36

Loks. . . . Konstantin Grigoryevich Loks, university friend of Pasternak's.

Page 39

Goslar . . . *like a medieval coal-miner.* . . . The German town of Goslar is an ancient mining town.

Page 40

"The Terrible Vengeance." . . . The title of a story by Gogol.

Elizabeth of Hungary. . . . Countess Elizabeth of Hungary became the patron saint of Marburg; she was famous for her kindness. She died at the age of twenty-four in 1231 and was canonized in 1235.

Giordano Bruno. . . . Italian philosopher (*ca.* 1548–1600), traveled widely, teaching and writing. He was arrested by the Inquisition in 1592 and burned at the stake eight years later.

From Maclaurin to Maxwell. . . . Colin Maclaurin (1698–1746), leading Scottish mathematician; James Clerk Maxwell (1831–79), Scottish mathematical physicist.

Page 41

Lomonosov's. . . . Mikhail Vasilyevich Lomonosov (1711–65), scientist and writer; sometimes referred to as the "father of modern Russian literature"; referred to by Pushkin as "himself a university"; important in the founding of Moscow University in 1755. After studying at the Slavo-Greco-Latin Academy in Moscow, he was sent to Marburg, where he studied philosophy, physics, and chemistry under the philosopher Christian Wolff from 1736 to 1741.

Page 42

Hans Sachs.... German poet and dramatist (1494–1576).

Elend, Sorge.... German words meaning "poverty," "care"—probably the names of disused mineshafts.

Page 44

The recent Spanish revolution.... A reference to the uprising in Barcelona in 1909.

Hartmann.... Nicolai Hartmann (1882–1950), German philosopher, professor at Marburg University from 1920 to 1925.

Critique of Practical Reason.... One of the major works of the philosopher Immanuel Kant (1724–1804).

Page 45

the V—— sisters.... The Vysotsky sisters. It was to the elder, Irina, that Pasternak proposed in Marburg, and he later dedicated some of his earliest verse to her.

Abélardian.... Pierre Abélard (1079–1142), French philosopher and theologian, secretly married Héloïse and thereby incurred the anger of her uncle, Fulbert, whose hirelings mutilated him. Thereafter Abélard withdrew to a monastery, was persecuted for heresy, and died on the way to Rome to present his defense.

"magic stick." ... Pasternak has *palochka-ruchalochka,* a variant of *palochka-vyruchalochka,* the name of a Russian children's game. It is a kind of hide-and-seek in which one child, the "leader," covers his eyes while the others hide. If, when he looks up, he sees one of the others, the two of them run to grasp a stick that lies in an agreed-upon place and say, "Little stick, help me!" (Palochka-vyruchalochka, vyruchi menya!) Whoever is beaten in the race for the stick becomes the "leader," and the game recommences.

Page 46

Kreutzer sonatas.... "The Kreutzer Sonata" is the title of a very influential story written by Lev Tolstoy in 1890: The hero kills his wife out of jealousy and a peculiar rage against her as a sex object; he argues that all sex, even within marriage, is bad, and that in the interest of morality, self-control should be practiced, even though it would lead to the extinction of the human race.

Tolstoys and Wedekinds.... Tolstoy is here referred to as the author of "The Kreutzer Sonata" (see preceding note); Frank Wedekind (1864–1918), the German playwright, as author of the play *Frühlingserwachen (Spring Awakening),* which is about young people whose lives are spoiled by the prevailing repressive attitudes to sex and pleads for greater naturalness and freedom.

Page 48

In Russian "to fib"... *"to deceive."* ... Pasternak uses the two Russian verbs *vrat'* and *lgat'. Lgat'* means more plainly to tell lies; *vrat',* while having this meaning, also implies to "talk nonsense," "tell stories."

Page 58

Nettelbecks.... Joachim Nettelbeck (1738–1824), Prussian patriot who helped defend Kolberg against the French in 1807.

Page 60

G—— Gorbunkov, a student associate of Pasternak's who maintained a sporadic friendship with him throughout the latter's life.

Page 62

Narkompros. . . . A Russian acronym for Narodny komissariat prosveshcheniya (the People's Commissariat of Education). Established in 1917, it later became the Ministry of Education.

Page 63

Michelangelo's Night. . . . A reference to the sculpture *Night* in the Medici Chapel.

Page 65

Funduki. . . . Plural of *funduk,* Russian for "hazelnut." *Fondaco* is Italian for "warehouse."

Page 73

Addressed by their patronymics. . . . Instead of using simply his first name or surname, the polite form of address to an adult Russian consists of the first name and the patronymic. Thus, if his first name is Boris and his father's name is Ivan, he will, at an appropriate age, be called Boris Ivanovich.

Page 74

Kommissarzhevskaya. . . . Vera Fyodorovna Kommissarzhevskaya (1864–1910), celebrated Russian actress.
In 1905. . . . The year of the "first Russian revolution."

Page 75

Renamed the "Aleksandrovsky." . . . After Aleksandr I, who was reigning at the time of the war against Napoleon.
Serov. . . . Valentin Aleksandrovich Serov (1865–1911), artist.
The Yusupovs'. . . . The princely family of Yusupov, renowned as patrons of the arts.
The Kutepov edition. . . . Colonel (later General) N. I. Kutepov, a devotee of the throne and in charge of the household management of the imperial palace, published a luxurious book to which major Russian artists contributed pictures on the subject of the imperial hunt. It appeared in four volumes from 1896 to 1911.
The Kasatkin family. . . . Nikolai Alekseevich Kasatkin (1859–1930), artist.

Page 76

Mayakovsky. . . . Vladimir Vladimirovich Mayakovsky (1893–1930), Russian Futurist poet. He signed the first Russian Futurist manifesto in 1912 and was one of the movement's most outstanding members. Arrested for revolutionary activity more than once before 1917, he was a strong supporter of the Bolshevik government and devoted much of his poetry to its cause. Disenchanted and oppressed by personal and artistic setbacks, he committed suicide in 1930.
A Trap for Judges. . . . A literary almanac produced by the Russian Futurists in 1910; its publication marked the first emergence of the Futurists as a group. The

title is ambiguous and might also be translated as "A Breeding-Ground for Judges."

"Lirika"... *"Tsentrifuga."* ... Pasternak made his professional literary debut with the "Lirika" group, which was Symbolist-oriented; in early 1914, however, the group was reconstituted as an "innovatory" Futurist organization under the leadership of Sergei Bobrov and set up as a rival to the more extreme Cubo-Futurist school of which Mayakovsky was a member.

Shershenevich. ... Vadim Gabrielevich Shershenevich (1893–1942), Futurist poet.

Bolshakov. ... Konstantin Aristarkhovich Bolshakov (1895–1940), Futurist poet.

Page 77

Bobrov. ... Sergei Pavlovich Bobrov (1889–1971), Futurist poet and literary critic.

Page 78

His yellow blouse. ... A regular part of Mayakovsky's Futurist dress, designed to shock the public.

"The Golden Cockerel." ... A folktale in verse by Pushkin, also an opera by Rimsky-Korsakov.

Page 79

Khodasevich. ... Vladislav Felitsianovich Khodasevich (1886–1939), poet.

Pages 79–80

"Vladimir Mayakovsky" ... *"A Cloud in Trousers," "Backbone Flute," "War and the Universe," and "Man."* ... *"150,000,000."* ... Titles of major poetic works by Mayakovsky.

"At the top of his voice." ... "At the Top of My Voice" was the title of Mayakovsky's last major poetic work, a work similar in spirit to the earlier works Pasternak had admired.

"With the oaken feet of its lines." ... This is an allusion to a phrase in the first draft of Mayakovsky's "At the Top of My Voice." In that passage, Mayakovsky claims that the strength of words is such that "coffins tear themselves open / To go galloping on all four of their little oaken feet."

Page 81

Nikolai Aseev. ... Nikolai Nikolaevich Aseev (1889–1963), Futurist poet, a friend and follower of Mayakovsky's for some time.

the S—— sisters. ... The Sinyakov sisters, one of whom Aseev married.

Khlebnikov. ... Velemir Khlebnikov was the pseudonym of Viktor Vladimirovich Khlebnikov (1885–1922), a Futurist poet who experimented with and theorized on language; one of the four signatories (with Mayakovsky, Kruchyonykh, and Burlyuk) of the first Futurist manifesto.

The Baltrushaitises. ... Jurgis Baltrushaitis (1873–1945), Lithuanian poet and diplomat most of whose literary output was in Russian; he was an important member of the Russian Symbolist movement.

Vyacheslav Ivanov. ... Vyacheslav Ivanovich Ivanov (1866–1949), Symbolist poet and philosopher.

Bread and salt. . . . The traditional Russian peasant's gift offering to a guest as a sign of hospitality.

Evgeniya Vladimirovna Muratova. . . . Muratova (née Lurye) was later to become Pasternak's first wife.

Page 83

One of the S—— sisters, Z.M.M. . . . Zinaida Mikhailovna Mamonova, the eldest of the five Sinyakov sisters; another sister, Kseniya (Oksana), married the poet Nikolai Aseev; Nadezhda Sinyakova, the youngest sister, who was a musician, had a brief love affair with Pasternak.

Dobrovein. . . . Isaak Dobrovein, conductor and pianist. After the October Revolution, he was granted an exit visa after playing for Lenin and emigrated to the West.

Esenin. . . . Sergei Aleksandrovich Esenin (1895–1925), poet celebrated for his evocations of the Russian countryside. He became disillusioned with the Bolshevik regime, which he felt was alien to the "peasant Russia" he loved, and committed suicide.

Selvinsky. . . . Ilya Lvovich Selvinsky (1899–1968), poet.

Tsvetaeva. . . . Marina Ivanovna Tsvetaeva (1892–1941), poetess. She left Russia in 1922, returned in 1939, and committed suicide in 1941.

Tikhonov. . . . Nikolai Semyonovich Tikhonov (born 1896), poet.

Severyanin. . . . Igor Severyanin was the pseudonym of Igor Vasilyevich Lotarev (1887–1942), a poet of the Ego-Futurist movement.

Lermontov's. . . . Mikhail Yuryevich Lermontov (1814–41), Romantic poet and author.

Page 84

Lilya Brik. . . . Lilya Yuryevna Brik (born 1891), wife of the Formalist critic Osip Brik, and a close friend of Mayakovsky's for many years. Much of Mayakovsky's poetry was dedicated to her.

The Bronze Horseman, Crime and Punishment, and Petersburg. . . . All three works are connected with Saint Petersburg: The first, a narrative poem by Pushkin, deals with the 1824 flooding of the River Neva; the second, Dostoevsky's novel, is set in Saint Petersburg; likewise the third work, a novel by Andrei Bely.

Page 85

Akhmatova's. . . . Anna Andreevna Akhmatova (1888–1966), poetess, wife of Gumilyov, associated with the Acmeist poetic movement.

Shestov's son. . . . Lev Shestov was the pen name of Lev Isaakovich Shvartsman (1866–1938), a philosopher and literary critic.

Page 86

Gorky. . . . Maksim Gorky, the pen name of Aleksei Maksimovich Peshkov (1868–1936), writer and publicist.

The Captain's Daughter. . . . A novel by Pushkin that deals with the eighteenth-century peasant uprising against the throne that was led by the Cossack Pugachyov.

Page 87

Over the Barriers. . . . A volume of poems by Pasternak, published in 1917; a second revised edition appeared in 1929.

My Sister Life. . . . A volume of poems by Pasternak, written in 1917 but not published until 1922; this volume won Pasternak his first popular renown.

Sivtsev Vrazhek. . . . The name of a street in Moscow.

Page 88

The Kornilov revolt. . . . General Kornilov marched on Saint Petersburg in September 1917 in an unsuccessful attempt to seize power from the Provisional Government.

Lipskerov. . . . Aleksandr Lipskerov, Futurist poet.

Page 89

Balmont. . . . Konstantin Dmitrievich Balmont (1867–1943), Symbolist poet.

Erenburg. . . . Ilya Grigoryevich Erenburg (1891–1967), Russian Jewish writer and journalist.

Vera Inber. . . . Vera Mikhailovna Inber (1890–1972), poetess.

Antokolsky. . . . Pavel Grigoryevich Antokolsky (b. 1896), poet.

Kamensky. . . . Vasilii Vasilyevich Kamensky (1884–1961), Futurist poet.

Burlyuk. . . . David Davidovich Burlyuk (1882–1967), artist and poet, one of the founders of the Russian Futurist movement.

Versty. . . . A volume of verse published by Tsvetaeva in 1922.

Page 90

The Contemporary. . . . An important nineteenth-century literary periodical, founded by Pushkin in 1836, the year before his death.

Exhibition of twenty years' work. . . . This exhibition was opened on February 1, 1930, at the Moscow Writers' Club.

A foreign passport. . . . Mayakovsky had been trying for some time to obtain a passport to travel abroad, but without success.

Pushkin. . . . Both Mayakovsky and Pushkin (1799–1836) died violent deaths—Pushkin in a duel—and both at the same age. Both died when they were experiencing great success and their creative powers were apparently still at their height. Mayakovsky mentions Pushkin in a number of his poems, and in one, "Jubilee," writes of himself as an equal of, and in some ways similar to, Pushkin.

Page 91

Terrible world. . . . No doubt, an allusion to the title of a volume of poems published by Aleksandr Blok in 1916.

Page 94

O.S. . . . Olga Grigoryevna Petrovskaya, widow of Vladimir Aleksandrovich Sillov, the Proletcult theorist who had been arrested and killed shortly before the death of Mayakovsky.

Chernyak. . . . Yakov Zakharovich Chernyak, critic, literary scholar, and editor.

Romadin. . . . Nikolai Mikhailovich Romadin (b. 1903), artist and fellow student of Pasternak's first wife.

Zhenya.... Pasternak's first wife, Evgeniya Vladimirovna Lurye.

The famous telephone call from "A Cloud." ... Pasternak refers to a passage in Mayakovsky's poem "A Cloud in Trousers." The passage is quoted a little later.

Page 95

Kirsanov.... Semyon Isaakovich Kirsanov (1906–1972), poet and translator.

Whether a telegram had been sent to Lilya.... Lilya Brik was at that moment in London.

L.A.G. ... L.A.... Lev Aleksandrovich Grinkrug (b. 1889), art critic and friend of Mayakovsky's.

Page 96

Bathhouse.... Mayakovsky's play *The Bathhouse* was performed at the Meyerhold Theater in March and April 1930; Mayakovsky himself was present at the performance on April 10. The play was damned by the critics.

THE MARK OF APELLES

This is Pasternak's earliest published short story. It was written in 1915 and first appeared in *Vremennik "Znameni truda" (Banner of Labor Chronicle)* in 1918. Pasternak later republished it under an Italian title, "Il Tratto di Apelle."

LETTERS FROM TULA

Although written in 1918, this story was not published until 1922, in the almanac *Shipovnik (The Wild Rose)*.

Page 121

Klyuchevsky.... Vasilii Osipovich Klyuchevsky (1841–1911), eminent historian, author of one of the standard histories of Russia.

The Time of Troubles.... Designation of the period in Russian history, in the late sixteenth and early seventeenth centuries, when dynastic undertainties led to foreign intervention, the appearance of a series of "false Dimitriis" as claimants to the throne, and a peasant uprising.

The Kremlin.... The Kremlin referred to here is the one in Tula (the Russian word *kreml* means "fortress"). The Tula Kremlin was taken by false Dimitrii I in 1605, and by some of the peasants in revolt in 1607.

Pyotr Bolotnikov.... The leader of the peasant revolt was in fact *Ivan* Bolotnikov (?–1608).

Page 122

Astapovo.... The railway station at which the author Lev Tolstoy died.

Page 124

Ozerov or Sumarokov.... Vladislav Aleksandrovich Ozerov (1769–1816) and Aleksandr Petrovich Sumarokov (1718–77), dramatists.

WITHOUT LOVE

This early prose fragment was first published in *Volya truda (Liberty of Labor)*, an obscure and short-lived Socialist Revolutionary newspaper, on November 20, 1918. It was not republished until after Pasternak's death.

Page 128
Aida.... A Tatar word meaning, roughly, "Let's go!"

Page 131
Breshkovskaya.... Ekaterina Konstantinovna Breshko-Breshkovskaya (1844–1934), one of the founders of the Socialist Revolutionary Party, nicknamed the "Grandmother of the Russian Revolution"; she emigrated to Prague after the Bolshevik October Revolution.

THE CHILDHOOD OF ZHENYA LUVERS

This story was written in 1918 and first published in issue number one of the almanac *Nashi dni (Our Days)*, in 1922.

Page 148
"ю", "я" *and* "ѣ." ... The Russian letters "yu," "ya," and "yat" (pronounced "ye").
This Russian letter "ы." ... This letter has no exact equivalent in French or English; it corresponds most nearly to the "i" in the word "will."

Page 149
"полѣзный." ... Pronounced "polyezny," meaning "useful."

Page 150
"Springing like a lioness with shaggy mane." ... This and the quotations in the next few lines are all from Lermontov's poem "The Demon." This particular line is well known for the poet's unfortunate zoological error: A lioness has no mane!

Page 168
Onegin.... The hero of Pushkin's celebrated novel in verse *Eugene Onegin*.

Page 172
Karamzin.... Nikolai Mikhailovich Karamzin (1766–1826), author and historian.

AERIAL WAYS

First printed in *Russky sovremennik (The Russian Contemporary)*, number two, in 1924, this short story later gave its title to a complete collection of Pasternak's prose published in 1933.

Page 185

Liebknecht.... This may be either Wilhelm Liebknecht (1826–1900), the German Marxist journalist and politician, or (more likely) his son Karl Liebknecht (1871–1919), the lawyer and Communist leader.

Page 186

Cheka.... A Russian acronym for the words meaning "Extraordinary Commission," the name of the Soviet political police from 1917 to 1922.

THREE CHAPTERS FROM A STORY

These short prose fragments were first published in the *Moskovsky ponedelnik (Moscow Weekly)* on June 12, 1922.

Page 191

Are you familiar with night in the Ukraine? ... This is a line from Gogol's story "A Night in May."

The flying muslin was illuminated.... The completion of this sentence is unclear owing to a mistake in the Russian typesetting. Unfortunately, no manuscript survives to which reference can be made.

Page 195

Rusalka.... The title of an unfinished drama by Pushkin.

THE STORY

This work was first published in the journal *Novy mir (The New World)*, number seven, 1929.

Page 198

Some of them found their way into print.... Pasternak probably has in mind "Three Chapters from a Story," though "Without Love" would also fit this description.

The Stroganovs.... A family of merchants who in the sixteenth century developed large-scale industries in northeastern European Russia.

Page 201

You haven't got a limp at all.... Pasternak himself sustained a leg injury in childhood, which later rendered him unfit for military service. This is mentioned in *A Safe-Conduct,* and the same motif also occurs in the second of the "Three Chapters."

Page 204

An important past.... In other words, involvement in the student demonstrations that helped precipitate the 1905 revolution.

Page 205

The Russian Word.... An important newspaper of the period.

Women's Senior Courses.... Higher-education courses for women, who were normally denied entry into the official university courses.

Page 206

Leonid Andreev.... Leonid Nikolaevich Andreev (1871–1919), the writer, achieved success and notoriety in the first decade of this century with his violent and naturalistic stories and plays.

Page 214

Fixed wax seals.... A reference to the Tsarist (and Soviet) police's habit of sealing up the doors of apartments lived in by people under arrest.

Page 219

The Triumphal Arch.... A ceremonial arch in Tverskaya-Yamskaya Street, built to celebrate the Russian victory over Napoleon. The arch originally stood near the old city gates of Moscow, but it was moved farther out to a site alongside the highway to Leningrad.

Page 220

Raskolnikov.... A reference to the hero of Dostoevsky's *Crime and Punishment,* who murdered an old usurer and took her money.

Page 221

"Aufschwung." ... or "Flight," the title of a well-known piano piece by Schumann.

Page 229

Cagliostro.... Count Allessandro di Cagliostro was the assumed name of Giuseppe Balsamo (1743–95), a celebrated Italian imposter. He traveled widely, posing as physician, alchemist, magician, and Freemason, and committed numerous acts of fraud to obtain money.

"The Egyptian Nights." ... The title of an unfinished narrative by Pushkin.

A DISTRICT IN THE REAR

A shortened version of this fragment appeared in *Literaturnaya gazeta,* number sixty-nine, in 1938. The completion of the text was printed in Boris Pasternak, *Fragmenty romana* (Fragments of a Novel), published by Collins and Harvill Press in London in 1973.

Page 243

"Peruns." ... Perun was the old heathen Russian god of thunder.

Kumyshka.... A homemade wine, brewed from fermented bread.

Page 246

Zemstvo.... A local-government institution that was created as part of the Great Reforms in Russia in the mid-nineteenth century.

Page 252

Tarantass. . . . A springless four-wheeled vehicle.

BEFORE PARTING

This text, unpublished during Boris Pasternak's lifetime, first appeared in Boris Pasternak, *Fragmenty romana (Fragments of a Novel)*, published by Collins and Harvill Press in London in 1973.

Page 254

Pugachyov. . . . Emelyan Ivanovich Pugachyov (1726–75), the Cossack leader of a popular revolt in the Volga area and Urals during the reign of Catherine the Great.

Page 255

The Living Corpse. . . . A play by Lev Tolstoy.

SOME PROPOSITIONS

This document was written in 1918, within about a year of the poems of *My Sister Life* and *Themes and Variations*. However, as happened to those poems, its appearance in print was delayed for almost four years, and it was first published in issue number one of the journal *Sovremennik (The Contemporary)* in 1922.

Page 261

Chastelard. . . . In his late twenties, Pasternak made a complete translation of this part of Swinburne's trilogy, and the translator referred to in the next paragraph is himself. Some of the translation was presumably completed in 1915 in Elabuga on the River Kama; Pasternak spent a considerable part of World War I in this area. The translation was never actually published; it was lost at some point by one of the Moscow publishing houses. Pasternak later returned to the theme of Mary, Queen of Scots when in 1957 he translated Schiller's drama *Mary Stuart* into Russian, and also the Polish dramatist Juliusz Slowacki's play of the same title, which was published in Russian in 1960.

APROPOS OF THE CENTRAL COMMITTEE'S RESOLUTION ON LITERATURE

The Central Committee's resolution "On Party Policy in the Field of Literature" was adopted on June 18, 1925, and publicized in *Pravda* and *Izvestiya* on July 1. Pasternak's response, together with the comments of several other Soviet writers, appeared in the tenth issue of the magazine *Zhurnalist (The Journalist)* for that year.

Page 264

Smenovekhovstvo. . . . A cultural and political movement among the Russian émigré (and also part of the Soviet) intelligentsia. It took its title from *Smena vekh (Change of Signposts),* the name of a journal published in Prague in 1921. Its adherents regarded the Revolution as only one of several stages in the Russian historical process and envisaged a further transformation of the Soviet state into a more bourgeois and democratic one.

Populism. . . . An ideological movement among the Russian intelligentsia that began in the 1860s. Its followers included both radical revolutionaries and liberal enlightenmentists, but the general aims and principles of the movement were to liberate and educate the Russian people and by peaceful or revolutionary means to replace the autocracy with a popular government.

ON THE CLASSICS

This short note was published in the journal *Na literaturnom postu (On Literary Guard),* issues five and six, in 1927, in a section headed "Our Contemporary Writers on the Classics."

ABOUT MYSELF AND THE READER

This short essay in two parts was written in 1928 and published in the fourth and fifth issues of the magazine *Chitatel i pisatel (Reader and Writer).* It was composed in response to a questionnaire issued by the magazine's editors.

Page 267

"Poem of the End." . . . Tsvetaeva's "Poema kontsa" was written in 1924 and published in Prague the following year.

"Man." . . . Mayakovsky's poem "Chelovek" was published in 1916.

Pugachyov. . . . Esenin's play about the eighteenth-century popular uprising was completed in 1921.

Autobiographical fragments. . . . This is the work that eventually would appear as *A Safe-Conduct.*

Zvezda . . . *Krasnaya nov.* . . . (*The Star* and *Red Virgin Soil*)—the titles of two prominent Soviet literary journals.

Boris Pasternak achieved a permanent place as one of the truly great writers of both poetry and prose in the Russian language. That he was awarded the Nobel Prize for Literature is an indication of his status as one of the world's premier literary artists of the twentieth century.

Pasternak's stellar reputation had two distinct high points. In the 1920s, he was recognized throughout his native land as one of its leading poets. Then, in the 1950s, his classic panoramic novel, *Doctor Zhivago,* brought him to new heights of recognition in the world at large—particularly in the West, where the difficulties of faithfully translating verse had kept his poetry from being accorded the renown it deserved.

But Pasternak's genius has still a third dimension. And this anthology presents it to the English-speaking public as has never before been done. In Pasternak's short fiction, his matchless lyric gifts are combined with the humanity, sensitivity, and narrative skills displayed in his famed long novel. They are gems of highly concentrated poetic prose, and the splendid, meticulous translations in this volume do unprecedented justice to the elusive magic of his art.

he. collection begins with a vivid new
ᴈ in English of Pasternak's auto-
al memoir *A Safe-Conduct.* Eight
follow, some of which have never